"It's too shall we do to fill in the time?"

Samuel laughed abruptly.

Realizing the implication of her innocent question, Caitlin blurted, "Oh, I didn't mean *that*. I—I just mean I wasn't weary enough to be packed off to bed like a pesky child."

"Cat, I'd *never* put you to *bed* like a child."

Caitlin saw that special glint appear as his eyes rested on the swell of her breasts, which suddenly began to feel too large for her bodice. She found it increasingly difficult to breathe, and she was wondering what would happen if she dared to lean slightly forward.

Sam circled her with his arms and pulled her onto his lap.

Dear Reader,

Emily French is fast gaining a reputation for the incredible emotional impact of her stories, and this month's *Bogus Bride* is no exception. It's the story of a young woman who gives up everything to travel to America and marry a man whom she has loved from childhood, in spite of the fact that he is expecting to wed her younger sister. Don't miss this wonderful story.

Haunted by their pasts, a gambler and a nobleman's daughter turn to each other for protection against falling in love in Nina Beaumont's new book, *Surrender the Heart*. And a Federal Marshal on the trail of a gang of female outlaws doesn't realize that the woman he's falling in love with is their leader in Judith Stacy's heartwarming Western, *Outlaw Love*.

Our titles for the month also include *Knights Divided* by Suzanne Barclay. In this medieval tale from one of our most popular authors, a young woman finds herself embroiled in a maelstrom of passion and deceit when she kidnaps the rogue whom she believes murdered her sister.

Whatever your taste in reading, we hope you'll find a story written just for you between the covers of a Harlequin Historical novel. Keep a lookout for all four titles wherever Harlequin Historicals are sold.

Sincerely,

Tracy Farrell,
Senior Editor

Please address questions and book requests to:
Harlequin Reader Service
U.S.: 3010 Walden Ave., P.O. Box 1325, Buffalo, NY 14269
Canadian: P.O. Box 609, Fort Erie, Ont. L2A 5X3

EMILY FRENCH

Bogus Bride

Harlequin Books

TORONTO • NEW YORK • LONDON
AMSTERDAM • PARIS • SYDNEY • HAMBURG
STOCKHOLM • ATHENS • TOKYO • MILAN
MADRID • WARSAW • BUDAPEST • AUCKLAND

ISBN 0-373-28961-8

BOGUS BRIDE

EMILY FRENCH

A living passion for the past, combined with the sheer joy of writing, has lured Emily French away from the cold ivory tower of factual academia to warm, heartfelt historical romance. She likes her novels to be full of adventure and humor, her heroes to be intelligent and kind, and her heroines to be witty and spirited.

Emily lives on the East Coast of Australia with her husband, John. Her interests are listed as everything that doesn't have to do with a needle and thread.

To my first readers, Robyn Lee and Debra Spratley, whose encouragement made a miracle seem possible. Thanks, girls.

I hold the Fates bound fast in iron chains, And with my hand turn Fortune's wheel about. Christopher Marlowe —*Tamburlaine the Great*

Prologue

Cornwall, England, Spring 1842

"A letter, Caitlin. Papa has a letter from America. From Samuel!"

With a passionate rustling of silken petticoats, Caitlin was on her feet. "Give it to me," she commanded, her cheeks on fire.

"I may not see so well these days, but it is addressed to me," her father said bitingly, "and your sister shall read it."

Caitlin swallowed hard. There had been times when she thought that Samuel had forsaken her, that she would be a spinster for the rest of her life. But now the longed-for letter had come. She could wait.

The flimsy envelope held a much-crumpled letter, as if the writer had altered it many times before daring to send it. Caitryn gave her sister a small apologetic glance and sat on the settee beneath the tall silver candlesticks. It was a long letter, crossed and recrossed, and she spread out the sheets where the light would fall upon them. Her sweet face shone with anticipation and joy as she began to read the letter aloud.

Caitlin stood at the window, spine stiff, fingers interlaced too tightly, and watched the expression on her younger sister's face. It was as if Caitryn believed that Samuel had penned the pages with a heart full of love for her and that what he had to say was for her eyes alone.

Samuel wrote of all that had happened to him since he had left Cornwall, ten years before. Then he went on to say that he had entered the lumber trade and had prospered mightily. He was now a man of means, with everything a man could wish for, except a wife.

Sir Richard grunted. Samuel was the only son of the local doctor, and it had been decided that Samuel should also become a doctor. But Samuel, though possessed of all those attributes desirable in a doctor—a warm heart, strong nerves, charming manners and an unshakable faith in his own judgment—had been a reluctant recruit. Samuel had preferred examining the earth and the trees that grew upon it, and the changing seasons that died and renewed themselves.

Dr. Jardine had cursed and sworn until Samuel gave in and began his medical studies. Then, somehow, he had bungled a simple prescription. The patient had almost died, and the good doctor had ranted and stormed. Rightly so, thought Sir Richard. But Samuel had flung his stethoscope in his father's face and decamped to America, where he had completely disappeared.

Now here was a letter from this prodigal son!

"'And so, sir, I come to the purpose of this letter,'" Caitryn continued reading aloud. "'I have often thought of your beautiful daughter, Caitlin. No other woman has ever taken her place in my heart. If she is not wed, and is willing, would you permit her to travel to Maine and be my wife? I enclose a short note to her regarding arrangements for the marriage, and send my kindest regards to yourself and Mrs. Parr. Signed this Third day of May, 1842. Samuel Jardine. P.S. A bank draft for passage is enclosed.'"

There was a moment's silence. Caitlin hurried forward. "The note!" There was a loud rushing in her ears that made her own voice sound faint. "The note Samuel wrote for me myself. Where is it?"

Caitryn blinked at her. She looked...different, somehow. A slight trembling shook her body, and her fingers groped upon the table as though her eyesight, as well as that of Sir Richard, was failing. Her face the color of ashes, she silently handed a small sealed note to her older sister. It was addressed to Miss C. Parr.

"The damned cheek of it! Thinking to wed one of my daughters, after dead silence for ten years! Arrogant young pup."

With shaking fingers, Caitlin opened the personal note Samuel had written especially to her. Her heart slammed to a stop, and she felt the air leave her chest in a rush.

My dearest Caitryn...

Caitlin saw the words with eyes that burned, blurrily, as if from a great distance. In her mind, she tried to flee, but her legs would not move. It was like being stuck in quicksand. She was in a waking nightmare. For one instant, she thought her entire world had disintegrated. It seemed that even her heart had ceased to beat.

Then the fingers of one hand closed convulsively over Samuel's letter, and she thrust it into the bodice of her dress, safe from prying eyes. The crackle of the paper set her mind leaping fiercely upon another track.

Each night, for ten long years, before she retired to bed, she had knelt in the window seat and found the North Star. The sight would bring a smile to her lips, while the memory of Samuel, fluttering through her mind, would lift up her heart like a flight of butterflies.... Now, standing by this window in the year of 1842, Caitlin felt out of patience with Samuel for his absurd confusion over the similarity of names between her and her sister.

"What an absurd to-do about nothing, Papa," she said,

managing to laugh lightly. A pox on doubts. Samuel loved *her*. Confidence flared up, welcome, fortifying, reassuring. "It was courteous of Samuel to write to you, but, as I am of age, there was really no necessity."

Sir Richard's jaw flexed. "No, by God. No daughter of mine will marry a man who deserted his father, a common lumberman, a fellow no better than a lackey."

To stand before the altar with Samuel—that had been the goal of the whole of her life. Well, most of it, at least since she had been sixteen. Caitlin's chin rose a notch.

She *would* go to America. She *would* marry Samuel.

"I am sorry, Papa, but that is exactly what your daughter intends to do."

Chapter One

Bay of Fundy, Summer 1842

Caitlin stood and braced herself with one palm against the ship's bow. The world was filled with cold, blustery movement and the steady surge of waves. Her eyes crinkled against the sharp, cool, salt-laden moisture that sprayed her face. She leaned into the motion, the rail pressed against her waist, enjoying the breeze.

Great gray gulls tossed screaming in the upper air. Below her, the water whooshed by, pale, ribboning in the sunlight, swirling against the ship's prow. They were within hours of landing, and to Caitlin, the clipper ship seemed swept along with steely purpose.

The ship's port of call was Saint John. Once she and Samuel were married, they would journey to River de Chute before setting off for the small backwoods settlement of Fairbanks, where Samuel operated his lumber business. She had spent much time preparing to be a good wife, but it was hard not to feel just a little afraid.

Not for a moment did she think Samuel would have changed. Not at all. He was still only thirty.... She saw him as she had seen him last, in the *Savannah*'s dinghy as it skimmed across the harbor, tall and broad and straight, with big shoulders and a fine, strong, square face, his clear eyes fixed on her, and her alone. Ah! Had she not looked into their depths and there read love for herself?

That was the image of him that she had carried in her heart, and she had no difficulty in imagining the image of herself that he had carried through all these years, the image of a spirited woman whose steadfastness would be his redemption and whose love would be his salvation. For she loved the man to whose side she was hasting with a love that had neither height nor depth, nor any other measure, but was just all of her.

Caitlin's heart danced a little jig. Elation surged through her. If even the thought of her had upheld him through the years of loneliness, what would her presence do? She felt a glow of delight already at the thought of the bliss of their mutual love, and the sweetness of home life together.

"Had no idea you were wantin' to get married this side of the border, old son. Why all this cloak-and-dagger charade?"

Groaning inwardly, Samuel Jardine turned around at the sound of the soft Irish accent. Leaning back against the wall, his arms folded over his belt, his partner and best friend looked challengingly at him.

Liam Murphy was above average height, with hair the color of a midsummer wheatfield and piercing blue eyes. He had a snub nose and a deep dimple in his chin, as if someone had poked him with a finger and left an impression in the flesh.

Samuel smiled thinly. It was the sort of smile he would give to a stranger.

"Some things are meant to be kept to oneself, Murphy." Even to himself, his voice sounded harsh. He struggled to lighten it. "I had to make sure that you came to Saint John,

Liam. We have a contract for delivery of a million feet to sign, remember?''

Murphy looked blank for a second. Then he grinned. "We've five limits untouched, and we can scale around ten million feet of first-class timber from any one of 'em, so Conrad Hatt's contract is no great problem. It's more than that. Feeling nervous, Sam?''

"Not a bit," Samuel answered, feeling the heat invade his cheeks. Was he nervous? Surely not. To cover his embarrassment, he poured strong black tea into a tin mug and pushed it across the slab-timber tabletop. Murphy smiled back, showing very white, very strong teeth. He held out his hand, palm upward.

"Mother Mary, you should be. All the best husbands are nervous on their wedding days, just as all good wives are nervous on their wedding nights.''

A black look speared Murphy. When Samuel spoke, it was without inflection. "It's a bad time for investment, and I want all accounts squared. We've got to get the timber out of the woods and boomed in the water, ready to tow to the mills, before we can thumb our nose at Sagamore and his henchmen.''

A look of concern crossed Liam's cheery face. "The *Angelica* docks in an hour. Maine's a rough country, and with trouble brewing between the rival lumber camps, perhaps it'd be best not to take a wife upriver. If you have any regrets, there is still time to change your mind, Sam. The wedding arrangements can be canceled.''

Samuel didn't want to speculate on that. He stood upright with a jerk. "I'm not changing my mind about anything, Murphy." He spoke succinctly, and smiled the smile of a captain prepared to go down with his ship. "There isn't a man anywhere in God's universe who knows what he wants better than I do. My bride has waited ten years and traveled three thousand miles for this marriage," he said, in a tone that meant "And *that* is *that*.''

* * *

Sunlight glanced dully off the thick, low bollards and the secured mooring lines. Crowds of visitors—men, women and children—lined the wharf. Eyes wide, Caitlin anxiously scanned the blur of faces.

Could she venture among the crowd, she wondered, to meet and greet Samuel, before so many interested and curious eyes? Her heart beat, and her eyes swam in a happy mist at the prospect. Steadying herself against the rail, she tried to focus on the dock, and sweep its limited space, so that she might find the figure she sought.

The letter in which he had fixed the day of her arrival lay in her reticule. It had been only brief, and hinted at, rather than expressed, the passion of his soul. When he saw her, he would tell her that he cared, and how much. After all, there had been neither bond nor promise between them, not even an ordinary goodbye.

"Cat!"

She leaned over the rail. A little gasp came from her lips. There was Samuel! Yes, it *was* him, pushing through the crowd on the quay, his hat in his hand. His hair was the same tossed, untidy chestnut mop, but his strong, lean body seemed larger, more overpowering than she had remembered. And his face looked sterner. The arched nose and high cheekbones seemed more prominent, the line of the mouth harder.

"Samuel! Samuel!"

Caitlin scrambled to the wharf level. Impossibly tall, terrifying in his imposing presence, he stuck out his strong, square hand as he would to a long-lost friend.

"Good to see you, Caitlin. You haven't changed at all. You're a picture in your fine gown."

What was wrong? she wondered, watching Samuel's aloof face from under lowered lashes. He was behaving as if she were someone he had just met. She smiled as she gripped the hard fingers. His hand seemed to dwarf hers, and the top of her forehead barely reached his shoulders.

"You look different," she managed breathlessly. "I hardly recognized you."

"A man doesn't get anywhere on his appearance in this country, Cat, especially when he's a lumberjack. He shucks off a lot of things he used to think were quite essential," he answered, with just a ghost of his remembered smile.

It was a strange and unfamiliar Samuel who looked toward the clipper, his figure set and still. The shadow of something came and went across his face. A soft breeze ruffled his hair, and then it was calm again. He looked her over again.

"Where is Caitryn?" His voice sounded a little stilted.

Caitlin smiled as she saw the deep furrows appear on Samuel's forehead. She wanted to throw herself into his embrace, but was paralyzed, while vagrant feelings she could barely comprehend rose and fell within her. Love, excitement, joy and, above all, sheer nerves reduced the moment to one of almost unbearable rapture.

She extricated her hand from his. "She could not come."

Samuel's face went dead white. There was an odd, shuttered reticence in the high cheekbones, the arrogantly arched nose and the proud mouth. He looked out along the inlet of the bay at the sun-sparked waves, the small fishing boats scudding along with the wind, as if they were objects whose purpose he could no longer quite comprehend.

What was wrong? Caitlin wondered desperately. Why was he treating her with this distant courtesy? Had she been wrong? Had he truly intended that letter for Caitryn? No! Her mind rejected that notion.

"Samuel!"

Samuel turned back to Caitlin. He slanted her a hard-edged glance. His strong jaw clenched as he watched her. He didn't touch her, but she could feel his intent gaze, as if he were probing her inner thoughts.

The sensation made her uneasy. A strange awareness settled in her. Was he sorry that he had sent for her? She swallowed.

He hesitated a moment. "I had thought she would come."

Something in Samuel's voice made Caitlin say, "She is to join the Little Sisters of Saint Teresa, and wanted to prepare herself through prayer and devotions. I'll tell you all about it later."

There was a distinct pause. His expression hardened. He stood there like a stuck image, his face set. Sudden, irrational fear gripped her. This blankness, this cessation of eagerness, disturbed her. He seemed strangely alien.

Caitlin looked away from him, seeking the indistinguishable line where sea met sky. She licked dry lips. What was it? Anything was possible, and it was always dangerous to jump to conclusions.

Apprehension went through her. Had she been wrong? Could her father have been right? If Samuel had truly cared, would he have waited ten years to write? Did he simply need a wife?

Caitlin's own attraction was like a pulse, a living thing existing deep inside her, separate and undeniable. She shook her head in bewilderment. Surely he could feel it? Or was that wishful thinking? Had she miscalculated the depth of his feeling? Had she made her attraction, her desire, his? The questions sent a small chill down her spine.

True, she had none of her sister's fair beauty: golden hair, blue eyes, and small, delicate mouth. But she had added strengths, an enviable mastery of language and art, a more profound knowledge of medicine and science than even Samuel's father, and she was fiercely protective of her lover. In truth, she suspected that she was the only one who understood Samuel.

Her eyes flicked to his face. He looked so...remote. She ruthlessly squashed her doubts. Come the night, she would be married to Samuel, in a place more appropriate to direct speech, with full honesty. Now wasn't the moment for frank discussion.

He looked singularly uncomfortable. She could feel his discomfiture; it was like rubbing up against a rusty scow. What should she do?

She resisted the urge to touch him. Instead, she clasped her hands tightly together. It was going to be difficult curbing her own far more dynamic, often impulsive nature. She took a deep breath, let it out in a rush.

"What are you waiting for? Aren't you going to kiss me, Samuel? Is there something wrong?"

He looked at her with surprise, as if he had forgotten she was there. His hand closed upon her shoulder. Caitlin seemed to feel the whole man vibrate behind it, like a steel spring. She watched him with an expectant, eager expression, curious as to how his kiss would feel.

Then, just as suddenly as he had frowned, his face cleared. The serious look left his mouth, to be replaced by a lazy smile. He was once more her Samuel, the Samuel she loved.

Very gently, he took her in his arms and kissed her. It was the merest brush of his lips over the trembling warmth of her mouth. Before she could encircle his neck with her slim arms, he had pulled away.

He traced the delicate line of her cheek with the knuckles of one hand, and sighed. "I'd best sort out your baggage, and get you to the hotel. You'll have time for a rest. I've arranged for Kate Flaherty to help you dress. The marriage ceremony is at seven. The river steamer leaves at first light."

Caitlin did not demur, but stood and watched Samuel disappear down the companionway amidships, to see about her luggage. She felt a little dazed, for some intuition warned her that something had gone amiss.

Was this the welcome of a man passionately in love? If

he did not return her love, the bonds would be those of duty and obligation. That was not what she wanted, to be trapped by her impulsive, sensual nature into a lifetime of guilt and bitterness. Then she shook the doubt away.

It was not the greeting or the embrace she had expected, but the immense tenderness of it was very sweet, more suited to a public place than passion. Of course, this was perfectly logical.

What she hadn't expected was the change in Samuel.

This man was not the same person she had loved so passionately ten years earlier. This man was taller than she remembered, his face harder, stronger, his skin burned brown by the wind and sun.

Ten years of pioneer life had changed Samuel almost beyond recognition. He was not the slim, cocksure youngster willing to be tormented by the nearness of a silly young girl. No longer would he be easily led into mischief, or easily provoked to anger.

This man was a stranger. He would go where he wanted, and do what he wanted at the time and place of his choosing. He was in control of himself, and he would not be manipulated.

When she thought of Samuel, a curious fluttering warmth uncurled in her stomach, leaving her heart pounding and her knees weak. Caitlin supressed a shiver, appalled at the wildness of the emotion that flooded her.

What had she done? What had she done?

She was here, and that was that, with an ocean between her and home, with a man she had not seen for ten years. In a panic, she wondered wildly what she would do if he sent her away. She would survive, of course, but, she asked herself, to what purpose?

She was trying to calm her frantic thoughts when she felt his hand touch her arm. Ever so gently, he stroked the inside of her bare elbow. Suddenly, as if by magic, her legs stopped trembling and her breath fluttering.

She smiled faintly, with relief. She knew she had no need to fear. She was there. The bridegroom was there. Pride was there, as well. The wedding was prepared. There was no need to feel concern. She'd take her chances.

Now on to getting married. The sooner the better.

In the church, only trivial things caught her attention. The scrubbed wooden floor, the plain glass on the windows, and the single red flame that burned before the altar.

Fiercely she concentrated on the lamp's mystic glow as she repeated everything that was said to her in a low, almost inaudible voice. She felt Samuel move beside her and wrenched her eyes from the behavior of the solitary sanctuary lamp to look down as he slipped the gold wedding ring over her knuckles.

Caitlin's eyes opened, flared. Samuel made a small, hoarse sound, as if his voice were clotted with emotion. With a shock of surprise, she realized that he was taking her arm. The service was over and she hadn't heard a word, nor did she remember making the necessary responses.

Married... Married... It was done. Her confidence came up with a surge. It had been easy enough, after all, becoming Mrs. Samuel Jardine, by name at least. As for the rest—the triumph that flooded her at the thought of her audacious success shut out any thought of what was to follow.

Astonishing. It was done. The terrible finality struck Samuel Jardine. He had married the wrong woman!

Samuel took a long draft, half draining the glass he clenched in his hand. He grimaced. Straight whiskey never did appeal to him, but it might help unravel his knotted stomach.

Hell and damnation! What had he done to himself? Walked into it with his eyes open, as well. How could he have been such a fool? Such a goddamned honorable fool? But he had been unable to resist the appeal in Caitlin's wide eyes and trembling lips. In that brief moment when he could have, should have, spoken the truth, she reminded him of the child of yesteryear whose generosity and wisdom had changed his life, and of today's child, Zoe, who needed the same big heart and clear vision. Had he been mistaken? He'd never had a thought like that about Caitlin before.

Sudden, irrational fear gripped him. He felt savage, mortified to the marrow of his bones. His fingers clenched almost white on the glass. *What do I do now?* The chaotic thought whirled around in his brain. Everything in his body and brain and blood screamed out to him to run, to save himself. Too late.

His thumb moved along the glass. He frowned, his eyes focused on the bottom of his glass. He was not at all accustomed to impulsive action on his own part, and yet he'd married Caitlin Parr an hour ago.

Dammit. Why was nothing ever easy? How had it happened?

Samuel put his glass down on the polished timber bar and ran a hard, callused finger slowly around the rim. What a fool I am, he thought. There was no future for them. Not when his bride should have been her sister, Caitryn.

He heaved a great sigh. He'd written to Caitryn. At least he'd meant to write to Caitryn—not her sister, Caitlin.

Despair gripped him. How could he have been so stupid as to confuse the names? But, of course, he wasn't stupid at all. On the contrary, he was considered very shrewd, with a reputation from Montreal to Philadelphia for his sound business acumen. And he certainly was under no illusions about which sister he had wanted to marry—and it was not the sharp-tongued Caitlin.

In fact, he had never been able to be in the same room with Caitlin for more than ten minutes without finding her an aggravation. She was as irritating as a burr in a man's breeches, and here he was shackled to her!

Liam Murphy's voice cut across Samuel's thoughts.

"Don't look so glum, Sam. A wedding's meant to be a joyous occasion, not one for soaking yourself in whiskey."

Samuel stiffened, his back going ramrod-straight. "What would you know?"

"I thought I knew you, Sam, an' now I have me doubts. You're not a drinkin' man, so you must be the jealous type who resents your little woman dancin' with every jobber in Saint John. Am I right?" Liam asked with a smug look. He raised an eyebrow archly, as if amused at his own foolish witticism.

Little woman. The phrase grated. Caitlin was small, Samuel could not deny that. Almost fragile. But that was deceptive. No one knew better than he that Caitlin's delicate exterior hid a tough, shrewd interior, one that was resilient and held its own secrets. The innocence, the sweetness, were all Caitryn's—which had been one of the reasons for his offer of marriage.

He flicked his eyes toward the dance floor, where his bride was dancing a reel with one of their wedding guests. Her face was aglow with enthusiasm, and even from this distance her eyes sparkled like the sun cutting across shards of ice.

One must admit, she was an elfin creature, all dark hair and wide eyes. Though one could not approve the nuance of recklessness in the faint tilt of the green eyes, one had to admire the porcelain skin, heart-shaped face and deeply etched, sensual lips.

The movement of the dance created an empty space between them, and they gazed at each other across it. Her head was tilted back now, her long cat eyes watching him.

Jealous type. The truth came unbidden and unwelcome, hitting Sam like a blow to the stomach. Dismay, stupefaction, guilt and desire swept him up in an intolerable chaos. His male hunger simmered just below the surface. It filled him with hot blood.

It was irrational, this surge of desire. This is Caitlin, not

Caitryn, he reminded himself. He shook his head. She might not be his first choice as a bride, but Caitlin was certainly delectable. She made this so damn difficult.

Samuel didn't know what it was about the woman that disturbed him. The idea of taking her to bed was driving him to distraction. The heat leaked up from his neck to his cheeks, circling his ears. He prayed Caitlin didn't notice, but that was too much to ask.

As she was spun into the dance, Caitlin rotated her head so that she could keep him in her line of vision. She raised her delicate eyebrows in a subtle challenge. The woman had a way of taunting him without even opening her mouth.

Samuel had the oddest feeling that those extraordinary green eyes were seeing right through into his thoughts. He hoped not. He had to force himself to look away.

"Don't be ridiculous," he snapped at the Irishman. His voice lacked conviction even to his own ears. Murphy made a wry face.

Samuel considered taking refuge in silence, then changed his mind as he looked at the Irishman. He'd have to do better, or Liam would be on to him.

"It's not very civilized in Fairbanks, so this is probably the only chance Caitlin will have to show off her city finery." He was glaring at Murphy now, so hard his eyes ached with the effort. "A logging camp in Maine isn't exactly Paris."

The wide smile disappeared. Liam eyed him thoughtfully, hesitated a moment. "I was only joking." Murphy took a long swallow of whiskey. "Then again, maybe I wasn't. My advice is to let the little lady have one last fling, 'n' enjoy herself with all them handsome young bucks twirlin' her about the dance floor, before she's claimed by her lover and has all them wifely duties to attend."

Awareness hit Samuel immediately as a tremendous surge in his loins. He felt it right in the center of his stom-

ach. Like a kick. *Claimed by her lover.* The words echoed
n his head.

What was he letting the woman do to him, for God's
sake? The answer was far too disturbing. His whole body
was seething with unreleased tension and sensual excitement.

Mentally he chastised himself for his own weakness but
the unexpected response of his body was unnerving, as was
the strangely possessive, yet uncomfortably vengeful, sensation he was experiencing. Setting snares for women apparently wasn't his forte.

At that moment, Samuel decided to get drunk. Soaking
himself in whiskey was exactly what he needed. In spite of
everything, his mouth curved faintly.

"Sure, why not? The end result will be the same. She is
my wife."

Murphy narrowed his eyes at Jardine's display of male
possessiveness. "You're not worried about Sagamore, are
you?" It was a statement, not a question.

Just don't screw up now and ruin everything, Samuel
finished wryly in his head. Something in his mind shied
away from abandoning the project he'd planned for his bogus bride. It was becoming very important to make it work.

He shook his head once, very determinedly. "An uppity,
unpredictable, difficult female like Caitlin will send that
jackass on his way with a flea in his ear."

"Sounds like you're having regrets already."

There was a sharpness to Liam's tone that startled Samuel, and the bland innocence in the Irishman's gaze made
him decidedly wary. He made a disagreeable sound in the
back of his throat.

"Certainly not. I haven't seen Caitlin for ten years, and
I'm feeling a mite nervous."

Murphy made a face. "There's a paradox there somewhere, but I'm damned if I know what it is." His eyes
flicked to the dance floor. "Just know if it was my missus,

I wouldn't have time to be nervous. I'd have her in bed quick smart 'n' let nature take its course. And I wouldn't be sittin' here swilling whiskey like some drunken fool an' abusin' her feelin's.''

A faint tingling warning came alive in Samuel's head as he scanned the dance floor with his eyes, seeking his bride. The reception room was crowded. Saint John society adored parties, and guests danced with eager faces, the men in formal dress, the women bright as flowers, their hair bound up with silver combs.

There she was, dancing with Martinus Soule, the tails of the banker's frock coat flying out as they spun about the floor. Samuel clenched his teeth and absorbed the scene.

As he followed her progress through the dance, he experienced a sense of déjà vu so acute he felt momentarily dizzy. She was wearing a gown of white satin with a pale green sash and a low bodice from which her breasts swelled in becoming fashion. Between them, shifting and gleaming with each movement of her bosom, was the simple silver crucifix he had given her on her sixteenth birthday....

They'd sneaked out of that party so that Caitlin could show Samuel the mare her father had bought for her. A full moon had shone through the barred windows of the stable. In his mind, he saw her face dappled in moonlight, moving from shadow to shadow.

She'd stumbled, and he'd reached out toward her. "Careful, Cat. You're such a tiny thing—a real shrimp. I'll bet you've got the hem of that gown all dirty.''

"Who cares about a silly old dress. And you can find a better thing to call me than a shrimp, surely?''

Her face had shone like a playful puppy's, all innocence and light. Samuel had felt a shared intimacy, and it had made him careless. He'd been thinking of her in an oblique fashion. He would be twenty-one in another week, but he would be gone by then. Somehow his imminent departure had triggered in him an intense sadness.

"A pixie? An elf? A fairy? A sprite? A witch?" Each question had been interspersed with a kiss. The first on her forehead, the second on her nose, the third on her ear, the fourth on her neck, the fifth on her mouth.

By that time, his knees were weak, his hands less than steady, and all he was aware of was the heavy weight between his thighs. Desire was a physical ache. Her mouth was open, all moist, warm invitation. She had been so wild, so sweet, that he wanted to part her soft thighs and feel that honeyed warmth wash over him.

He was, in short, so enchanted that when she took his hands and pressed them to her breasts, taut with passion, he savored the sweetness beneath his fingers. They kissed long and deep, their tongues exploring for the first time.

It was madness, he knew, and for a second he began to pull away. But then he felt her fingers undo the flap of his trousers, move across his flesh, saw that languid, lustful look in her eyes, and he melted inside.

Caitlin's sleek head came forward, through bars of shadow and light. He saw the pink of her tongue tip, bright and shining as it passed through a swath of light just before it touched him. A sigh like a cloud riding high on warm wind and sunlight escaped her lips as she traced his long length upward.

"Go on," he said thickly. His chest heaved. "Go on."

His eyes closed in exquisite pleasure as she explored the nerve on the underside of the thickening head. Her open lips engulfed him slowly, slowly and so wetly. Spirals of ecstasy swirled with each swipe of her tongue, and he groaned deep in his chest as liquid heat rushed up his body.

Her lips lifted and she stared into his face, her eyes huge and glassy. "Love me, Samuel," she said to him. "Love me, now."

And Samuel, his manhood quivering with tension, slid to his knees, moved against her. But that was as far as he got.

Sound brushed through Samuel's mind. A noise at the stable doorway. It was Caitlin's father. Caitlin scrambled up, retreating now to the mare's stall. Streamers of hay flew from her skirts, attaching themselves to his broadcloth trousers.

The squire had given him an ultimatum. Get out of England or his father would be told of the incident. As he boarded the *Savannah*, he had had the taste of ashes in his mouth as the sight of Caitryn exacerbated his guilt. She had not even said a word to him. Perhaps he had called out to her. He did not remember.

He thrust the memory away sharply, turned again to the dancers. Elfin Caitlin might be, but she had a nice shape, curves in all the right places. She had an unconscious grace, and her slim hips swayed in an enticing manner. He did not think she did it on purpose. She always had been a spritely creature.

Samuel idly swirled his drink and watched the candlelight spinning off her glossy black hair as she tilted her swanlike neck to the music. The arch of her throat made him feel heavy in his chest. Her vivid smile generated conflicting emotions deep within him. His hunger was like a pulse, a living thing existing deep inside him, separate and undeniable.

Samuel knew now that nothing would permanently slow or alter the quick, impatient way Caitlin moved. What was she now? Twenty-six? Twenty-seven? Her character was volatile, complex, and her restless intellect reached out for knowledge that was neither attractive nor necessary in a woman.

It was ridiculous, of course, but he felt the tension growing inside of him. He felt his insides clench, and he could hear the rushing of his blood in his inner ears as if it were part of a spring thaw. His hammering heart seemed to be threatening to choke him.

God, this was torture! He had not lain with a woman in

a long, long time. Another dismaying thought flitted
through Samuel's mind. What of Caitlin? Why had she
come all this way to marry him?

Chapter Two

Caitlin's eyes strayed to the corner where Samuel was leaning on the counter and conversing with Liam Murphy. She felt her skin tighten and tingle all over. Though she could not like the way he was paying more attention to his business partner than to his bride, she had to concede he did look very handsome in his dark blue evening coat.

She also had to concede that Saint John, at least, was above her expectations. Samuel's letter had hinted that this country was crude, full of inconveniences and uncouthness, and that she would need all her strength for what lay ahead of her.

On the contrary. The hotel ballroom was as grand as any in London. From the lovely green-papered walls to the fine trio of crystal chandeliers that hung from the high gilded ceiling, the room reflected elegance and refinement.

Caitlin was partly amused, partly provoked, by Samuel's harsh evaluation of his new country. She hoped that his opinion of her destination would prove as inaccurate. Until this journey, her childhood dream of having a true adventure had seemed unattainable. She sighed with pleasure, feeling a delicious sense of anticipation.

Samuel suddenly looked up, directly at her. She experienced again that queer breathlessness whenever he looked in her direction. He studied her for a moment, an intensity revealed beneath those half-closed lids that shocked her. It was as if there were a kind of vexation there, a frustration, held in check.

A heartbeat more, and he inclined his head. A smile appeared and vanished on his lips, so quickly that Caitlin was not sure she had actually seen it. The noise in the ballroom seemed distant, dreamlike, unreal.

It was happening again—that disturbing feeling was back, deep in the pit of her stomach, an awareness of the pressing softness of her shift across her breasts. She couldn't pinpoint the feeling. All she knew was that it made her uncomfortable. Very uncomfortable.

She felt her face warm, certain that it was wrong. Sinful. Caitlin was fully informed as to sex and reproduction. She had seen and studied things that would make any modern young woman blush, but she had never felt this upsurge of *femaleness* before. Perhaps it was simply that she was viewing Samuel as—

"Mrs. Jardine." The banker's voice interrupted her train of thought. "Your charming presence will be missed when you travel north. It is a shame you could not stay longer in Saint John."

What was she thinking? Not wishing to appear impolite, Caitlin smiled demurely. "It's a long journey, and Samuel is anxious to show me my new home."

She wanted nothing more than to retire for the night and be alone with Samuel. But he was preoccupied with men's business, and a squire's daughter did have some sense of the proprieties. She understood, and she would wait for him. She had always waited for him, from the beginning.

As if he followed her thoughts, Martinus Soule's eyes twinkled. "Ah, young love. It warms the cockles of my old heart. Here am I hogging you, when you're no doubt wishing it was your young scalawag who was on the dance floor with you."

That was true enough. Were her own feelings so transparent? The thought was appalling. Caitlin's breath quickened, and she was acutely aware of a soft blush creeping up her cheeks. She shook her head.

"Samuel and I have all our lives ahead of us, Mr. Soule."

The banker's voice lowered earnestly. "We are rather apt to forget that our destinies are not always in our own hands—even for such a winsome beauty."

Was the statement rhetorical or serious? Caitlin's brightest smile flashed across her face. She couldn't imagine what lay before her, but she embraced it with all her being.

"Beauty will pass—but love lasts forever."

The banker smiled indulgently. "You are still very young."

"Oh, yes," she murmured, accepting the edict without reservation. "Quite young. But Samuel and I have known each other since childhood, and been pledged these many years past. I just wish—" She broke off, catching herself before she said the unthinkable.

"I wouldn't like to see you hurt."

Caitlin drew her delicate eyebrows together. "How can Samuel hurt me? He doesn't gamble, and he has courage and genius and works hard—that's what it takes to be successful in the lumber business—and you know he's carved a fortune out of the wilderness, made a name for himself."

"Too big a name for peace and comfort, and there are other faults a man can have. Sam Jardine is a mere man, not a god to revere." Martinus Soule smiled as he said it, but his black eyes held a warning that was genuine. He cleared his throat before continuing. "Now, it's time he rested on his laurels and settled down."

Something in his expression caused Caitlin's heart to flutter painfully. There was a sense of disapproving judgment, and the banker's bland insinuations had created an uneasiness in her.

She wanted to hear about Samuel, about the tall timber that he said was like a vast green sea, endless, enduring, stretching into infinity. She felt that she would trade her soul for a few more bits of information out of which she could fashion her dreams.

With outward calm, she asked, "What are these awful faults?"

"Oh, he's simply been a bachelor far too long, and in the past he has had other goals to occupy his attention."

In America, a man has a chance to better himself, Samuel had told her. *Promise to remember me,* he had said to herself and Caitryn on that long-ago day.

And she had. During the weeks, the months, the years, that passed. Time had blunted her hope, and driven her to more practical matters, but she had gone on doggedly preparing herself until she had done all she could.

Then the letter had come, with its confusion of names. Her deceit would be all right. Caitryn had wanted her to go. Had she not said, "I wish it. It must be so. Samuel has sent for you and I know you love him. I wish to devote my life to God, but can I rest quiet in the cloister, knowing you lie alone at night?"

Caitlin raised her gaze just in time to see the hint of a smile register on Samuel's face. She inclined her head. The immediate tightening of his jaw rewarded her. She felt a pulse flutter in her throat, and a sudden weakness in her knees.

"Of course, but that is past, and who knows how God and fate work? None of we poor mortals, to be sure. So I won't let it gnaw at me. Samuel is married now, and I think I'm going to enjoy Fairbanks."

Fairbanks...even the name was enchanting.

The banker laughed suddenly. "You sound so certain, Mrs. Jardine."

A small frown touched Caitlin's forehead. She was beginning to feel quite neglected by her new husband. His consideration in sharing his bride as a dance partner was touching, but surely he should have claimed her by now. Her lips set in a stubborn line.

"I am," she replied.

Samuel watched the whole scene unfold before him as if he were watching a melodrama. Caitlin floated around the room in her fancy gown, partners attracted to her like bees to a honey pot.

A succession of uninvited pictures flashed through his head. Caitlin in his bed. Her black hair had slipped its bonds and now whirled about her, a dark mantle. Ivory and charcoal.

His single-minded vision of the future was transformed. Within it was Caitlin Parr—no, correction—Caitlin Jardine. His bogus bride.

For the first time, he realized that, should his wife simply refuse to cooperate in his plans, he would feel horribly embarrassed, not only in front of Sagamore, but also the entire population of Fairbanks. Pride was a definite burden at times, and Samuel knew he had his full measure of it.

He had good reason to be proud. He had done damned well. He had found his vocation, and his life, but only after the false starts, the shameful error that had led to his expulsion from medical school not three months before graduation, and the headlong restlessness that had flung him into the arms of Caitlin that day in the barn.

His expression relaxed into one tinged with humor. "Perhaps I'm just being prudent, Liam. Good for the character, prudence. You should try it sometime," Samuel said, in a voice that he hoped hid his own inner tension.

Murphy nodded, his eyes thoughtful. He raised his glass in salute. "Marriage is a gamble."

Samuel's smile tightened, and he picked up his glass. "It's a calculated risk, I admit." He took a long, deep pull on the whiskey and felt its warmth spread across his chest.

"Now we get down to it, Jardine. Risk. You're addicted

to risk, Sam. Look at this impulsive marriage. Sending for a woman you haven't seen in ten years. What if a logging camp in Maine don't suit her? You may wake one morning to find the bride has taken to her heels.''

That was her problem, Samuel told himself. She had contracted the marriage willingly enough, and now she was stuck with it. He shrugged mentally. So was he, for that matter. A man set standards and lived by them, and if fate cast a die with a single spot, so be it.

"Even if her religion didn't prevent a divorce, it's not the Cornish way to break a bond.''

Samuel's tone cut through the space between them. Liam Murphy's thin eyebrows lifted, but he said nothing, contenting himself with a sip of whiskey. The two men sat in silence for a while, united by unspoken contemplation of marital obligations.

Murphy lifted his glass in the faintest of salutes. "You are sunk deep in thought, my friend.''

Samuel brushed at his trousers, staring absently at his hand. "The border dispute must be settled. There's been more trouble. Heard Morgan's boom was busted.''

"There's hiring at Sagamore's.''

"How many?'' That Sagamore's was hiring surprised him, since most lumber mills were not. Only two weeks before, the deCarteret mill had dismissed fifty workers, because shingle production had fallen.

"I don't know how many they're taking on. I'm trying to find out.''

"If Sagamore's recruiting this early in the season, seems he must be expecting a big consignment. It can only mean the land agents intend turning a blind eye to trespass and cutting on Maine territory for yet another season.''

"Very active, these trespassers, Sam. I don't like it.'' Open indignation tinged Liam's voice.

Samuel shrugged. "We'll deal with them, if we have to.''

"Hush, Sam. Don't say the words, else sure it is that you will wish them unsaid tomorrow." Even when he was serious the Irishman's lips seemed to quiver with a barely controlled smile.

"It's what comes of Tyler's bein' president," Samuel went on, peering at the bottom of his glass in disgust. "Despite election promises, it seems Fairbanks is too far away to serve legal processes and too expensive to employ military ejection."

"I thought we weren't going to mention that." Murphy spoke easily, his voice deep, but there was a stiffness in his features.

Samuel let out his breath in a long sigh. His partner had a timberman's suspicion of any type of federal intervention. "Politics is a complicated affair. It's a big country, but the lumber trade is a small community." He held out his empty glass for a refill. "I've no political sympathies, only instincts, and they shy away from cheats."

As Murphy poured in a generous measure of whiskey, Samuel's eyes moved slowly to settle on Caitlin's face. She was watching him, her pointed, fawnlike face lit as if from within. It was as if she were drawing him into herself, so that he had no will of his own. Soon, he thought, he would have to go to her. Samuel knew he could not delay much longer. He was running out of time.

He sighed and took another drink. He would go to her. He would do his duty. Yes, duty, that was what it would be. He saw that clearly now. This marriage would be a constant reminder to himself that he was a deserter, that he had shirked his duty when his father needed him. Yes, it was fitting.

Chills ran up Samuel's spine. Somehow, in retrospect, every major turning point in his life had been associated with Caitlin Parr. He had known her since childhood, though he knew that this did not make her any more easy to understand.

Some things never changed.

Caitlin Parr—no, Caitlin Jardine—had been a strong-willed, reckless girl from the moment he had met her. She'd burst into his life like a miniature whirlwind, disrupting the even tenure of his existence.

Samuel winced, remembering.

He had been only a boy of thirteen when his father went to Cornwall to set up a medical practice in Port Isaac. Samuel had been born late in his parents' married life, and his delicate mother had not recovered from the difficult birth. She had taken to her room until her death some ten years later, and her son had grown up without a woman's soft, gentle touch.

For all his height and strength and the maturity of his thirteen years, he saw no reason for a tidy house, no purpose in study, no sense in putting on clean clothes that would only become soiled, and no logic in trying to tame his shock of curly chestnut hair. Never was a male so much in need of female attention or so blissfully unaware of his need.

Dr. William Jardine, a massive man with rough-and-ready manners, possessed a notoriously incendiary temper. He could intimidate the bravest man, but he could not understand or handle his obstinate son.

They were in the middle of a loud argument when a ball came bouncing through the open door of their cottage. Later, it occurred to Samuel that the ever-curious Caitlin had only been angling for an opening, an excuse to cross into forbidden territory.

She danced across the threshold on eager little feet and took in the room in one glance: the cracked stone floor, the peeling paper on the walls, the armchairs with the stuffing oozing from torn leather like purulent wounds, the shelves stacked with interesting bottles, and mysterious odds and ends strewn over the table. She glanced at William, at Samuel, then grinned and came forward with a little hop, skip and bounce.

Caitlin halted in front of Samuel. She made a sympathetic murmur, then hid her mouth behind one hand. "You sound as though you were on the losing end of the argument."

Samuel made no attempt at reply. He froze inwardly. Green eyes. He had never seen green eyes before. He searched those bright, intelligent eyes, transfixed.

Tense silence fell.

Samuel realized that he was holding his breath and staring, and he let air out deliberately and breathed in again. A new voice, unmistakably feminine, distracted him.

"Cat?" A beat of silence, then the sound of feet approaching the door. The lyrical sound of a young girl's soprano floated through the open shutter. "Cat? Where are you?"

Dark lashes lowered to partially conceal the green gaze. Caitlin took a step, stopped, and said over her shoulder, "It's safe, Cait. You can come in." It was her expression that told Samuel she was far from pleased about something.

There was the sound of feet. Caitryn crept in like a frightened mouse. She was like an angel, a real-life cherub, with fair ringlets, great blue eyes and dimpled cheeks. She looked at Samuel. Then she lowered her eyes from his face and quickly looked away, as if it hurt her to look at him.

Not so the bold Caitlin. That one took a step closer. She scanned his father's rooms. There was a sense of reckless energy about Caitlin, a dynamic, almost rash force that, Samuel later came to understand, was an intrinsic part of her nature.

"Oh, how disappointing. I thought there would be blood and guts everywhere. Being a doctor's surgery, and all that." The surprise in her tone was obvious.

Samuel made a soft noise of disbelief. William Jardine crossed his arms. He fixed a forbidding stare on Caitlin.

Her heavy, dark hair had escaped its ribbons and was lying tossed and untidy in joyous disarray across her shoulder. She did a little jig—like an intoxicated little bird.

William snorted and glanced around his chamber. There was a line, thin and deep as a knife cut, between his eyebrows. He stroked his beard. "It lacks a woman's touch. My wife is dead. Which is why my son neglects his chores," he replied brutally.

His heavy face looked as if it had been carved in wood, so still and stern it seemed. It was an expression that brought excuses immediately to Samuel's lips.

"It is clean—only a little untidy," Samuel said, bravado elevating his chin. He knew he sounded insolent, but he could not help himself.

Caitlin seemed not to notice the threatening atmosphere. She treated William with a casual irreverence that Samuel could only marvel at, and certainly could not hope to imitate.

"I am Caitlin Parr. This is Caitryn, my sister. The squire would not be averse if your son joined us for lessons, Dr. Jardine. He says all children should have regular lessons. Our tutor knows Latin and Greek, and Mama would see that he changes his shirt and bathes frequently. It would be good for him." She spoke primly. Even at nine years, her clear brain led her to make an unerring attack upon the paternal sense of duty.

Samuel had stood there, crimson-cheeked with mortification. He studied the rather grim expression on his father's face, and decided that the girl's preposterous suggestion was being considered very seriously, as if there were some question about whether or not it would be accepted. He shrugged. It was all one to him. He didn't care.

"Caitlin and Caitryn. Too much alike. Cat and Cait. Too confusing," Samuel said, determined to be perverse. He knew he was beginning to sound rude, but he couldn't help it. The green eyes bored into him. For a gleeful instant, he thought she was going to blow up.

"Would you come? I've always wanted a brother." Caitryn smiled a smile that gripped Samuel smack in the middle. What sweet words. His shy, lonely heart lightened, lifted.

"Oh," he said with soaring joy, forgetting his vexation with the angel's older sister. "I'd consider it an honor to be your brother, Caitlin."

"I'm so glad!" She smiled all over her little cherub's face. "But you've mixed us up. She's Caitlin. *I'm* Caitryn."

Caitlin gave him a furious look, as if she'd taken a grip on her resolve. She found an unexpected ally.

William's voice was stern. "That's settled, then! You need proper schooling, Samuel, else weakness of memory and confusion of brain will land you in a fine mess one of these days."

Caitlin cast a glance at William. "If I am ever so quiet and well behaved, Dr. Jardine, can I come and watch, and—maybe when I am bigger—help you?"

Samuel almost laughed, seeing how disconcerted his father looked, as if he thought that the girl was an alien creature. He felt a flare of grudging admiration for her impudence.

To his surprise, William laughed. "I'll think about it," he said, but Samuel knew him well enough to see that he liked Caitlin's bold approach.

And so, the Parrs took Samuel in, and Caitlin won over William Jardine with her high spirits and rebellious nature.

Grace Parr had been so taken with the life of King Henry VIII and his many wives that she had named her daughters after the ill-fated Catherine Parr. The similarity in pronunciation confused the child Samuel and, much to everyone's amusement, he was forever getting their names mixed up.

The large, rambling house, hunkered by the edge of Bod-

min Moor, had soon become a second home to the doctor's
son. His hair slicked back, his face scrubbed and polished,
his jacket brushed, he'd visited the Parrs as often as possible. While Caitlin teased and tormented, Caitryn had
smiled and soothed.

Samuel topped up his glass from the bottle of rye resting
on the counter. He tried not to think ahead. Yet an unwilling dream enveloped him. He saw Caitryn waiting. He pic-
tured her opening his letter with hope in her face....

He took a mouthful of the strong liquor, and wrinkled
his nose. A voice in his head told him he had indeed had
more than enough whiskey, but a louder voice cried out for
more.

He made wet circles on the polished timber counter with
the bottom of his glass. Why the hell was he thinking of
the past now? It must be the whiskey. Too much grog made
a man maudlin. And while drink was not one of his vices,
he needed something to dull the pain.

In life, Samuel knew, one not only had to cross bridges,
but one had to cross them at the proper time. Around went
the empty glass. The trouble was, he had just burned his
bridges. He shoved the empty glass toward Murphy with a
violent motion.

Caitryn was the woman he should have married. Not
Caitlin. Caitlin had been the bane of his life.

Damn, he needed time to comprehend the merging of
past and present, to let the scattered pieces fall gently into
place. Besides, he was in too far for backing out, now that
he'd taken vows in front of the altar.

Samuel took a deep breath, exhaled it slowly, accepted
the refilled glass. His bride had a lot to answer for! He
could still remember his father's anger that his son of nine-
teen years had endangered the lives of the thirteen-year-old
Caitryn and her fifteen-year-old sister.

And it hadn't been Samuel's fault. Even after all these
years, the injustice of his father's accusations still rankled.

It had been Caitlin who suggested taking the dinghy over to the cove and exploring the caves. And it had been Caitlin who went gaily tripping off into the hollow caverns and twisted her ankle, the delay caused by rescuing her making it impossible to leave the cove once the tide had turned.

Samuel was now convinced Caitlin's sprain had been all pretense, but at the time he had been a gullible fool and believed her fabrication. Unfortunately, he did not even have the consolation that time had taught him wisdom. He might be that much older, but he had still fallen for another of Caitlin's falsehoods. *The letter...*

Samuel settled on the situation at hand.

Caitlin. She was a part of that life he had pushed into the dark recesses of his mind, that life that included the mortification of the anguished secret that gnawed at him.

Caitlin. She had become like a many-armed octopus, her tentacles weaving themselves into every crevice of his life. Yet he saw no remedy. Now he was married to her.

He should not have waited this long to fetch Caitryn. It had been a shock to him when recently he calculated her age and realized that by now she might already have married, and be nursing children. He could not picture it. He had not wanted to picture it. He had not wanted Caitryn changed.

For the first time in years, he'd felt the desolation of the exile, the poignant ache for home; thus, he had penned a letter to Sir Richard. It had been a long letter, the scrawling script telling them of all that had happened to him since leaving Cornwall, explaining how successful he had become, and that he wanted to wed their daughter, Caitryn.

Only the wrong sister had come. It was Caitlin to whom he was now married.

Samuel looked at the whiskey at the bottom of his glass. What was it about the woman that made him so vulnerable? Was it the brain that was too quick and hard and brilliant for her sex? Or was it that small, indomitable chin, or those firm lips that were the physical evidence of a passionate temper?

Samuel took another long swallow. The memory of the day he had realized Caitryn was the eternal Madonna and that Caitlin was the true daughter of Eve was crystal-clear. It had been one of those magical summer days.

He could recall the querulous sound of gulls calling overhead, the sounds of the sea surging and retreating, and Caitryn, his gentle Caitryn, sitting in the shallow crescent of the stony cove, diligently painting. She had turned her shoulders just enough so she could see both him and the sea.

Light had spilled out over the bay, chopped by the waves into splinters. The air had been strange, as if it had been combined with mist or syrup, and Samuel had watched Caitryn, transfixed. He had been young, and he had been susceptible.

She was like an angel, all pale skin and hair, her soft, harebell-blue eyes staring at something on the other side of the bay that Samuel could not see. Her eyelids fluttered, but her gaze never wavered.

Samuel, rapt as he was, longed to see what she saw, to know what she was thinking, to understand the nature of her spirit. At thirteen, Caitryn had a sweet, generous nature and a cherub's smile.

"Stop dreaming, Samuel! Come and explore!"

Caitlin positively beamed. Her open mouth showed perfect white teeth. She seemed to mock him. The magic spell was broken. The sun seemed less warm now.

Samuel felt himself flushing at Caitlin's evident amusement. He stared straight ahead, ignoring her.

Caitlin was not a beauty like her sister, although she was arresting, in an exotic way. There might have been beauty in her green eyes, had they not been so needle-sharp.

Abruptly as a shark's dorsal fin rising from water, there was the sound of a scream. That scream vibrated in his gut like a hard-driven blade, tearing into his mind, his heart, making him rush off to be the hero.

It had been Caitlin. Caitlin and her devious ways. A sham, a cheap trick—and Samuel had fallen for it! Lord, his stupidity, his utter gullible imbecility, to have been taken in by the green-eyed witch.

And she was his bride. His bogus bride.

Now, Samuel stared at the back of her head, with its heavy knot of midnight hair, at her slender back, at the graceful curve of her waist, and the sweet flare of her hips. Deep inside him, something rippled. He tingled with the force flooding through him, which caused Samuel to groan inwardly. *Have you no shame?*

His lips set hard. "Canvass an extra team tonight, Liam. The new crew can join us on the trip upriver tomorrow." He placed a hand on Murphy's shoulder to brace himself as he struggled to his feet. "It's more simple and more effective to be ready for any trouble."

Marshaling courage, Samuel pushed himself away from the table with one knuckled fist. He needed time to deal with the problem. Time he didn't have. Heart pounding, he moved to claim his bride. He put out a hand, clasped hers. Caitlin flashed him a brilliant smile. Her eyes behind their sooty lashes shone intensely green.

He took a deep breath to keep the quiver of emotion from his voice. "My dance, I believe?"

She accepted with a shade of restraint. In Samuel's arms, Caitlin lost all sense of time and space, as if the music had thrown her free, displaced and rushing with the wind.

"The last time we danced together was on my sixteenth birthday. You trod on my gown. Remember?"

Samuel closed his eyes to the memory. The hotel ballroom seemed to ebb and recede, a surging in his ears wreaking havoc with his balance. He stumbled, and Caitlin took his arm.

"Are you sure you're all right?"

Samuel looked at her. She stared into his face, her eyes huge and liquid, their green turned dark as the forest. Her long lashes threw tiny shadows into the soft hollows of her face. He merely nodded.

"You're an imprudent man, Samuel Jardine."

Her tone managed to convey both a solicitous care for his well-being and a repressed anger. His expression darkened. She was probably riled both about his neglect and his inebriated state, but it couldn't be helped. Samuel skated swiftly over the thin ice.

"It's late. We should turn in."

"You're right." Caitlin slid her arms around him, leaning her cheek against his chest. "You're always right." That was a lie, but no one wants to make a false start, she thought.

"Right." He took a breath that momentarily lifted his chest. "Let's go," he said, the words a thick, hot jumble in his mouth.

A silence heavy with significance stretched between them as they slowly made their way to their room. Caitlin felt his fingers moving across her flesh, saw that languid, lustful look in his eyes that made her melt inside. A burst of happiness exploded inside her. She would tell him that she cared, and how much.

At the door, going up on tiptoe, she began to kiss him. Her lips parted as he angled his mouth to hers. His kiss was wide, wet and demanding. He tasted of whiskey, not a bad taste. One arm came up, enfolded his head, stroking.

Samuel felt her body, strong and supple against his, the ripple of her breathing, the warmth of her breasts and belly. He touched her cheek, the side of her neck, the hollow of her collarbone, the flat planes of her shoulder. He put his lips against her neck.

Everything should have been rosy. He was young and strong. His blood howled and leaped through anguished veins. A liquid heat rushed up his body. Trouble was, the world kept sliding out from under him on an oblique tangent, away from now, toward what he couldn't, shouldn't, mustn't, remember, so that he was no longer sure of anything. Except that she *was* his wife. Completely, unequivocally.

Chapter Three

The usual confusion prior to departure from the wharf at Saint John was in full swing. There came a clang of a bell from the shallow-draft riverboat. The sound ricocheted under the iron roof of the pilothouse and echoed across the poop deck and along the quay.

People descended the gangway to the squat and powerful craft in a rapid stream, and a flood of mingled French and English reached Caitlin's ears. From her vantage point on the poop deck, she watched a dozen men stringing in from the road, bearing bundles and bags and rolls of blankets.

They were big, burly men, unshaven, flannel-shirted, with trousers cut off midway between knee and ankle so that they reached just below the upper of their high-topped, heavy laced boots. Two or three were singing. All appeared unduly happy, talking loudly, with deep laughter.

It dawned on Caitlin that these were loggers. They were a rough lot—and some were very drunk. The men began filing down the gangway to the bulwark amidships. One slipped, and came near falling into the water, whereat his fellows howled gleefully.

Caitlin shivered, glanced up, and found Samuel watching her. He raised a well-defined auburn brow, managing offense and amusement at the same time. Her mouth com-

pressed. "It's plain folly employing such ruffians, pictur-
esque though they be."

He shook his head slowly. A grin eased up along one
side of his sculpted mouth. "A strong back and a good
sense of humor is all that's required in a lumberjack. Come-
liness is not a requisite."

Caitlin felt hot blood go to her face at the mild rebuke.
There was an edge to his voice that disturbed her. She felt
as if he had dealt her a light but very decided buffet in the
face. Again it struck her that Samuel had changed in some
indefinable fashion.

Perhaps it was simply the aftereffects of the liquor he
had consumed last night? While she must make allowances
for the excitement of getting married, she must ensure that
he did not indulge in such intemperate behavior on a regular occasion.

The Samuel she thought she knew was not a drinking
man, and manifestations of liquor were most inconvenient,
especially when it came to marital intimacies. Her eyes,
refusing to obey her edict of caution, drifted downward,
taking in the long, muscular line of his thigh, outlined by
his breeches. She swallowed, wanting nothing so much as
to reach out her hand and touch him right there.

Caitlin touched her upper lip with her tongue, excited
and a little perturbed at the shocking drift of her thoughts.
She saw Samuel's eyes flicker to her mouth at the movement and linger there.

He was very close, so close she could see the pulse beat
in his throat. She released a shuddering breath. He swallowed hard. Then he cleared his throat and shifted his feet.

Studying him, her heart swelled anew with love and did
a mad dance along her rib cage. The pose of polite calm
was a facade. Underneath, he was as tense as she was.

Samuel's eyes found hers at last. She lifted one hand a
little toward him, and let it fall helplessly. The shadow of

something came and went across his face. It was impossible to tell what he was thinking.

Caitlin's mouth went dry, her palms damp. For a moment she wished she could look inside him, and just see for once what he was actually thinking.

There followed a long, tense moment when nothing happened. He did not smile. His brown eyes did not waver. But they were alive, hot—and hungry.

It came to her suddenly that he wanted to kiss her. Her heart did a little flip of anticipation. The blood surged in her ears, and her breath was in short supply.

But he did not.

There came a rumble and sputter through the boat's side as the valves of the steam engine plunged into the pistons, and the steady thrum of its power reverberated through the wooden craft.

Samuel looked away. Deep creases formed in his forehead. He looked as if he were in pain. What was the matter with him? Perhaps he had the headache? Of course, that was perfectly logical, she told herself. After all, he'd consumed a considerable quantity of liquor the previous evening.

Caitlin's initial rush of relief at this interpretation quickly started to fade. It was beginning to be followed by doubts. Samuel looked, if anything, a little annoyed. Maybe she'd been wrong about him?

After all, she had not had a great deal of experience with Americans and their strange ways. And her husband had been in this country for nigh on ten years, sufficient time to have assimilated thoroughly its culture and habits.

What was certain was that his virile handsomeness was quite different from the insipid, pale-faced young men she had known in Cornwall. Most likely, the foolish notion that he wanted to kiss her had been all her imagination, she counseled herself.

No, she realized, with dizzying relief. She had not imag-

ined the way he looked at her, the tension, the desire that
seemed to vibrate in the air between them as loudly as the
engine.

Samuel was a considerate, genteel man—even if he was
forced to associate with ruffians. He was trying to act with
propriety. This was not the time and place for a gentleman
to kiss his wife. He would wait until it was appropriate.

Caitlin swallowed the thick knot of love that pushed high
in her throat, understanding what he felt, overcome that for
Samuel it should be as splendid as it was for her. She
slipped her hand around his upper arm and hugged him,
leaning her head against his jacket. She could smell the
deep, male scent of it.

"How true. It's always best to be chosen on your merits,
nothing else. Otherwise you're just a player in a masquer-
ade. All show." She made her voice very cool, in order to
mask her emotion.

Samuel did not reply. Perhaps he had not heard her. He
stood, hands on the rails, idly watching a wagon from
which goods were being unloaded. A motley array of passengers trailing around the wagon were forced to dodge
barrels and casks as two men piled its cargo aboard.

Caitlin stood next to Samuel and took deep breaths, in-
haling the crisp fragrance of the morning air. A small smile
played around the corners of her lips as she fantasized life
in the future.

There would be Samuel, a pleasantly ordered home life,
and, of course, a variety of social activities. They would be
delightfully happy. If she had remained in Port Isaac, except for the matter of being married, things would have
moved along the same pleasant channels. But what else did
women do in this country? she wondered.

And, abruptly, the thought triggered in Caitlin a doubt,
a welling of uncertainty, of the mind's apprehension, that
she had allowed a girlish infatuation to trap her into the

narrow, conventional mold that she had tried for years to escape from.

There had been a time when she thought Samuel had forgotten his promise, and she began helping Dr. Jardine. At first, she had washed bottles, folded linen, ordered supplies and sent out accounts.

Gradually, things had changed. She had a quick and eager mind, and Dr. Jardine, somewhat to his own astonishment, had found himself not only acquainting her with medical facts, but also initiating her into the practical aspects of medicine.

While she had not been permitted to go to Edinburgh and sit the examinations needed for formal qualifications, she'd been able to work with patients, instead of just learning theory from books. It had been many years since the sight of Caitlin Parr perched up beside the good doctor as he made his rounds raised eyebrows in Port Isaac.

What was her life to be? While marriage was all well and good, she hoped Samuel would understand that he had acquired a wife whose horizons had been broadened by none other than his own father.

The hush between husband and wife allowed normal activities to intrude on her thoughts—the creak and groan of the timbers of the sturdy riverboat, the shush of water beneath pilings and a man's laugh. The clang of the ship's bell brought her out of herself.

Caitlin looked around, catching sight of the drunken loggers. Their actions were theatrical—even melodramatic. They reminded her vaguely of a pantomime. Precariously they negotiated the slanting passage. All but one. This beefy, bearded, dirty-looking brute sat himself down on his bundle at the slip head and began a quavering chant.

Samuel's mouth set in grim lines. His breath hissed out, and she saw his chest rise and fall with a deep, controlled breath. He hailed the logger sharply.

From below, his fellows urged the recalcitrant one to

come along. When the call went unheeded, Samuel excused himself, then removed her from his path without the smallest ceremony, and was gone before she could protest. A man of action at all times was Samuel. A couple of passengers smiled at her, but she quickly looked away.

The ship's bell sounded again. From the bridge, the captain called, "All aboard!"

Samuel ran lightly up the slip. Arms akimbo, he stood before the logger. He spoke now with authority, impatiently. "Hurry aboard, Raoul. We're waiting."

The logger rose, waved his hand airily, and turned as if to retreat down the wharf. Samuel caught him by the arm and spun him to face the slip. "Come on, LeFeuvre," he said evenly. "I have no time to fool around."

The fearsome creature drew back his fist. Evidently he was angry at Samuel's decree. This looked serious, which didn't come as a surprise. It *was* serious. Somehow it seemed an irresistible force was about to meet an immovable object.

The crowd at the rail watched, stilled either by fear or by anticipation. Something quaked in Caitlin, and her heart fluttered painfully. She went still, her breathing labored, as she steeled herself for imminent disaster.

The logger was a big, barrel-chested man. But if he had it in mind to deal a blow, he failed, for Samuel ducked and caught him with both arms around the middle. He lifted the logger clear of the wharf, hoisted him to the level of his breast and heaved him down the slip as one would throw a sack of bran.

The man's body bounced on the incline, rolled, slid, tumbled, until at length he brought up against the boat's guard, and all that saved him a ducking was the prompt extension of several stout arms, which clutched and hauled him to the flush poop deck. He sat on his haunches, blinking.

Then he laughed. So did Samuel and the lumberjacks

clustered on the boat. Homeric laughter rang out in an explosive roar, as at some exceedingly funny jest.

The man who had taken that shameful descent clambered unsteadily to his feet, his mouth expanded in an amiable grin. "Hey, Sam!" he shouted. "Can y' throw me blankets down, too, while yer at it?"

Samuel's rich laughter spilled across the space. He caught up the roll, poised it high, and cast it from him with a quick twist of his body. The woolen missile flew like a well-put shot and caught its owner square in the chest, tumbling him backward on the deck—and the laughter rose in double strength.

The captain called, "Got a schedule to keep. All aboard!" The bell clanged again. The sudden jarring was so overwhelming it set Caitlin's heart thumping—or was the reaction caused by the sight of Samuel, still on the wharf? She felt a moment of panic when the boat began to swing.

Arms flung wide, Samuel ran down the length of the gangway. At the very brink, he leaped the widening space as the steamer, chugging steadily, drew away from her mooring. It seemed impossible that he set down on his feet, for from here, the distance seemed vast, but for all his size and hard muscle, he was as graceful as a dancing master.

Caitlin's breath came a little faster. Her lips parted, and her heartbeat leaped wildly within her bodice of green sprigged cotton. The fingers of one hand moved to the underside of one breast, as if to keep her heart confined within her body. A shuddering breath fell from her.

For a brief moment, her heart sank, as she looked at her husband and let herself think of the gigantic step she had undertaken. What in the world had she stepped into? Caitlin wondered.

Everything had changed. Nothing was the same as it used to be.

She stood there with her eyes closed, and was glad of the support of the rail, or she probably would have fallen.

Footsteps sounded behind her. Samuel caught her arm, and spun her around. He stood before her and grinned like a little boy who'd just done a magnificent feat.

"Cat, you should see yourself, standin' there all in a panic, wonderin' whether you'd be a widow before becomin' a wife." His voice still held traces of laughter.

Before she could answer, a voluble French family of four crowded against them and they were overwhelmed by a clatter of tongues, which, for the next few minutes, made any further conversation impossible. What was there to say?

Even after the riverboat had set its course, some time elapsed before their fellow travelers began to subside, and Caitlin contented herself in the interval with gazing out at the landscape. Somewhere distant along that stretch of water was to be her home.

Standing at her side, Samuel felt a confusion of emotions such as he'd never felt before. Guilt at marrying a woman he did not love, chagrin at his earlier uncharacteristic drunkenness, irritation at himself for his primitive male weakness in wanting to bed Caitlin. To top it all off, his head ached dully.

He looked down at the water that rushed past and felt physically sick. The river was like a sheet of silver that reflected and enormously magnified the sun. He could scarcely bear to turn his eyes toward it. The piercing, metallic sheen of it was unendurable.

He let his eyes blank out the bright daylight that hurt his already throbbing head, but he turned his head too fast and grimaced at the resulting pain. He sucked in a sharp breath.

There were a thousand questions he wanted to ask her about the previous night. She'd been in his arms, dancing across a floor of glass, while he drowned in the green depths of her eyes. There'd been smiles and kisses, even sweet words, but none of the words reached his brain now.

He could still feel the warmth of her pressed against him, the soft dampness of her. His last coherent thought had been how she clung harder when he pushed his knee between her legs and thrust...

The churning of the engine below had begun to recede. The boat seemed to be rounding a bend.

Samuel became aware that they were being watched. As if suddenly mindful of the loggers staring at her, Caitlin turned toward him.

Samuel took her hand and held it for a moment, marveling at its smallness. It seemed to go to nothing in his grasp. He rubbed his thumb absently over the back of her wrist and watched goose bumps ride her skin, which prompted him to ask, "Sure you're warm enough?"

She nodded. He cocked his head to one side, his eyes focused on her mouth. He watched her with the same hungry eyes she'd seen before. There was silence between them for a few moments. Then a sudden tremor shook him.

Caitlin gave him a weak smile. "Samuel! People are watching."

Samuel took a step backward. Damn. This was going all wrong. Her sharp green eyes made him tense. He inhaled a deep, slow breath. "Cat, let's go somewhere and talk. I have a great deal to tell you—and I want to talk about last night." His voice came out low and muffled.

Understanding, and a silent message to be cautious, met his gaze. Again he was struck by the self-possession that seemed to go oddly with her fragile appearance. He drew a shaky breath and ran a hand through his hair.

"Let's not talk about anything unpleasant on this lovely day."

She met his gaze steadily, and without flinching, and certainly never had she looked more attractive and alluring. With her dark hair slightly ruffled beneath the fringe of her bonnet, she looked even younger than when he had left Cornwall.

Caitlin was exquisitely made, and her sprigged gown gave her a fairylike aspect. Around her slim waist was tied a green satin ribbon to match that on her bonnet. Wide white skirts, like a puffy cloud, were lifted by the breeze, while the bodice hugged her slender frame and pressed firmly upward on breasts that rose and fell sharply.

Samuel didn't want to argue with her, but suddenly he wanted all his cards on the table. "I think we do need to talk." He held his arm out to her. "Shall we go?"

Without waiting for her agreement, he guided her gently toward the row of cabins reserved for first-class passengers. The glare lessened as they reached the accommodation area. There was a good deal of bustle and, apparently, some difficulty in finding accommodation for all the passengers.

Caitlin knew she was looking distracted as they walked along the deck. She had just caught a glimpse of a woman who had a fragile new baby, and who had lost two of her four other children on the voyage between Plymouth and Saint John. When she and Samuel were settled in their cabin, she would go find them in the mêlée of trunks, bags and milling people and renew their acquaintance.

It had been Caitlin who stood at her side when the two small bodies, almost too weightless to sink, were slid into the curling waves. At twenty-five, Eliza Freeman had already borne her phlegmatic husband, Tom Freeman, five children. Now three survived, and Caitlin wondered what the new country would do to the remaining children.

She was deep in thought when a familiar, throaty laugh sounded from one of the cabins. "Wait and see how things'll change now that Sam's taken a wife. No more late nights drinkin', no more cardplayin', no more visits to the Indian camp. Anyways, I made sure he had a good start t' marriage. Ol' Sam drowned his sorrows like a man."

Caitlin stumbled, halted, and applied a bit more pressure

to the arm she was holding. Samuel narrowed his eyes and studied the woman by his side. Her green eyes widened and a red glow spread across her cheeks, and Samuel knew without asking that she'd already comprehended Murphy's words. Ouch, he thought, was he in trouble.

Someone replied in a high-pitched feminine voice that echoed along the passageway, "Are you crazy or something? Don't try to kid me that encouragin' Sam t' drink himself blind was for Sam's own good, Liam Murphy!"

Murphy and that hellcat Kate Flaherty! Samuel swore under his breath, and his gaze shifted for the briefest moment to Caitlin's face.

"Sure it was. I was only tryin' to be of some help! A desperate man's an irrational man, Kate. Sendin' for a woman you haven't seen in ten years is a foolish t'ing t' do."

"Sam Jardine didn't *need* your help, you idiot! Succeed too well, and you fail completely! Sam's quite capable of tending his own affairs. He may have been a little too far gone to handle straight logic last night, but he could still handle a woman."

"Let's not be downright churlish about this, Kate! Even if he didn't disgrace himself last night, it's going to be a little difficult for Sam to explain away little Zoe."

Samuel winced inwardly. That insensitive turnip-brain! Now what was he to do? He pushed past the cabin, dragging Caitlin with him.

When she tried to jerk free, his fingers tightened. She glanced down at his hand, and then her eyes slanted up at him. Her green eyes glittered, as if she were trying to decide how to deal with this unexpected and puzzling information.

Samuel frowned, leaning forward slightly to study her upturned face. Her head was so close to his that he could smell the fresh scent of her hair. "You'd better walk very carefully," he said, "because it's rather slippery." That was true enough. "You're wondering what happens next, aren't you?"

She looked at him fiercely. "Yes." The word was barely a whisper, a muted feminine sound that caught him off guard.

Samuel lifted his hand and brushed a strand of hair from her forehead. His sun-browned hand looked very dark against her pale, delicate skin. "It's a bit complicated, and you're just going to have to trust me!" His fingertips lingered at her face.

He gently traced the outline of her face, pausing at her chin and tilting it upward. He groaned inwardly. He badly wanted to kiss those wet, shiny lips, not to confess some past indiscretion.

Dammit! What was the matter with him? Why was this so difficult? He wanted very much to tell her the truth, but just as he was about to do so, he paused, biting his lip.

Why should he confess? That was the honorable thing to do, and he was tired of honor. Wasn't it better to let Caitlin find out the truth about himself now, rather than a couple of weeks from now?

Caitlin ran her index finger along the back of his hand. Samuel was strangely astounded at the incredibly erotic effect the simple caress had on him. And he certainly shouldn't be having these feelings now.

If he once gave way to this raw emotion, he'd burn like straw. He could not accept it. He concentrated grimly on controlling his arousal. It was not easy. He took a grip on his resolve.

Caitlin stiffened imperceptibly, her mouth becoming a tight line. "Those in glass houses can't afford to throw stones. Who am I to judge?"

Samuel cursed under his breath. Obviously, what he had been thinking showed on his face. Embarrassed, he turned away and ushered her into their cabin.

The small, musty cell contained several narrow wooden

bunks, all of them shorter than Samuel's length by a good six inches. A small commode stood nearby, atop which was a cracked porcelain bowl and pitcher.

Standing erect, Caitlin could easily touch the planked ceiling. How could a man possibly be comfortable in such a small cubicle? At the thought of sharing one of those bunks with Samuel, her insides turned upside down, and there was a strange, trembling sensation in her knees that she couldn't explain.

Not a very sound medical diagnosis, she knew, but it did describe how it felt. What she needed was an explanation of Liam Murphy's insinuations and innuendos.

"Care to share your thoughts?" he said from the doorway.

Caitlin looked away from her husband, so that he couldn't see her face. She wanted to give away nothing of what she was feeling. Pain...betrayal...nothing she wanted him to see.

She thought quickly. If she framed her answer carefully, she could be honest, yet not tell too much. She gave a little laugh. "Actually, I was just thinking about the lack of accommodation. I was wondering where the little ones were going to sleep. Very unromantic thoughts, I assure you!" She was talking too fast, and she knew it.

Samuel's lips curled into a lopsided smile. "You like children?" His tones were unfathomable.

Caitlin's eyes darted to his eyes, and once again she found him looking at her. She wasn't sure how to describe the look he gave her. Intense. Penetrating. Probing. It made her nervous.

"Don't look at me like that," she said in a small, defensive voice. "It's natural that the children should be in my thoughts. Young ones are very vulnerable to the damp night air."

"Caitlin, you'd best sit down." He paused, as if trying to decide how to phrase his next words. "We must talk."

His face wore a curious expression. It was what Caitlin was beginning to think of as his "American" look—a look in which humor and sheer savage determination were very oddly mingled.

The wooden floor planks creaked as she took a seat on a bunk. She stared at the husband who had become a stranger. "What is it that you are so determined to talk about? Does it have anything to do with the absurd conversation we overheard just now? Or the fact that you fell asleep last night at a most inopportune moment?"

Both were questions he had feared. Samuel settled himself so that he could look straight at her. Seated, he dropped his laced fingers between his spread legs and raised his eyes to her face, where a smile that he could not interpret seemed only a challenge. He said nothing for a moment, sitting in silence while he gathered his thoughts.

Actually, he didn't have a thing to say. It had simply been a wild idea that he must tell her about Zoe before they arrived at Fairbanks. Better to wait until they were home. He let the silence grow.

Caitlin made a sharp movement of protest, and scooted so close to the edge of the bunk, she was in danger of falling off. She hugged her knees. "I may be naive, but I'm not stupid. Are you not going to tell me there was some mistake, some exaggeration? That the friends you invited to the wedding are not friends?" she asked, with an odd rasping note in her voice.

"Enemies come to your wedding. Friends come to your funeral."

"With friends like yours, who needs enemies?" Caitlin swallowed the lump in her throat and blurted out, "Is Zoe your mistress?"

Samuel shook his head and said absolutely nothing, but she could see the change in his red-brown eyes. They held a speculative, half-amused look. It was like being slammed into a brick wall.

"So why don't you deny these allegations? Why won't you even try to defend yourself?" Caitlin choked out. She was so angry she felt she might burst.

Samuel stood up. "Caitlin, I'll thank you to stay out of my—"

"Your what? Your affairs? After what just happened, how you can even think about—"

"Caitlin, I didn't ask your opinion. Zoe is not my mistress. It is a simple matter of trust. Either you are with me or you are against me. As my wife, you have no other options. I will tell you that much."

"What is it exactly that you want from a wife?"

Samuel's brown eyes were cautious. He shrugged and said, "Oh, I want a woman who is so besotted with me that she won't worry over who or what I am. She won't care what I have done in the past and will enthusiastically embrace every project I undertake in the future. She'll be a faithful helpmate, a mother to my children, and never give me cause to suspect her loyalty...."

Samuel fell silent. His mouth twitched a little, as if in self-ridicule, but Caitlin did not find the expression reassuring. Her breath was coming fast, and her hands were balled into fists at her sides.

For a moment, she almost voiced her own sentiments, then her ever-present sense of humor came to her rescue. She suppressed a giggle and fixed him with a meek, understanding, dutiful look.

"You want a woman to follow you barefoot wherever you choose to lead?" she asked, a little too sweetly.

"Exactly," he agreed, obviously pleased at her perception.

Caitlin caught her breath. The temper she had tried to control flared, and she did nothing to control it. Grabbing for a weapon, her hand curled around a metal candlestick. She hurled it. He didn't so much as flinch, even when it hit his shoulder.

"You sound as if you want a doormat, you great oaf. Murder and mayhem sound very attractive to me right now."

His brown eyes widened, and then he half smiled, teasing. "To love, honor, and *obey*..."

She took the point, but faced him undefeated. "You've had the only promise you're getting. Go take a walk, else I shall be converted into a doormat instantly."

"I just might do that." This time he dodged the missile, which hit the door frame. His rich laughter followed him down the passageway.

Chapter Four

Zoe. Zoe. Zoe. The name spun like a fiery litany in Caitlin's head, sharp and painful, keen as the blade of a sword cutting through her sensibility, releasing those wretched twin failings of hers, anger and pride.

Don't think about it, she told herself fiercely. She stood in the center of the cabin, shivering, alone with the empty bunks, and fought to put one coherent thought in front of the other.

She was being too intense again. Overreacting.

Zoe. Zoe. The name kept ringing in Caitlin's mind, an interior thunder drowning out the rational words she kept trying to think of, to cling to.

For a little while, she thought Samuel would come back to her. That he would smile, and she would run into his arms, and angry constraint between them would dissolve.

But he did not.

A deep shudder ran through her body, and she knew she should have kept her mouth shut. Why was she so cursed with vinegar on her tongue? Because she felt indignant and resentful about a woman she had never seen, that was no perverse reason to attack Samuel.

Caitlin glanced down at the narrow gold band on her finger, and her mouth set in a contrite curve. Poor Samuel.

The linkage of his name with this mysterious Zoe had obviously caught him off guard, and his wife had driven him away with her petulance and sharp words.

It was just that the shock had staggered her to the core and scattered her sensibilities. And now, in the aftermath, she was embarrassed by the viciousness of her attack, ashamed for the way she had spoken to him. The destructive power of words was as deadly as a gun, she mused.

She clasped the crucifix that hung about her neck and promised that she would do penance for her faults the first chance she had. A week of celibacy should do it, she thought with a revival of humor.

Caitlin let out a little giggle at this absurdity. In the intoxication of her rage, she'd forgotten that, in his youth, Samuel had often been the prodigious clown. He would become embroiled in any foolish scrape, so that his father had dared not contemplate which tales were true and which were false.

Unexpectedly, a vivid memory of Samuel came to Caitlin.... It had been the feast of Saint Francis of Assisi. The blessing of the animals.

Poppies red against the white altar cloth, sunlight fanning through the stained-glass windows, reflections of gold and delicate rainbow hues spilling like treasure on the gray stone floor, worn over the centuries to the sheen of polished pewter. It was stuffy and airless in the church, and Caitlin wished they would open the door.

Heads were raised during the singing of the hymns and bowed during the blessing. The ceremony seemed to go on forever, with every parishioner bringing along some creature to be prayed over. It was so boring, until Samuel let the doctor's white mice out of their cage right in the middle of the church service.

Later, when all the fuss was over, he excused himself, saying he'd thought it'd liven things up. Caitlin grinned. It sure did.

Farmer Johnson's wife fainted away right there and then, and silly Margaret Reade climbed onto a pew and held her petticoats up so high that all the boys could see her drawers. Samuel and the other boys crawled round under the pews, ostensibly trying to catch the terrified mice, while getting a great lesson in what women wore under those voluminous skirts.

Later, saintly Caitryn stoutly agreed that Samuel deserved a medal for liberating the poor dumb animals. At the time, she cowered in the aisle with the other girls, gasping in horror, as if a great wickedness had been committed. It was foolish Caitlin who was caught standing with the open cage clutched between her hands and a guilty expression on her face.

Caitlin could picture Samuel plainly the moment he realized the enormity of his stunt, and somehow the memory of it now made her smile. He'd been parchment-white, his freckles bright as threepenny pieces on his face. But with an unflinching, reckless, scornful courage, he'd taken the empty cage from her, taking full blame for his actions.

"That was very stupid, Cat. My old man won't like it one bit. I reckon he'll just about raise the roof!"

Caitlin had stood in great anger against the wall. "Don't speak to me, Samuel Jardine!" She had found it difficult to speak, knowing he would be beaten for his actions. "There's nothing I want to say to you!"

She found a bright side to this unfortunate recollection. People did not change. Samuel was as honest now as he had been then. Would he have sent for her after all these years if he had another woman? Of course not!

A sly thought intruded, instinctive and unbidden. But what was the basis of these allegations? Truth? Fabrication? Both? Neither? she asked herself angrily.

In what manner had Samuel contributed to the sordid gossip? Surely the rumor could not be all fabrication?

Part of Caitlin was appalled at these pernicious thoughts.

It was irrational. She knew it. But knowing didn't stop the aggravation seething inside her. Somehow it seemed disloyal to Samuel to even consider such wicked notions.

Well, then, don't think about such things! she berated herself.

Common sense reasserted itself. She reached down, picked up the candleholder from where it lay in silent reproach by the door and returned it to the narrow shelf. There was no point in wasting energy in worrying over false accusations. Work was always a panacea.

She untied the ribbons beneath her chin, pulled the dainty bonnet from her head, and tossed the frivolous confection onto her brass-studded trunk. Pulling up her sleeves, she set about making the tiny compartment comfortable.

Try as she might, while she folded linen industriously, her mind was elsewhere. How many times, as a young woman, had she dreamed her dreams and wondered what would happen if they came true? To be touched, to touch Samuel, to savor the textures of his hair and skin...

Caitlin shivered deep inside herself. She glanced at the narrow bunks, one above the other. Surely they could never, never be shared? That could not possibly be, she thought. Could what she had been told about the marriage act happen *here?* The thought sent a tiny thrill of excitement down her spine.

And what of Samuel? The brown, piercing eyes, as hot as the flame burning in the altar lamp—ah! Had she not looked into their depths and there read love for herself? Or had that been the product of her own imagination, a sort of wishful thinking on her part?

Stronger and stronger within her grew the certainty that she had already learned why Samuel acted as he did toward her. Little things. Simple things. The knowledge lurked somewhere inside her, hiding. Perhaps if she had eavesdropped longer, or even listened to the banker...

Somehow Samuel's hesitation in greeting her at the dock

now seemed ominous. She had put his odd behavior down to his nerves. To her excitement. She had thought she knew every passing mood of his tough, masculine features, but now she realized she did not know him at all.

Try as she might, she couldn't dispel the thought. All because she had overheard a stupid conversation that was not intended for her ears, and which Samuel had claimed was false.

No. Samuel had not said that, another little voice whispered in her head. Samuel had simply made the disclaimer that this mysterious Zoe was not his mistress.

If the woman was not his mistress, who was she? And why was this unknown woman's flamboyant name linked to Samuel's in such a dishonorable way? That was what she'd wanted to ask, but she couldn't. She was afraid to know the answer.

The nagging sense of feminine impotence began to irritate Caitlin. She sought to counter it in the only way she knew. She got angry again.

Damn Samuel for compromising himself like this, she thought fiercely. The idea infuriated her. He always had been a powerful fool, but he was not a simpleton.

Caitlin's back teeth clenched in sudden tension as she deftly inspected the bundle of bed linens. If only the bunks were a decent wide double bed, with high pillows and enveloping sheets and blankets. She tried to ignore the discomfiting thoughts that washed through her, leaving her stranded with cold, solid facts.

The truth was, she was wicked and selfish, part of her admonished, while another part resented his leaving her here, alone in the cabin—even if she had provoked him and told him to go. As he had done once before. The world slid out from under her again in a belly-churning swoop and shudder.

Caitlin's sensation of déjà vu was so strong that for a moment she staggered, and she had to grab the upright edge of the mahogany-and-brass trunk in order to keep herself from stumbling over the floorboards. She leaned her head against the wall and closed her eyes.

Once before, Samuel had left her, and though she knew the circumstances had been different, still he had gone at her command. Now, after all these years, was history about to repeat itself?

For an instant, Caitlin closed her eyes and thought of nothing at all. Then she recalled what Dr. Jardine had told her about loving Samuel, and his son's determination to do any outrageous thing that he willed, with no care for the cost.

There are times, Caitlin, when you gain more by letting go, William had told her when Samuel left Cornwall. *You are young now, but believe it or not, you will be glad Samuel has chosen his own path. It may be unfortunate, but one must at times make compromises, painful and uncertain though they may be.*

Recalling William Jardine's homily, Caitlin made a conscious effort to put aside her indignation. How could she speculate on Samuel's former exploits? How could she believe a hot-blooded man hadn't taken care of his needs? Better men than he had buckled under the strain of living in the wilderness.

Whatever she might wish, Samuel was a man among men, and he put his all into everything he did. He would get over her harsh words, she tried to convince herself. After all, there was no smoke without fire. And she hadn't forced him into marriage, had she? He had no choice but to brazen the thing out.

It was all his fault, anyway. Let him straighten it out.

Another dark and disturbing realization struck Caitlin. It was just her pride that had been touched. It simply galled her pride to have her husband's name denigrated. The Jardine name meant something in Cornwall. She meant to see that it remained that way.

With a shudder, Caitlin turned away from her thoughts, finished tidying the cabin, and glared at the door. She was angry at herself. She had never considered herself an intolerant woman, or an uncharitable one, and she found she was extremely discomfited by this sudden bitterness.

A noise at the door, footsteps and muffled laughter, tore her thoughts from the dark route they had taken. She straightened and went to peer along the dim passageway. Nothing unusual. Nothing at all.

Caitlin stared blindly in the direction her husband had gone. She wanted him—his closeness, his warmth, his strength, his immense desirability. How could she pretend otherwise? It had never, ever crossed her mind that she would travel three thousand miles to argue with her beloved Samuel within twenty-four hours.

She wanted to shout, in a frenzy. Instead, she must act the complacent little wife. She would not give the gossip-mongers the satisfaction of knowing they had created a rift between herself and her husband.

Devious adversaries demanded devious measures. Somehow, she must give Samuel time to consider and to reflect that she, Caitlin Jardine, was here, and that anything that had gone before was over.

Caitlin stood at the door, put on her bonnet and tied the broad green ribbons decisively beneath her chin. She had a plan. Her blood began to sing. It felt good to have a purpose again, to be caught up in stratagem and challenge, to have a cause to follow.

She would take one step at a time. She hurried past the cabin where they'd heard the laughter and wicked slander.

It was not long before she began to wonder if even one step at a time would prove to be too much. The moist, humid atmosphere wrapped itself around her like a damp towel as she stepped out of the dark passageway.

Above, the vast bowl of the sky, a breathtaking blue so lucid it seemed infinite, reflected itself in the sunlit water.

It wasn't just that it was hot; it was the humidity that made it uncomfortable. The deck smelled of humanity, and bilge water, and tar.

At several points along the length of the deck were small groups of people. A few steps from the passageway, a man in a woolen cap was stringing up hammocks, and Caitlin stood for a minute to watch.

Farther along, she saw a mother with a young baby in her arms, her husband and two small boys gathered around their baggage. The woman had a sweet face, though it was a little wan and tired, and there were dark circles under her eyes.

The woman's eyes were piercing, and dwelled on Caitlin's bonnet with an intentness that began to disturb her so palpably that she proceeded to move away, out of the range of her vision. She didn't feel up to initiating a conversation with strangers right now.

The deck reeked of unwashed humanity, but overall there was a feeling of energy in the atmosphere. The air was alive with arguments and laughter. Two loggers were shouting at each other and jabbing their fists into the air, as if impaling flying insects, while another sucked on an orange, spitting the pips overboard.

Caitlin skirted several huddled forms. As she made her way forward, no one spoke to her, although several of the passengers cast glances at her and exchanged whispered comments.

Near the rail, a half-grown boy in a tatty blue waistcoat and black trousers he'd outgrown was supervising three squabbling children. All the sour smells that rose from the unclean bilge eddied about them.

A brown-bearded, brown-jacketed man, hurrying by in the manner of an anxious squirrel, muttered an apology when they nearly collided. The heat and the smell and the boat's slight rocking motion began to nauseate her.

It must be her tense state of mind, combined with a lack

of sleep, that made her slightly indisposed. She would feel better presently. She wiped her forehead, and when she took her hand away her glove was wet. This place was impossible!

And where was Eliza Freeman? Caitlin returned stubbornly to her search.

As the riverboat plied its way at a steady speed up the river, Samuel busied himself with pretended work in the cargo hold, checking Caitlin's mountain of luggage and ensuring that the teamster had penned the livestock securely.

In this new perception and knowledge, his feelings were beyond endurance. He'd turned down Liam's offer of a round of poker and conversation. His excuse was that the manifests needed to be in order for the next leg of the journey. He was certain Murphy wasn't fooled.

Shut inside the hold, he inspected the bill of lading with an aching head, a sour, dry mouth, and the knowledge that he had done something there might be no forgiveness for. His mind refused reality, and he concentrated on the physical activity. By midmorning, he had gotten his breathing under control, and with it his temper.

In spite of his assurances, Samuel wasn't sure that Caitlin was entirely satisfied with his denial of Liam's foolish prattle, but he had made no further attempt to improve it. After his first denial of any relationship to Zoe, he felt devious and awkward, unable to think of any word of reassurance that was not a lie.

It seemed better to say nothing. He had not even taken the Irishman to task. When Liam found him, he'd looked startled, then stricken. "Oh, God, I really stepped in it this time. Damn my big mouth, anyway."

Samuel had given his friend a narrow glance that spoke volumes on the subject of loose lips, but he hadn't said anything. There was no point in taking offense at Murphy's ideas of humor.

He stretched, every one of his senses taut and alive. He could not deny the pulsing in his body. All because of a woman, one with whom he had no business ever having involved himself. His intense physical attraction to Caitlin still surprised him. He was beginning to feel some slight uneasiness as to what the outcome might be.

All chickens eventually come home to roost. Whatever the future, he must accept it now. He had no option. Then Samuel remembered that it was his fate that had brought him this far. The marriage was his, just as his fate was his. He was its creator.

The headache didn't go away all morning, even when he busied his mind. Checking the manifest did not ease the pain. He decided it might be best to keep from drinking too heavily too often, for it made him very slow-witted the morning after.

It was a temptation to go back to Caitlin, but he resisted. It was a battle within himself, but this was not a time for half measures. Instead, he thought of her. He thought of the touch of her lips on his, the smell of her and the feel of her.

Temptation indeed.

It had been a long time since he had had a woman, and his body was reminding him of that fact. Summer Dawn had died two, almost three winters ago, and he had been without a woman all that time. He had missed Summer Dawn so much.

Never could he tell Caitlin of the anger, the betrayal, the bitterness, the despair, that had conceived the vile plan that resulted in the letter that was never meant for her.

Better that she knew nothing.

Samuel let out his breath in an explosive sigh. But to abandon all his honor? Then what? He was utterly guilty, even if he regretted nothing of what he had done. He still was not sure why he had done it. Or rather, if he knew why he had done it, he still did not know why he had not stopped himself.

Indeed, for all of yesterday he had debated whether to tell Caitlin of the tumultuous circumstances that had led to that letter to Caitryn. He had determined to tell her the truth before the wedding ceremony, give her a chance to renege. But his mind had slowly changed, or had it been made up all the time, without his knowing it? He wondered now.

He was aware of a tremendous mixture of emotions. A sense of horror with himself for what he had done, for his misconceived missive, for his misjudged marriage, mingled with an enormous elation at the understanding he had just gained of his wife's character. And mingled with that was a fierce determination to continue with the arrangement for as long as was necessary.

Or was there more to it than that? And what lay at the end of it? He spent the second half of the day's journey deep in thought, his shoulders hunched and his eyes focused on the middle distance as he stared at the countryside that marched by the riverbank, and tried to shake the spell of her away.

Minutes—hours?—later, the vibration of the riverboat's powerful engine changed, deepening to a liquid gurgle as the craft hugged the outer limits of the waterway and, taking a long, sweeping curve, commenced a slow, almost ritualistic confrontation with the river's strong current.

Samuel straightened. There was nothing especially exciting in the scenery, and it was getting late. He felt he had allowed Caitlin sufficient time to get over her ill humor, so he made his way back to their cabin. From past experience, he knew she did not stay mad long. Her tongue might be sharp, but she did not sulk.

In any case, he badly wanted a wash, and he was hungry.

Heart pounding, he hurried down the passageway, which was lit by a single lantern suspended from a deck beam.

The beams themselves were so low that Samuel had to bend to avoid striking his head.

Repentance was not a familiar sentiment for him, and he wanted to get it over with. He began rehearsing suitably contrite phrases under his breath, the words of confession and forgiveness forming on his lips, even as his mind revolted at his intent.

On the threshold, some inner sense made the hair on his neck seem to prickle, and he checked his stride. He stood before the closed door, his hand on the knob. There was a moment's hesitation, and then, throwing caution to the wind, he flung open the door.

The words died on his tongue. He could not stem his swift intake of breath.

His eyes skirted the tiny compartment. Boxes and trunks seemed to take up every available inch of space. A pale-faced woman, dressed in an unbecoming shade of brown, sat on a battered trunk and nursed an infant. On her head was a narrow-brimmed bonnet trimmed with feathers. But the crown of the bonnet was crushed out of shape, and the feathers were limp.

A stooped, rawboned man of medium build, whose cheeks bore the scars of a childhood bout with smallpox, stood beside her. Two scruffy children sat on the floor at their feet, playing with some jackstraws.

Caitlin knelt beside them, her skirts bunched in a wild rumple about her. Samuel was so dumbfounded, all he could do was stand in the doorway and stare at his wife stupidly.

"Oh, Samuel." Her head came up. She swallowed and lifted her eyes to his. He could see her cheeks were flushed. "This is Eliza Freeman, her husband Tom, and their children. They traveled with me on the *Angelica*."

There was a depth of emotion in Samuel that he couldn't touch, dared not feel. Right now, what he wanted most was to be alone with Caitlin. He wanted *her*. That much his body was telling him.

He tensed all of his muscles, got his breathing firmly under control, and ducked his head as he stepped inside. He carefully negotiated his way round the children, and held out his hand.

"Evening, Freeman," he said, with a slight questioning tilt of his head. But the rough, pockmarked countenance regarded him with an odd expression, as though the fellow were gathering his courage.

Tom Freeman smiled respectfully and took his hand, but said nothing, as if he were not brave enough to speak. Caitlin looked uncomfortable, suddenly. Now Samuel wondered what she had done—if she had done anything.

Samuel suddenly went cold all over. He was not going to ask. He didn't want to hear what this family and all their baggage were doing in his cabin.

Caitlin sprang to life. She rose to pace the room, circling the children with quick, nervous steps. She stood before him, half defiant, half afraid, and thoroughly desirable. Desire started a slow coil in his gut.

She grasped Samuel's arm and stood on tiptoe to kiss his cheek. The touch was so light, it was almost more imagined than real. Yet he felt it all the way to his knees.

And so did she. He knew it. Her eyes were like gemstones, glittering with green fire. For a few moments, he stood there, enjoying the sensation of her body pressed against the length of his own.

"Oh, Samuel. Tom and Eliza are in difficult circumstances. There's no adequate accommodation..."

He felt the shifting surface of her body against his as she sighed. His mouth brushed over the tender skin behind her ear, touching it with his tongue. He wanted to close his arms around her, enfolding her. His hands began to move. He caught himself in time.

"...no place to sleep except on deck, and with the baby and small children, well..." Her voice trailed off.

Samuel stuck his thumbs in his waistcoat and said nothing. So that was it. Instinct told him Caitlin was getting some strange female idea in her head, one he would not like at all. He felt a bit like that unfortunate French king, Louis, whose head they'd cut off. It must be like this, he thought, when you waited for the guillotine to fall.

"Samuel. I had..." She paused to lick her lips. A certain rigidity had come into her stance, which had nothing to do with her stays.

There was something in that erect figure, the shining gaze, that made Samuel uneasy. He looked away from her, so she couldn't see his face. He made a neutral sound. He wanted to give away nothing of what he was feeling.

"I suppose I should have asked you first, but you were not here, and it was getting late and the baby needed to be fed, and I've invited Eliza and the children to share our cabin." She was speaking very quickly now, the words tumbling one over the other.

The implication of her words hit him, and he felt the blood chill in his veins. It changed everything, and nothing. "You'd best be joking, sweetheart. After all, we were only married yesterday."

He knew that was the wrong thing to say the moment the words were out of his mouth, but he decided to stay with the argument. It was, in part, true.

Caitlin jerked as though she had been struck. For an instant, Samuel thought he saw pain on her face, but it came and went so quickly that he decided he had been wrong. She lowered her head and found something fascinating to stare at on the floor.

"There is no rush, Samuel. I don't..." She could not quite get it out.

Samuel made a sound that was halfway between disgust and amusement. Tension surged in him. He could think of nothing to say to her. All his words stopped in his throat, sounding idiotic and churlish. He waited. He was reduced, finally, to asking outright.

"I take it Freeman and I are de trop?"

Caitlin looked quickly up at him, her green eyes glittering. Samuel became aware of the intense anxiety radiating from her. She gripped her fingers together, as if she weren't to be put off so easily. He knew she would not abandon her determination now.

"It will be a trifle overcrowded, I daresay, but I am sure we will manage. After all, it is only for a few days." She stopped and looked embarrassed.

Samuel gave her a quick, hard glare. He felt a little angry with her. He did not believe she was thinking clearly. If he had her in his arms again...

He watched her breathing catch, an intake and a long pause while her skin grew pink. She gave him a little curving smile, her lips moist and soft.

A sudden intense spike of desire ran through him. The woman was unique, magnificent in her protection of the vulnerable Freeman family. Would she be as generous to Zoe? Let her mean it, he thought, setting his jaw.

Deep within him, a tiny seed of hope was beginning to grow, even as his blood rose in a deep, powerful surge that made him tremble. His muscles, his breath, his mind, his whole carnal self, urged him to oust these intruders.

"There are times when good reason overrides passion. This is one of them."

The rise of his own violent emotions took him by surprise. It was only with an effort that he prevented himself from biting his lip. "Do forgive me my lamentable lapse of manners."

"I once read that sensual pleasures are enhanced by doing without them for a while," she said in a muffled voice. Her small chin tilted. "Maybe you should try it."

Tension laced the room like fog. Samuel felt a little

shocked by Caitlin's outspoken words. He felt himself turn red beneath his tan. A long moment passed.

Nobody moved.

Taking a deep, fortifying breath, he finally said, "At least I know the true measure of my blame." Another deep breath. "Unless, of course, there is some element of self-punishment in it."

The expression on Eliza Freeman's face made him repent instantly. It was one of considerable sadness, a crumpled look of weariness and disappointment. He found, to his chagrin, that the look cut him far more deeply than was reasonable.

Caitlin said nothing more. She didn't have to. Every line of her slender body rejected what he'd said. She pursed her lips, those soft, curvy lips, and looked at him sideways. She stared at him for a moment or two, then unbuttoned and rebuttoned her gloves in a jerky little gesture. Another wave of heat swept over him.

Samuel waited for a long moment, and then he caught her hand. The fingers twitched, closing convulsively. Her breath came out in a little gasp.

"I don't know what you mean, but I'm sure no one can expect to be right all the time." There was a question mark in Caitlin's eyes, if not in her voice.

Samuel met her wide, shining gaze, and the vague tension that had been gnawing at him for several hours suddenly coalesced into an almost overmastering urge to take her into his arms and wipe some of that feminine promise out of her eyes.

But no. He could wait. She was his wife. She would be worth waiting for. Instead, he saw his opportunity to retreat, and seized it. He shrugged. "Don't fret, my love. There are other nights." He kissed her, quickly, on the tip of the nose. "Come on, Tom, I believe there's a card game in progress somewhere on deck. We'll leave the ladies to enjoy the children's company, while we bunk down with the men."

Chapter Five

It was the falls that stopped the riverboat. Five hundred feet away, the cascade frothed down the steep mountainside. White water snarled and sucked against sharp-toothed black rocks. One huge pinnacle, already worn and ravaged by the endless flow, stood, a grim and silent sentinel against the sky. The shallow-draft vessel rocked quietly upon the water, feeling only the gentle swell, an afterthought of the spill upstream.

Come a freshet, and the falls would become a rushing force, water seething and racing, coffee brown streaked with white, thundering in its rush to the sea. Great clouds of spray would shoot skyward, with beautiful rainbows wreathing like goblins in the mist. But today, the falls were restrained, genteel, allowing the passengers to disembark in comfort.

Caitlin was pleased to touch land again, even if they were still a long way from Samuel's home in Maine. The Freemans were to remain in this little straggling township, where Tom had accepted a position as a schoolteacher.

River de Chute was an untidy collection of shacks and sheds and river wharves, but there was a good guesthouse there, a large wooden building that stood by itself on the outskirts of the town.

After saying their farewells to the Freemans, she and Samuel crossed to Le Renard Rouge, where Samuel engaged a room. They ate a hurried meal in the inn's dingy, smoke-filled dining room, before Samuel went off and busied himself arranging transport for the morning.

Upstairs, in the largest and best bedroom Le Renard Rouge possessed, the walls were boarded and distempered with white paint. By the fireplace was a dark varnished washstand. A single rickety chair, a mirror and a massive sawn-oak bed, covered with a rose-patterned comforter, completed the decor. Over the bed was a sampler, with roses on it, and the legend The Lord Is My Shepherd.

The room was dark and smelled of camphor and carbolic, familiar, pervasive odors that brought back many fond memories of Caitlin's childhood. She remembered sitting quietly for hours on a high stool, watching Dr. Jardine mix his medicinal potions and learning his vast pharmacopoeia.

A vision flitted across her mind's eye, of Samuel laughing as he grabbed her off her perch, tossing her almost up to the surgery's high ceiling, then catching her as she came down, kicking and shrieking with outrage. The easy way he handled her weight had served to underline his strength and her vulnerability—a vulnerability she stubbornly refused to acknowledge.

Never had a boy tormented a girl more. Caitlin suspected Samuel enjoyed teasing her. Her mouth curled into a smile. It was understandable. After all, she did bite so beautifully.

Out the window, with its rose-patterned curtains, there was a view of the mountains, a mirage of wavering greens. Caitlin looked out over the rim of trees. There was nothing but forest, though just beyond the mountain, she knew, lay Maine, with its farms and settlements, a kind of civilization. She stretched, and took a sharp sniff of pine-scented mountain air.

Somewhere in that vast green range her future lay. One day she would know the outline of those mountains as well as she knew her own face in the mirror. But today they looked alluring and secretive and misty; and she had a sense at last of having arrived somewhere, after a month of rocking boats and seeing nothing but horizons and skies and surging water.

Insects droned in and out of the window as Caitlin tried to calculate how many days it would be before they reached Fairbanks. She had never thought of the rigors of taming the wild frontier before.

How difficult it has been for Samuel, she thought, carving out a living for himself in this vast land, without the succor and support of the woman he loved. It would be different now. She was there.

The sky had darkened. Over the river, a flock of black scoter ducks circled, like the ashes of a burned newspaper, and then vanished. Ripples on the dull surface shimmered in the waning sun.

Caitlin crossed to the washstand and poured some luke-warm water into a china bowl. She looked at herself in the smeared mirror and wrinkled her nose at the wide-eyed woman reflected there.

"There is something wrong, I can tell. I may be naive, but I'm not stupid. I think Samuel is annoyed with me. He spent the entire trip upriver 'attending to business.'" Caitlin cocked her head. "Why?"

A faint flush of color showed beneath the flawless skin. Tangled locks of dark hair framed the delicate features. The woman stared back and gave a convincing show of mulling over what Caitlin was asking. Her chin high, she tapped her long forefinger against the double ridge of her pursed lips.

"Now just assuming that I was interested in such a physical phenomenon as the difference between a man who is alive and one who is dead—the only way I've seen a man who was fully naked—as you well understand, I'd want to know some things."

The woman in the mirror faked a look of innocence. "No, you don't. Better to remain in suspense. Curiosity killed the cat."

"You don't know...you can't even guess what it must feel like to be loved so. Someday you'll laugh at this. I'm sure of it," Caitlin told the woman. "Someday, but not tonight."

From the woman's frown, Caitlin knew that wasn't what she'd wanted to hear. She shook her head. "I think you're nervous, and that's why you jumped at sharing your cabin with a bunch of strangers."

Caitlin smiled. The woman smiled back. "I guess I am at that. I never supposed a woman felt this way, that the marriage act is not solely for the purpose of procreation, but an act of love and lust. You're not going to tell me what to do, are you?"

A faraway look came into the green eyes. "I don't think it can be explained," the woman said. "It's got to be learned."

After this sage advice, Caitlin attended to her ablutions. As soon as she had freshened herself, she climbed onto the bed and tentatively bounced on the feather mattress. There was a great crescendo of springs, and the bed groaned like a huge, creaking raft.

Caitlin caught sight of herself in the large engraved mirror over the washstand. Hair flying, she looked like a wild creature. Her face hot and rosy, she quickly slid her bare feet back to the floor.

The doorknob made a click. Caitlin looked up sharply at the sound. Samuel was leaning against the door, his hands in his pockets, his jacket stretched tight across bunched shoulder muscles.

There was an awkward moment in which neither seemed to have anything to say. Caitlin curled her bare toes against the cool, rough wood, feeling foolish.

Samuel stood there a moment, looking at her with narrowed eyes. For all his casual pose, she sensed that he was disturbed about something. It was as though something dangerous were prowling the room, an almost definable rippling of the atmosphere.

As she listened to his raspy, heavy breathing, she wondered if he was ill. She started to ask what was wrong, but held her tongue. He was staring at her with that intense look in his eyes again, and she found her hand straying self-consciously to her hair, which she had tied out of the way, so that it flowed down her back in a soft cloud.

For a long time, there was only silence and the rushing sound of the distant cataract. Then Samuel moved abruptly, straightening. He came into the room and closed the door behind him.

Perversely, Caitlin made no move. Motionless, she waited for him to say something. His footsteps echoed on the unpolished floorboards. The careful deliberation in his movement carried an air of purpose. He looked at her over his shoulder.

"Well, here we are," he said. There was a dangerously forbidding set to his jaw and mouth that was making her blood shimmer wildly through her body, leaving confusion in its wake.

"I'm glad. Even if—" Caitlin broke off. She stood still, feeling weightless, breathless—uncertain of what she wanted, unable to move, to so much as take a step. She ran her tongue over her lips and saw him instantly fix his gaze on her mouth.

"Even if what?" Crossing to the rickety chair, he sat down and began to remove his boots. "Even if we do have another tedious three days' journey ahead of us?"

His fingers fumbled at the laces a little, for his eyes never left her face. She found herself following the small action, spellbound. Those hands…

Caitlin gave a shiver. She caught herself in the middle of it, but not before Samuel had seen the movement. His glance shifted to the pulse that beat erratically at the base of her throat. He was watching her with that strange intensity that made her breath shorten.

This, she realized with a shock, was what she had been playing for since he had arrived just now. He'd spent the past four days avoiding her. Today, without understanding what she was doing, she'd been determined to make him aware of her.

Now that she had succeeded, she wasn't sure she could handle it. Something unexpected smoldered in the red-brown depths of his eyes that was banked down and hidden before she could retreat from it. She retreated just the same, worried that her wanton thoughts might reveal themselves in her face.

Striving for an idleness she did not feel, she said, "At least this smells better than the riverboat, and we won't have to share it with—" she faltered as the keen eyes met hers again "—a-any—anyone."

Caitlin heard her own stammering and willed her unruly tongue to behave. She felt as if her heart had leaped into her throat and lodged there. It was unnerving being so close to him, especially knowing the huge bed was there... waiting.

"A good night's sleep will be most welcome. I've not had much rest recently."

In the quickly fading light, she could see that although his eyes were serious, a wry smile touched his lips. She flushed with embarrassment. It was as though he had read her mind.

It was immodest, she was sure. But it felt so right. So good. She'd been waiting all her life to be stirred like this, impatient like this, filled with this strange eagerness that only led to a deeper need.

Caitlin lowered her eyes and self-consciously smoothed her gown. Its rustling seemed a loud shriek.

Not now—not yet.

Surreptitiously she glanced up from beneath her lashes. She moistened her dry lips. He was still looking at her. Her heart was pounding again, filling her ears in the sudden silence. She tucked a strand of hair behind her ear and asked, "Does Mr. Murphy accompany us on our journey to Fairbanks?"

Samuel's hands stilled. A muscle in his jaw twitched. He shifted his glance. The corners of his eyes crinkled slightly.

"Only as far as the Presque Isle Stream depot. The new crew will work from there. Timber has to be cruised, and tote roads prepared while the weather holds. And that—" a hint of iron crept into the smooth tone "—means we'll be on our own for the last leg."

Caitlin heard the edge in Samuel's voice and wondered if he was still angry about her trick in sharing their cabin with the Freemans. Or maybe there were dangers and hazards on the journey about which he was concerned and about which she knew naught?

She could not fathom what was in his face. Only that he looked tired and angry.

Her fingers curled into the palm of her hand as she stood very still. "You...you speak a language I don't understand. What does cruising mean? And what's a tote road?"

"We speak of measuring timber as cruising. That can be standing timber, logs, or even sawn lumber at the mills."

The boots thudded to the floor. The chair creaked raucously as Samuel stood to divest himself of his jacket and cravat. His eyes never left Caitlin's face as he absently draped the jacket over the back of the chair and began unbuttoning his shirt. As he moved, she watched the play of bulging muscle; there seemed to be no slack in the shirt at all.

Caitlin could feel the blood racing through her veins. She hurriedly busied herself with lighting a candle. Her hand trembled as she lifted the taper, but she knew now that the die was cast.

"A tote road is clearing the right-of-way from the se-
lected stand of timber to the river. Stumps have to be cut
low enough to give clearance for the tote wagons—and
before you ask, a tote wagon is a flat wagon used for trans-
porting logs. It's hauled by a team of oxen." His voice was
too low-pitched, too thick, telling of some deep-seated dis-
turbance within.

Caitlin carefully placed the candle on the washstand. She
did not look up for a moment, because she knew she was
blushing. She waited a beat, a second beat, for the heat to
fade from her cheeks. Then she looked up over her shoulder.

A frisson of carnal awareness laced with feminine caution spread through her nerve endings. Samuel had tossed
his shirt in the general direction of the jacket and was beginning to unclasp the leather belt at his waist.

The soft candlelight poured over him, highlighting the
sharp planes of his face, the sensual lines of his mouth and
the sheer power of his body. Gold dust shimmered as his
arms moved. Muscles tightened and relaxed, making light
slide over his skin with each supple movement of his body.

Caitlin felt a primitive urge to run and hide from him,
and an equally primitive urge to reach out and touch him.
He kept watching her as he stepped out of his trousers. A
thick nest of russet hair framed his heavy, aroused manhood.

Excitement washed over her at the sight of him. It was
as if there were a bright core hidden deep within her, a
molten river flowing with need. She tried to tear her gaze
off his hard, pulsating masculinity, and couldn't. She
opened her mouth. Nothing came out. She couldn't have
spoken if her life depended on it, bemused that this much-
loved man should so blatantly exhibit the physical evidence
of his love for her.

It was a love so different from that of parents or family,
or the adoration of a young, inexperienced adolescent. This

was a mature, virile, impassioned man who desired her. As she thought of the word *desired,* small pulses began to beat in her body.

But this time Caitlin wasn't dismayed. This time she admitted she was nervous and uneasy, so vividly aware of him as a man. She hoped he didn't realize how totally inexperienced she was, that dissecting cadavers and examining patients wasn't the same as standing next to a living, breathing, near-naked male who made her blood hum.

Even in her imagination, Samuel had not looked so overwhelmingly male. The naked reality of his strength fascinated her. He was large and wholly male, a creature built for taking what he wanted in life. Wide, muscular shoulders, flat waist, lean hips, long legs, the flesh sun-browned, hard and smoothly muscled.

On the washstand, the candle softly flickered, and the thick hair on his chest gleamed with metallic golden highlights. His eyes were glittering like the red-hot center of a furnace. Caitlin's lips opened on a warm outrush of breath, a throaty sound.

Ten feet between them, and it might as well have been one. She could feel him as if he already had his arms around her, as if she were already naked. Nothing in her past had prepared her for this rush of emotional intensity. The flood of feeling washed over her like a swoon.

He was watching her with eyes that burned. Muscles stood out rigidly along his jaw, and the pulse beat too quickly in his throat. And she had the satisfaction of seeing that he shook, too—that he wanted her as much as she wanted him.

Caitlin walked to him. There was no hesitation in her stride. She made no pretense of hiding her eagerness. She felt excited. Every nerve, every part of her, was alive, burning, screaming with the desire to be touched, caressed.

Stopping short, she reached out with her hand, touching him first on the shoulder, tracing the rigid muscles of his arm with one finger. What she really wanted was to wrap her arms around him.

But if Samuel realized what the action had implied, nothing was revealed on his face. He made no response. Only those red-brown eyes seemed alive, with a fire that threatened to consume.

Caitlin, abruptly dizzied by an intense stirring inside her she could not define, drifted against Samuel for an instant. She gently moved against him in what she hoped was an arousing, sensual manner.

He was fully erect, his body hard and fiercely aroused. She felt the vitality of the man, encompassing her, enthralling her. Even through the cotton of her dress, the brush of his hard warmth against her thighs left her trembling. She could feel it spreading through her like the slow infusion of a sensual elixir.

"Samuel?" she whispered with uncertainty. Why did he hesitate when she was so obviously willing?

His hands grasped her shoulders. "I can't explain... Not now. Not yet. God, you don't know what you're asking," he said, his voice raw and harsh.

Caitlin stared up at him, stunned by the intensity of his words. She couldn't breathe, couldn't think, in this hammering, melting, whirling closeness. *Touch me...touch me...*she willed him.

She spread her fingers across his broad shoulders, feeling the ripple and flex of his muscles at the touch. "Maybe this is as good a time as any for us both to find out." She broke off abruptly, swallowing hard. She was annoyed to feel herself turning pink.

Samuel said nothing, but his expression altered, and Caitlin abruptly found herself confronting the hard, intent, hunting look of the sexual male. He stood still, staring at her. She could feel the sensual driving force within him, and knew it was focused totally on her.

A silence sprang up between them that had a quality

Caitlin could not define. *He wants me. We're married. So why won't he even kiss me?* She wondered what she was missing.

Caitlin eyed Samuel carefully. She recognized the controlled hunger there. In a blinding flash of awareness, she realized that he was waiting for her to make the first move.

So what was she supposed to do now? Her knowledge was the unfamiliar matter of the books she had read. Instinctively she moved closer. The thought of being kissed by Samuel made her blood shimmer wildly once more.

Unashamed, unafraid, she lifted her hand. A fingertip traced its way down the line of his jaw. She put her palm against his cheek, savoring his warmth and the masculine texture of his skin.

Words crowded Caitlin's throat, all but choking her. She spoke none of them, but the softest sound, as of a breath being slowly released, floated in the air.

She rose on her toes to kiss his lips. A cautious kiss. His mouth felt hot as it slid against hers, and she whimpered. At last she knew what to do. She need only open her lips like this, strain to him like this, and the rest was easy.

It happened all at once. Her breasts shook with her body's shivers as their lips crushed together. His mouth held hers in a deathless grip, never letting her go as she clung to him.

They kissed long and deep. Her hands buried themselves in his thick hair. His hands seemed to be everywhere, stroking, caressing, removing clothing. Within moments, her dress was in a heap beside them. She felt his body strong and supple against hers, the ripple of his breathing, the warmth of his chest and belly.

He put his lips against her neck and caught hold of one of her wrists, pushing it down to where the thick bar of his manhood pressed against her stomach. Suddenly breathless, Caitlin tried to free her hand, but he held it where he wanted it, groaning thickly as she cradled him.

"Oh!" The sound was filled with hidden depths, promises of unsaid delights. "Samuel..."

He let out a sigh like a cloud riding high on warm wind and sunlight as she traced his long length upward, became familiar with the shape and size of him. A liquid heat rushed up her body at the touch of that silken flesh. Slowly, she traced an intimate path with her fingertips, her uncertainty giving way to a thrilling excitement as he responded to her.

A low groan rumbled deep in his chest, the vibrations passing back and forth from one to the other. He lowered her trembling body onto the turned-back bed. Coming down beside her, he touched her cheek, the side of her neck, the hollow of her collarbone, the flat planes of her shoulder, the most intimate parts of her soft, womanly secrets.

Still she sensed him holding back, even through the veil of her own unending passion. Such a bothersome thought was ludicrous. Or perhaps not, considering his strange behavior since her arrival.

To anyone else, Caitlin would have said, "It's impossible that he didn't send for you. You've got your facts wrong." She knew Samuel too well, and had known him too long. Again the sensation of missing something vital rose in her.

Think, she berated herself. She was trying very hard not to let her thoughts run away from her, but the instant they came together, all coherent thought was flung from her mind.

Dream, fantasy and reality met in a terrifying swirl of emotion as he thrust himself deeply within her. Caitlin was aware of herself and Samuel only, linked by the rising pool of pleasure, like ripples in a lake, spreading outward endlessly. She lost all sense of time and space, as if her passion had thrown her free, displaced and rushing with the wind.

Guttural sounds emanated from her, a siren's song of lust

and love, entwining passion with the emotional bond without which sex soon sours. And, as it did so, she felt the gathering storm within his thighs.

The core of the sun burst inside her, bringing her joy beyond description. She laughed with it, elation and ecstasy combining, filling her with life.

She heard the sound of his deep, heaving breaths and felt his face as he buried it in her hair. When she fell asleep, it was with one brawny arm wrapped around her waist, holding her as though he would never let her go.

But in the granulated light of dawn, when she awoke, soft and shy, Samuel was gone. It was just as well, she thought. There was so much between them, so much unspoken, the darkness and the light, the questions and the answers, and the questions without answers.

Suddenly feeling chilled, she reached for her paletot, lying on the trunk, and slipped on the stylish jacket that her mother had had made for her. Grace Parr had always liked her daughters to wear pretty clothes, and the paletot and dress she now wore were elegant and expensive, far different from the serviceable garments Caitlin herself had stowed in her baggage.

It took a little time to pack what she would need for the three-day journey, after which she wrote three letters, one to her parents, one to Caitryn, and one to William Jardine. That done, she donned her bonnet and went to find Samuel.

Although it was early yet, there was already a motley assemblage of farm wagons, carts and drays gathered outside Le Renard Rouge. Samuel seemed to be everywhere, organizing the teamster, shouting at the loggers, pulling on ropes, checking the balance of the load.

The journey to Fairbanks must now be undertaken overland. Caitlin's baggage occupied three wagons. Her wardrobe trunk and her boxes of linen, medicines and books were securely fastened with lengths of rope. In the train of supply wagons that followed were stores of flour, molasses, salt pork and spices.

Behind the town and the dark stands of pine, thick and creamy cumulus clouds lazed away the morning, waiting for the cooler winds of the evening before they rose up to bring a summer thunderstorm, and rain. A thread of early-morning fog drifted low over the river.

Moving with short, determined strides, Caitlin pushed through the crowd gathered on the sidewalk. Once clear of the throng, she came to a halt. In her path, two people were having what seemed to be an altercation. She recognized one of them as Liam Murphy. The other was Kate Flaherty, the girl who had helped her dress for her wedding.

The Irishman was standing with his back to her. Facing him was the blond girl. Wisps of her hair had come undone, fluttering now against the skin of her cheeks. Her face was white and pinched. She was talking rapidly, though not loudly. Murphy's response was low, vehement. The girl shook her head like a dog coming out of the rain.

Caitlin stood very still, staring at the pair. She could not make out any of the words, but it was now evident that they were having a heated argument. She was just deciding what action to take when the conversation erupted.

"Liam, it would be wiser not to disturb my brother with news of this.... Surely he will blame me for allowing you to..." Her voice tightened up, and she put her hands over her face. Caitlin could hear her weeping softly. "I'm sorry," she whispered. "I'm sorry."

"Damn, I hate it when you cry." The Irishman swung away and almost bolted down the sidewalk.

He pushed past Caitlin. She tried to evade him and lurched badly, losing her balance. She clutched at his brawny arm to stop herself from falling. She stood upright, with care. No harm was done.

"Look what you've done now, you lack-witted, clumsy oaf." As the words left her mouth, she was astonished at

herself for having said them—but not sorry. It was this
quarrelsome pair who had borne false witness against Samuel and caused such pangs of jealousy as to disturb the
journey north.

Liam, who had never in his life been talked to in this
way by a woman, was momentarily tongue-tied. He took a
deep, shuddering breath, his head nodding spasmodically
like an ill-worked marionette's. He did not evade the
charge. "I'm sorry, Mrs. Jardine." He extended an awkward hand. It was broad in the palm, and capable.

"Such gallantry! There's no point in thinking you can
bully the weeps out of a woman, Liam Murphy. Only a
fool would think that."

"'Tis a poor fool that I am, then. Spoutin' off me mouth
like an idiot, and upsettin' poor Kate." Caitlin allowed his
fingers to enfold hers. Liam swallowed hard, tried again.
"Anger does terrible things to a man's good nature. Makes
him say and do what God and his holy angels count as a
mortal sin."

"Well, at least you're honest." She smiled. "I myself
have a shrewish tongue when things don't go exactly as I
planned them. Good morning, Kate," she said, acting as
though she hadn't noticed the woman's tears.

The girl's face flamed. "Good morning, Caitlin." She
turned to the Irishman. "I'm sorry, Liam. 'Twas my own
folly that brought the argument about. Now, if you'll excuse me, I have some things to do." In another moment,
she was gone.

"'Tis nothing, ma'am." Liam gave out a nervous guf-
faw. "A storm in a teacup, and Kate's a bit high-strung at
the moment."

Caitlin looked at Murphy levelly. She was a little surprised to detect a shadow of sorrow in his blue eyes. "Then
why do you argue in a public place? You don't look to me
as if you're an uncaring man."

Murphy could sense Caitlin bridling. Her voice was

sounding downright prim. He kept his face impassive. "I suppose you were expecting me to—"

Caitlin cut in. "As a matter of fact I make it a habit never to expect anything. It makes for clear thought and pure reaction."

"Instinct, eh?" The Irishman nodded. Then, abruptly, he laughed. "It may be that everything I've heard about you is true."

"Well, I suppose it depends on who is telling the tale. But then, so much depends on the storyteller, doesn't it?"

"I gotta get crackin'. There's a lot to do." He eyed Caitlin carefully, hesitated a moment. "You know," he said slowly, "Sam said you was full of pluck, and a little bit irreverent. He was right. I'm glad you never took our tomfoolery out on Sam. He's a good man."

Liam looked toward the wagon train. He was filled with a depression that he could not shake off. He looked across the square to Kate Flaherty's house, but the door was closed. He felt as if he, too, had been shut out.

He wished she hadn't chosen this morning to tell him about the baby. He wished...

It had been in his mind to attend mass and confess his sins. Yet what was he about, thinking of going to church, with the sun high in the sky, and the road before him? Better to apologize to Sam and get at least one load off his chest.

Caitlin smiled at him. He tugged at the brim of his cap, then went on his way. He found Samuel checking wheel rims.

"Sam," Liam said, the moment he was sure he could not be overheard, "I gotta apologize for talkin' out of turn the other night."

Samuel thrust his hands into his pockets. "Forget it, Liam. We're all human."

"'Cept you, maybe. I been thinking about what you did, sharin' your cabin with those poor kids—and that you must have powerful strong feelin's for Zoe, to wed a woman you haven't seen in ten years."

Samuel smiled tightly, and balled the fists in his pockets. He did not deny it. He could not deny it.

"I don't know why I was thinkin' of the little 'uns. Maybe to take my mind off of...what I gotta do today. Kate's brother..."

Liam looked away, toward the pale light of morning filtering through the clouds. "He never liked me much, anyway. It's gonna be very hard, Sam. Very hard." He shrugged, turned back. "Anyway, I've just been after telling Caitlin that I'm glad you two got together all right. She seems to be a logical creature—most unusual in a woman."

Samuel sighed, caught, as always, by his affection for his friend, who rarely had an unspoken thought. He lifted a hand, waved Liam's words away with a joke of his own. "Woman's logic and emotions are often very confusing."

He leaned on a wagon shaft and watched Caitlin. His eyes followed her every move. Just watching her lithe figure dip and sway as she busily adjusted her baggage set his heart pumping faster.

Oh, Christ, how had it gotten so out of hand? How had he let it? He cursed his insanity, his lust, and the miserable, stupid way he'd handled things. Here was a woman who was worthy of a better man than he was.

But no, he'd botched it up, started kissing her—wanting her, feeling the blood rush through him—and more, so much more. It had been a long time since he had responded to a woman like that—quick and hot and hard, suddenly filled with a need as elemental as breathing itself.

Plans did not always go as a man wanted them to. He had allowed her to seduce him. She'd made it so damned difficult. And he, Samuel thought, was hardly blameless.

Samuel fought to control his breathing. He could feel his heartbeat, strong and heavy, in his throat. He swallowed.

He'd set forth on this path, and must walk it now.

Chapter Six

Under a sky showing sunlight with ominous storm clouds behind, the tall pine-clad mountains rose in their eternal vigil. Golden sunlight streamed down upon the mountainsides, revealing tree lines and sparkling, slender cascades of water.

Transfixed by nature, Caitlin stood perfectly still and watched as a zinc-colored cloud tore itself to shreds along the snaking peaks. Like the unseen fingers of a carnival trickster, the wind plucked the riven fragments away. Then, having allowed herself this minute treat, she turned her full attention to the preparations at hand.

Nearby, a thickset farmer struggled to load a crate of squawking red-colored chickens between two squealing black-spotted pigs. Helping him was a boy, a head shorter and an age younger. On his head was a blue bobble hat that had seen better days, but he seemed happy, Caitlin thought, because he whistled quietly as he worked.

Across the road, a redheaded woman with ringlets like curly apple peelings was standing twisting her gloves around and around. Beside her, a thin-backed, dreary-looking man with mustaches like two skeins of wet wool kept up an incessant harangue as the wagons were being loaded. The odd couple was not near so happy, she decided.

As Caitlin hurried along the sidewalk, she nearly collided with a young man who suddenly stepped out of a doorway. If it had not been for the sullen expression in the eyes and the smoldering discontent on the face, she decided, he might even have been considered good-looking. He had the fair look of Kate Flaherty about him, and Caitlin guessed the man was her brother.

Kate Flaherty! The girl with blond hair and blue eyes and the earthy sense of humor. It was obvious her brother didn't share this trait. He stood, arms akimbo, his chin stuck out pugnaciously.

Caitlin shrank back against the wall. She did not need a second look to tell her that the fellow had come to make trouble. He stood immobile, the weak sunlight behind him casting a wavering shadow that was bigger by far than he.

Samuel's loggers were a motley lot, as rough as any Cornish seamen it had ever been Caitlin's fortune to meet—and some of those had been wild and woolly—but it seemed that they were mild in comparison to the men of the new world. These men relished conflict.

"What are you doing here, Irish?" Flaherty said challengingly to Liam, his voice curt and hostile. "I told you last time what would happen if you came to River de Chute, sniffing around my sister."

"I've no argument with you, Ned." Murphy stood with his arms folded across his chest and spoke in his soft Irish brogue. He was not a man who needed to raise his voice or bang his fist on the table to make his anger felt.

Ned Flaherty smirked. "And if I don't agree?"

"Then, Ned, you are free to knock my head off, sure enough."

Murphy grinned, and so did the younger man. They both had a powdery-dry sense of humor and, it seemed to Caitlin, they took great pleasure in winding each other up.

The group of loggers burst into deep-throated laughter. Few among the watchers expected any surprises. The fight would surely last only until Liam Murphy had subdued his opponent. Second only to Jardine, Murphy was the best and fairest fighter there was in all of the timberlands, and Ned Flaherty was at least forty pounds lighter, if somewhat quicker on his feet.

Flaherty waited for the laughter to die away before he moved.

As Caitlin watched, the younger man slowly shifted his stance, revealing a gun just enough for the light to play along its barrel. His right hand remained at the level of his hip.

There were a few heavy sighs from the audience. Liam's lip curled scornfully. Sullenness slipped like a dark shadow over Ned Flaherty's fair features.

"My sister's brought shame to our house. If Pa were alive, he'd want me to avenge his honor."

Liam faced him steadily. He leveled a look at the younger man that would have felled a less obstinate foe. "Don't be a fool, Ned. In the wrong hands, those things are fatal. 'Sides, Kate's with child, and if she'll have me, I intend to marry her, all right and proper."

Kate's with child.

It explained a lot. Too much.

"You just get yourself the hell out of here, Liam Murphy, and if I ever see your face around this town again, I'm going to make sure that it never gets recognized again, not by anybody."

"You can try." Liam Murphy did not lift his voice. It was not necessary. As he stood on the sidewalk, he conveyed an impression of strength in every line of his solid body. Even the corduroy trousers he wore folded into his short laced boots seemed to have fallen into wrinkles that expressed power.

They stood toe-to-toe, two rigid bodies braced for a fight, two pairs of eyes flashing danger signals. For a moment, neither of them moved. Then the fist by Ned Flaherty's hip clenched. He flushed angrily.

"Just get the hell out," Ned Flaherty repeated. "I don't want no Yankee lumberman marryin' my sister."

"It's not up to you. I don't need your permission. Let me pass, lad." There was a cutting edge to Murphy's voice.

It happened all at once.

Caitlin saw Ned Flaherty reach for the gun. The weapon swung through the air. Caitlin saw the fingers of his left hand grip the stock, the forefinger insert itself awkwardly through the trigger guard and squeeze down.

Gasps went up, cries from the watching crowd.

The world exploded.

Liam Murphy dived sideways, even as Caitlin saw the bright flash. A loud crack, and a bullet chipped at the wall just above the Irishman's head.

Another man in his situation might well have panicked. Liam stayed calm. Always a man of action, he was quick to take advantage. In seconds, he was on top of Kate's brother, jamming the heel of his right hand underneath Flaherty's jaw, grasping the hand holding the gun with his left hand.

The two men rolled.

Ned grunted, swung forward and down, striking Murphy on the side of the face with the butt of the pistol. That was when Liam slugged him. He punched upward hard, just below the rib cage, and, as Flaherty began to double over, pushed him violently aside.

Ned grunted heavily as the back of his head struck the rough wood of the sidewalk. He fell into a clinch to get time for recovery. Liam jolted him out of it with a short-armed left below the chin and followed with two slashing rights to the face.

Ned went down again.

"*Enough!*" Samuel's voiced boomed to the side. Out of the corner of her eye, Caitlin saw movement behind the two antagonists. It was Samuel, sprinting, closing the gap between them.

"That's enough, Murphy." Samuel's voice suddenly contained an edge of authority. "Give the boy a chance. I don't care if he was foolhardy. You've hurt him enough. Let him go now."

"S'pose you try minding your own business, Jardine. I'm gonna fix Murphy for good." It was a last growl of defiance from Ned Flaherty.

The next few seconds were bedlam.

There was a brief glint of metal as the sunlight struck the upraised pistol. Caitlin heard the soft but unmistakable *snick* of a trigger as it hit a firing pin. The sound turned her blood to ice.

A muffled explosion.

The Irishman gave a convulsive jerk and went limp.

Samuel moved then, very fast. Coming in low, his shoulders hunched, he charged, struck Ned Flaherty on the side of the neck with the edge of his hand and, and the same time, lunged out and grasped the young man's wrist as tight as a metal vise.

Holding up her skirts, Caitlin ran to the Irishman. He lay still, ominously so. She knelt, feeling an icy hand clutch at her heart. She put her hand on his shoulder.

He groaned, struggled to roll over. Her hand stayed him. "Easy now—"

Panting, Samuel turned quickly, just in time to see Caitlin do something odd. She had the skirt of her dress bunched up, with no care for modesty or constraint. Unashamed, unafraid, she was tearing at the linen ruffle of her petticoat.

Samuel had a flash of impending dread. With every ounce of control he could muster, he slowly approached the small group on the sidewalk, his head held high and his eyes fixed on the still figure.

It was a scene from hell.

Liam's chest was awash in blood, the red fluid ribboning like bunting blown in the wind. His face was a deathly white.

Samuel stood there, swaying, for a few seconds, a horror growing inside him. He felt as if a cannonball had struck him in the gut. He stood numbly, not knowing what to do or even what to think.

In the background, a jumble of voices, and an odd sound, indistinct, caught his ear. Samuel strained to make out what it was.

Caitlin was kneeling beside the Irishman, endeavoring to stanch the wound. Her movements were sure, confident, steady. Obviously, she wasn't going to come apart in an emergency. She calmly slipped something under Liam's blood-soaked shirt, pressing down with the flat of her palm.

Samuel, abruptly dizzied by an intense stirring inside him that he could not define, thought it was a wad of her undergarment. Scented with honeysuckle and feminine essence. He had to fight the irrational sensation that he could feel it on his lips, cheeks, forehead, eyelids. Pressing down. *Stop it!* he told himself.

But Samuel's straining ears picked up the odd sound again, and identified it: Someone trying to breathe. It was Ned Flaherty. Ned lay gasping for air like a fish floundering on the beach—a thick, ugly sound.

Samuel's eyes swung away for a moment, before centering on Liam again. Blood was running out of Ned's nose and all down his mouth and chin, but Liam had gotten the worst of it.

He lay unmoving.

Samuel's eyes crept back to lock with Caitlin's. "Is he all right? Or—?" He bit his lip, unable to voice the terrible thought.

Caitlin said nothing, and this frightened him all the more. His heart plunged. He closed his eyes for a moment as he fought to keep his emotions under control. He opened his eyes, took his worst fear and verbalized it.

"Is he dead?" It was an explosion of breath. Panic clutched his throat. He seemed to have difficulty moving his lips, and his tongue felt like cotton batting.

Caitlin hesitated a moment, then shook her head. She did not take her eyes off the Irishman. There was a lot of blood, but the bullet had passed cleanly through his upper shoulder.

A woman screamed. It was Kate Flaherty. She threw herself through the onlookers in a wild, sweeping rush. "Liam! Ned! You've killed Liam!"

Liam opened his eyes, and saw Kate's face. He shook his head from side to side. "I'm not so easy to get rid of."

Kate's eyes were liquid. "Forgive Ned, he didn't mean it!" She collapsed onto her knees, cradled Liam's head in her lap, sobbing like a child.

Desperately Liam tried to recall the Savior's words about loving one's enemy, turning one's other cheek and forgiving assorted trespasses. Unfortunately, his brain could not get past the business of loving one's enemy.

"Do not fear for me, colleen. It'd take more than that young fool to do me in." His mouth twisted in a semblance of a smile. Then a bright lance of pain ripped through him, and his grin turned into a grimace. "Don't get blood on your dress. It'll stain."

A most unfeminine snort greeted his statement. "Bother the blood! Liam, I love you!" Kate said.

Caitlin, hands busy, ignored them both. Her small, shapely hands were both capable and graceful. It came to Samuel that his wife knew what she was doing. She seemed to have taken all the surprises they had to offer in this strange territory well in stride.

Murphy gritted his teeth against the agony. He seemed unable to catch his breath. Once more, pride rose to the occasion. "I love you, too, Kate, but one can't touch pitch without paying the penalty."

Caitlin let out a very unladylike expletive. "Shut up and lie still—or you'll bleed to death."

Samuel glared at them all. By heaven, he didn't need this! He hadn't been expecting trouble, and when it came, it had come from an unexpected source. He'd been caught off guard.

Slowly he lifted his eyes to Caitlin's. He tried to read her expression, failed. There was a look in her eyes that he had never seen before; it alarmed him, as if he had been witness to something he should not have seen.

The world, for a few endless heartbeats, came to a standstill. He realized that his stomach muscles were clenched, and wondered if caring was supposed to make a body feel all faint and queasy inside.

The silence was ghastly, palpable. With a set-jawed, straight-ahead stare, he met her unfathomable eyes. In a slightly strangled voice, he asked quietly, "Is it a mortal wound?"

Her eyelids drifted down. Samuel melted inside, like a tallow candle. *Please, Lord...*

"...wagon."

Samuel made a soft, startled sound deep in his throat. "What?"

"Times like this, I wish men had a bit of common sense. Don't just stand there like a great lummox, Samuel Jardine. Get my carpetbag from the front of the wagon." Her voice was calm, assured.

More shaken than he would have cared to admit, he resorted to anger. "Dammit, woman! Is that all you can say?"

She gave him a withering look. "Don't swear at me, Samuel. And don't tell me what I can or cannot do! This is an emergency. Time is running out," she said, waving him away. "If you don't go and get my medical kit out of the wagon, this man *will* bleed to death."

Caitlin shifted her position until she was on her knees. She leaned over Liam, pressing hard with both hands. Murphy made a short, savage sound. It was a sound of agony. And a distraction.

"Now, Kate, stop that sniffling, please. Run and get a pudding bowl, or some such container, and fill it with hot water. Get some clean towels, too."

Her face red as an autumn apple, Kate gulped and ran to do Caitlin's bidding. Samuel stared at his wife uncomprehendingly, at Liam's blood dripping from the edge of her fingers, at her gown, sprayed with it. Then he, too, did as she asked.

He even handed her the necessary instruments and watched her as she deftly cut the blood-soaked fabric away. A spurt of blood hit his shirt. With an automatic action that was as natural as if they'd been working in tandem for years, Samuel pinched the artery with his fingers and held it.

The loggers stood over them, barely giving them room, as Caitlin threaded a needle. While Samuel held the wound open, she tied the artery, then closed the long, deep gash in Liam's shoulder. Each stitch was precise and exact.

Crouched beside her, watching her hands, Samuel remembered the hundreds of times they'd threaded bait for each other, gone fishing for whiting off Pentire Point, or dug winkles at Port Isaac Bay, sharing their catch over an open fire on the beach, with Caitryn sitting between them. Time was wrong, twisted. Had it ever been correct?

Samuel had been knocked into a freezing stream once, bludgeoned in the back by a log freed from a jam, in the days when he was learning how to survive in this wild land. It had arrested his breath, centered all his consciousness on exploding pain, annihilated him—and he had had to go on, to keep afloat, to move when his body was paralyzed.

He did it now. He functioned on discipline and nerve alone. All the time he crouched there quietly, he fought to keep his stomach under control and his hands from shaking. His mouth was dry, and he could feel a pulse ticking in his temple.

It made Samuel furious to think that he had failed his father. That the education William had paid to have tutored into his stubborn son had seemingly been thrown over by him without a thought.

Caitlin had taken that empty place in the surgery. He had known it all along. But he had never, until today, come face-to-face with what it would mean.

It was almost too much to bear. Almost. But, dammit, *she* needn't to know that!

"I think he'll be all right," Caitlin said, pouring a dash of alcohol onto the wound. "He's lost a lot of blood, but if he pulls through from the shock, I think he'll make it."

What could he say? He heard again his father's voice.... *One can't run from pride, son. It follows like a shadow— the brighter the sun, the darker it looms.*

But Samuel had run. If only he could go back and do things differently. He had made his choice in a moment of panic. It hadn't seemed so wrong at the time.

And then he saw the image of a younger Caitlin, in her honeysuckle-yellow gown with the doctor's stethoscope stuck in the waistband, standing atop Pentire Point, saying to him, *Life isn't worth the price of a loaf unless you take risks, Samuel. Remember that. Without risk, you might as well settle down, put your blinkers on and count the days until you die.*

He had gone at Caitlin's bidding. Turned his back on Cornwall and his father's profession, and begun a new career. A career where he was one with the sun, the earth, the mountains and the tall trees. A career in which a man's life—or death—did not depend on his ability to read and write.

As a child, the written language had eluded Samuel; the world of radicals, strokes, compendiums, lexicons, phonetics and recensions was beyond his grasp. The effort to learn how to read and write had caused him nothing but rage and frustration.

Literacy was an impenetrable wall, and books were a closed universe. The characters undulated like snakes before his eyes, reversing themselves, moving around on the page and speaking gibberish to him, where they spoke eloquently to others.

But he had not been entirely deterred. Through native intelligence and sheer will, he had found his own secret key to the hidden world. He had developed a mathematical formula that, applied to a written page, revealed to him enough of the page's contents to enable him to form an approximate interpretation.

With practice, he had learned to perform the calculation mentally in the same amount of time it would take to read a page. Though the finer nuances of meaning still occasionally escaped him, his technique worked well enough that he had been able to conceal his deficiency from all but his business partner, and Liam Murphy, loose-mouthed though he was, would never reveal the secret.

In writing to Caitryn, he had taken great care to get the words right, promising not undying love, but a straightforward proposal of marriage. It had been such a masterful plan, and it had worked—up to a critical point. Caitlin had received the letter, not Caitryn.

It struck Samuel as ironic that the most difficult and potentially disastrous part of the plan, the acceptance of his marriage proposal, had been accomplished with relative ease—and the part that he had thought would follow logically had been fouled.

The injured men suddenly filled his vision, sweeping him from the past. He stared at Caitlin, could not help himself, felt more and more helpless as he watched her swiftly moving fingers. And the minute she had tied the last knot and he was sure she was finished, he grabbed her arm and pulled her upright.

"You don't need to be here, Caitlin," he declared as he took the brightly polished utensil from her hand.

"Nonsense. There is still another patient to attend."

Caitlin turned to Ned Flaherty. The boy was shuddering, and with every inspiration he made a harsh crowing sound. The gun dangled from the broken finger, already swollen so thick it would have to be forced through the trigger guard.

"Here, stanch your bleeding with this." She handed Ned her scarf, which he pressed against his bloody nose. "Samuel, make yourself useful, please. You hold, I'll pull, then we'd better deal with that hand."

Calmer now, Samuel gripped Ned Flaherty's wrist tightly while Caitlin slowly freed the poor swollen finger and set the broken bone. A dose of laudanum and brandy helped Kate's brother bear the necessary pain, but nothing could keep Samuel from breaking into a cold sweat at that soft sound of success.

Caitlin eyed him intently, suddenly remembering his aversion to his father's profession. She watched his breathing catch, an intake and a long pause while his cheeks grew pink. When she lightly touched the back of Samuel's hand, the muscles of his forearm bunched. He closed his eyes and then opened them again, very wide, as if bringing the scene back into focus.

"My gracious me. Samuel, you look dreadful! Go on, now. I'll deal with the rest. It's almost done."

Samuel let out the air in a little rush. He blinked twice. He made a stilted gesture with the bowl he still held in one hand.

"I'm sorry. Don't worry about me," he said. His voice was sounding downright unnatural.

Caitlin could see that his lips were pulled back in a com-

bination of a smile and reaction to the shock of seeing his
friend wounded. She stood up then, as he rose beside her
on shaky legs.

He attempted nonchalance. "I can make it." But he took
two steps, and collapsed. He grunted, having landed on the
pistol, which still lay on the sidewalk.

Caitlin pushed his head between his knees. She made a
soft sound, as of exasperation. "The last thing I need is a
fainting man on my hands! You sit there until I say you
can move!" she ordered.

"Yes, ma'am," Samuel said meekly.

Without bothering to reply, Caitlin examined Ned Flaherty, then strapped his ribs so that they wouldn't suffer
more damage.

"Bloody hell." Samuel surged to his feet. Then he began
muttering words she had never heard before, pungent words
that told her he was very cross.

Caitlin straightened and stared at her husband, uncertain
how to take the intensity of his tone and the grimness of
his expression. Tension surged in him. He looked almost
angry. Her mind raced over the list of potential areas of
trouble. What was it?

A customs officer rode up and dismounted. Up close, he
was a huge man in his heavy serge uniform. A tree stump
would have been more expressive. He stood there, arms
crossed over his massive chest, and stared at the blood-
stained sidewalk. Slowly his glance moved over the injured
men, to Kate and Caitlin, in their blood-spotted gowns. He
lifted his eyes to Samuel, who stood, hands curled into fists
at his sides.

"There's been a shooting."

It was a statement, not a question, and no one made an
answer. They seemed to be frozen, like statues. His eyes
met Samuel's briefly, and an unmistakable challenge passed
between them.

The officer cleared his throat and dropped his voice to a

dramatic tone. "Will this two-legged vermin survive?" He nodded down at the Irishman.

Samuel's back and shoulders grew tight. "Survive? Of course he'll survive," he repeated, a hard edge to the word. "Liam's as strong as an ox." The quiet voice was inexorable.

Disappointment flickered over the officer's face, then was gone. She would have expected satisfaction—but disappointment? Probably because he would not be able to charge Ned Flaherty with murder and string him up from the nearest tree!

Well, she was disappointed, too, but not for the same reasons, she told herself. She was disappointed because...because all this violence seemed to beget violence, and all hell was fixing to break loose in about two minutes. A man could get himself hanged if this official chose to exert himself.

Caitlin racked her brains. How utterly absurd that love was the cause of all this savagery and upset. Surely, if the hand of friendship was extended, then peace and goodwill would follow? As no one else seemed inclined to try it, she just might have a go at it herself!

She stepped forward, smoothing her skirt awkwardly. She looked down at her husband's large, thick-soled boots and placed her own, much smaller high-buttoned shoes squarely beside them. Deep inside herself, she began to shake. She wet her lips.

"Samuel...what if I...we...you were to ask Kate and her brother to come stay at Fairbanks for a spell?"

When Samuel didn't say a word, Caitlin looked up. A pensive look had overtaken his face, and was still there. She felt the tension in him. Maybe she ought not to push the matter further, she thought, but only for a moment.

"Kate would be grand company for me, and it'd give Ned a chance to get to know Liam," she said brightly into the silence, and waited for the fireworks.

It didn't take long. "Have you lost your *mind?*" He spoke through his teeth.

Caitlin made no comment on this. With the single-mindedness that was typical of her, she pushed on with her own line of thinking. Obviously, the man was unaccustomed to dealing with any radical or ingenious suggestions, especially from a woman.

He had a lot to learn.

But still, she did not want him to think that she could manipulate him. He alone must make the decision. He must be made to see that quite clearly, and that meant—because men were such obtuse, limited creatures—on his own terms.

She hid behind a facade of light banter and mockery. "According to Father Gabriel, temper is one of the many paving stones on the pathway to hell. Pride is another, and debt still another. I reckon Liam owes Ned for seducing his sister, Flaherty owes Murphy for losing his temper and going off half-cocked about it—and if you ask me, the pair of them are too proud to admit that the only one to suffer for their sins is poor Kate!"

Caitlin had taken this bantering line because she imagined it might be the safest. She fully expected to see Samuel lose his temper and give her a tongue-lashing in return, so she was taken aback to see his eyes warm with mirth.

"It's a good-natured gesture, sweetheart, but you know nothing of what you're saying," Samuel said matter-of-factly.

"Well, since you think so little of me, I don't suppose you would grant my request as a wedding boon?"

"Must you mock me, madam?" he drawled.

"But you so often deserve it." The insolent words slipped out before she could control her unruly tongue. She smiled to take away the sting. "I'm telling you, Samuel, the way I see it, that's the easiest way to steer clear of trouble from a certain quarter."

His mouth hardened into a grim line. "You mean the law?"

"Yes. Anyone can see Kate's scared half out of her mind that her brother will be charged with attempted murder. Under the circumstances, she could miscarry—lose her child."

No one spoke, but her suggestion made the onlookers come to life, and they began to clear their throats, as if trying to cover her outspokenness. Caitlin felt her face grow warm. Felt her whole body glow with heat. Taking his arm possessively in hers, she gave a little tug and pulled him to one side.

Stubborn, *stubborn* woman! Samuel looked at his wife and felt a surge of irritation so heavy as to almost choke him. She looked up at him, her little chin set at a defiant angle. Since she had been a child, Caitlin had always been a rebel. Her crusades had often managed to get him and Caitryn into trouble.

While the others watched in varying degrees of astonishment, Caitlin bent and picked up the pistol. It felt heavy and cold in her palm. She straightened, idly twirled the barrel, and looked back at him with a slanting, defiant smile. She managed to add an additional half inch to her stature with the tilt of her head.

"Unless I'm mistaken, the government requires an awful lot of scribbling to be done when there's any sort of ruckus—especially in these border towns. If the culprits were removed to Maine and out of Canadian jurisdiction, there'd be no paperwork to worry about. Am I right?"

"Caitlin." The word was involuntary, a response torn from the depths of him, a shield and a defense against an unseen enemy. Did she suspect his flaw, his weakness, his defect? Or was her reasoning simply a lucky strike?

Caitlin ratcheted her chin up another notch, daring him to argue. Her skirts swished around her ankles as she tapped an impatient foot on the boarded sidewalk.

Samuel followed his wife's gyrations and sighed. It
seemed that when she decided to do something, she could
see nothing but her goal. He felt walls closing in on him.
Nothing on earth could stop her. He sighed again, deeply.

At least this cause was a worthy one.

Chapter Seven

The Canadian official frowned, and Samuel could hear the irritated click of his tongue against his teeth. They were in dire straits and Samuel knew it. These skirmishes were becoming more frequent, adding to the general unrest along the border, and the trooper was more angry than he appeared on the surface.

Samuel's first impulse was to say no. The mere thought of having to do all that figuring and calculating on paper was a nightmare. Unbidden, the memory of his struggle as a youth and his ignominious flight from Cornwall entered his mind. It had tainted the past ten years.

I can never get away from it. The thought swirled through his brain in a pulse beat before reason returned. He had run all his life, he realized. Run from the shame of his disability. But he could not, would not, run any longer.

What had she said? *Go to America, Samuel. You know you have the strength of purpose...to do anything.*

Caitlin's idea wasn't out of the question. In fact, it was a godsend. With Liam out of action, he *must* deal with his defect, else he would never resolve his deceit and dread, and become the kind of man she imagined he was—and the kind of man he wanted to be.

Not that he was going to let on immediately.

Heart hammering against his rib cage with such force he could feel himself trembling, he frowned down at Caitlin. She was watching him, her green cat's eyes huge. He could feel the aftermath in his body of the alertness, the exertion, the excitement, of the fight. It would be expedient to direct that excitement into other channels.

Perhaps he should give up a frontal assault and try to outflank her? A heady prospect.

Samuel took a deep breath, said slowly and distinctly, "What if either Liam or Ned's wounds get infected? What's going to happen then?" His voice betrayed none of the emotion he felt energizing him.

Caitlin waved her hands in dismissal. "I'll make a poultice."

He saw his opportunity and seized it. If he'd learned anything today, it was that his wife was resourceful. On the other hand, he liked challenges, and it would be interesting to go to the Presque Isle Stream depot with a new team, test out her astuteness—and face his nemesis. He still hadn't had time to churn over in his mind the dramatic way in which she affected him.

"We're already behind schedule because of various unavoidable delays, and now we're down a key man. At the moment, I need a surgeon more than I need a wife or cook. I need someone who can deal with accidents and emergencies, as well as the various ailments one would expect to find in a lumber camp." Samuel said it as though he were trying out the idea. "Can you do that?" he demanded.

Caitlin drew a long breath. "Try me. I'm a quick learner."

Her voice had that faint exasperation that Samuel was learning meant she was upset, or uncertain. The inflection was the most enchanting sound he'd ever heard. Full of glee at the way she had snapped up the bait, he tried to look stern.

"It's not a common job for a woman. It will be your

choice, but I don't want you to make it out of ignorance. It could shock some.''

Caitlin bridled visibly. "So, it will shock them. Let it then, and have done with it!'' she whispered fiercely.

"They are already shocked. River de Chute has never seen a female doctor before." It was time to tell her, he decided. No more excuses. If she turned from him now, she could return to Saint John with no loss of dignity. She had already proved herself. She deserved the truth. "Caitlin, there's something you should know…"

He hesitated, and she broke in. "One day, women doctors will be as commonplace as the pines in Maine."

Samuel heard the rush of her breath as she smiled, and inhaled her perfume in the same instant. Dammit, she smelled of honeysuckle, and something indefinably feminine! When it came to that womanly smell, it seemed his brain could still get soft and a certain unruly extremity could still get hard and take over the brain work.

Holy Mother Mary, it wasn't decent for a man to feel this way about a woman in broad daylight, and in company, even if she was his wife! There was a time and place for everything!

Forcing himself to think in more practical terms, Samuel placed one callused hand over her slender fingers. Without moving, standing utterly still, her body seemed to vibrate with feeling.

You never get time for a second chance, he thought to himself. You have to seize your time and seize it tight, and that was why he was here, married to Caitlin, when in all truth his wife was supposed to have been Caitryn.

Samuel cleared his throat and decided what he had to say could wait for a few more days. After all, he was already working within an emergency situation. Ned Flaherty had seen to that. He felt another flare of anger at Ned for his attack.

Caitlin looked up and met his eyes. Her eyes were spar-

kling, and her curving smile was lighting her face. He
watched her take in a deep breath and slowly release it. He
swallowed one of those choking surges of desire that she
always aroused in him, and smiled back.

God help him! Would he ever forget last night and the
way the lamplight had captured her nakedness and held him
spellbound with her perfection? She'd come to him wild
and unpredictable, unashamed and generous, in her womanly passion. Her enthusiasm had more than made up for
her lack of experience.

Trembling like a leaf in a gale, she'd gasped as he
plunged into the core of her, her head thrown back, her
palms against his chest, the tips of her bare breasts crushed
against him. He'd allowed their natural movements to move
her against him slowly, achingly, until at last she abandoned herself to his masculine demands, flowering open to
him, drawing him into her liquid depths.

In his mind's eye, he kept glimpsing her face, contorted
with passion; thinking about her hair, and how it strayed
like a soft, flowing waterfall across his shoulders. He kept
seeing her eyes, and the deep, warm shadow between her
breasts.

With a jolt, Samuel realized his pulse had become rapid
and erratic, his breathing shallow. He could not deny the
pulsing in his body. Somehow, he must control these unbidden desires. He was *not* going to think about all that
black hair that had fanned his arms last night with feathery
softness. He must take command, and immediately, so he
did the only thing he could.

He surrendered.

"All right, Caitlin." He squeezed her hand tightly.
"We'll bend the rules on this occasion. Ned and Kate Flaherty can go to Fairbanks with Liam. You and I will attend
to the Presque Isle Stream depot."

He was rewarded for his surrender with a smile as wide

as the Grand Falls, a smile so bright it made him blink. He tried to concentrate.

"Samuel, where you go, I go. I have made this resolve. And remember, we fight in harness, now and always."

He was silent for a moment, and then Caitlin was astonished to hear him chuckle. The sound went through her like the quivering echo of a church bell through fog.

Her smile widened.

The tension dissolved, and the Canadian officer suppressed whatever savage emotions he might still be feeling. "Everything's fine then, ma'am. No harm's been done. You may leave the official explanations with me." He reached across the space to shake Samuel's hand. "Allow me to congratulate you, Jardine, on wedding such a remarkable woman. Knows how to negotiate in a sticky situation."

It was difficult to decide whether he was thanking her, or reproaching her for what she had so obviously been doing. Either way, he was smiling broadly, sun glinting off his square, white teeth and the brass buttons on his uniform.

Caitlin heard the rumble of laughter in Samuel's big chest. She had made him smile; it was an expression she loved. His face was transformed by it, and him with it. In fact, he was grinning from ear to ear. "I wouldn't dispute that. She should be a politician."

Caitlin couldn't help but smile back. She hugged Samuel fiercely. Against all reason, her voice came out all breathy and hoarse, as if she were suffering a congestion of the lungs. "Now that would be tempting providence and fortune. I just might become the first female president."

Samuel quickly wiped the grin off his face. Didn't he know the truth when he heard it! He spun around and gave the orders for men and a wagon while Caitlin prepared a medicinal compound.

"How's your head?" As Caitlin asked the question, she handed Murphy a glass of the restorative brew.

Face set, the Irishman muttered, "I'll live."

"Really? I'll bet it aches. This'll help."

Liam looked dubious, but he swallowed the draft Caitlin was pressing on him. He screwed up his face like a sulky schoolboy at the bitter taste. Using his left hand, he pushed his torso from the sidewalk.

"Sam," he said, as evenly as he could. The entire morning was rotating about his head, but he had gotten his breathing back under control. "Have you heard the rumor that Sagamore is putting a team on Quaggy Joe Mountain?"

Samuel shrugged slightly. "I've heard a rumor, but have largely discounted it, in view of the season. Besides, at this time of year, there's too much to be done to worry about that oaf. Don't worry, I propose to deal with Sagamore when the time is right—and hopefully rid the world of a rogue."

The morning rotated more and more. Soon he would faint. Soon. "Damnation. You'll not do it, Sam. It was *my* gun, not Ned's."

Samuel muttered. "Well...I suppose I can go down to Presque Isle Stream and supervise the fitting-out myself— let Caitlin go on to Fairbanks with you and Kate. I have waited ten years for a wife. What is a month here, a month there?"

"Bloody hell! Are you bent on self-destruction, man? You're a dead man if you go it alone. Sure, this wound will heal in no time at all, and I'll be out on the swings checking that scoundrel's pulpcutters' pile. I want to be there when the devil's caught red-handed."

"Now, Liam, you must be patient. Why work up a sweat? We'll get a dam built on the confluence of Presque Isle Stream and the Aroostook and foil Sagamore's schemes. You just wait and see." Samuel's voice was clipped, foreclosing any other discussion.

Liam sighed at the warning in Samuel's voice. He looked

up at the sky, and the scudding clouds. "I don't like it, Sam. The road to perdition is paved with good intentions. The better the intentions, the deeper you go."

"I don't think life's like that." Samuel grinned, as if torn between amusement and appreciation. "I think it's more like a circle...or a chain.... A man receives a favor, and passes it on to someone else. We have a limited set of options, and *you* will take the only alternative offered."

"And you?"

Abruptly Samuel's face changed. "Me? I have not even the wit to enjoy the pleasures which are thrust at me. I was lost years ago."

"And nothing I can say will change your mind?"

Samuel shook his head. "Nothing, old friend."

"The hell with it. I'm not in any shape to knock sense into your thick skull. But to be sure, it is in my mind. You're the truest friend a man ever had, Sam Jardine." Murphy chuckled. His left cheek was bruised and split, and Samuel appreciated the effort it must have cost him.

Somewhat discomforted by the Irishman's emotional outburst, Samuel took refuge in supervising the transfer of the invalids. The loggers loaded the injured men carefully into the wagon. Both men had been given the restorative spirit that Caitlin had laced with laudanum.

"It's going to be rough once we hit the low ground. Hold them as best you can, Emil," he told the teamster, but it was the thought of losing Liam Murphy that concerned him.

Kate Flaherty scrambled into the wagon and knelt between her wounded lover and brother, covering them with several colorful Indian blankets. Liam smiled up at her face. She touched his forehead, stroking his hair back with loving affection. She kissed both his cheeks, then raised her head and looked at Samuel with tear-streaked eyes.

"I'll stay here with Liam and Ned," she said in a quavery voice. "I'm enormously grateful to you, Sam, for rescuing Ned from his own folly."

Samuel did not answer her at once. Then he lifted a finger, smoothed a drop of moisture from her velvety cheek. "It's all right, Kate. Ned'll be fine at Fairbanks. I figure he and Liam have a lot in common. They're both as stubborn and independent as a pair of mules."

"It's right glad I am you and Caitlin didn't take offense at Liam's nonsense. He talks the hind legs off a jackrabbit, but means no ill."

"Liam does talk a mite foolish at times, but I don't count it against him. 'Sides, Caitlin's a sensible-headed woman, and not one to get out of harmony because of a bit of tomfoolery." The hand on Kate's shoulder was firm and steadying.

Kate made a soft, husky sound. She reached up and clasped Samuel's wrist. "You're a good man, Sam."

"Don't worry, honey." He said it softly, because she'd started to cry again. "Liam and I are old friends. We go back a long way. A hell of a long way."

Caitlin felt something clench in her stomach at the gentleness she heard in her husband's deep voice. Was that all it was? Surely one did not experience this pulsing of feminine desire simply because one suddenly imagined one's own finger smoothing a drop of moisture from another's velvety-soft skin? Her nerve endings were on fire at the thought.

She tucked a blanket firmly under Liam's shoulder, telling herself she was intent only on distracting her patient until the laudanum could take effect. Somehow, this activity counteracted her fluttering heart. Steadied, she smiled cheerfully.

"Well, such friendship is too rare nowadays for me to criticize it. But if you ever do anything like that again, Liam Murphy, so help me, I'll let you bleed to death. I don't hold with violence."

"Yeah. Sure," Liam said thickly.

Caitlin put the flat of her hand against the Irishman's temple. She was not yet worried about infection and fever, though she couldn't help but feel concerned that he might have a slight concussion. There was a wicked bruise on his jaw, and his eye would be black by morning.

"Dizzy? Double vision? Nausea?" Her eyes fixed him with a very straight look.

"No. I have a hard skull. Thanks for your concern." He smiled at her again, and she felt that his smile was meant to be reassuring, but he winced a little and closed his eyes.

There was very little time for much talk after that, as they busied themselves with last-minute activities. By the wagons, the loggers were also assembling, getting themselves ready to leave. They were indulging in a good deal of chaff, and not all of it was good-natured. Caitlin guessed they were at once uncertain and exuberant, realizing that the fracas, however foolhardy, had been a signal victory for the Americans.

Justice was the prerogative of the strongest, and on this side of the border, the Canadians held the winning cards. The inevitable consequences of such a clash had been avoided only by the timely intervention of Sam Jardine's woman.

But the loggers were beginning to wonder whether the situation here was actually more critical than they had been led to believe. They were entering disputed territory, and could be in danger of their lives if the border rivalry escalated.

"You goin' straight to Presque Isle Stream depot, Sam?" Liam asked suddenly.

Anger and grim laughter warred within Samuel. Hell and Lucifer! Damaged as he was, the Irishman was still as full of chatter as a flock of finches. "Reckon I will. I'll leave you to settle accounts with Ned, the best way you can, seeing as how you got yourself into the goddamned mess in the first place."

Liam opened his eyes. His mind, freed of the network of pain within which it had been gripped, was floating. "The Lord moves in mysterious ways. If Summer Dawn hadn't gone off, leavin' Sagamore's off-cuts, you'd never have had to set your mind to figurin' how to keep those discarded bits of scantling all legal-like." His eyes were glassy, turned inward, his voice hoarse. The laudanum was beginning to take effect.

"That's enough, Murphy. Hold up and rest your tongue, else Caitlin will think you've lost your wits." Though Samuel's tone was carefully neutral, Caitlin picked up a subtle undercurrent, and a warning siren went off in her head.

The preoccupied expression left Murphy's face. His eyes focused, and he looked at Caitlin with startling intensity, as if he'd just then seen her standing there. He groaned.

"You still here? Thought you'd be hightailin' it back to Saint John. Not many want someone else's off-cuts...only great men...like Sam." His smile was bleak and tired.

Samuel's mouth flattened. He thrust his hands into his pockets. "Trust an Irishman to exaggerate."

Caitlin looked up, surprised by the sudden edge in Samuel's voice.

"Thanks for getting me off the hook. I owe you one."

"Like hell. I'll probably get my head bitten off for taking my bride to a house that hasn't been lived in for nigh on three years."

A laden look passed between the two men, then Liam gave her a sideways glance. He lay there blinking for a moment, and then his jaw flexed. "Better to face trouble head-on than wait for it to sneak up on you."

Caitlin had the feeling it was a warning. Liam closed his eyes and opened them again. The brief thread of tension was broken. "I'm sure Liam's very well-meaning," she said, puzzled by their intensity.

Liam blinked his eyes fully open. "Well-meaning be damned! Sam is a good fellow—a great man—one in a million. Promise you'll remember that when he's balancing his accounts?" He was speaking more quickly now, the words slurring as they tumbled one over the other like logs over the falls.

"Of course I will," Caitlin said, soothingly. She smiled at Samuel and laced her fingers through his.

Liam blew out a rasping breath and closed his eyes. This time they remained shut.

As Caitlin prepared to mount the wagon for the last stage of the journey, she noticed the woman in the drab brown dress who had stared so fixedly at her bonnet on the riverboat. She nodded. The woman nodded back, smiling bashfully.

Caitlin had changed her blood-spattered traveling costume and was now wearing her prettiest cream-and-burgundy bonnet, all ribbons and lace. On impulse, she untied the ribbons and ran across to the woman, thrusting the confection into the woman's hands.

"I'm not going to need this where I'm going."

"Oh, thank you, ma'am! It's beautiful! Chipped straw and red satin ribbons. Oh, my!" The woman's face was radiant.

So it was on a note of joy that Caitlin resumed her journey. She felt strong and confident, ready for what she knew lay ahead. At the head of the column, Samuel sat astride his roan mount. How splendid a figure he made, dominating a score of men, riding a horse or, indeed, striding the boardwalk, she thought.

The sunlight transformed his hair into spun copper. His voice drifted over the rows of wagons like the wispy fog that still lay in thin strands across the river. Caitlin could just make out the ghost of a smile curling his lips. To think that she had married that splendor!

Samuel had other things on his mind. Valuable time had

been lost, and they were later getting away than he had planned. It was a long, difficult trail to Fairbanks, but he determined that they should get back as quickly as they could—provided the injured men could stand up to the strain of the journey.

Liam lay with his eyes closed—either feigning sleep or in a drug-induced stupor. Ned said nothing but coughed in thick, racking spasms; sometimes clutching hold of the wagon rail as if that were the only way in which he was going to be able to draw breath again.

There was a grandeur about the pine-clad hills, a vastness that was awe-inspiring. They traveled between tall, fragrant pines, between columns of purplish shadows, and the mountain air grew crisp. There was a smell in the air of pines, and smoke, and rotting vegetation—so different from the moors, Caitlin thought.

It was a long, uncomfortable trip. The hooves of the horses rang like a bell on the hard trail, the iron-rimmed wheels of the wagon clattering and shaking as the wagon creaked and bounced and rattled. The rig had no suspension, and so by the time they had covered half a dozen miles along the stony track, Caitlin's back was jarred and her head felt as if it had been clapped between a door and a door frame.

By the time the mountain sky was stirring itself into a sunset that looked like black-currant jelly stirred into a bowl of blancmange, she ached in every joint. She sighed audibly when Samuel said it was time to stop and prepare to camp for the night.

It was a strange supper. Caitlin only half listened to the tall tales told over a hastily prepared meal of bacon and potatoes. She was too busy eating, with an appetite that must owe itself to the fresh air, she thought.

The campfires crackled and smoked in the evening wind, and the stars began to come out, thousands of them, prickling the night. The wolves yipped and howled at each other, across the warm breadth of the Aroostook Valley. Fear rushed like a stream through her, and for a moment she was so dizzy that she thought her knees would not hold her. She had to remind herself this was frontier country.

After supper, Caitlin gave another large dose of laudanum-enriched spirits to Liam and Ned. Neither was feverish, and she offered a silent prayer of thanks for that. Barring complications, they should make it. She was suddenly aware of Samuel's sidelong glance.

"Expecting a rough night?" His raised eyebrows said volumes, but Caitlin refused to commit herself to a prognosis.

She kept her explanation vague, allowing no hint of any doubts to creep into her voice. "A precaution only. Ned's ribs need immobilization, and if Liam does any tossing and turning, his stitches could come undone."

Soft and shy, she wanted to go to Samuel, curl up at his side, have him run his fingers through her hair, kiss and caress her. She wanted to reassure herself that last night had truly happened.

That they had made marvelous love.

But she didn't. How could she, with a full team of lumbermen nearby, watching, listening? Instead, heavy-limbed and stiff with weariness, she settled herself against the sacks Samuel had removed from the back of the wagon and watched the flickering fire.

The moon swung higher in the sky, its silvery light giving a cool glow. The wind had risen and sounded like the sea. Caitlin gazed toward the dark line of the forest, fathomless and mysterious.

Trees, stiff and straight, seemed to move out of it toward them, silently. The sturdy livestock, tethered to tree stumps, loomed in the darkness like gigantic mushrooms. She stifled a scream as a great brown night bird swooped overhead, giving its harsh cry.

Samuel turned to her and took her hand. He gave a low chuckle. "It's only an owl."

As Caitlin curled her fingers in his, she tried to stave off the feeling of anxiety that washed over her. She tried to concentrate upon her happiness in becoming Samuel's wife, but still the anxiety crept in, like an unwanted thief in the night. Her thoughts were going in circles, and her nerves crackled alarmingly. They had all day.

Forcing herself to relax, she became painfully aware of every stiff, aching muscle in her own body. She was too tired to think much about it. She was even too tired to think of this aching need to press herself, the whole length of her body, against Samuel. In fact, she was too tired to think of anything at all.

Tomorrow would be soon enough to think. Tonight was purely for sharing the simple pleasures of life—moon, stars, woodsmoke—and Samuel.

A casual shift of position, and her head brushed his shoulder. He was breathing deeply, steadily.

"It will be daylight soon, so we'd better get some sleep."

A warm arm curled around her waist. Heat sang in her veins like a chorus of archangels, until the universe shifted and the stars twirled oddly in the sky.

God, but she was tired! She nestled against him, and closed her eyes, and the night passed like the closing of a shutter.

For the next two days, they doggedly followed the southern bank of the river, rising at dawn and making camp at nightfall, and making do with as few stops as they could manage. But when the road divided, one fork going on along the river and the other through the forest, the convoy separated.

Amidst much grumbling, Caitlin had two of the men remove the largest of her mahogany-and-brass trunks from its place, and transfer it to Kate Flaherty's wagon. She stretched out her hand.

"Kate, this is my wedding gift. Most of the contents have not been worn, and the gowns may be a bit short or a bit firm, but that's no disaster. Just let out the laces and tuck in a scarf until you can alter them to fit properly."

Kate's pale face flushed. She sniffed and gulped. "Oh, my." She stood, hands clasped together, palm to palm.

Samuel looked up from adjusting his saddle girth and frowned. He knew Caitlin was trying to be helpful, but she was going about it all the wrong way. Her besetting sin was this insistence that her way was the right way—the only way. He wanted to yell at her to shut up, but he desisted. For a single moment, he thought she looked artless, sincere.

Ignoring his sister, Ned said aggrievedly, "Kate don't want no charity! She can't take your clothes. It ain't decent!"

Bullheaded, stupid man! Caitlin didn't know whether he was overtired, or overwrought, or slightly drunk from the double portion of her special restorative potion, but she stared at her with such violence in his eyes that she couldn't help flinching. Nevertheless, she determined not to allow him to browbeat her.

"If it's pride that ails you, Ned Flaherty, consider the practicalities. Kate's run away with what she managed to cram into one chest—and half of that is probably yours."

Samuel could see tears forming in Kate's eyes again. How much water did a body hold? Buckets, by the look of it. The woman had been leaking on and off for three days. Her face was as pale as a midsummer moon, and her nose was as red as a grosbeak's breast.

There was no stopping Caitlin. She pointed to the small, rope-handled wooden container. "You can guarantee that Kate's wardrobe won't be enough for a woman who's increasing. Nowhere near enough. You take my advice, Ned

Flaherty, and stop being a dog in the manger. When Liam is himself again, he'll thank you for it.''

Ned struggled to sit up, his lips pursed. "Begging your pardon, ma'am, that's none of your business," he said stiffly.

Caitlin didn't try to hide her vexation at that. "What an absurd notion, and you know it! Who do you think saved your wretched life? You owe me one, Ned Flaherty, and I'm calling in the favor." She knew her voice sounded sharp.

"Ned!" Kate's lips framed the word as if it were a toad from one of the Grimms' fairy stories, crawling dangle-legged from the mouth of the unkind sister.

"I didn't mean— That is, I hadn't actually—" Ned broke into a fit of coughing.

Caitlin's eyebrows went up a little and stayed there. Challenge glinted from her eyes, in the tilt of her pointed chin. There was challenge in every line of her body.

"No? If you'll forgive me for saying so, what do *you* know about the needs of a pregnant woman?"

Something flared in Ned's eyes, but was swiftly damped down. His lips clamped tight.

Samuel put his hand over his mouth so that she wouldn't see him smile. It seemed she had bluffed Ned Flaherty right proper! When he looked back at Caitlin, he knew his face was as rigid as an Indian mask, his mouth set in a firm line.

Caitlin was in full flight now. "And I'll lay guineas to gooseberries that there's no fripperies in Kate's baggage. Seems to me she might want something fancy to wear if she's fixing to get married."

For a moment, neither of them moved. Then Ned coughed and pulled a grotesque face. "I figure your offer ain't as patronizing as I first thought, and it wouldn't do no harm to accept a gown or two." His voice was very little more than a croak.

"That's better. Now, Kate. My mother was so pleased to get rid of me, she ordered far too many clothes for my trousseau, and most of the gowns are in styles and colors more suited to my sister's fair beauty than my dark countenance. Imagine me in blue chiffon ruffles!"

Kate hiccuped a laugh between her tears.

"Look on the bright side, Ned. Your sister will have something to think about, apart from crying and getting herself red eyes. Besides, she'll look real pretty in blue chiffon!"

Ned gave another wheezing cough. "I guess every cloud has a silver lining, so to speak."

Samuel lowered his head and tightened the cinch strap. A slow grin spread over his face. Sharp-tongued, impulsive, and bandbox-beautiful, Caitlin was an intriguing creature: a calm and efficient doctor, a passionate and generous lover, a compassionate and kind friend.

Yes, his bogus bride was really something, but he wondered what sort of an enemy she would make.

Chapter Eight

Oh, saints be praised, this was *it?* Caitlin's heart plummeted. *This* was to be her new home? This Spartan, inhospitable dwelling? Dear Lord, it was like a nightmare—a hideous denial of everything she had imagined. Here was no trim painted cottage and velvet lawn.

Lichen and yellow stonecrop flushed the unpainted wood-framed walls, and there were blank patches on the roof that shingles had once covered. A little orchard of sturdy fruit trees separated it from several other crude shanties and barns, all dominated by a blockhouse, which isolated the depot from the forest and held it close to the water's edge.

The front door gave entrance to the timber-floored main room. This room was empty—stark and primitive, cool and dark as a sea cavern. There were no floor coverings, no pictures, no comfortable furnishings. It was just a bare, damp, inhospitable cell, and it reeked of filth, and a strange odor that Caitlin couldn't even begin to guess at.

To the left was another large, raftered room. A great oak table, with chairs to match, stood in the center of the room. Bales of hay were stacked to the ceiling. There was a wide window, and a fireplace that could have been homely, but was currently filled with trash. A perfect haven for spiders and ants, she thought.

Then a worse notion intruded. Mice and other indescribable vermin had probably made their nests there. The small hairs on the back of Caitlin's neck lifted. Her skin crawled. Proudly, she gave away nothing, except perhaps a flicker of her eyes.

When Samuel took her on a further tour of inspection, her heart sank. The kitchen was dull and small and smelled fusty. It contained a scarred slab table, a large oak dresser and a small potbellied stove. On the blackened stove was a frying pan so covered in grime that it looked as if it had grown fur.

Samuel tried hard to open the window, but it stubbornly resisted his efforts, and he stood back to dust his hands. "Item number one," he said slowly, and turned to find Caitlin surveying the fire oven with wrinkled brows.

One slender hand lifted, then fell like a dying butterfly. "Am I supposed to cook on that?" she asked, as if the thing were going to leap up and bite her.

At the skepticism on her face, Samuel turned away, his shoulders shaking. He moistened his lips and spoke in a voice devoid of all expression. "There's nothing else. Don't you think you can manage it?"

Caitlin continued to stare at the stove for a moment, then gave a sigh. If there was one lesson she'd learned, it was that one must do today what could be done today. There was no point in wasting time railing against fate, hoping tomorrow would bring about an improvement and worrying that it wouldn't.

"I'll have to." She thought her voice sounded a little high-pitched. Her chin went up in a stubborn thrust. Stop bellyaching and get on with it! she berated herself. She looked around. "What we need are a fire, plenty of hot water, a good supply of soap—and a sense of humor."

Samuel put his blunt index finger on the tip of his chin. "Yeah, like Aunt Lizzy and her seven sisters."

Aunt Lizzy and her seven sisters were imaginary figures conjured up by Samuel, Caitlin and Caitryn when they were young. They had helped them to let off steam after they were reprimanded for some misdemeanor.

Now those memories swept over him with the force of waves. He vividly recalled a hot summer's day when they had rattled around the village green in the undertaker's black barouche while the mourners had knelt and prayed beside the coffin in the white-spired church. Several passersby had shaken their heads in dismay.

Caitryn had clasped her hands together, her eyes like smashed sapphires, and her fine skin glowing as if God had already dusted it with angel powder. Not so bold Caitlin. That one had pulled a funny face, and bugged her eyes, drummed her little button-up boots and giggled so much that she almost had a coughing fit. She had prodded Samuel sharply in the small of the back with her parasol, urging him on.

Aunt Lizzy and her seven sisters had been much in evidence for days after that incident. Suddenly, Samuel was laughing, and after a moment Caitlin was laughing, too.

Caitlin straightened her shoulders. "Let's explore a bit further."

A narrow flight of stairs from the kitchen led to a loft with a sloping ceiling and odd nooks and crannies. It, too, was home to stacks of hay. The main sleeping area was the only other room in the house. It had a narrow window, shuttered now, that Caitlin guessed overlooked the river. A second fireplace told of cold evenings and wood fires glowing red and smelling sweetly of resin, but this, too, was filled with refuse. Against one wall was a wide pine bed, almost invisible beneath a pile of dried animal hides.

Caitlin didn't shudder, but she came close. She waved

her hand round the room. "It all needs burning." She said it with more venom than she meant to.

Her head turned so that Samuel could see her profile, the light touching her lashes; and he felt then that he entered the room on a wave, rather than walking, a wave that surged him forward until he was standing close behind her. He put his hands on the curve of her waist, and gently slid them down across her stomach.

"Is it that bad, Cat?"

Caitlin hesitated for a long while, and then she started to stroke the back of Samuel's hand with a gentle circular motion, around and around. She shook her head slightly.

"No, not bad. Just—I don't know—*homespun*, if you know what I mean. I think I've been a bit spoiled, that's all. I never realized...well, I never dreamed I'd have to rough it on my own."

Samuel was silent, listening, feeling the endless circling movement of Caitlin's fingertip on the back of his hand. Sometimes, he thought, the dream was better than the reality.

Take now, for instance.

The lightness of her touch and the closeness of her and the scent of her made him close his eyes and feel for one strange, light-headed moment as if he were completely contented, as if this were all he ever wanted to do, for the rest of his life. He stood in silence delaying, for a few precious moments, their separation. Out of the silence that followed, Caitlin murmured, "Even dreams have obligations. Especially to the people who dream them."

Samuel was beginning to feel aroused. Their bodies were very close. He kept thinking of kissing those soft lips, and feeling those slight breasts pressing against his chest.

Fire surged through his body at the thought. He was tempted, oh, so tempted. But some of the men would be arriving shortly, and it wouldn't do to be caught in the act, even if the woman was his wife.

He moved his hands to her shoulders and turned her to face him. He touched his lips to her cheek.

"I guess everybody has obligations, after all, if only to be peaceable to his friends and neighbors, and nothing else," he finished, putting his fingers lightly over her mouth, knowing she had been ready to protest.

Samuel replaced his fingers with his lips in a kiss that began in affection, lingered, and turned to fire. He drew away and smiled. "If we had more time, I'd enjoy what those lips promise," he said softly.

A slow smile spread over Caitlin's face. Her eyes opened wide, and Samuel knew that she was about to suggest something outrageous.

"Do you remember the fun we used to have on Bonfire Night? I propose we celebrate Guy Fawkes Day, even if it isn't the fifth of November."

Samuel struggled not to laugh. Caitlin was impossible. A world unto herself. The wicked light in her eyes reminded him of the carefree days of his youth.

"Not a bad idea, either, Cat."

When Raoul LeFeuvre, accompanied by two other men and three wagons loaded with great piles of boxes and luggage, arrived at the clearing about three o'clock, he let out a low whistle of amazement. The wind was blowing gently toward the river, and on the grassy bank a fire was burning cheerily, while from the house came sounds of great activity.

He continued to stare as Moses Livingstone, one of his logging team, emerged from the shadows of the doorway, with arms full of stiff bearskins, which he cast on the flames. Standing well back to watch for sparks, another of his men, Silas Crane, poked at them with a long stick.

Raoul jumped to the ground and went to investigate. He bit his lip. "I do not understand this. What happens here? Why do you burn the happy home?"

At the expression on the lumberman's face, Samuel

turned away, his shoulders shaking. "Some people have queer ideas as to how to clean a house."

LeFeuvre's great-knuckled hands curled and clutched at the air, making hairy fists. "And mad, as well!" he gasped, in such a strangled voice that Caitlin knew he was having difficulty controlling his emotions. That look was on the faces of all the men.

Caitlin ignored this flippancy. "It's lousy—and it smells." She smiled cheerfully. "I suspect it's infested with mice."

"Is that so?"

A significant pause stretched between them. LeFeuvre looked at Samuel. Then he looked at Caitlin. He stared at her in silence for a long time, then shrugged his heavily muscled shoulders.

"I have it now. I understand. I think."

Sam grinned. "It's going to take a bit of work to get this place in order. Raoul, can you let me have two or three men for a while?"

"There's wheels that still need greasing, and there's an axle loose on one of the wagons. We're three men down as is—what with Emil and an offsider goin' to Fairbanks with Murphy. Last thing I need is to lose more good men to some damned fool female notion of cleanliness."

Samuel gave a smothered exclamation, but Caitlin was made of sterner stuff. "There's no cause for profanity in the presence of a lady, and let me tell you, cleanliness is next to godliness."

LeFeuvre swung around, and his gaze was baleful. "Bathin' regular gets a man into terrible strife."

"If more people washed themselves and kept a clean house, there'd be a sight less sickness for the likes of me to attend."

Raoul pursed his lips. "It's on account of smellin' so sweet that Murphy got his wick stuck where it had no right to be—and look at all the hassle that's caused!"

Another sound came from Samuel, a short, thick noise, quickly strangled. Out of the corner of her eye, Caitlin saw him shake his head at Raoul. The wretch was in stitches trying to contain his mirth!

Caitlin was infuriated. She gave Samuel a look that spoke volumes. She wished she were Medusa and could turn him to stone with a mere glance.

"I have never heard anything so absurd in my entire life."

A long moment passed. Nobody moved. Samuel just smiled his infuriating wide, white smile. That made her even madder. She looked around for a weapon. If she'd had a skillet handy, she'd have hit him on the head with it!

Suddenly she could take no more. "If you'll excuse me, I have a house to clean," she sniffed, and stalked off with as much dignity as she could muster.

The men waited until she disappeared into the cabin, skirts swishing and rustling, before they burst into laughter, but she heard their howls of merriment anyway. So much for her good advice, she thought as she viciously scraped a pile of ash out of the fireplace. Just wait until one of them was sick and needed her and she wasn't available. They'd laugh on the other side of their faces then!

Her hand hovered over the pan of ash, itching to pick it up and throw it against the wall, but Samuel's laughter came back to her, and she only glared at it. Damn his arrogance. She was going to have to get even with him.

Looking around at the atrocity he'd offered as a home, she rubbed her hands together. She'd show him. When he walked through that door this evening, he wasn't going to recognize the place.

Caitlin had washed all over in a basin of warm water and donned a clean gown in her favorite shade of green. She'd twisted her hair and pinned it into its usual coil, but with no looking glass, it was impossible to do much in the way of grooming. Luckily, vanity had never been one of her besetting sins.

By the time Samuel had taken a seat, she had her plan all worked out. First she would feed him, something delicious, served up on her best china. The menu was not the most delectable of fare, but beggars could not be too pernickety. At least the flour for the biscuits had been fresh, with no weevils in it.

Opening up the small meat safe Moses had kindly assembled from bits of sawn timber that were stacked in a pile at the rear of the blockhouse, she produced a pound of bacon. The man at the wangan store had assured her it was home-cured right here at the depot.

Caitlin believed him, because she'd had to skirt the pigsties, cow byres and outhouses to get to the store that supplied the wants of the small community. She wasn't so sure about the stove though. It seemed a bit on the cantankerous side, hotter on one side than the other.

The draft from the stove did not work efficiently, so smoke parched the air. There'd been a bird's nest in the chimney, and Silas had had to climb up on the roof to clean it out. Of course, that had been after she lit the wretched thing and black smoke belched back into the room and made the place even filthier than it had been.

Samuel leaned his elbows on the table and watched her lay the rashers of bacon in the pan. With all the fascination of a healthy, hungry male, he scrutinized closely the way they curled and spat. He leaned forward, sniffed at the cloth-covered tray. Biscuits!

She turned quickly, startling him. "It's lovely having this comfy cabin to ourselves. If we lived in a grand house, there'd be servants hovering, and we'd never have a chance to be ourselves."

Caitlin was laying the table with an Irish linen cloth and napkins she had unpacked from one of her many boxes. Though he was sure the serving utensils and cutlery were good English silver, he guessed the decorative porcelain dishes were from France.

Samuel strongly suspected that the fancy setting was to distract his attention from the food. It didn't look too appetizing.

Caitlin bent down to kiss him lightly on the cheek, and walked away. She knew he was watching her go, and she swung her hips, just a little more than usual.

As she placed a dish heaped with steaming victuals in front of him, she gave him an impish smile. "My cooking could be a darn sight worse. I don't know how, but I'll let you discover that for yourself."

Samuel's worst fears were confirmed. The bacon was underdone, and the biscuits were burned black on the bottom. He wondered if his stomach would stand the strain. He picked up the fine china cup, drank the contents without tasting it.

"The tea's strong, and crunchy biscuits are nice!" Although he was trying to be nonchalant about it, he could hear the constriction in his voice.

Grinning across the table at him, she mocked, "I may not compare with one of the great chefs of Europe, but I think I can manage to cook a fairly tasty stew or broth, provided we have fresh meat. Moses says the woods abound with game."

"Before it gets dark tonight, I'd better set a few snares."

It was a strange supper. As they slowly ate their meal, Samuel found that Caitlin was a complicated mixture of innocence and experience, self-assurance and complete artlessness. He also learned that she never admitted defeat. Never.

She chattered of all sorts of inconsequential things, from the spring fashions in London to the skylarks on Bodmin Moor and the number of fishermen drowned off Pentire Point in last winter's storms, but she never once mentioned his father, Caitryn, or the afternoon's episode. It was as if she were avoiding any contentious subjects. She reminded Samuel of a skittish doe.

Caught off guard by the aching sense of need that shot through him, he decided to distract himself by creating a crisis, as there would have to be one anyway, eventually. In the mood he was in, he'd welcome almost any diversion.

"There's been some trouble while Liam and I were away. Unfortunately it hasn't worked itself out yet. I need to give the situation some more time," Samuel fell silent as he heard his own words.

In the ensuing silence, he heard the mournful cry of a loon calling its mate. The sound was unnaturally loud, hanging in the air for what seemed an eternity. It made him unaccountably nervous.

"Just what is the situation?"

Samuel swirled the dregs of his tea around in his cup. Something he couldn't grasp or understand had subtly changed between them. He disliked this tension between them.

"The situation can be summed up in two words—Henry Sagamore."

"The man who owns the lumber mill at Westfield? What does he want?"

Samuel rubbed his neck. He stirred uneasily. "He wants me."

"What does he want you for?"

Samuel stretched out his long legs. "Because Sagamore's company is involved in a number of sensitive export deals and this border dispute continues to fester, Sagamore's anxiety level has reached the boiling point."

Something inside him gave off a long sigh. The best lies, he thought, always contained a core of truth—or a version of it. "I've heard rumors he wants me brought up on charges, and our contract with Conrad Hatt terminated forthwith." He almost told her the whole truth. Almost mentioned Summer Dawn.

Caitlin looked at him, astonished. "What kind of charges could he possibly hit you with? I am sure you have done nothing illegal."

Samuel chuckled. He knew Caitlin well enough. Her sense of fairness was acute, as was her sense of loyalty. She was a fanatic about both, in fact. He steepled his long fingers, looked up at the ceiling.

"Your faith in me is touching, Cat. Trespass and cutting timber from his block on Quaggy Joe Mountain is what Henry Sagamore'd like to hit me with."

"I know you. You wouldn't—"

"Eye of the beholder. George Buckmore doesn't think so. He's the surveyor attached to Governor Fairfield's staff."

Caitlin felt her heart lurch. Her anxiety level was escalating dangerously. "So what are you saying?" she asked.

"Sagamore has to be stopped from blocking the movement of log booms. The only way to do it is to get that dam built as quickly as possible, then we can coordinate joint drives. It might be best if you keep close to the depot for the next few days. Silas and Moses can be spared for any jobs you want done."

"Well, maybe you're wise. It'll give me time to go through the things I had shipped out here. Set up some sort of surgery. If the situation is as bad as you suggest, there could well be casualties in need of my skills." A grim note that was not without a touch of humor crept into her voice.

A faint sense of disappointment went through him. He'd looked forward to her sharp tongue spitting out things he knew she'd regret later. An argument would have been a welcome distraction.

He looked up, met those magnetic green eyes and felt the weight of her gaze. He could almost see his own reflection there. His body tightened. It seemed that when he was with her there was a heaviness between his legs that never went away.

A strange awareness settled in him. Caitlin's eyes were betraying her again. It was as if she were fighting the powerful attraction she felt for him for all she was worth, which at the moment didn't seem to be much. His traitorous mind dared to wonder if she was as nervous as he was.

"Don't be too disappointed if no one comes. A female physician might be a bit radical for this rough lot."

Caitlin made an unconvinced sound. A stubborn line came into her jaw. At times, she could be frustratingly stubborn and obtuse.

"They're not fools, either. Most of them can't afford to pay for a fancy doctor. Silas told me the men are paid in tokens that can be exchanged only at the wangan store."

"That's because they'd gamble away their wages. When their contracts are finished and they're ready to go home to their families, the tokens are traded for currency."

"If they have nothing else, they can pay me in gratitude."

Samuel heard something in her voice, but he was too distracted to dwell on it. Her waist was so slim and supple, he thought. He wanted to put his hands around it. He could see the sweet curve of her breasts beneath the fitted green bodice. He wanted to put his hands on them, as well.

Samuel lowered his gaze and studied the shifting runes of the tea leaves. The questions he'd avoided all evening rushed in upon him. What would be her reaction when she knew the truth? Could she forgive him? How foolish could he be?

I'm a fool. I know it. But I can't stop wanting her. And I can't give her up, either. There wasn't any answer to the problems that circled relentlessly in his mind, arguments and hopes repeated endlessly, with no solution in sight. No matter how many times he thought about Caitlin and himself and the future, he had no answer he wanted to live with. He didn't want to think the thought. It unsettled him.

Unsettled was too gentle a word to describe how Caitlin

felt. She could not take her eyes off him. The lamplight turned his hair to molten copper and caressed his face the way she wanted to.

Dear Lord, he was so handsome—and he was her husband. To distract herself, she signaled with the teapot. "Another cup?"

Samuel grunted, but did not otherwise reply.

Caitlin put a refill in front of him. His sleeve brushed her arm. Her skin glowed. Her heart was thundering in her ears. There was soft warmth between her thighs, and her limbs were tingling with life. It seemed to her then that the burnished gleam from Samuel's hair reflected the warm glow inside her.

Again, that silence, relished as slowly as clear molasses.

Samuel drained his cup and sat staring into the dregs, as if he found them fascinating. Caitlin stirred herself, and began to gather the dishes. "It's too early for bed—so, what shall we do to fill in the time?" She'd had to say something, anything, to break the mood.

Samuel laughed abruptly.

Realizing the implications of her innocent question, she blurted, "Oh, I didn't mean *that*—I—I just meant I wasn't weary enough to be packed off to bed like a pesky child."

"Cat, I'd *never* put you to bed like a *child*."

Caitlin saw that special glint appear as his eyes rested on the swell of her breasts, which suddenly began to feel too large for her bodice. She found it increasingly difficult to breathe, and she was wondering, just wondering, what would happen if she dared to lean slightly forward.

They stared at each other. The silence was thick with tension. Caitlin's heart pounded erratically. His eyes were fixed on the rise and fall of her breasts, held tight within her dress. She was quite certain that he knew exactly what she was thinking.

With an effort, she ignored the challenge and hastily removed the dishes. She stacked them into a large enamel pan, sprinkled on some soap shavings and added water that had been warming in a bucket on the stove.

"In all my grand vision of life in America, I never once took into account the very mundane chore of washing dirty dishes. Life can be interesting at times, can't it?"

"Very interesting." As she walked by him, his hands went out in one fast swoop and he pulled her close against him, so that her scent came to him and a wave of her thick black hair brushed his cheek.

God, she was tiny, like a schoolgirl, though the breasts that pressed against him were those of a woman. Warmth began to suffuse him. He circled her with his arms, and he felt big and clumsy. He could feel her breathing, and he touched briefly the pulse at the hollow of her throat. A thick wing of hair passed across his face, smelling of honeysuckle and citrus. He inhaled deeply, pulled her onto his lap.

Hell, this was torture! He would put the future out of his mind, concentrate on the present, he told himself.

Afterward, he would tell her about the mix-up in names. Afterward, he would tell her about Zoe. Afterward, he would suffer the consequences.

For now, he would yield to the serpent of temptation. For now, it seemed to him as if he had the sun in his lap, instead of this small, dainty female. The heat had targeted one specific source in him, where her buttocks wiggled enticingly against him. His loins were burning up. He was as stiff as stone.

Caitlin was keenly aware of his maleness, in every interesting inch of his body. His big body pulsed against hers. His lips were parted. His face was so close to hers that she could taste his breath. He watched her mouth with an intensity that left her weak.

He had only to touch her and she felt as though she were coming down with a fever of the blood. Did her touch have the same effect on him?

Suddenly she wanted to touch him, to trace every ridge and swell of flesh, to know again the compelling male textures of his body. She moved her hands across the planes of his torso. Slipping the heavy embroidered suspenders that he wore down over his shoulders, she began to unfasten the buttons on his shirt.

Somehow, his knee had slipped between hers, and his thigh had aggressively inserted itself against her buttocks. The evidence of his desire was there, a rigid cylinder, pressing into her leg. It was a good feeling.

The pads of his thumbs rubbed her nipples, and she gasped, burying her head in his shoulder. He tilted her head up, captured her mouth with his lips. Her lips flowered open, and she moaned a little as she felt his tongue twine with hers.

Imprisoned by his knees, she felt one of his hands edge up beneath the hem of her skirt. He unfastened the tapes of her underskirt and let it drop to the floor.

His hand wove patterns down her belly and below, finding the slit in her drawers, sliding beneath. His fingers teased the soft, delicate flesh at the top of her legs, creeping around to the inside of her thighs, stroking rhythmically back and forth until her loins began to melt and she felt her hips move forward.

The backs of his hands brushed against the soft triangle of curls, and he inhaled quickly. Abruptly his biceps began to quiver and jump. His forearm muscles were giving little twitches, and his fingers shook as they attempted to unknot the laces of her drawers and demicorset.

In the end, Caitlin was obliged to help him. Stepping out of her garments, she exhaled, aware that she had been holding her breath. She reached out and touched his cheek with the flat of her hand.

"Samuel...?" Her voice was low. If they had not been so close, Caitlin believed, he would not have heard her.

Suddenly Samuel shifted. He scooped her up, carried her

over to the bed. The mattress was as soft as down, though the cloth case was filled with her thick winter garments.

Caitlin could hear her own breathing now, harsh and ragged. She smiled at him, welcoming him openly. Then her legs opened and she was drawing them up the outside of his thighs. Her invitation was unmistakable. He was so strong, so handsome, to her. And she wanted him.

She heard him groan, his body shudder, and she lifted her legs, fitting him to her. His need was raw and powerful, but he sank into her so slowly there was no discomfort.

A shudder ripped through him, yet his gradual penetration didn't hasten. Gently he rocked back and forth, until she felt him deep inside her, like a second heartbeat, his pulse accelerating as he slid farther and farther up into her. His hot breath was in her ear.

The pleasure as he bucked up against her was a solid filament reaching all the way up to the top of her head. She was on fire. Her thighs were trembling, her breathing as broken and rapid as his own.

Caitlin's head went back. She gasped air out of her lungs, and her eyelids fluttered. Her thighs closed inward as she welcomed the deep physical interlocking.

She felt his hips give a ragged lurch inward, and then he was expanding deep inside her, so that she couldn't tell where she ended and he began, for there was no distinction, no division, no difference, as they were made double, made whole.

Samuel convulsed against her, the shudders going on and on, like echoes through his body, while he emptied himself inside her. She was flooded with an intense heat. Her insides had turned molten. The filament disintegrated. She melted, her eyes closed, and the shivering, shimmering ripples of pleasure consumed her.

Time was suspended, locked in an endless moment. Her mind was blank, her eyes were glazed and unseeing, open wide, as their shared body shuddered in a joyous rhythm of ecstasy.

And when Samuel awoke near dawn, he was lying with one leg thrown across her thighs. He felt the thick sheaf of her hair against his cheek, the sweetness of her breath. He put his lips against her ear until he felt her stir.

"Cat, I want to tell you—"

Sleepily she snuggled closer to him. Samuel sighed and kissed her eyes and cheeks. Her body was relaxed, surrounded by his warmth.

The smell of their mingled musk was potent. It underscored the guilt that gnawed at him. He sighed again, deeply. When a man's mind couldn't rise above his groin, he was in serious trouble, he thought.

His own lust had led him into this predicament. Period.

Chapter Nine

Neither Silas nor Moses spared himself in the next few days. They set to work with a will, and soon the Jardine household resounded with the banging of hammers, the tearing of wood as the floors were ripped up, and heartfelt bursts of profanity.

On the fifth day, after Caitlin managed to wreck a perfectly good trout, Samuel brought Mulligan over to teach her how to gauge the heat in the oven. The inarticulate Mulligan showed her how to stoke it up so that the heat was evenly distributed. Best of all, he showed her how to make flapjacks.

"I've never had flapjacks," she told him.

"Then you haven't really lived."

Caitlin soon acquired the knack, and began cooking all sorts of delicious treats for Samuel, which she shared with Silas and Moses, much to their secret joy.

No grumbles now.

The men, excited and charged with the spirit of high adventure, leaped over the roof, like hounds on the leash, asking only to be released. Toward the middle of the second week, the floorboards and roof shingles had all been replaced.

The window in the sitting room had been widened, and

when he returned with the news that Liam and Ned were
well on the way to recovery, Emil brought with him a pane
of glass cushioned in hay. Caitlin now had a view over the
stream, and of the mountain that towered to the north.
Every evening and every morning brought new variations
of weather clouds and different shadows on the hills.

Caitlin loved to watch the colors flare. The sun sank in
reds and yellows and golds, and it rose in pink, lilac and
lemon. Green lay the forest, brown and silent the moving
river. The land lay still, brooding, expectant, but she had
no time to sit and brood. The time for dreaming was past.
Now was the time for doing.

The days passed as swiftly as a hawk diving for prey.
At the depot, Caitlin rummaged in boxes, unpacking all
manner of things that, when in Cornwall, she had deemed
essential for survival in this remote wilderness, and Moses
turned his attention to the room Caitlin had earmarked for
her medical practice.

A change was made here, an addition there. Moses
erected cupboards and shelves in every place Caitlin considered suitable, and she filled them with all manner of jars
and bottles. In the end, the whole of one wall was taken
up with shelves labeled with abbreviated Latin names, and
a ladder ran on a rail so that she could reach the top row
of shelves.

It was the custom for Hugh Mulligan, the cook, to rouse
all the camp at six o'clock with a tremendous banging on
a piece of boiler-plate hung by a wire. Long before that,
Samuel had stirred. Each morning he was gone at dawn,
not returning until the sun began its downward curve across
the sky and the western face of the hill was all in shadow.

One night, Caitlin looked across the table at Samuel as
he poured some brown, viscous liquid all over his plate of
steaming buckwheat flapjacks.

"What is that?"

He stuck a forkful of flapjack into his mouth, held up

the pottery beaker he had purloined from the mess house. "Maple syrup," he said. "It goes over the flapjacks."

Caitlin put down her fork. "I don't think I..."

"You must," Samuel insisted. He swiped up the last of the syrup with the last wedge of flapjack. "They're not the same without the syrup. The two go together in a very delicate chemical process."

Caitlin gingerly poured some over her pancakes, took a bite, and was instantly converted. "Hmm...where does it come from?"

"The Abnaki over on the promontory. They trade maple syrup for cloth."

All in all, Caitlin found herself remarkably content with her new life. Only one thing plagued her. No customers came to her surgery. It seemed the inhabitants of Presque Isle were inordinately healthy.

Samuel, on the other hand, found himself torn apart. He hadn't expected the intense sexual arousal that accompanied his marriage to Caitlin. The indescribable physical hunger she both kindled and appeased vied with the horrible fear that she would reject him when she discovered the truth.

Perhaps it was lack of fortitude, Samuel thought, that held him from confronting Caitlin. Perhaps it was prudence that argued, in the growing contentment he found in the marriage, that getting on with his plans and thinking through his problems might grant him some useful leeway—not only with Caitlin, but with his archrival, Henry Sagamore. There was no way he could explain anything to her yet.

Samuel hoped to buy enough time to hobble Sagamore. So he concentrated on getting the splash dam built. A series of ponds, lakes and interlacing marshes would provide storage sufficient to raise the water level several feet. This, together with numerous fin booms, would protect the an-

nual river drive from slack water and eddies and facilitate
getting the logs to the Saint John.

As succinctly as he could, Samuel told Caitlin what he
was doing, and why. He hoped it would stop the political
bickering and let the rival lumbermen sort out their differences. He recognized that frontier lumbermen from both
sides of the border entered the woods with the conviction
that the trees belonged to those who cut them.

Last winter, Sagamore had made a foray into the Fairbanks Logging Company's Quaggy Joe timber limit. The
theft had been minor, but Samuel was determined to stamp
out this practice before the pillaging became significant. He
had the feeling that Sagamore would back off now that
there was a stalemate between the two governments on the
border issue.

"Surely there are enough trees for all?" Caitlin broke
into his dark thoughts. He studied her for a moment. As
ever, looking at her brought an odd tightness to his chest.

"Sagamore suffers the sickness of blind greed."

"What I can't fathom is this personal determination to
stop him. Why not leave him to his own dirty business and
let the authorities deal with it?"

"It's just not possible."

"You mean it's not practical."

Samuel sighed, knowing he would not win this argument
with Caitlin—if he even wanted to. Caitlin, with her sharp,
probing mind and her equally sharp tongue, was an enigma.
So frail of body, so strong of will. For the life of him, he
couldn't figure her out.

There was the calm, cool physician who dealt with a
gunshot wound or a broken finger with equanimity; there
was the passionate lover who gave herself to him freely,
generously and unhesitatingly, in uninhibited sensual ways
he'd never before known a woman to do; there was the
impeccable fashion plate; and lately there was all this fre-

netic domestic activity, as if she wanted to subdue this wild frontier territory.

He nodded, wordless.

It was good that she was too busy to think. Let him get the dam built first. Then he could worry about Caitlin and all the confessions he had to make. Only a fool would jeopardize the order of things.

Somehow, Sagamore must be made to stop his illegal depredations before the boundary dispute escalated. It was essential that Maine lumbermen have access to free navigation on the Saint John. Without it, Aroostook's timber was virtually worthless.

The idea was for licensed timber to be sorted and passed to the Saint John, while the trespass timber was to be landed on the banks above the dam. This would settle arguments about ownership before the politicians became involved and boundary negotiations broke down.

Henry Sagamore was against construction of the dam, probably because most of the large cribwork piers were to be built from confiscated timber—most of it Sagamore's. His opposition to the scheme seemed the height of folly to Samuel.

Of course, this intransigence could have as much to do with Henry's longtime bitterness over losing Summer Dawn to his archenemy as with any business rivalry with the Fairbanks Logging Company, Samuel thought. The first round had definitely gone to Samuel. Summer Dawn had come to him. He had taken her in as his woman, and given the child she carried the protection of his name.

Could he retreat now, claiming he had been duped—knowing the consequences? No. He could not.

He could not remotely justify it.

If Caitryn had come to Maine, as she was meant to do, she would surely have taken little Zoe to her heart. It had been Caitryn's Madonna-like image that spurred Samuel to send for her. Instead, she had joined the convent, and Caitlin had become his bogus bride.

Caitlin professed to love him. He was consumed with his need to possess her. She welcomed him. That was more than enough.

So why did he feel so damned guilty?

Uneasily, he considered his options. To confess meant to risk conflict, and possibly lose Caitlin. To say nothing meant she might stumble on the truth of her own accord. The decision would have to be made soon, and the weight of the burden lay heavy upon him.

Tomorrow, he promised himself, he would decide....

And tomorrow came and went...and still no one came to Caitlin's surgery.

Then, one morning, the Chinese gardener, Li Foo, arrived. A round-faced little man, bandy-legged and potbellied, he wore a loose cotton tunic and wide-legged trousers. He simply stood there and fixed her with an unnerving stare.

"What is the trouble?"

He shuffled forward. "Yesterday, Li Foo carry wood for firebox of little missy." The high, quavering voice hung momentarily on the still air, then silence...

"That's right, Li Foo, and now the wood box is full." Caitlin lifted a hand. She studied the old but still intelligent face, the slanted black eyes. "Thank you very much."

"Li Foo carry wood for little missy on his back. Now there are many splinters, and Li Foo can't reach them to dig them out." His voice was as brittle as rice paper. "Li Foo puts himself in your hands. He is trusting you. But no one else!" For the first time, he raised his voice above a whisper.

"No one," he repeated, more softly.

He stared off into the distance, frightened a little, but not wishing to show it. His loss of face would be incalculable...and to a barbarian woman. It was unthinkable!

Caitlin recognized the strain of anxiety in his face and turned quickly to the instrument tray, making a pretense of arranging the supplies to give him time to find composure. He turned back to her, rubbed his palms on the front of his tunic. The black almond eyes were without expression.

"A thousand pardons, but, if little missy is not afraid of fire-breathing dragon, maybe she would remove splinters?" He removed his tunic, hung it carefully over a chair and hoisted himself onto the table.

As Li Foo lay on his stomach, the braided queue that began in a knot on the crown of his otherwise smoothly shaven head fell to one side, and Caitlin looked for the first time at the old man's back.

Mercy! She took a deep, shuddering breath, her gaze riveted on the reddish blue swirls that adorned his spare frame. He resembled a splendid work of art. His skin was like gold leaf, and from neck to buttocks his hairless flesh was indelibly decorated with colored ink in the design of a huge, writhing dragon. Surrounded by meticulously drawn flames, it seemed to be alive.

How Li Foo must love his native land, to have its symbol tattooed on his back! Caitlin tore her eyes away from the awesome sight.

The splinters were not very big, or in too deep, but she removed them with great care. The gardener was old, but in the way of the Oriental. His skin had yellowed, like the patina on parchment, and seemed to have grown thin, so translucent that the blue veins in his temples showed clearly. "I'll try not to hurt you. I promise."

Li Foo bore her ministrations with stoicism. Her touch was light and deft, but she knew her probing hurt. He spoke only once, in a voice as soft as a leaf falling onto a wet sidewalk.

"Li Foo joss is good. Little missy is not easily frightened."

Caitlin swabbed the area with alcohol. She smiled at the back of his head. "All done."

Li Foo struggled to sit up, and she reached to help him, pulling his tunic down, allowing the layer of cloth to conceal the indigo scrolls. Politely, she kept her eyes averted from his, and groped for words to break the awkwardness.

"May I offer you a cool drink?" Caitlin asked, wanting to put the old man at his ease.

Something passed across the impassive face; the slanted, hooded eyes became tightly closed slits in the wide and wrinkled brow. He stood back, clapping his hands over his small, round belly, and shook his head.

"Thank you, velly kind, but no. There are many plants here that Li Foo grows, plants used for medicine in other countries. Li Foo bring to little missy. In such way, good joss multiplies itself." The old man touched his hands together, bowed deeply and backed away through the door.

Caitlin watched him walk away and felt a vitality rush through her, a feeling that her joss indeed was good, and that soon, very soon, the benches Moses had made for her waiting room would be filled.

Happy with that thought, she accepted the fresh vegetables that Li Foo left across the doorstep each morning.

Caitlin wondered if this simple gesture contributed to the deep sense of belonging she experienced at Presque Isle. She did not know what the residence was like at Fairbanks, but this little settlement in the backwoods was beginning to feel like home.

But although Li Foo kept her supplied with fresh vegetables, there were no further patients.

As was his custom, Samuel woke early. He lay still for a moment, blinking into wakefulness. The sunlight streamed through the glass-paned window. Beside him, Caitlin stirred.

Turning carefully onto his side and bracing himself on

his elbow, Samuel looked at his wife. Her right arm was beneath her head, the hand buried to the wrist beneath the crumpled pillow. Her waist-length hair tumbled down over her face and across her shoulders, a solid curtain of blackness.

He lay there for a while, listened to her soft, even breathing. Her face was very close to his. Nuzzling her neck, he smelled the sweet scent of her, all mixed up with the fragrance of honeysuckle. She gave a little wriggle, muttered something, then settled again.

With a little sigh, he gently pushed back the deep blue embroidered blanket, swung his feet to the floor and padded to the door. It was a bright, crisp morning. The sun was just beginning its climb above the sky-scraping pines, casting long, dancing shadows on the grassy verge between house and stream.

For some reason, he felt strangely edgy. The air was cool and moist, and he breathed in deeply, savoring its freshness. Suddenly he knew what he needed to work off this uneasy restlessness.

Samuel strode with a long tread across the grassed area and went down the crusty scree to the glimmering stream. Voices, small yet distinct against the vault of the forest, echoed from the cookhouse.

Slowly, the Presque Isle Stream depot was awakening…

The wide water stretched before him, half-veiled in fog. There was no one to see him; he stripped and plunged in, gasping, for the water was icy.

Caitlin came awake with a sense of anticipation. Eyes closed, she used her bare toe to locate Samuel. When she realized that the bed was empty, she sat up, blinking. Samuel was already up and gone. Swimming, no doubt. It was a regular custom.

Ten minutes later, she stood on the bank of the stream. There was a slight chill in the wind, which was nevertheless invigorating. It bent the corn in the garden, scattered the pine needles and blew Caitlin's dark hair into her eyes. Watching Samuel, she marveled at the flex and resilience of his body as the lean, muscular frame cleaved the water.

Someone was watching him. It was a sensation Samuel had become accustomed to, bathing as he did. Usually it was the loggers, who seasoned their gazes with jokes about his odd habit of bathing regularly. He whipped about, body supple, strong and quick.

Caitlin stood on the bank. He stared at her, back erect, hair billowing, eyes like wells out of time, filled with an unconscious appeal.

Samuel felt a surge of wild delight that she was here with him. "Right on time," he called. "I like that."

She gave a mock pout. "You left me so early, I rolled over and tore the sheets into ribbons."

"Really?"

"Really." He saw the light in her eyes, that slight parting of her lips that he loved so much, when there was something on her mind and she was working out the best way to say it.

She tucked a trailing strand of dark hair behind her ear. "I hugged your pillow and wished it were you."

When she was like this, she made his mouth water. A smile he couldn't prevent stole across his lips. "What did you think about?"

"I shouldn't tell you," Caitlin went on in a soft, mischievous murmur, "but I dreamed of you doing all the delicious things to me I lacked the courage to ask you to do last night."

He laughed out loud, enjoying Caitlin's quick tongue. "You don't seem to me the kind of woman to lack the courage to ask anything."

"What kind of man needs to be asked?"

Samuel heard the invitation in her voice. His body stirred eagerly, the familiar hunger beginning to seize him. He shook his head, spraying cold drops everywhere. Already partially erect, he strode, uninhibited, to where she was standing, placed wet hands on her shoulders. "It's Sunday. Let's play hooky."

The red-hot gleam in his eyes made Caitlin feel weak. She started to say something, then forgot what it was as a jolt of deep longing knifed through her. The naked grace of his physique fascinated her. Every masculine curve of his body, every movement of sinew and tendon, made new formations of light and shadow.

Blinking, Caitlin tried to gather her scattered thoughts. She reached around his waist and held him tightly, her cheek against his wet shoulder.

Samuel ran his fingertips down the long arch of her neck, and touched her, so softly that she scarcely felt it, down the ridge along her spine. "Make up your mind. It's your call," he said in her ear, then licked it with the tip of his tongue.

She poked him in the ribs and scowled. "You're playing a game with me."

He grinned knowingly, kissed her hair and reached for his clothes. "If I am, you're winning."

They went through the woods, heavy with summer smells, the forest floor spongy with pine needles, sunlight filtering through the branches. Hand in hand, they circled the segment of inlet, and watched a raccoon methodically washing some prize for her three cubs at the water's edge, while beyond them loons vanished and reappeared in odd aquatic wizardry.

Climbing a low, rocky point, they found themselves a nook against a fallen tree, the odor of moss and partridge berry in their nostrils. Back in the lee of the high promontory, they were sheltered and alone, with only a chickadee singing its silly two-note refrain above their heads.

Beginning where they sat, tree trunks rose in immense brown pillars, running back in great forest naves, shadowy always, floored with green moss laid in a rich, soft carpet.

Far through the woods behind them, the wind whistled and hummed among swaying tops of pumpkin pine. Downstream, to the west, past a long curving slice of land, the dam was taking shape with its cantilevered confines and toe-piled wings.

As the sun rose, its heat intensified and the last chill of night quickly surrendered to the golden fire. Samuel put his hands behind his head, his long legs stretched out, savoring the washed-gold flood of sunlight against his face.

Caitlin reclined on an elbow beside him with the sun in her eyes. Her long lashes threw tiny shadows into the soft hollows of her face. Wisps of her hair had come undone, fluttering now against the skin of her cheeks in the warm breeze.

She put her palm along his cheek. "Hear the wind rustle in the treetops, Samuel. It's like cathedral music."

"I know." Samuel ran his fingers through the raven's-wing cascade of her hair. He kissed her fleetingly, closing the distance between them until there wasn't any at all.

Caitlin slipped to her knees, deftly undid his trousers. Slid her hand along the length of him, curling her fingers as she went. Felt the powerful muscles along the insides of his thighs begin to jump and convulse. Then, she stopped.

"This seems rather decadent. I wonder what Father Gabriel would say?"

Samuel's heart rolled over, and he could not catch his breath. "This is evil, what you do, my children," he said in a shaky voice.

Caitlin let out a deep groan, her forehead pressed against his chest. She could feel the thunder of his heartbeat. She thought of the boundless energy of the sea.

"Does it seem so to you?"

Samuel's fingers stroked her face. "Would you believe me if I told you that whether I tell you the truth or lie to you, it is the same?" Now it was his turn to whisper.

Caitlin put the palms of her hands on his chest, pushed

her head away from contact with him. Her green eyes peered at him as if they would see into his mind. "No."

"But it is." He moved slightly, sliding his leg between hers. "There is no difference."

Caitlin put her hands on the round, hard muscles of his shoulders and slid her fingers along his arms until she lay on top of him, then lifted again and came down until he was all the way inside her. With the unselfconsciousness of a cat, she rubbed the sensitive tips of her breasts against the rough hair on his chest.

Samuel gasped air out of his lungs. Her heat was incredible. She engulfed him in a pool of liquid fire. He felt as if he had walked into a furnace. "This is crazy. Suppose someone came hiking along here."

"I know. Isn't it a delicious thought? I've never had the chance for any real honest-to-goodness decadence, Samuel. It's rather fun."

"Caitlin," he said helplessly as she drew him closer.

The passion in her began to rise, replacing the levity and the laughter. She pressed her body closer, pulling him to her. He heaved like the ocean, and the sounds of ecstasy were like the wind in their ears.

And then they came together in a way that was wholly different from the ways they had merged before. And far more intimate. Somehow, in that moment of ultimate fusion, they were one.

The music they heard, saw, scented, felt, was the harmony of their souls twining...

...becoming whole.

The sun, ripe and golden, was stretched through the treetops like a web when Caitlin heard a sound outside the surgery and went to investigate. A tall man with an athletic build stood in the open doorway. Sunlight glinted off smooth, dark hair.

He was young, in his midthirties, Caitlin judged, with a

great curling mustache shining with wax. Fashionably
dressed in a cutaway coat and dark trousers, he wore a
striped waistcoat and a patterned cravat.

"May I help you?"

He ducked his head under the low door, took one careful
step across the threshold and squinted into the surgery. Inside, it was cool and still. He blinked, struggling to get his
eyes adjusted to the dimness of the immediate environment.

"Who's in charge here?" He asked that as one might
make any commonplace inquiry, but his quietness did not
deceive Caitlin.

"I am." Her tone was calm, but inwardly her heart had
skittered. He was virile, handsome, but her intuition told
her this man was up to mischief. And it was *bad*. Surely
not.

Caitlin was startled by the effect he was having on her.
She knew there was no rational explanation. This disturbed
her. The irrational, Caitlin believed, was what manipulated
events. Like currents in a stream, unseen but felt, the forces
of the universe worked to a purpose. Were these forces
trying to tell her—warn her—of something? If so, what?

He lifted a brow. His eyes swept over her body, taking
in the piled-up hair, the delicate structure of face and chin,
the tiny silver crucifix nestled in the vulnerable hollow of
her throat, the soft, feminine curves of bosom, waist and
thigh.

Caitlin's heart felt as though drenched in ice-cold water.
She was wearing a day dress in a striking shade of light
green, the bodice of which was decorated with flat, pleated
folds that descended from the shoulder to the center-front.

He looked again at Caitlin, devouring her with his eyes.
His blue eyes followed the line of pleats. It seemed as if
they stripped away the bodice trim and probed the delicate
flesh beneath. Stupid thoughts, surely, she tried to reassure
herself. Nonetheless, she felt herself shiver.

As he stared at her, he rubbed his mustache with a long

finger. His head came close to hers. "A passionate mouth." A merry grin was on his lips. "Made for kisses."

Caitlin flushed with a mix of fury and embarrassment. The stranger was both base and brazen, and it seemed he liked to feel superior. She forced herself to look straight at him, to meet his gaze.

"What seems to be your problem?" Her voice was clipped and precise, but she did not raise it even a note.

He looked at her, surprised, for a moment. Then he gave a laugh and shrugged a heavy shoulder. He took a hand-rolled cigarette out of a pocket of his jacket, spent some time lighting it, sucked in some, then said, "Sam Jardine," as he exhaled.

She trod down the fear that surged up in her bosom. Her fingers touched the crucifix at her throat with a fingertip, and she felt her courage renew.

"Samuel's not here, and you're wasting my time. Please leave my surgery," she commanded, surprised at the authority in her voice. She wished Samuel were here beside her. Not to tell her what to do or even to reassure her, just to be here. She began to turn away.

He chuckled, deep in his heavy chest. "Well, ain't you Miss High-and-Mighty? You callin' yourself a doctor, and expectin' the folks around here to come to you?" His voice was very soft, his smile menacing. "They won't, you know, not when Henry Sagamore spreads the word that the new doctor ain't nothin' but a bit of fluff. No man's gonna come for any doctorin'—though he might come for somethin' else."

Caitlin grew angry at this. She didn't think her incivility would matter now. "Aside from the fact that most folks in Aroostook County wouldn't care to insult Sam Jardine's wife, I guess if a body hurts enough, he won't care who works on him, Mr. Sagamore."

Henry looked at her in renewed surprise. Sam Jardine's

wife! He studied the woman more carefully. She was very
sharp. He wondered just how sharp she was. He cocked his
head and took another drag on the cigarette.

"What is it you've been trying to prove, Mrs. Jardine,
in wanting to become a surgeon? That you're the equal of
a man? Because you're not, you know. No woman is."

Caitlin was partly amused, partly provoked. She had
spent much time and effort in grooming herself for the role
of wife to Samuel Jardine, but she was also accustomed to
skillfully handling her own affairs without male interference.

She looked him up and down in an insolent way. She
knew Henry Sagamore didn't like it, and that had she been
a man and looked at him in the same way, the fellow would
have knocked her down.

"Contrary to the male's mistaken way of thinking," she
said smoothly, "women do not want to be men."

His mouth tightened. He was no longer amused. "No?"
His tone was challenging and skeptical. "Then what is it
they *do* want, since equality isn't in the cards?" He examined the dying end of his cigarette.

She contemplated him for a time before answering. "Just
a measure of respect, and the chance to prove themselves.
That isn't so much to ask, is it?" There was an edge to her
voice.

"What are you suggesting?" he asked, suppressing a
hard smile, as he leaned closer to her. The woman was a
challenge. He shrugged his big shoulders. You're either
very smart or very stupid, Mrs. Jardine, he thought to himself. I wonder which one it is?

Caitlin remained silent, eyeing the enigmatic face in front
of her, judging whether the man would be an ally or an
opponent. Their glances held. His grew dark. What she
needed was in his face.

She smiled broadly at him. If he saw even a tiny chink
in her front now, he'd roll right over her.

"Tell you what. Any of your men get hurt real bad, I'll come over and see whether they'll let me try to fix their hurts. If they do, you'll call off this stupid vendetta you seem to be having with my husband. Bail out. Resign."

Then, as quickly, her smile vanished, and she looked straight into the eyes of Samuel's sworn enemy. "If not, you have my permission to go the whole hog. Let the Sagamore juggernaut have its day. Let it destroy what it will—Fairbanks Logging Company and Samuel Jardine. How's that for a deal?"

In the silence that prevailed, Henry Sagamore flicked his butt into the empty fireplace. He seemed to have made up his mind.

"The best I've had all day."

Chapter Ten

The sun was already lost in the foliage and long shadows were making lacy patterns on the grass when Caitlin made her way to the wangan store. Smoke issued from the stovepipe of the cookhouse, and a white-aproned man, who eyed her with uneasy diffidence, stood framed in the doorway.

She stopped to chat with the Chinese gardener, Li Foo. The wide mouth of the Chinese broadened into a grin as she stood and admired his small walled garden. Flowers blooming along the outer edge of the vegetable garden lent bright bursts of color to the green plants. Why the sight should be so unexpected, or so striking, she did not know, but for some reason it made her catch her breath.

"Little missy like blossom?"

Li Foo seemed to take great pleasure in cutting her some flowers. He sat on his heels and clipped a bouquet of black-eyed golden rudbeckia. His small, bony hands worked deftly at this task and, though he must have been over eighty, Caitlin could detect no unsteadiness in those fingers.

"Thank you. They are beautiful, Li Foo."

The aproned cook hailed her with a nonchalant air, a cigarette resting in one corner of his mouth. His fleshy face was very florid, dominated by a waxy nose. His high cheeks were pocked, and a scar ran down like a tear from the corner of one eye, so that it appeared lower than the other one.

"That your doctorin' bag, ma'am?"

"It sure is, Mr. Mulligan. There is an old saying—If the mountain won't come to Mahomet, then Mahomet must come to the mountain," Caitlin exclaimed, as much to herself as to Mulligan.

Mulligan's bare arms were slick with sweat, and Caitlin saw the yellowing bandage covering his left forearm, discolored with the grime of ashes and cooking lard. She pressed her lips together with disapproval.

"What have you been up to?" She gave him a sharp questioning glance.

Mulligan shifted from one foot to the other. "Well, see, I got this wee bit of a burn on me arm, 'n' it seems to have become infected. Wanna have a look at it?" He said it in a halting, protracted manner, and it was obvious that it was difficult for him.

"I'd best come in."

Caitlin found herself following him into the dark, stuffy warmth of a large kitchen that reeked of onions. She let her eyes wander over the room—the wide hearth, with its cooking pots and fire irons, the sparse and simple furnishings—gradually becoming accustomed to the dark after the brilliance of the day outside. The mess house had the saving grace of cleanliness—according to logging-camp standards.

Mulligan took a seat, pressed his knuckled fist down onto the table, his arm rigid as an iron bar. "All yours, Doc."

Caitlin removed the filthy bandage, flinching a little at the odor. *A wee bit of a burn.* Were all American men as casual as these lumberjacks? Caitlin frowned deeply. Mulligan's forearm was horribly burned, the blisters cracked and purulent. It was not a pleasant sight. Grimly she bent to her examination.

"Sometimes a hurt can look worse than it is."

"I concoct an excellent salve, Mulligan, but if infection

gets into the blood, there is little I can do. This has to be kept clean." She scowled blackly at the cook. "I suppose you know what a bath is—and there must be no drinking while this is healing." Her voice was tart and peppery.

"Not a chance." Mulligan winced a little at the pain.

Caitlin looked at him. "You know, Mulligan, sometimes men are like children. All they need to see the error of their ways is to be given parameters."

"Parameters?"

Caitlin bent over him, working on the wound. "If a man senses that he has no limits—that he will be allowed to do whatever he wishes—he will push to see if it's true. He does this, because with limits comes the sense of security that all men and all children need."

"You don't mind if I don't take your word for it…at least not yet." Mulligan waved away her words.

"Keep still." Her hands were suddenly motionless, then began again. So did her scolding. Occasionally she rummaged in the open bag beside her.

Mulligan listened to all her instructions with an air of great attention, stretching his neck forward like a reptile about to strike. Two spots of color appeared high on his cheeks, accentuating the whiteness of the pockmarks. He kept his body very still, but she heard him suck in his breath.

Caitlin's fingers probed and pushed, moving over the blackened flesh. Mulligan stared at the ceiling, at nothing. But his muscles had a will of their own, and they betrayed him, jumping in pain under the slender fingers.

Somewhere in the screen of woods, a whistle shrilled. Caitlin could hear Mulligan let out a little breath. "Oh, Christ," he said. "That's the donkey blowing quitting time. Men'll be in soon." His voice seemed hoarse and raw.

"Just hold on. I'm almost finished," she said, having already cleaned his arm thoroughly.

By the time she had finished applying some salve, she

heard the voices of men. Looking out through a window curtained with cheesecloth, she saw Samuel's logging gang swing past, strong men all, with thick necks and shoulders, grimy with the sweat of their labors.

She watched them cluster by a bench before the bunk-house, dabble their faces and hands in washbasins, scrub themselves promiscuously on towels, sometimes one at each end of a single piece of cloth, hauling it back and forth in rude play.

"Why, who's that?"

Her ear had caught a low, throaty laugh, a woman's laugh, outside. She looked inquiringly at Mulligan. His expression remained absent, that of one concentrated upon his own problems. She repeated the question.

"That? Oh, Winter Moon, I suppose," he answered. "Abnaki band camping around the point. The girl does some washing for us now and then. I suppose she's after Sam for some cloth or something."

Caitlin stared out of the window. At the office door stood a short, plump-bodied girl, dark-skinned and black-haired, dressed in a brightly flowered chintz gown. Her pointed breasts rose and fell against the fabric with her breathing. It was obvious she wore no corset, for the glow of her firm, dusky flesh warmed the color in spots.

Why Caitlin was surprised, she did not know. If she had been pinned down, she would have admitted that she had probably expected the girl to be garbed in beaded buckskin. And that was because her preconceived notions of Indians were vague, and colored by the stories of brutal savagery and fierce customs she'd heard in Cornwall.

"Why, she speaks English," Caitlin exclaimed, as fragments of the girl's speech floated over to her.

"As good as anybody, 'n' probably better than most. Why not?"

"Well, I guess my knowledge of Indians is rather limited," Caitlin admitted. "Can they all talk English?"

"Most of 'em," Mulligan replied. "The younger generation, anyhow. Say, Mrs. Jardine, can you cook apple pie?"

Winter Moon's teeth shone white between her parted lips at some sally from Samuel. She stood by the door, holding a small child on one hip. Her hair had a bluish luster when the sun caught it.

"I think so," Caitlin rejoined guardedly, wrapping a clean bandage over the burn. She took a deep breath. "That Winter Moon's real pretty, isn't she?"

"Yeah. Not as pretty as her sister, though. Summer Dawn was a real dazzler."

The child giggled, squirming until Winter Moon set her down. She went across to Samuel, put her hands on his knees, said something in Abnaki. He grinned, hoisted her over his shoulder so that she squealed in delight. They went inside.

"Was?" Why was her heart hammering so? Her fingers scooped into the bag, came out, set to work again.

"Yeah. She's dead now."

Samuel came outside again, put the child down and handed Winter Moon a parcel done up in newspaper. As the pair walked away, Winter Moon gave a nod to some of the loggers sitting with their backs against the bunkhouse wall.

"Why were you asking if I could cook?" Caitlin inquired, when the woman and child had vanished into the brush.

"Every third Sunday the Jesuit priest comes from Caribou, 'n' after mass we have a bit of music, 'n' the men enjoy a bit of a spree. I wondered if you'd like to make some proper home-baked apple pie—or some of those nice Cornish pasties that Sam's been tellin' us about."

Since the pasties had been as tough and dry as an old piece of boot leather, Caitlin wondered at the veracity of

Samuel's tales. "I daresay I could manage," she returned dubiously. "How's that feel?"

"Better," he said. "Thanks."

Voices, quickening. Caitlin glanced into the messroom, saw that the tables were filling up with the first wave of diners.

"Just be careful of that arm, Mulligan. Keep it clean, especially, and lay off the liquor for the next few days."

She hurried across to the depot office. The sun was coming down, sending deep gold shafts slanting into the room. It was a magpie's nest of old newspapers and record books—a regular clutter.

Samuel was poring over some figures, but he pushed aside his pencil and paper when she entered. "Cat, what are you doing here?"

"Waiting for you."

Some hard edge in her voice made him wary. What has happened? he asked himself. Immediately he was struck by a lance of panic. Had Winter Moon—? No, no, that was impossible. Caitlin did not even know about his relationship with Summer Dawn.

"Hardly necessary, but I'm glad you're here," he said at last, conscious of the light-headed sensation of hovering on the edge of a fateful decision.

"Perhaps you won't be when you hear what I have to say."

His brow lifted ever so slightly. "I don't understand."

"I had a visitor today. Henry Sagamore."

"What the hell did he want?"

Caitlin loved to see that perplexed look on his face, as if his heart had skipped a dozen beats. It was partly because it happened so infrequently, partly because there was a thrill in knowing that she caused it. "He didn't say."

Instinctively his eyes slid over her head, over the block-house roof, in the direction of the Abnaki camp, a little way around the point. It could not be seen from here, even in good weather.

"Whatever it is," he said, "doesn't concern you."

"Whatever concerns you concerns me, Samuel. But on this occasion, his visit seemed to concern me. Henry Saga-more's convinced that no man in his sound mind would go calling on a female doctor. Seems to think that women are good for only one thing."

In a flat, low voice, he said, "That sounds like him, all right."

"Sounds like who?" Caitlin's eyes burned up at him from under the dark, winged brows. There was always something to learn in what he said, as well as in how he said it.

"You said Henry Sagamore, didn't you? He always uses people."

Caitlin's jaw set. "Well, I'm not afraid of him, and I'll show him that he can't control the blood and bones of ordinary people." Her voice roughened, her lips went tight with scorn. "He's nothing but a robber, anyway, stealing your lumber." She dumped her bag on the desk.

"Oh, for God's sake, Cat, you sound like my father! Next you'll start ranting about the land sharks and crimps—"

"Have you got a better word for him? Do you? He's the enemy." She ground out the words. "The *enemy*..."

"In that case," he returned hotly, "then so am I!"

Caitlin looked at him as if he'd struck her. "Samuel, what are you saying?" She thrust the bunch of rudbeckia through the bag's handle and crossed to his side.

"It's true, Cat." Samuel couldn't have stopped himself now if he'd wanted to. He was thinking of his father. What would he say to him? Of course, his father would under-stand. "Who do you think you married? A bloody angel? I'm as bad as the next man. I'm intolerant of restraint and I break regulations that prove inconvenient."

Something subtle shifted in Caitlin's already severe expression, a narrowing of the eyes, a tenseness in her lips. He grinned at her consternation. "Even formulate new ones to apply, and I hunt out of season. It's a rich, rough, tough country, where it doesn't do to be finicky about anything."

Caitlin digested this in silence, but it occurred to her that this mild sample of lawlessness was quite in keeping with the men and the environment. There was no mechanism of law and order visible anywhere. This had colored the frontiersmen's point of view.

"You don't like Henry Sagamore, do you, Samuel?"

"*Like* him?" His eyes stared unseeing, up at the underside of the roof. "Hmm, I never considered *that* alternative. Let's just say I don't approve of his methods, period."

"Didn't you just say that your methods were a trifle unorthodox? Same thing when you come down to it."

Samuel sat on one corner of the desk, one booted leg dangling down, one braced on the floor, as he studied Caitlin. She wore a celadon-green gown with just a thin line of deep hunter-green piping.

"It's not as though we commit murder or mayhem, Cat. No—" He put a finger across her mouth. "Don't say anything. Right now, I need you to listen to me. Whatever is happening here is all connected, in some way I haven't as yet begun to understand. But the important thing is that it's no longer business. It's personal."

"Just don't sell your soul for thirty pieces of silver."

Was that what had happened, or was this delicate strand of circumstance and coincidence a figment of his imagination? Caitlin's eyes, so close to his, were large and luminous, and she was still watching him strangely, as if she sensed something as yet unsaid.

He lifted a hand to brush back the hair from her forehead. His fingertips lingered on her skin. "You have not always been so self-righteous. I remember when we stole apples from the orchard."

Caitlin's lips twitched. "That was not all. Think of the time we changed the labels on every bottle, jar and box of medicine in the pharmacy. We almost killed old Lady Ransome when her husband took one of your father's herbal aphrodisiacs instead of the medicine he needed for his gout."

Samuel laughed. "I remember that very well. After several strokes of my father's razor strop, I couldn't sit for a week. And we had to change the labels back again. In the end, we knew what was on those shelves better than my father did."

"I can still remember. First shelf—betony, periwinkle, goldenrod, tansy, rue…"

Samuel's arms slid around her. Her face was but a breath away from his. She was so close to him that he could inhale her scent, a bit like honeysuckle, a bit musky. He felt her warmth and more, the pulse of her. He felt as if he had downed a bottle of whiskey in one thirsty gulp.

Light-headed, unable to catch his breath fully, he drew her closer. He buried his face in the hollow of her neck. She smelled of summer and sunlight. Or perhaps those were the triggers she set off in his mind? His head came up.

"Second shelf—meadowsweet, dittany, foxglove, mignonette, heartsease…" Her lips were only a handbreadth away from his. She tried to break away.

"No, no, Samuel. Mignonette came before foxglove."

It was as if a shotgun had gone off inside Samuel's head. To stop her saying another word, his mouth closed over hers. Her lips opened beneath his. Her tongue twined with his. He felt her moan into his mouth.

"Samuel." Her body clung to his, as if they were fastened from shoulder to foot. He felt her heart beating. It reached out and encompassed him. It was as if her pulse were his pulse, as if a spiritual force were linking them.

The echoes, spreading now, like ripples in a pond. The years seemed to melt away. It was as if he was back in

Cornwall, the error in mistaking the dangerous digitalis—also known as foxglove—for the innocuous mignonette existing only in some ephemeral future that might or might not yet occur.

Samuel felt his heart open, felt the shell of bitterness that had surrounded him slough away like a reptile's dead skin. The physical and the emotional were both supplanted at this moment. But by what, he could not have said. Only that he seemed whole and alive again.

He dropped his arms, took a moment to clear his throat of all his roiling emotion. "This will have to keep until later. At the moment, I believe we need something to drink," he said with soft decision. "Something restorative."

Caitlin bowed her head in concession. Samuel was right. This was neither the time nor the place. Glass in hand, she let her eyes wander over Samuel's domain, the sparse and simple furnishings. Against one wall, at eye level for a man of average height, was a bookshelf, on which stood a row of books.

Curiosity led her to see what they were. There were several heavy-looking volumes on geological subjects, and a stack of Maine Acts and Resolves, as well as a number of Annual Reports of the Land Agents. There was also a newspaper that looked relatively new. She screwed her head round to see it better: the *Bangor Daily Whig & Courier* for September 25, 1842. Little over a fortnight old, then, suggesting that a delivery of mail had arrived.

Caitlin touched it with the bottom of her glass. "Any news?"

"Sagamore's having trouble with his boom again. He's got some of the best lumber territory in New England, and he's barely pulling his weight. His outfit's way under quota."

"Does it matter? I mean, whether you cut more this month than he does?"

Samuel glanced at her in frank surprise. "Why, of course it does, Cat. It's a matter of economics, plain and simple. That's why the quota's set by contract."

"But *why* does the quota always have to be increased? Can't the timber just—well, be cut when and how it's needed?" What a cumbersome implement the law had become! It was worse than useless.

"Because that's the way it has to be, Cat. That's progress. That's what this country's all about. You can't sit still, marking time—you either grow or you shrink. That's business...."

"I see."

But she didn't, really. It seemed to her part of some diabolical conspiracy devised by madmen. She wanted to say, "But isn't there a breaking point somewhere? Surely everything isn't meant to expand *infinitely?*" She could also have added that, if the quota kept being raised, in a few years the trees would all be gone, and there'd be nothing left.

Frightening thought. Appalling thought. But she said nothing. She knew better than to continue this line with Samuel. Doubtless he'd have an answer for that one, too— he genuinely believed the sky was the limit, and no horizon lay beyond landfall....

Caitlin made her way down the track from the depot, coming to where the sheltering belt of trees marked the eastern border of Fairbanks Logging Company land. Here, where the fringe of pine met Presque Isle Stream, it was already deeply shadowed, with a cold wind setting the leaves rattling overhead. From her vantage point, she could see the dam site.

Out in the sunlight, two canoes were drawn up on the shingle above the water's edge. Several small figures played on the gravel, and sundry dogs prowled along the bank. Her wandering gaze came to rest on a wigwam top showing in the brush. Smoke went eddying away in the wind. The Abnaki camp where Winter Moon lived, Caitlin supposed.

She had an impulse to view the Indian camp at closer range, a notion born of curiosity. She was just about to do so when her movement was arrested by a faint crackle in the woods behind her. It was the sound of boots crunching through the understory.

Someone was coming. A man emerged from the forest shadows, headed almost straight toward her. Across his shoulders he bore a reddish gray burden, and in his right hand was a gun.

She began to move, then froze. It was Ned Flaherty. Bowed slightly under the weight of the deer, he passed within twenty feet of her, so close that she could see tiny droplets of sweat glistening like cut diamonds on the side of his face. Close enough to see that the load he carried was the carcass of a deer.

He did not see her, and in a minute or so, he had thrown the deer into one of the canoes and pulled away north along the shore. She watched him until he rounded the point, paddling with strong, even strokes.

Oh, dear God. Where was Samuel? How she wanted him here, just to hold his hand, to know that he was with her. The fact was, Samuel was out with his loggers. But knowing that did not stop her wishing for it with all her might.

A barge, invisible around the bend of the river, hooted, and Caitlin shivered. What was Ned Flaherty doing visiting the Abnaki camp? Did it have anything to do with the strange things that had been happening in the Aroostook Valley lately?

There had been a considerable increase in violence, not out in the open, like the usual drunken brawls between the men, but in the woods, on the tote roads, behind the almost completed dam. At several of the logging sites, the men had arrived to start a new day's work to find vital equipment or wagonways smashed beyond use.

More seriously, several of the loggers had received menacing threats from other lumberjacks in rival camps. One of the crew had been battered unconscious by several men. He could not remember the incident when Samuel plied him for details while Caitlin tended to his hurts.

"Mistaken identity," he said in a reedy whisper. "Thought it was you. Must have been the galluses. Very distinctive."

Caitlin wondered briefly if the blows had addled the lumberjack's brain, since what he said seemed to make little sense.

"Ned Flaherty would recognize them suspenders."

Caitlin saw Samuel's face sharpen, and LeFeuvre's.

"That's ridiculous," Samuel said, but even Caitlin recognized the lack of conviction in his voice.

In the eerie silence that followed, thunder rumbled, at some distance from them. Caitlin rewound a bandage.

LeFeuvre smoothed his beard with his fingertips. "There's a lot of bad blood between you and Henry. That is difficult to forget—or to face. The accounts are not yet balanced."

A second man gave Caitlin a quick sidelong glance. "That Murphy thinks he's a regular gilded rooster, shackin' up with Kate Flaherty, but truth is, it's a bit like invitin' the fox into the henhouse having Ned Flaherty around."

"I'm not so sure," LeFeuvre answered. "Murphy's a fancy talker, but he's a top-notch cruiser, and Ned's young enough to put the past behind him."

"I don't care about the past. Only the future." Samuel shot Caitlin a peculiar look. "The other matter is over and done with," he said. "As for Ned Flaherty, your suspicions of him are quite ill founded, I'm afraid. Don't you agree?" There was a note of warning in his voice.

The man swallowed, nodded.

Caitlin closed her bag and stood up. "I'm an outsider, a newcomer to your valley, but I have a real interest in this community. You know what it says in Ecclesiastes—how agree the kettle and the earthen pot together? For if the one be smitten against the other, it shall be broken."

There was a brief, horrified hush. Then they all spoke at once.

"I gave up religion years ago. Bad for the chest, religion."

"Yeah. All that singing by gravesides."

"Well, then, gentlemen, let this be your personal penance. Invite Sagamore, Morgan, deCarteret and their crews to the service on Sunday, and suggest they stay for the festivities after mass. Perhaps the problem could be sorted out if people mixed on a social basis."

Caitlin was aware that she was talking too much, that her husband was staring at her, but she could not seem to stop herself. She felt the anxiety like a knot inside her; it was as if she had become infected by the loggers' cold rage.

"Cat!" Samuel roared, in a voice that his crew would have recognized as one to which they should come running on the double. Not being one of his loggers, Caitlin crossed the floor at her usual seductive pace.

Samuel could not help admiring Caitlin's composure under pressure. She would have made an excellent foreman. He smiled, and his eyes began to glitter. He took her wrist firmly in his and tugged her out of the bunkhouse.

"One of these days, Cat, your penchant for interference is going to get you into trouble."

Caitlin took an undignified little skip with each step, almost running, and he smiled at her again—but he didn't slow his stride. She felt, rather than saw, that many in the group watched her go, though whether with sympathy or malice, she could not be sure.

Once inside their own sitting room, he released her. "Now what was that all about?"

It came out angry, and he hadn't meant that. Caitlin instantly took two steps backward and began to rub her wrist.

"Haven't you always said when in a difficult situation, you must use your initiative?"

Samuel heaved a sigh and thrust his hands in his pockets. He was tense; he had had the self-restraint scared out of him with this morning's brutal attack. He was ready to lose all patience.

Instead he said mildly, "I know you've done your best, but when it comes to Sagamore, I'll make the decision and you'll abide by it."

Caitlin's brow furrowed. "I hope I haven't given the impression that I don't support your authority, Samuel."

God help him, he thought. "No, of course not. Let's skip the postmortem and have some breakfast."

"How can you think of food, when that man has been beaten?"

Caitlin had a habit of doing that to conversations, he decided, once you tried to change the subject, defuse an argument. He stuck to his guns. "It's simple. I'm hungry."

"Your logic is unassailable, but don't you understand that—" She gasped, a short, small intake of breath, and Samuel's heart froze. "Oh, Mother Mary, Kate! What did she say on the riverboat? *Succeed too well and fail completely.*"

Samuel gave a shiver. The whole damn situation was already too dangerous. He stood there with his skin gone to gooseflesh. He couldn't read what was in her face.

Another shiver shook him. A warning bell went off in his head, but he could not think why. The only thing that was clear to him was that Caitlin had some maggot in her head. Caitlin, with her poised and elegant body, her strange, erotic allure.

His frustration hit new levels at the thought. Impulsively he reached out, put his hand over hers. Her marriage band disappeared beneath his palm. "Kate also says the little people talk to her. That's the luck of the Irish."

Caitlin stood where she was, her hand in his. She lifted her face to his, and the early-morning sun streaming in the window bathed her features in light. Her green eyes glittered like gems. They made the recipient of that scrutiny think of everything he'd done in the past thirty hours.

"Liam claimed the gun was his, when Ned shot him. Where was the sense in that?" Her cheeks were pink. All this, and brains too! She was one of the most complicated and interesting women he had ever met.

Samuel gave a rueful smile. "Liam's got four left feet, and he keeps them in his mouth most of the time, but he's a fine man and a good friend. It's the curse of the Irish."

Caitlin could hear the truth of those soft words in his voice. "And of the Cornish. How often have you told me that I suffer from foot-and-mouth disease?" It was a weak attempt at teasing, but she was pleased to see it pull a faint smile from him.

"Cheap philosophy."

She regarded him with a troubled frown. "So what is the answer, Samuel? Is Ned to be trusted?"

A more difficult question. "If your sister had a gun, and your father threatened me—whose side would you take?" He hadn't phrased it quite right, of course, but Caitlin seemed to understand.

"Is that what Liam and Kate were talking about—on the riverboat?" Her implacable stare was on him.

He looked for an escape. A dozen explanations logjammed in his throat. "I don't know," he said, not altogether truthfully.

Another of Caitlin's long, sober stares. Her eyes were the clearest, most incredible green. Like glass. Just as expressive. "Don't concern yourself, Samuel. I have confidence in your instincts. The secrets you and Liam keep are in no danger from me."

He couldn't fault that answer. It was entirely reasonable. Everything was.

Which was a worry.

Chapter Eleven

The mists of morning had dissipated, leaving the skies clear and bright. A light wind was gusting across an oyster-colored sky as Caitlin took a shortcut through the woods. Ahead, the trail wound higher up into the pine forests, where the felling gangs were hard at work.

All around her, it seemed, birds twittered and sprang from twig to branch. Every so often, she spotted a squirrel or other small animal scurrying through the brush. Once she was certain she caught a quick glimpse of the rear end of a deer, bolting from her line of sight.

Now, oddly, in this isolated spot, her head was filled with a thousand unanswered questions. Such as Liam's message: *Sam is a good fellow—a great man—one in a million. Promise you'll remember that when he's balancing his accounts?* What had Liam meant? And where had she heard that there were outstanding accounts between Samuel and Sagamore? What was their nature?

When she got to the crossroads, she saw a drag to which were attached the big red roans from Presque Isle Stream depot. Knowing the driver, who had been a long time in Samuel's service, she stopped to inquire whether he was going back to the depot.

The man touched his woolen cap. "Yes, ma'am. Just got

to call in at the Abnaki camp 'n' drop off some candy cane
for little Zoe.''

Zoe! That name again.

"Fine. Then you can take me," she said, and the next
moment she swung herself, with her usual agility, to the
high seat.

Rattling along, the driver did most of the talking, Caitlin
nodding and occasionally asking a question. Her mind was
busy elsewhere.

The thought crossed her mind that Samuel would not be
pleased. She could almost hear him saying, "Cat, I wish
you'd consult before making impulsive decisions.''

She knew *that* response. *Keep out of other people's business.* And maybe it was excused that he be angry, and that
this Zoe person was none of her business, that Samuel was
entirely justified in not revealing any secrets, but she was
too curious, and the answers to the riddle were tantalizingly
close.

Disquieting question. If the answer to the puzzle was not
at the Abnaki camp, where would she find it?

On one side was the point, on the other the dam. These
two were stretched out like arms, and within their shelter
nestled the Abnaki camp. Securing the reins, the driver alit,
scooped up a packet and quickly threaded his way through
the network of lodges to an open area in the center of the
compound.

Caitlin followed at his heels like a shadow.

A group of women were seated in a circle, fingers flying
as they deftly threaded twists of horsehair and colored
beads into an intricate design. They paused to smile at him,
white teeth flashing in their dark faces. Winter Moon rose
to her feet in a single lithe movement.

The driver held out the bulky, beribboned packet. When
the small child who'd accompanied her to the depot pulled
at her sleeve, Winter Moon took it, squatted, and invited
the child to open the present.

Caitlin watched her for a time. The child had skin like gold leaf, much lighter than that of the other children, who clustered around for a piece of the sticky sweet. This close, it was obvious that she was of mixed blood.

The sound of children's laughter was strong in the air and, unconsciously, Caitlin touched the firm flatness of her lower belly, imagining a little life growing there. She felt a longing deep inside her.

"Zoe. Only one piece," Winter Moon said, taking possession of the packet.

"Zoe?" Caitlin stared, astonished, and the youngster looked up at the sound of her name. She stood unmoving, her big round eyes wary and curious. From the corner of her eye, Caitlin saw the teamster shrug. He didn't answer.

"Summer Dawn's child. My niece belongs here." Winter Moon offered no explanation of her remark. Perhaps she was supposed to have asked something, Caitlin thought, but imagination failed her. She was too scared of the answers—scared of her own ignorance and her own failure to figure out what the silence around her was saying.

Her mind snapped back into focus, and Caitlin examined the patterned braid the women were weaving. "That is an unusual design." A far more innocuous topic.

"It's an ancient Abnaki pattern."

Caitlin stared down at the weaving as if it were a poisonous thing. She could feel herself shaking. Her pulse rate rose, and she felt a tremor in the side of her face.

"It's identical to the design on Samuel's suspenders."

Winter Moon nodded, and gave her an expressionless stare. The short hairs at the nape of Caitlin's neck began to stir.

"The women here make such things. This particular braiding is their design—it symbolizes the bond between a woman and her husband."

Coincidence?

Liam's voice came back then, a low, quiet burr. *A des-*

perate man's an irrational man... No more visits to the Indian camp... It's going to be a little difficult for Sam to explain away little Zoe.

Then the battered logger saying, out of breath, *Ned Flaherty would recognize them suspenders.*

Suddenly Caitlin felt her stomach turn over. Something, lodged in her memory like a pebble, broke loose, rising to the surface. She remembered Samuel's odd intimacy with the child that day at the depot, and all her suspicions burst open like a wound. She looked up, a sudden intuition flooding her.

Zoe... Mother of God! The answer had found her. Irrevocable, from this point. But Samuel...

"This can't be happening," she whispered. A wash of anguish swept her, so profound that it threatened to collapse her knees.

How can I bear it? was the thought chasing through her mind, scattering saner notions. She looked from one brown face to another, careful to keep her emotions under control, but, *damn,* she was angry, with a peculiar, stinging kind of anger that added up to a hurt so painful it took her breath away.

"Is something wrong?" Winter Moon asked her.

A difficult question. Caitlin bit her lip. There was a painful lump in her throat, interfering with her rational assessment of the situation. "I think you already know," she said simply.

The silence hung there. Winter Moon looked at Caitlin without speaking, without an expression on her face. Then she turned courteously to thank the driver for his gift.

Caitlin heard herself say, "There is to be a feast on Sunday, with food and music. You are all invited." Should I say something more? Caitlin pondered, growing anxious, self-conscious in the combined gaze of the Abnaki women.

Winter Moon's eyes were as round as Zoe's. "Have you spoken with Samuel about this?"

Caitlin made a short, thick sound that was too harsh to be a laugh. "It will be all right. Everything will work out fine."

The women bid her farewell, their gesticulating hands expressing the amiability of their feelings. Then, with a final grin and flicker of the fingers, they again became garrulously absorbed in their weaving. Their talk, rapid, dramatic, rising and falling with a soft musical inflection, drifted after Caitlin as she took her place on the drag.

The short trip to the depot settled the nausea churning in her stomach. When the teamster stopped at the storehouse, she clambered to the ground. Walking swiftly, shivering, she headed for the house. The pines surrounding the depot were shivering, too, caressed by a fitful wind, and the dwindling day had a lucent gray sameness.

Once in the house, she stirred the embers in the fireplace, added another log and set about preparing a meal. But her mind would not let her be.

Zoe is not my mistress. No, but she is your daughter! Zoe. Summer Dawn. Samuel.

The logs burned down and fell, showering sparks up the flue. Temper flared up. Or a sense of muddled desperation. She could feel the anger; it moved like a living thing inside her. Her chest seemed full. She fought it, but it was there.

Damn Samuel's wicked, deceitful soul! Play her for a fool, would he? Well, that great hulking creature would discover it wasn't such a wise thing to do! Before this day was over, he'd be sorry he'd ever thought of marriage, and he'd be lucky if she didn't hit him on the head with the frying pan!

Half in apprehension, half in defiance, wholly in anger, she set out to find her husband. And all the while, she heard her sister Caitryn's voice echoing in her head: *Curiosity killed the cat.*

"I have found her!" Caitlin announced, as if she knew

she must spill out her news before she had a chance to bite it back.

"Who?"

Samuel looked up from the paperwork he had been poring through. His head turned, just enough so that Caitlin could see that he was smiling. Her insides turned to water. He had the most endearing habit of canting his head to one side.

In the pool of soft light, his thick auburn hair, gleaming richly, fell in a coil over his forehead. Her fingers itched to thread themselves through the unruly curls. Caitlin's tongue clicked against the roof of her mouth. She mustn't think of such things now.

"Zoe!" She spat it out as if it burned her tongue. Their eyes locked for a moment, her eyes fixed, impaling him on their unwavering gaze. "You have a child!"

Samuel looked away, fast, like a wild creature bolting. Then, deliberately, he returned her gaze. "I know it must be a terrible shock, but—"

A small silence built itself in the room, and the air seemed to get thick and difficult to breathe. He moved papers off to the side, seemed to be studying something.

His hesitancy eased Caitlin's anger, and she found that her heart was no longer beating so erratically. "Is there a reason why you withheld this information from me?"

The implication of this question took a moment to sink in. He pressed his fingers against his eyes. "I don't know," he said. "But I have an idea that the reason is straight out of a nightmare." He looked at Caitlin. "Why do you ask?"

"Haven't I always been honest with you?" She ignored the little voice in her head that reminded her that she still held a secret, still kept one truth from him.

Caitlin's question startled him with a vengeance, and he stared at her for a full minute in silence. He sensed the core of her resentment, and understood, but how to deal with it?

Samuel wasn't a man who floundered for words, but he hadn't a clue how to answer.

"I suppose that this was inevitable." He rubbed his hand down his face. "The time has come for me to tell you the truth."

She took a deep breath. "Tell me the truth, not what I want to hear." Her voice was so clotted with suppressed anger that she abruptly broke off, began again. "You've been so good at that."

"The truth." He said it as if it were a foreign word that he could not quite fathom. Shadows fell across his cheek, spilling downward, like a river at night.

"Yes." Caitlin gestured impatiently. "The truth."

This was surely the crucial moment. His only chance was to avoid the conflict. To convince her...

The silence hung there. Samuel steeled himself for what was to come.

Truth had its own rewards, but in this case, he dreaded what he had to tell her. She might hate him for it, or she might disbelieve him. Either response, he knew, would have devastating results, not only for him, but for her, as well.

He was struggling with a truth of his own. He definitely hadn't expected to be attracted to her. But he was. He didn't want to lose her. He rose and went to the window.

Outside, he could hear a loon's iterative call. He inhaled deeply, scenting rain. It was still some distance away, but it was coming. As he watched, the darkness came alive with the forked flicker of lightning. When the second outburst licked downward, he judged the distance.

"The rain will not last long," he said, even as the first rumble of thunder echoed in the hills. When she made no reply, he turned from the window to contemplate her. She stared at him wordlessly.

"The fact is that Zoe is the child of Summer Dawn. Three years ago, when Summer Dawn came to me, she was with child by another man." How the admission seemed to stick on his tongue.

Caitlin did not move. Emotion, stirring and fleeting, transformed her face. Her green eyes glistened.

"The truth is, I did the only thing I could." He found, after all, that it was not difficult to talk, at least not while it was simply a matter of recounting facts, bare and mundane. "I said the baby was mine, and hoped it was not too much a chip off the old block. That way, no one would figure it was one of Sagamore's..."

He paused, as though Caitlin were supposed to divine more of the story on her own. It was then that she remembered Liam Murphy's cryptic reference.

"Off-cuts," she said. Caitlin gave a sound very much like a whimper. There were tears trembling at the corners of her eyes. "Tell me about Summer Dawn."

"She was little more than a child herself, the youngest daughter of White Cloud and Morning Star. Summer Dawn reminded me of Caitryn. They shared the same spirit-self, the same calm, unruffled way of viewing life's little irritations. She died giving birth to Zoe."

The implications of this reply took a moment to sink in. They were both quiet for a time. It was as if invoking Summer Dawn's name had made the past return, and undermined their certainty about what the future would bring.

"Did you love her?"

"It would have been hard not to have loved Summer Dawn. She was a fine woman."

How could so much pain be wrapped up in loving someone? Caitlin wondered. She watched Samuel's face carefully. On his face was guilt. A hint of his thoughts and his motives? She wasn't sure. The corners of her mouth tightened. It hurt her to press the issue, but she did.

"Your love for her will never die." It was a statement, not a question.

Caitryn and Summer Dawn. Much to his dismay, Samuel

discovered that he could not think about the one without thinking of the other. He wanted to lie, but could not. He had done nothing but deceive her. He gave a grim smile, and passed a hand over his face, as if he could scrub away the remembrance.

"One comes to a kind of inner peace. An ending to the hurt. Memories possess a power all of their own, Cat. Sometimes it's easy to want someone, so hard to love them."

In that moment, the rain began to lash itself against the windowpane like a swarm of angry bees. At the sound, the serpent of suspicion left Caitlin. She emitted a deep sigh, and when she spoke next, it was in a tiny whisper.

"You're wrong, Samuel. Love is the easiest emotion, because it takes no learning. You have to be taught how to hate."

Caitlin stood staring at him, giving him the feeling—he didn't know why—that she had just raised the subject of their marriage. Samuel realized he had entered very shaky ground. But he hadn't lost yet. He hadn't made a fatal mistake. There was still a slim hope that he could retrieve the situation.

"Are the two emotions necessarily contradictory? They have more in common than you know."

When she spoke, her voice was soft and low. "You have answered your own question."

"I speak only the truth."

"You have changed, Samuel. You are less...open."

"Yes. And do you have any idea why?"

What could she say? She had to think about it, and she didn't find the answer she'd wanted—couldn't even locate the young man who'd set off for America, couldn't believe this man and that were one and the same.

Caitlin stood facing Samuel across the width of the room. He stood stock-still. It was impossible to tell if he was even breathing. Outside, a crack of thunder reverberated nearby. Caitlin started, her head jerking around.

"No. I just know everything has changed. Now we must begin all over again to forge a trusting relationship."

Fine, Samuel thought. So she's making an extraordinary gesture. The stakes go up. He thought about that for a moment.

"Won't you give me a chance to explain? Or have you tried and convicted me already?"

Caitlin's first thought had been that she never wanted to see him again, that she was going to leave him. Now she saw that he was as disturbed as she was.

And yet...she suspected that she had made a mistake, not in falling in love with Samuel, but in persisting in loving him. That he was attracted to her, she was certain, but she did not think that would be enough. She came slowly toward him, her heart hammering because she still did not know what he would say.

"Do you want me?" She said it so softly that she could almost believe that it had been a whisper in her mind. There was humiliation in giving of yourself so unselfishly, and getting so little in return.

Samuel took a quick step toward her, not knowing what she would do, or even what she meant by that short, strangled sentence. Was there some deeper, more sinister desire lurking at the back of her mind?

Was a man ever so beset? Hell, if this woman were only as fragile as she looked! He was on dangerous ground. Very dangerous ground. He sensed, perhaps, the core of her resentment. He wasn't sure. But he had come up against Caitlin's convoluted female logic before—it was known territory. He looked her straight in the face.

"I would not be a man if I did not."

A little smile at that. And a sober next question. "Or did you want me for the child?"

She pressed herself against him, so that he could feel the

trip-hammer beating of her heart. Instinctively he put his arms around her. It would be better—far, far better—if he left the truth unearthed this time.

He made a soft, derisive sound. "Oh, yes, of course. And, of course, that is the only reason. And, of course, there is more than one child. Didn't you realize that I collect other people's offspring the way gardeners collect those hideous little stone gnomes?" he asked, trying to make her smile, or make her angry—anything but to have her eyes blank and her voice flat and expressionless.

Caitlin put up a hand. "I've argued with myself, listing all the reasons why I should be angry. Now you're here, silencing my questions with nothing but your presence— and your poor Cornish jokes."

Samuel let out a long breath. He found it difficult to speak. "Is that a yes or a no?"

She lifted her face to his and moved closer. Her lips were half-open, and her sweet breath fell upon his cheek like spring rain. His hand caught itself, straying, on her thigh.

"When I was a girl, there was a prayer I said before I went to sleep each night. You taught it to me, Samuel. It went, 'Yes is a wish. No is a dream.'" She smiled as she reached up to touch his cheek. "So now I must use yes and no. Allow me to keep hidden the wish and the dream, so that someday I may be strong enough to do without them both."

He stared into her green cat's eyes. She looked steadily back at him, silent, while her eyes told him her true feelings. She gave a great shudder, and her eyes fluttered closed.

"Cat—"

Thunder boomed, rain beat its rapid tattoo. He held her face between his hands and kissed her softly. When he drew away to look down at her again, her eyes were a blaze of green.

"Do you see now why I couldn't tell you everything

when I met you, why you had to understand it a little at a time?''

She looked at him—gave a small, strange laugh. A second later, he had her locked in his hungry embrace. Her mouth parted easily beneath his as she pressed against his muscled body, and urgently his hands roamed over her slim form.

Caitlin had an entirely unwelcome thought. Why couldn't the infant have died with the mother? She chastised herself for even thinking such a terrible thought.

Her nerves twitched to distant thunder, sending her thoughts darting this way and that way. Why had Samuel felt compelled to take someone else's off-cut and claim it as his own? The thoughts kept running, proliferating, tangling. Not unless he loved the mother above all reason, beyond life itself.

Putting Samuel's intentions in question...

Caitlin panicked. Mother Mary, her mind was going. She was raving, irrational, not making sense, and not making sense was pathetic and stupid. She caught a quick breath—caught up the pieces of her sensibility—and acted.

''No!'' With an inarticulate cry, she broke away from him and ran across the length of the room. ''I need to be alone.''

Samuel caught up with her just as a violent streak of lightning forked downward overhead. ''Cat, I—''

Caitlin raised her head, looked at him through tear-streaked eyes. Then he realized that she was swaying, her pent-up emotions breaking through the barriers of icy iron she had erected. He could only imagine what was going through her mind.

She waved him away before he could say anything. ''Don't say a word, and don't make me say things I'll regret later. Leave me be. I want to be alone tonight.''

''You'll regret what you're doing now.'' He ground out the words. ''You always regret your actions, later.''

"Not this time." Caitlin stood, looking off to the window. Into rain spatter and nothing. Her eyes were very wide and very bright. "Time." She hugged herself tightly, began to shiver. "Just give me some time. Right now, I don't know how I feel."

Lightning flashed, burnishing the walls with orange. The window rattled, an eerie, unsettling sound.

Samuel's stomach contracted, turned over. Time. Perhaps that was what they both needed now. Life was not neat and predictable. It preferred to come up and kick you in the stomach while your attention was elsewhere. It was regrettable, but unavoidable.

Slowly, he thought, gagging on the rush of words he longed to speak. He wanted to tell her again how sorry he was. But he sensed that words would be ineffective. Too much had happened all at once.

Samuel felt as if he had lost all sense of himself, as if his heart had stopped beating without his knowledge and now he stood, breathless, staring at the wreckage life had brought. *Go slowly or you'll lose it all now.*

He put his head closer to hers. Her face was but a breath from his. He felt the air between them, tasted it, heard it, saw through it, and took a deep breath, collecting himself.

Light-headed, unable to catch his breath fully, he reached out, and his fingers stole along the inside of her wrist until they wrapped themselves around her forearm.

"Don't you touch me!" she said in a quavery voice, then jerked herself free and rushed out into the rain.

"Cat!" Samuel ran after her. The heavy cascade of her hair fanned out. Rain danced off her face, flew through her hair, as if both were part of the wind.

"You used me." Caitlin's tone was accusatory. The dark was all around her for a moment, and she lost her balance—caught herself, heart thumping, with a hand on Samuel's rain-wet shoulder.

"What difference has that made to you?" It was a loaded question, and they both knew it.

"Something crosses my mind, but I don't think you'd like to hear it."

"I want to know."

"Why?" Abruptly she felt put-upon. "Why must you know everything? Do you tell *me* everything?"

"Yes. Of course. At least I would if you'd let me."

"You're a liar," she said hotly. "How do you expect me to put my trust in a liar? What kind of a partnership could that be?"

"Obviously, not one filled with trust."

"Where does all this lead us?" Her voice was skittish, swinging through the emotions.

Damn, *that* question again. He drew a breath to think about it. "Back to square one."

"Just like that?"

"Don't, take that righteous tone with me," Samuel said sharply. "It was my choice, my decision only, and I do not regret it." He looked away for a moment. Rain whipped into their faces, a mist thick enough to breathe. Rain spattered their hair and clothes. "Let's get out of here. In case you haven't noticed, it's raining."

Once they were inside, Samuel made a pot of tea while Caitlin changed into dry clothes. After he'd also changed, he sat down, closed his eyes, and let the sound of the rain surge around him. The draft from the fireplace did not work efficiently, so smoke parched the air. And at least it served to bring Caitlin back to her waspish self. And they needed to squabble right now, to let off steam.

Caitlin did not touch the cup of tea, which was dark and strong as liquid brass. Samuel always made tea so thick you could use it for lampblack, she thought idly. She kept her hands folded together, the fingers laced, in order to conceal their trembling. She did not know whether it was in rage, confusion, or frustration. She wasn't sure what it was, but it was getting the better of her.

Ever since they had come inside, she had gotten the impression that Samuel was spoiling for a fight. He also seemed somewhat nervous. "You've changed," she said.

Samuel stared down into the dregs of his tea. "As have you," he said at last. "I hope you still remember what it was like when we were together."

That pierced her like an arrow. It seemed that when the lots were cast, fortune and chance made their pick. She was beginning to see the pieces, then, in a crazed sort of way. It was difficult to be jealous of a dead woman, or to deny that Zoe had a right to know her heritage—both red and white.

"Is that what this is all about?"

He turned to her. In the corners of her eyes, liquid diamonds danced. "Is it so little?"

"Now you sound like a small boy who has lost his favorite toy."

Samuel shifted his position. He ran his hands through his thick hair. "I feel like a man suddenly losing a limb."

"I suppose you only have yourself to blame for that. I feel as if I have lost a part of myself, as well."

Samuel abandoned his seat and crossed the room to stand at Caitlin's side. He hunkered down on his booted heels.

"Cat." He said her name softly, then hesitated. "Caitlin," he said seriously, "I don't believe that I have sinned. It is important—essential, even—that you understand that."

She felt his presence as he knelt at her feet. Would the knot of pain ever go away? she wondered. She rejected the hand that tried to take hers.

"I will not—*will not*—debate the morality of this with you," she said sharply.

He received the barb without any sign of discomfiture. It was easy for him to show nothing on the surface. Memory—and emotion—tended to obscure the facts, as if they were the stuff of legends instead of, simply, his life. He hated himself for what he had done to her. What he still had to do.

It was at these times, when he felt most vulnerable, that he was afraid of her leaving him. He was standing on sand, as his father used to say. It was an irrational fear, to be sure. He had no doubts about Caitlin. She loved him fiercely and completely, even if it was with an independent will and spirit, and not with a slavish devotion. She loved him. Period.

Give me time, she had said. That was the least he could do. He turned away. "All right, if you like to put it that way."

Caitlin stood staring at him for a moment, and then on impulse reached out and caught his arm, not wanting them to part so painfully. "Samuel!"

He looked around, and halted.

"To answer your question, whatever you are has nothing to do with what I feel inside."

Then, without knowing who moved first, they came together, and he held her fiercely to him and kissed her, and she clung to him as if she could not bear ever again to let him go.

This morning, in Li Foo's garden, she had seen a black-and-yellow butterfly hover over some rudbeckia. It had touched here, there, never alighting for more than the space of a wingbeat. Below it, crawling over the green foliage, a caterpillar had made its slow, deliberate way.

Two such different creatures, Caitlin thought, winding her arms around Samuel. And yet, within the space of a week, there would be two black-and-yellow butterflies darting over Li Foo's plants.

Two such different creatures, she thought, and yet both are one. Like me. Today I am the caterpillar. Tomorrow I will be the butterfly. I will be transformed. I will be set free from this anger, this resentment, this jealousy.

And, knowing this, she could not hate him. She loved Samuel. And out of her own love for Samuel, she would be able to accept his affection for Summer Dawn and make Zoe part of her life.

She put her hand up. A fingertip traced its way down the line of his jaw. "This is the answer, Samuel. The only answer."

Chapter Twelve

Caitlin was restless and uncertain as she surveyed the kitchen the next morning. It seemed infinitely peaceful, an entire world unto itself, the homey clutter somehow comforting. A long thread of sunlight streamed across the floor. The wooden spoon was balanced on the blue-and-white bowl, waiting to be used. A row of apple pies, hot from the oven, sat cooling on the bench.

Across the room, the darkness of the bedroom filled the open doorway. That morning, Samuel had left without waking her, leaving only an indentation in the pillow and the scent of their loving. Even now, she saw his face, and remembered. He would normally have kissed her awake, ignoring her grumbled attempts to snatch a few more moments' sleep. Perhaps he had realized the extent of her exhaustion and been reluctant to disturb her?

How long ago it seemed that she had vowed that no one but herself should order her destiny. She would show herself stronger than fate. How arrogant! The new house of cards, frail shelter for her happiness and her heart, had toppled down, and she sat among the ruins.

Caitlin knew in her heart that she still loved Samuel and that the thing he had done on the rash and peculiar impulse of the moment was, in her eyes, of less account than dust.

It was already forgiven, and would be thrust forevermore into the limbo of forgotten things. But she needed time and space in which to recover.

That probably said something about her own flawed character, she decided gloomily. She did her best to think of other things—like the scent of a freshly baked apple-and-cinnamon tart that spiced the air. She shook an Indian reed basket, squinted critically at the inside. A faint sound, a movement glimpsed out of the corner of her eye...

Startled, she looked up. Samuel was standing in the open doorway, his eyes warm. Her body grew taut.

"Good morning, Caitlin Jardine."

Caitlin Jardine...the name had a sound, and it was a sound she loved. He moved, and she felt his lips, warm and soft at the nape of her neck, creating a melting deep within her.

"What's that marvelous smell?" The last word was muffled against her ear. Chills of pleasure shot through her. Her neck was warm where he had touched her, and she was very aware of her heartbeat. Desire had its own life and will.

"Pie." She peeped up at him. His smile was tiger-bright. She blushed like a guilty child, and pushed a deep breath out of her lungs to slow her hammering heart. "I'm so glad you got here in time to help me carry this."

"Changing the subject, Cat?"

Samuel made a little sound, a kind of rasping laugh. Caitlin shifted from one foot to the other, as if she had excess energy that she was unwilling to part with. She'd given him the brush-off. Pleasantly enough, but he still got the feeling that she was being evasive, that there was something she didn't want him to know.

Caitlin glanced up quickly. But his face showed no sign of displeasure. For some reason, she felt shaken and vulnerable as never before in her life, and she had to retreat, to put up defenses. She wiped her cheeks on the backs of her hands and forced her tone to tartness.

"Do you think the border troubles will get worse?"

"I don't think the local sheriff will let it go much farther," he said absently, putting out a hand to play with the tendrils of hair falling around her cheek. "He's turned a blind eye so far, because this is an election year and these people are his neighbors and friends."

"Can you honestly blame him?"

"For being afraid, no. Not even for his vacillation— that's part of the job. But soon he'll suddenly find he's got a conscience."

Caitlin could not help smiling. "Does that surprise you?"

"I don't surprise easy. You never know about people. Who knows? It may all be a storm in a teacup."

"Then you hope for some amicable settlement?" She wiped her hands and glanced around the kitchen. She picked up a clean dish towel, shook it hard and spread it as a lining inside the basket.

"The change in season will help. Passions run high, and tempers are fast to flare in the summer heat, especially when there's been a long spell with no relief. Are you expecting the entire valley for lunch?"

Caitlin packed the apple pies for the wedding feast with utmost care. The cloth lining the Indian reed basket felt as soft to her touch as did Samuel's hair. Unusual notion. But she had other things on her mind.

"While you're here, I'm going to tell you about a plan I have. One that will bring all the arguing parties together."

"Just like that, huh?" Samuel chuckled.

"A move well planned is a move half done."

Samuel gave a real laugh this time. "I know it's Halloween and you're running a trick or treat on me, Cat. Out with it."

Caitlin was caught off guard. She was quiet for a long

time. At last she said weakly, "You've always seemed such a law unto yourself, Samuel. I know you're wondering what Henry Sagamore is doing, and you're content to let the future take care of itself when he shows his hand, but I'm not like that. I want things settled."

"You're just feeling depressed and emotional. Hardly surprising, considering the circumstances. Stop worrying. Let's get Liam and Kate married."

"You stand there talking as if there's no problem, and all the while... Samuel, really, you've got to speak to Henry Sagamore—you've *got* to get this settled."

"I have no intention of backing down. I've never backed down from a confrontation in my life," Samuel answered with a lift of the chin and a quick squaring of the shoulders. His brown eyes were solemn, and his posture was a little stiff, saying, *Now for the lecture.*

"I'm not asking you to! Just listen!"

Samuel shrugged. "I'm listening."

"I don't believe you."

"I appreciate your interest, but I've too much to lose to let Sagamore get away with any more high jinks. Well-meaning as you may be, if you meddle, you will endanger the entire project. In fact, it would be best if you returned to Fairbanks with Liam."

"Not yet. Please, Samuel, not yet."

"All right." He sighed, jaw tight, and then nodded. "I assumed you wouldn't want to get involved in a vendetta."

She laughed softly, her breath brushing his cheek dark with stubble. "You are right there. Messy stuff, vendettas." She pressed her lips to his, and with delight felt him shudder. Her mouth opened; his arms went around her, and instinctively she moved against him—and felt him harden against her belly.

"Just look at the way I keep trying to give you advice, even though you have no intention of accepting it." She drew her head away from him, studied his expression.

Heat flared in his red-brown eyes. "I'm not a child, Cat."

She felt her own quick anger. "And you think I am?"

"No, but we're *acting* like children. I have to resolve this absurd situation in my own way." He stared at her, his face hardening in a way that she hadn't seen before.

Caitlin was drawn tight as a wire, filled with wild desire and wilder fear. "Don't." There was a shameful catch in her voice. She swallowed hard and added, more steadily, "You drive me crazy with wanting you, and you don't care. You don't think of anyone but yourself!"

He stared at her in outraged amazement. "I—? What about you? I've held back from a confrontation only because you wanted it."

"Only because I love you and don't want you or your reputation damaged! Why must you defend the entire valley's rights?"

"Because I care!"

She began to laugh, and suddenly tears streamed down her face and she choked, sobbing and laughing, and her arms went out to him, holding him fiercely, trembling. "Don't ever stop caring. Whatever happens, promise me you won't make that mistake."

Then, surprisingly, he beat back his temper. He laughed at her, as he would a child who was afraid of the dark, to dispel the innate foolishness of the notion. "I don't make many mistakes," he said. "And I never make the same one twice."

"Now there's a comforting statement," she murmured, her voice muffled against his chest.

"Must you always have the last word, Cat?"

Since the day was warm for the end of October, the men had moved the benches out into the courtyard, placing them in front of the blockhouse. The courtyard of the depot was filling up. Settlers and other loggers from the valley were arriving by cart or on horseback, parking their vehicles and animals in the shade of the big cedar and pine trees.

Silas and Moses were standing by the bunkhouse, hands in pockets and hats jammed down over their ears, staring with sharp eyes at the unusual crowd. Some of the men were playing horseshoes. There was a metallic clink of shoe against pin, and a quick burst of laughter.

An odor of roasting meat drifted on the breeze. The tantalizing smell rose from a barbacoa spit, where an old Abnaki was roasting a fat deer and a hog, basting the meat with its own drippings as he turned it. Buried in the coals were corn, pumpkin and potatoes.

Stacked on a long table were white biscuits sweetened with wild honey and red clover, together with Caitlin's crusty apple pies. The fragrance of coffee drifted across the courtyard. Mulligan was boiling it in the cookhouse. A man was tuning a fiddle, and loggers were dragging long tables into the courtyard and setting out pitchers of wine and flagons of apple brandy.

Mulligan was inordinately proud of his apple brandy, which he put out in kegs each winter, maintaining that the secret of his success was in the freezing. "Take a cup, ma'am? It warms the vittles." The cook patted his stomach serenely.

Caitlin took a polite sip, but the strong spirits were not to her taste. She thanked Mulligan, turned, and gave an undignified squawk.

Samuel stood in front of her, thumbs hooked under his suspenders. His eyes bored into hers. "Henry Sagamore sent word that he's accepted your invitation—the one you failed to mention."

Caitlin could hear the tension in his voice. The world blurred. Her hands were trembling. She let one clutch the other, trying to steady them. She had better luck with her voice. "Is he likely to make trouble?"

Samuel shook his head. "If he does, we'll give him a

charge of grape and send him back to Westfield. He's just another lumberman, rough and uncouth, though he does have the governor's ear and a bit of influence.''

Caitlin flinched, but the fact that she did so was scarcely perceptible. She pulled her glance away from Samuel, and looked at some spot on the ground. "I can see it's awkward. I should never have invited Mr. Sagamore and the settlers at the same time."

Samuel shrugged. He dealt with the problem swiftly, in his own way, throwing anger aside. "Ah, well, what's done is done. I'll have Mulligan pour enough brandy to keep them all in high spirits." His eyes fixed her with a very straight look. "You're always so certain of everything, Cat, but next time, you might consult with me first before you—interfere."

Caitlin flung down her own gauntlet forthwith. "I'm sure you must think I'm very young and foolish. But—"

"Perhaps we're neither of us very old or wise at present," Samuel said, interrupting her. He drew in his breath sharply. For a moment, his eyes searched her face.

The unspoken question hung in the silence. It might have been a physical object that Samuel had dragged from hiding and flung down between them. Do we love each other enough to overcome our differences? If they understood each other, as she had once imagined they did, that was the question they must answer together.

Their eyes locked for a moment, each trying to plumb the unfathomable depths of the other's. He drew back from her sharply, as though resisting a sudden impulse. "There seems to be a crowd arriving. Don't you think we'd better meet our guests?"

Caitlin lifted her chin. This at least is familiar, she thought. So she circulated among the guests, and began to talk and talk, though suddenly all she really wanted to do was to cry.

How had she been so foolish as to attempt to reshape

the world to her own specifications? Love was so very vulnerable. The mistake she had made was in being so quick and impatient to tie all the loose threads together herself without regard to fitness or proportion. She would do better in the future.

The Abnaki people had gathered near the wagons. The men, like Samuel's loggers and the settlers, were as solid and as rough as a log cabin, built for weather but with no extra trimmings. Caitlin watched the group for a moment, then crossed the compound to join them.

Winter Moon seemed glad to see Caitlin again. She smiled, and pushed her hand through her heavy dark hair. "Is it far to Cornwall? Samuel says it is over the green mountains and the ocean."

"That is so."

"Will you return?"

"For me, there can be no question of returning. Cornwall is behind me. I am married to Samuel. If he stays, I stay…and I want to stay."

"That is good," Winter Moon murmured.

Caitlin's gaze jerked to Zoe's face. The child's dark eyes were intent upon her face, asking something of her. She swallowed.

"We will build a new life in this land. Zoe will be part of that life."

In spite of herself, Caitlin crouched down until her face was level with the child's. How could any man reject such a bonny infant? Henry Sagamore was a fool. Still, an innocent child could not be blamed for the sins of the parents, and of course Samuel loved her.

"I was told I'd be given— That I'd get to go— I wish—" Caitlin closed her mouth, afraid to say more in front of White Cloud in case Summer Dawn's father did not approve of Samuel's plan to share in Zoe's upbringing.

White Cloud leaned against a tree. "Our ways are different from yours."

. "Would you deny a child half its heritage?" She brushed
Zoe's black hair from her forehead.

White Cloud waved an arm. His face was calm, almost
indifferent. "If you wish to know, you must ask the wind."

Caitlin stared at him, not knowing what to say. A lump
rose in her throat; she could hardly breathe. She probed her
feelings, surprised to realize how hurt she felt at the rebuff.
"I see," she finally managed to say. "Then I must wait
and listen for its answer, is that not so?"

The gray-haired Abnaki nodded his head. His eyes gazed
past her; his brow was furrowed. Caitlin seemed to feel his
expression on her own face, almost as if she were touching
his thoughts.

"There is a time for all things. The child of Summer
Dawn needs to learn the ways of her mother's people before she leaves, and to go when she is still young enough
to adapt quickly." There was no mockery in his voice.

Zoe had become bored with sitting still. She went over,
sat in Caitlin's lap. Without thinking, Caitlin put her arms
around the little girl.

"Hello," Zoe said, putting her face up to Caitlin's.
"Hello." Then she went on in a stream of Abnaki.

Samuel clasped a hand over her shoulder. "She is just
learning English."

Caitlin stiffened. Her answer came out in one breath.
"We are all just learning, aren't we, little one?"

Samuel was watching Caitlin with a kind of intense scrutiny. She glanced up at him, wondering why he had an
almost anxious look on his strong features. Was he really
concerned that she should accept the situation? He smiled
at her, and said, "I'm glad you invited White Cloud and
his family."

As she lifted the child off her lap, she whispered quickly,
"I must tend to Kate." She moved with a quick, graceful
swing of her skirts, and Samuel stepped aside to let her
pass. She hurried off before he could stop her.

The benches had been set in rows like pews, and everyone gathered for the marriage of Liam Murphy and Kate Flaherty. Samuel and Caitlin stood as witnesses.

Under the open sky, deep in the heart of the pinewoods, it was as solemn a ceremony as one conducted in a grand cathedral. Samuel was clearly moved, and he caressed her hand as he held it tight within his own.

Caitlin's spirits rose. The mountains and trees appealed to her, and seemed to thrust into the background all the meaner and smaller. A feeling of more settled happiness stole into her heart, and a smile played about her lips.

Father Kelly had just raised both hands and declared the marriage blessed when Zoe threaded her way through the crowd and ran to Caitlin, holding her own plump little arms high.

Laughing, Caitlin swung the child onto her hip. "This is one custom that crosses all cultures, little one."

Caitlin, not Samuel or Liam, saw Henry Sagamore. The lumberman was standing by the blockhouse, smoking a cigarette, watching her. Once the ceremony was finished and the crowd began to disperse, he sauntered over.

"Don't you think your playing little mother is a bit premature?" He exhaled the words along with the smoke, squinting at her.

"I doubt it," Caitlin said, setting Zoe on her feet. "I like children, and cannot have one of my own soon enough."

Henry's head went back in a quick, dry laugh. It was an explosion of breath. He shook his head. "You sound like you know already. Bit of a stallion is Sam?"

Caitlin felt the anger begin in her throat, spread with a hot flush to the roots of her hair, rush painfully to the very ends of her fingers. "I don't care for your...manners. It's not polite to speak so of your host."

"No?" He flicked ash on the ground. "The way you talk, I keep thinking you're one of those delicate city girls."

"Someday people around here are going to forget about the wrapping and look inside the package. Maybe some of them will be surprised. I know you were invited, but why have you come today, Henry Sagamore?"

"Well, I guess that depends on whether I came to praise Caesar or to bury him."

"Haven't you got that the wrong way around?"

"Spare me the lecture. Isn't it said that too much book-learning makes a woman sharp—or should that be weari-some? In any case, they challenge man's superior intel-lect." Sagamore's face wore a mixture of chagrin and amusement. He picked a shred of tobacco off his lip.

"Times change, and one must make way for the future," Caitlin said, as pleasantly as she could. "What if I prove to you that this negative opinion you nourish is unfounded? What if I prove to you that your natural good sense is warped by prejudice, and—"

Caitlin pulled herself up short. In the enthusiasm of the moment, she had said more than she meant to say, and already regretted the impetuous words that had escaped her.

"Oh, piffle," he answered coolly. "What's the use of talking like that? A bit of common horse sense would tell you I would never let a woman doctor tend me."

"It's a long road without a turn."

Henry glanced across to where Samuel was speaking with the newlyweds. "All this stuff about ideal love and soul communion and perfect mating is pure bunk," he said, tacking off on a new course of thought. "Marriage is more a game of chance, a spin of fortune's wheel."

"If that is so, then children are the consolation prize."

"It would serve *that* one right if he was blessed with another one just like himself later on, a daughter who wants educating."

Caitlin suddenly had an insight. *It is catching,* she thought, on the very edge of laughter. *Another month or two, and I could relish an argument or two, just to spike this man's impudence.... But wouldn't Samuel be cross with me!* She chose the soft answer.

"An interesting idea, Henry. It requires further thought." In her mind, she added, *Educate women at your peril, but they will be educated.* "Come, the meat is done to a splendid turn, the wine is already flowing. Let me give you a plate...."

Earthen plates were stacked high on a table by the roasting pit, and Mulligan was cutting slabs of juicy meat. The fiddler had been joined by an accordion player and a fellow who rapped on a rawhide drum. They were practicing together softly.

Samuel joined a group of men gathered around the brandy barrel. "Hello, folks," he said as he poured himself a drink.

"May I compliment you on your hospitality, Sam?" René deCarteret raised his pewter mug. "It's been a while since we've all had the chance to relax in each other's company. Good for morale."

"My pleasure, I'm sure." Samuel took no more than a ritual sip of Mulligan's brandy. He knew Caitlin did not approve of strong liquor, and while he did not subscribe to teetotalism, he was not addicted to the stuff and was quite happy to restrict his drinking.

René deCarteret shook his head. "Some of these men are such an uncouth lot."

Samuel caught sight of Mulligan, laden knife in one hand, spinning some outrageous yarn, and LeFeuvre, slapping his knee, roaring with laughter. Sawdust coated the logger's hat and stuck in a fine red dust along his eyebrows. Samuel knew Raoul would stink of sweat and pine, odors embedded forever in the very fabric of his clothes. Pity the man didn't believe in bathing.

"I count myself lucky they are my friends," he said quietly.

René deCarteret pulled at the corner of his mustache.

Sam Jardine was a power along the Aroostook, a dominant, hard-bitten woodsman who had gathered about him the toughest crew on the river. He controlled many square miles of big timber, and he had gotten it all by his own efforts in the ten years since he came to Maine as a hand logger.

"Hang it, I guess you're right. To be a leader of such ruffians demands not only courage but gall, the daring to challenge anything. You are such a man. You will not fail in this bid to stop timber poaching."

Samuel stared at his hands and flexed his fingers. "The word *failure* is not part of my vocabulary. I'm not going to allow an inch of leeway. There's five million feet ready for delivery, and every log will be checked, down to the last splinter, before the boom leaves."

"Isn't that hazardous?"

"The element of risk was—and still is—enormous. Time is money right now, but if we all pull together, we'll make delivery on time."

There was a violent commotion, and the music stopped. The chaff and laughter died into silent, capable action. People gathered in a ring near the roasting pit.

Samuel heard shouts, and someone cursing in French. He thrust his way into the mêlée. There was a muttering, a sullen undercurrent among the loggers. They drew a little aside, allowing him space. Caitlin pushed her way to his side.

LeFeuvre had stopped laughing. His eyes bulged a little as he leaned forward. His face was red from drinking. There was ugliness in him, and fury.

Mulligan glared at LeFeuvre hotly, hands on his hips. "You are a stinking fool, Frenchie."

"I ain't no fool, and don't you call me one," LeFeuvre said, as if he had just managed to get his thoughts together, and added distinctly, "I could beat the living daylights out of you." He began walking toward the table.

"Do not try me, Raoul. I have broken far better men than you—stronger men, wiser men."

"Do you think you could defeat me, you fat, flour-pushing bastard? A man a third bigger, and in prime condition?" LeFeuvre's voice was shrill; the brandy was talking.

"Well," Mulligan said at last, "ain't none of us got a crystal ball, now do we, you great, drunken booby?"

Raoul LeFeuvre's face had a tight, suspicious look. The cook had clearly unsettled him. He was hot-tempered, proud, a man who acted before he thought. Like me, Caitlin told herself with some trepidation and not a little amusement. Rather a lot like me. Now, if I had been a man...

LeFeuvre decided to challenge the slur. His hands came up, and then he came forward quickly, in a rush.

Too late.

Mulligan dodged to his left, swung at him and missed. Raoul's head snapped back with a sound like a popped shingle. He was spinning around—he'd crashed into something hard. It was the table's edge.

"Can you do anything?" Mulligan backed away, laughing.

Crouched on his hands and knees, Raoul shook his head. His eyes lit on the hickory-handled ax in a bucket by the roasting pit. He weaved to his feet, snatched the ax out of the container and whirled around, his left arm out, fending—to see Mulligan staring past him, his hands at his sides again.

Samuel was standing at the edge of the circle of men, Caitlin at his side. Liam Murphy was standing only a few feet away, thumbs hooked easily in the edges of his trouser pockets.

"I warned you, LeFeuvre. There'll be no brawling in the camp." Samuel said the words calmly, but the veins stood out on his muscular neck, and his body seemed tense. Caitlin knew he was chain lightning in action, a force to be reckoned with.

"Sam!" Raoul stared at him, startled. The sight of Samuel had jolted some of the drunkenness from him, but Caitlin knew the Frenchman was still not thinking clearly. Suddenly, he swung. It was perfect—the move, the swing—the ax high above his head coming down in an arc.

"You idiot!" Mulligan cried.

Caitlin pressed the back of her hand against her lips. Her throat tightened.

With a quick slap of his palm, Samuel knocked the blade over, out of line with his body. Then he took a quick step in with his left foot. Samuel's right leg hooked behind Raoul's, and his right hand smashed up, the butt of his palm under the logger's chin.

LeFeuvre's head snapped back, and Samuel's leg tripped him. He half turned and fell to the ground, his grip loosening on the ax. As he hit the ground, Samuel kicked it from his hand, then took it up. Raoul lay staring, shocked, expecting…what?

Samuel broke the hickory handle over his knee and flung the ax head back into the bucket, where it clattered on the tin.

Raoul groaned. "Someone shoot me…."

"I've a better idea." Samuel heaved the logger over his shoulder in a fireman's carry, over to the horse trough. "I'd love to oblige you, but unfortunately there's this little deal over at Fairbanks, and I need your…noble…presence!" Crouching, he dumped the logger into the trough.

"Oh!" LeFeuvre cried. His eyes flew open wide, he began floundering in the water, gasping, "Oh, oh, oh…" while Samuel held him down, watching him.

"Afterward, I'll be more than happy to shoot you. But right now you're going to get cleaned up."

"Let me up, Sam!"

"No."

"Let me up. I'm clean—"

"The hell you are. But you're going to be. I guarantee it."

There was a short silence. LeFeuvre looked at Samuel and grinned. "All right!" he said. "This is one hell of a party. I'm sorry, Sam. You too, Mulligan. Let's forget this damned foolishness and get back to enjoying ourselves."

"Fair enough. I'll go along with that."

Caitlin could no longer restrain herself. "You could have been killed, Samuel. He should be sacked!"

"Don't be so prissy." Samuel's throat moved as he swallowed. "There's no reason to sack a good man. I trust Raoul completely, and you should, too." He smiled—a quirk of the lips. In the brightness of the day, his voice carried a mildness that was, Caitlin knew, deceptive.

She wanted to cry out at the injustice of it, but the strength to do it deserted her. Her face burned with indignation. He was wrong, all wrong. How could she begin to tell him? *Later, later,* her mind cried silently, *I'll talk to him later.*

Caitlin didn't move. How green her eyes are, Samuel thought, like river water when the sun goes through it. There was a silence, broken at last by Henry Sagamore.

"Ah. Test of fire for the sweet young thing." He flashed a toothy smile. "How do you like life in a logging camp now?"

"Now you listen to me, Henry." There was a subtle change in Samuel now. His voice had lost that desultory, faintly derisive note. "And you listen hard and well. I'm unhappy with your Quaggy Joe operations."

Sagamore made a dismissing gesture. "My, you're bitter today."

"I don't like these rotten deals you're setting up. I don't like you pressuring the loggers, and most of all I don't like this latest dodge with Ned Flaherty. I don't like you using Ned to stir up mischief. I don't like it one single bit."

"Now, I say—that's coming down a bit hard," Sagamore said sharply. "I haven't done anything illegal. Everything has been aboveboard, and let me assure you that I will have access to the timber on Quaggy Joe."

"It is trespass, pure and simple, and I'll not have it."

"It is politic, Sam, to talk of what you hope to achieve, rather than what you will have."

Samuel glared at him. "As to what is politic, press the issue and you will find yourself in an untenable situation, in no position to demand anything."

"A ridiculous statement, if I may say so. This is *my* empire. I'll not be denied the right to cut timber when and where I will."

When Samuel spoke, Caitlin heard a harsh new note in his voice. "You know something, Henry? You can project, and analyze, and huddle with your legal jackals, and connive ways to slide around rules and regulations. But provoke trouble, and we may all well end up bankrupt."

Henry frowned. "Do you think you can wiggle out of putting my logs in the boom? Or has the governor's little ultimatum about stirring up trouble given you some divine insight?"

"Oh, nothing as grand as that. I've done my homework. You're getting overextended. You're in debt for supplies, behind in wages. Fall down on this delivery and you're finished."

"You don't know what you're talking about!"

"Yes I do. Big fish eat little fish, and I'm a little fish, but at least I own my own puddle. If this dispute is dragged out over two or three months, by the time the logs are sold, you might not have anything left."

"If you try to force me out, you're going to be in for the fight of your life—I guarantee it." The menace in Sagamore's tone made it quite plain what he had in mind, though he added, as if to leave no possible doubt, "I'll destroy that dam and you with it.'' His voice now actually alarmed Caitlin.

''Do not threaten me, Sagamore.''

''I *do* threaten you, Sam Jardine! I give you fair warning.''

Samuel only smiled at him, nodding—a faint, mocking smile. ''You're not going to win this one, Henry. Push me and you'll be sorry,'' he continued implacably.

Sagamore started, glanced at Caitlin swiftly, and grunted in annoyance as he turned on his heel and stalked away in the direction of the roasting pit. In a moment Caitlin saw him in genial conversation with Ned Flaherty.

''Well!'' Caitlin considered his back. ''What does that mean?''

''Don't meddle, Cat. You've done enough damage for one day.''

Chapter Thirteen

Meddle? Damage? The full import of what she was hearing swept over Caitlin as if she had been doused in cold water. How could he be so obtuse? Her head came around, and she glanced at him sharply.

"Samuel, for heaven's sake. Didn't you hear what Henry Sagamore said?" Her brows snapped together. "He just threatened to kill you. I am sure he meant it!"

Samuel gripped her by the shoulders. She shut her mouth, with a view to opening it again. She would have spoken, but he cut her short with stinging ruthlessness.

"No, do not say it." He bent forward, his fingers biting into the softness of her skin. "Now is not the time to interfere." His voice was low and compelling.

Samuel's lips tightened a little, and there was something in his voice that told Caitlin it would be unwise to argue with him further. She looked up into his face. Only by dint of her iron will did she hold her tongue. For a long, long moment they stared at each other, and the world seemed to vibrate and move, almost dizzily, around them.

He was cross. She did not blame him. Nobody wants to have another person meddle in his affairs. Perhaps she had seemed smug to him, though she had not meant to be.

An energetic young woman, she was accustomed to having her own way. One of her earliest delightful discoveries had been that she could nearly always get what she wanted by being eager for it and assuming that, of course, the others involved would recognize her plan as best, or at least would give up theirs cheerfully when she urged hers.

But Samuel was leaving her dashed and rebuffed. The hurt was not to her vanity, but to her feminine urges. The desire to save him from himself and his fate fluttered wistfully toward him.

"Call it a whim, but I think for the moment it would not be wise to let Liam realize his new brother-in-law may be involved in any trickery."

Caitlin frowned, annoyed that she hadn't thought of that herself. "So we do nothing?" The words burst out of her before she could stop them.

Again she had made a mistake. A small frown pleated Samuel's forehead. Though the ghost of a smile crept into his eyes, there was an expression of grim determination on his handsome face. But he didn't overlook her question this time.

"Not exactly," he said at last.

Caitlin gave a little sigh. It was all right for Samuel to disapprove, but she was not one to find plots and intrigues where they were not at all likely to be! She knew she had overstepped the bounds of what Samuel would willingly put up with by inviting both of his business rivals to today's celebrations, but what else was a body to do? Allow mischief to be fomented, just because no one had enough sense to bring the warring parties together?

In any case, what did it matter that Samuel thought she was meddling? At least for the moment he was safe, even if he didn't care to offer an alliance. Instinctively she flicked a glance at Henry Sagamore and Ned Flaherty. She wondered why there must be all this secrecy. It was so uncharacteristic of Samuel to be reserved, to refuse to even discuss a situation.

Caitlin parted her lips to speak, but Samuel shook his head. "One thing we can do is play for time. Humor me, Cat. Go and have the fiddlers strike up some dance music," he said, as if to end the subject.

Caitlin would have liked to ask questions, but instinctively she knew they would not be welcome. It was very annoying, but she decided it wasn't worth orchestrating a battle over the matter.

Instead, she reached up and brushed a red-gold curl off his forehead. And if her open smile was not an apology, it refused, anyhow, to be at variance with him.

Samuel was watching her speculatively. He had put both hands on her waist and was holding her, looking into her eyes. The moment seemed agonizingly intimate. A giddy rush of feeling went straight to her belly.

"I'll make it the bridal waltz. That will get Liam and Kate out of everybody's way." Her accompanying smile was bright as sunshine.

For an instant, she had the unsettling sensation that he was going to pull her into his arms. She felt the strength of his hands and the tension of his body. The very air around them was charged with its force. He said nothing, but Caitlin could feel the tug of his masculine magnetism. Her skin tingled, and her mouth parted in open invitation. Anticipation almost wrung a cry from her mouth.

Unfortunately, she was faced instead with yet further proof of the strength of his resolve and will. Samuel's hands dropped from her waist, casually, almost mechanically, and he nodded in agreement. "Not a bad idea, Cat. Save the last dance for me."

Caitlin's fingers dug into her palms. With a little feeling of exasperation, she watched Samuel move across to Liam Murphy. He walked quickly, like a man who dared not hesitate, lest he should turn back. What a stupid thought!

Why would he come back? To shake her, or to kiss her? The odds were even, either way, Caitlin thought glumly. It was depressing to think she had waited all these years for the wretched man, only to be dismissed by him as an interfering busybody. They were still too new at marriage, she decided. Samuel might be difficult, stubborn, and involved in any number of dangerous escapades, but he was her husband.

A sobering thought. At least now she knew where she stood. And even though she was conscious of a slight annoyance, there was nothing to worry about. They communicated quite well at the most basic level—in bed—and that was all that mattered. In bed, she had a breathless sense of her own power, at once jubilant and frightening.

It was just that she was impatient. She must trust Samuel to find a solution—and not one that he was rushed into by his wife.

Whatever the problems, she felt certain that Samuel could, in some miraculous way or other, surmount them. He got things done because he was so virile, so dominant. To look at the lines and movements of his sturdy body, at the straight mouth and resolute eyes, was to know him as a leader of men. The best she could do was to support him.

The afternoon sun was warm on Samuel's shoulders as he debated the matter in his head. Samuel had had too many years doing things his own way. He had forgotten what a minx Caitlin was. How she loved to poke her nose into his men's business. His wife was a diminutive tyrant, and he was tired of her ceaseless lectures. He was no longer a young fool tortured by rampant desire. No passionate interludes or physical satiation could compensate for her constant nagging.

And that, God help him, was the biggest lie he had told since he'd sworn to Squire Parr that Caitlin's ball gown was all mussed because she'd come to the stables to see the new mare—and him with hay sticking out of his hair and the flap of his trousers undone.

That, after a lapse of years, he could write home for a

bride, and then get the wrong one because he had confused
her name with that of her sister, seemed highly improbable.
But it had happened. And he had held his tongue about his
mistake.

He had honestly thought he could carry it off.

Even though she wasn't the bride he'd sent for, even
though she was a bogus bride, it had seemed a reasonable
solution. After all, he had known her during much of her
formative years. He had fished her out of an irrigation ditch
when she was ten. He had shown her how to tie knots in
sailing ropes, how to dig for winkles. It had been under his
direction that she learned to ride, to fish, to shoot.

Therefore, the solution had seemed simple. Marry her,
allow her a measure of freedom—he'd allowed her to set
up a surgery, hadn't he? He would honor his commitment,
sleep with her, make love to her when the urge came on
him, and then go about his business.

Only there was a flaw in his plans. He'd taken one look
at Caitlin when she stepped off the *Angelica,* at the slim,
vital girl confronting him with such passionate and feminine ferocity in those bold green eyes and that devil-may-
care tilt to her head, and he'd been a goner. Never mind
that he'd known she was up to her old tricks and was as
devious as ever.

He had wanted her then. He wanted her now.

Aware only of his own thoughts, Samuel went to the
table and took a piece of pie, dipped it in a bowl of cream,
munched on it. It was delicious, the pastry light and crisp.
As on other special occasions, the women had contributed
to the feast, but Caitlin had outdone herself. A whole row
of pies sat waiting to be eaten. A labor of love.

He heard himself say to someone, "A good gathering,"
and realized in amazement that he was smiling. It was as
if he were acting a part, but somehow had got into the
wrong play. *Who arranges our lives,* he thought, *that at*

this particular moment I know for sure that I never loved Caitryn, that it was all a dream?

Samuel looked at Liam and Kate, shaking the hand of each person who passed by, at Li Foo's wrinkled yellow face, at the familiar benches and the old horse trough, at the black-robed priest. Everything was so familiar, yet so unreal.

He picked up another sliver of pie. He dipped and bit into the succulent morsel. Caitlin's smiling face floated before him. How could she know his feelings, if he was too much of a coward to tell her?

Samuel wasn't a man given to admitting his shortcomings. When he discovered that unspeakable major flaw in his makeup, he'd tried to quash the knowledge of his affliction before it became widespread.

He'd thought he'd succeeded in fooling everyone. Now he suspected Caitlin had long been aware of his weakness. Those green eyes were too alert, too knowing, not to catch on.

Not that she'd ever said anything, but the evidence was there. When he stumbled during his reading, she'd cut in with the correct words. When the tutor went to correct his written work, she'd dropped ink blots on his laboriously constructed essays. In fact, she'd interfered constantly, until the tutor turned his attention away from Samuel to his more volatile pupil, whose father, after all, paid his wages.

The young Samuel had wanted to snap at her, but had held back. She had been a better student than he; she had helped him often, and tolerating her interference had been a small price to pay for that. He had been grateful to be able to keep his affliction a secret and pretend that any achievements were commonplace. It had been worth all the frustration and misery to see her expression when he'd succeeded.

And he had succeeded. He'd mastered the books—valued them the more, perhaps, for their cost in lonely labor.

And he'd done more with his common sense than most men. It had guided him through endless pitfalls.

It was Caitryn, the younger sister, who had soothed the agony within. Her sweet smiles and gentle ways had offset Caitlin's sharp tongue and teasing laughter.

The trouble was, Caitlin was a thorn that refused to be dislodged—an affliction that was as appalling, in its own way, as his difficulty in reading and writing. The name of the thorn was *love*.

The dreamlike memories evaporated like a mist. Henry Sagamore was saying, "You're good, Ned. Real good. You've done well. How good are you at taking direction?"

Ned Flaherty shrugged. "Depends on how I feel about it." His voice sounded strained.

Samuel was instantly alert. His mouth flattened into a hard line. His eyes roved and sought, piercing the distance between them. Against his will, he found himself listening. He had his own ideas of what they were going to talk about.

"A reasonable answer." Sagamore's voice was very soft. Samuel edged closer. "But what I'm suggesting is something quite different, but right up your alley. You get a piece of information and are…asked to act on it. You do so."

Ned Flaherty's sandy brows knit together. His eyes flickered. "I dunno. It all sounds so cryptic, like you're talking political. Like spies."

"Tell me, Ned, how's your financial situation these days?"

"Fine." There was absolutely no inflection in Ned's voice, and his face was a mask. But something in his posture, a minute stiffening, a straightening of the spine, sent a warning through Samuel's mind.

"That's not what I heard." Sagamore shook his head and smiled. "Rumor has it that you're too much a betting man, that you're in real bad shape, Ned. Very bad shape."

Samuel grinned suddenly. It was straight political technique, which he recognized immediately: Give the good news, and while the flush of pleasure is still on, tack on the bad. Like an amendment. A rider to the bill. To protest the latter would be to risk the former. Smooth.

Ned began to object, then stopped himself, but his freckles stood out in a crazy splatter across his nose. "So I gamble," he said, his back stiff as a lodgepole pine.

Samuel cursed them silently, the winners, the losers, and the vultures who preyed on both.

"Seems you're not very lucky. In fact, you're hard-luck-prone." Sagamore leaned forward. "I'm not talking out of school, but guess a thousand dollars would clear your debts—and I can't imagine my asking you to do anything that would go against your grain. We think alike, after all."

A peculiar look crossed Ned Flaherty's face as swiftly as a breeze. As Samuel thought that over, his grin widened. This time Henry Sagamore had outsmarted himself. He hadn't taken into account the real affection that the boy had for his sister, Kate—and Kate was married to Liam.

"What are you saying?" Ned's voice did not rise above a whisper.

"Business is not a fit subject while eating," Samuel said, interrupting. "That's what Henry is saying. That right, Henry?"

Sagamore stood by the table, relaxed and calm. "Sure. I make it a strict point not to mix business with pleasure, which is why I find I must leave this happy gathering. If you're in the vicinity in the next week or so, Ned, drop in to Westfield for a yarn."

Ned nodded. "I'll do that, Sagamore, I'll do that."

Without another word, Henry brushed past Samuel and Ned. In a few seconds, there came the sound of a horse trotting away down the track.

Ned faced Samuel, as if daring him, even asking him, to guess the truth. Samuel knew Henry Sagamore as well as anyone in the valley. He knew Ned. The boy stood there, sullen and sly, waiting for his judgment.

Samuel looked at Ned thoughtfully. He grasped at anger and felt it shrivel into nothing. He had to give Ned Flaherty the benefit of the doubt.

He wouldn't try to judge another man, Samuel thought. He'd bide his time and see which way the wind blew, and then he'd settle accounts with Sagamore, when the terms were in his own favor.

Samuel said at last, "There are always situations arising...which would benefit greatly from your expertise with explosives, Ned. Now more than ever, in fact."

"I'm sure there are."

There was an obvious pause. "How's the hand?"

Ned smiled. He opened and closed his left hand, flexing his forearm. As he moved, Samuel watched the play of bulging muscle.

"You know, Sam, Sagamore's right. I am a gambling man, and I'm damn proud of it. It comes of being Irish— our lineage, history, heritage." His blue eyes glittered slyly. "I've a sporting proposition to make to you. We'll have a little arm wrestle, and whoever's the winner can call the tune."

Samuel grinned. "Come on, Ned. Don't you know a losing cause when you see one?"

"Fortune favors he who dares." Ned lifted his thick forearm, flexed his biceps. He laughed. "What's the matter, Sam? Getting too soft—or too old?"

Samuel was over six feet tall, well muscled, and weighed in at one hundred and ninety pounds. In comparison, the younger man carried much less bulk. He stood very still for an instant before he slowly shook his head.

"No."

"The only way you'll get me is to whip me, fair and square." Ned moved so that the wooden table now stood directly between them. "One takedown. No rematches.

That's it. Period.'' He laughed again. ''C'mon, Sam, you must have a bit of the devil left in you.'' He paused, waiting.

Samuel took a deep breath, collecting himself. He was no longer certain that what he had planned to do was the right course of action. ''I guess I don't have much choice.'' He was relieved that his voice was easy, casual. He stepped back, rolled up his sleeves.

''This is gonna be a piece of cake.''

Both men seated themselves, and together they placed the points of their elbows on the tabletop. They gripped hands in a perfectly vertical position.

Ned thrust first, hard, in an effort to achieve an immediate advantage and build upon it. To a large degree, he was successful, though he encountered firm resistance. His confidence quickly blossomed, and he settled in to lay Samuel low as quickly as he could.

The ferocity and lightning-quickness of Flaherty's attack caught Samuel by surprise. As he felt the pressure on his wrist and the tendons of his arm, he recognized that Ned was a master of this game. Already he was feeling a sharp twinge in his shoulder where the unaccustomed strain was telling.

It had been years since he had done any arm wrestling, so it was some time before he thought of the law of leverage. As the loggers often said, *It's not the timber cutter's strength that fells the logs, but a tree's own force.* By that time, sweat was trickling uncomfortably down his sides, and Ned had him more than one third of the way over.

Samuel applied the principles of timber felling, altering them slightly to fit the rules of arm wrestling. He felt the answering surge of energy and, though Flaherty sweated and strained, their rippling arms were back at the vertical, where they had begun.

Now, Ned's once smiling face began to take on a morose and then a harassed look. His muscles knotted and his brow furrowed until his whole body began to tremble as he attempted to block Samuel's unexpected counterattack. He used every strategy he could think of.

Nothing worked. Steadily their straining arms slid farther and farther toward Ned's side of the table, until the rough wood brushed against his knuckles and he knew that, despite all the odds, all the muscle, all the youth, he had lost.

Ned staggered up from the table, walked stiff-legged over to one of Mulligan's flagons. His brow was beaded with sweat, and he was breathing hard. An odd animal noise came from his throat. He filled a pannikin with apple brandy and tipped it up to his mouth. He did not stop swallowing until he had finished it.

Then he refilled the mug, raised it. "Drink with me?"

Samuel went across to the barrel and poured himself a drink while Ned downed a third of the contents of his cup.

"You won fair and square." The gesture Ned made was as curt as his voice.

"Did you think I wouldn't?"

Ned waggled the flat of his hand. "Fifty-fifty. I had a bet with myself."

Samuel lifted an eyebrow. "Which fifty did you take?"

"The winning one. I'm always honest with myself."

Samuel grinned. "And very sure."

"Just what do you know?"

Samuel sipped at his drink. "Only what I overheard just now."

"Now, just a minute! You said…"

"Maybe we both have to listen sometimes, huh?"

"There's something else at work here."

"There's loyalty—"

"Loyalty never helped anyone's career."

"No?" Samuel asked. "I'm no organization man, Ned, and you're not on a leash. Do whatever you think is right." His voice, if not exactly filled with menace, had taken on a steely edge.

The air between them turned to lead. It was as if an entire world revolved on this one point, so delicate was the moment. There was a peculiar tense silence.

"You aren't going to ask me about my debts?" Ned's voice was low, but perfectly clear.

Samuel lifted his drink to his lips, then hesitated. "I learned a long time ago not to interfere in other people's lives. You're a grown man, capable of making your own mistakes."

Ned laughed and moved to another group.

"That's rather hard and unfeeling, Samuel."

Again Samuel lifted an eyebrow. It was Caitlin, come to meddle and interfere. He stared at her. She was smiling. Her smile was like sunshine, a contagion of warmth, a well of moisture edged with promise. He felt anew that odd, almost compulsive quickening of his blood that was so disturbing, and all the more intense because it was so unexpected. He put his drink down on the table beside him.

"It saves a lot of grief, though."

Caitlin made a soft sound deep in her throat. "Is that why you never tried to contact me? Did you decide it would save you a lot of suffering just to forget about me?"

He did not know he sighed until he had done it, and then he did not know why. "I wish I could have forgotten you."

She looked surprised by the sudden edge in his voice. Her eyes widened, and he saw himself reflected in their convex circles. Then her eyelashes swept down, concealing her emotions. But nothing concealed the change in her mouth, the smile gone so quickly he might have knocked it off her face.

Her eyelids slowly lifted. "You sound like you regret writing to me." She came closer, and then closer still, not stopping until she was so close that he could smell the fragrance of her hair.

Samuel began to realize she might be playing games with

him. Caitlin Jardine, for all her sharp intellect, was not above jumping to conclusions. He took a gulp of his drink.

"Or did you mix up my name with Caitryn's, as you often did when we were children?" Her voice was even, supple, almost amused, but her eyes narrowed on him accusingly.

Samuel reacted as if he were a kid caught with his hand in the cookie jar. He considered running, then reminded himself that she could not read his thoughts. He laughed.

"I believe I would have remembered that."

She gave him an all-too-brief smile, showing him just a bit of her even white teeth. Her sunny, careless expression belied her body's actions. Her spine was rigid. "That's not what I asked."

Samuel kissed her to make her be quiet, but she snatched herself away and was across the compound, the back of her hand against her mouth. She stared at him solemnly for a moment, and then she came back.

"Did you?" Her voice was very faint, but her mouth wasn't trembling, and her eyes were clear.

She never backed away from a fight, Samuel thought. Temptation smote him savagely. He could bear to fight with her. He grinned suddenly.

"We are husband and wife now."

"That's not an answer."

Her chin was high and her nose was in the air. God bless her spirit, Samuel thought, and his feeling for her came back, so hard and sudden it hurt. His arms came up, embraced her, leaving only a shadow of space between.

"For me it is." Samuel pulled her close, kissing her again.

"Samuel, we're in company!"

He looked down at her. Her eyes were very wide and very bright. Her tongue came out, touched her upper lip, moistening it. Hands on his shoulders, she pushed him back. *She* was on the defensive now, not he.

"So we are." He kissed her again.

There was a fluttering deep in her belly. Caitlin stirred uneasily. His body was very close to hers. She could see the gleam of sweat on his face, the short stubble of beard. But most of all she inhaled his masculine scent. Really, it made her feel quite weak.

There came a distant rumble out of the south, the sound of thunder. Weather moving in. Silas Crane's fiddle twanged from the mess house. The musicians had just begun a fast reel. With a violent jerk, Caitlin pulled free of him. She said nothing. What was there to say?

So the matter was dropped—but not very far. Caitlin turned on her heel. She took only five paces before he caught up to her.

"I've got a better idea." Samuel's powerful hand took possession of her elbow and half guided, half propelled her away from the celebrations. She had to run, skip and jump to keep up with his long strides. The fiddler's rollicking notes pursued them, bright and loud at first, fainter as he marched her past the mess house, around Li Foo's garden, across the short expanse of grass and on through her own front door.

Caitlin felt the coiled tension of his body, knew instinctively that he was on the edge. Because of that, she could not stop herself, wanting as she did to push him further, to provoke in him a response strong enough to prove to her once and for all that he truly cared for her.

"I don't think this is a good idea." His arms slid around her, and she put her hand over his. "Samuel, no—" She tried to break away.

"You won," he said. "Don't you see that?"

"Won what? This isn't a contest," she informed him righteously.

"Oh, yes." He smiled, watching her face carefully. "It's all a contest, and I can't match your efforts. You know that."

"What do you mean?"

"You ignore ten years of neglect, travel to Maine, marry me and forgive my involvement with Summer Dawn, despite the fact that you have forfeited a career that you wanted more than anything else."

"*Almost* more than anything else."

"*Almost* is the operative word. It is the *almost* that tells me how much you care. That's something I need, Cat." His voice was tight and clogged. "More than you could know."

"So you terrorize me to—"

"No." He shook his head. "You terrorized *me*. The moment you walked into my life and began to meddle with my future, I knew I must resist. I could never allow that to happen." She felt his breath on her face, saw his eyes, shining above her. "Now, I'd do anything..."

Caitlin wrapped her arms around his neck, her fingers gently caressing the nape, feeling the toughness and the resiliency as they moved slowly down the rigid contours of his back. When she reached his waist, she clawed his shirt free of the waistband of his trousers, ran her fingertips inside, upward. He gave a tremendous shudder.

"Give me anything I want?" Her voice was very soft.

"Yes." His voice was even softer as his arms tightened around her and he buried his face in the hollow of her shoulder.

Every part of Caitlin's body throbbed with self-awareness. Thighs, breasts, belly, ached with longing. She was filled up with love for him. Surely he loved her! It must be a sin to want anything so much.

"You could love me, Samuel. You could love me, now." Mouth open, she brought her face up to his. She wanted to give him her warmth, her passion, her love.

For a dizzying instant, he did not move. Then his tongue touched hers, while his hands reached down to cup her buttocks and she felt herself lifted up onto the tips of her toes, back arched, his fingertips lightly caressing her between her thighs.

Samuel pulled aside her clothes as Caitlin frantically opened his. At last they were totally naked, flesh to flesh. His head bent as his hands slid around her bare sides and gently lifted her breasts. He caressed her firm, ripe breasts at the same time she surrounded him with her fingers, gently stroking his length, urging him, teasing him.

He shuddered and drew her breasts against his mouth. His lips opened to encompass the point of first one, then the other. Caitlin threw her head back, her neck arched, her eyelids fluttering uncontrollably, as she felt the tender pulling, the origin of a fierce line of fire reaching down through her belly and into her feminine core.

Beside herself with passion, she ran her delicate fingers over the hard outlines of his gleaming bronze muscles. Finding that was not enough, she slid down his naked body. Her small tongue licked at him. She took him into her mouth, moaning with delight at his taste.

His fingertips traced the indentations of her spine, descending slowly. Her flesh tingled where his callused fingertips scraped her skin. The backs of his hands brushed against the thick thatch of hair in the shadowed dell between her thighs, and she inhaled quickly. His lips soon followed as he moved down her. The sound of her pulse rushed like a hurricane in her inner ears.

Caitlin's body undulated upward as the soft lance of his tongue traced the feminine length of her, the friction causing the moist, secret folds of her to open up like the petals of a flower. Her thighs trembled and her breasts shook with the racing emotions.

He spread her legs with his until they encompassed his hips, and he lifted her onto the bed. His hands went behind her, cupped her buttocks, and he pushed up into her. The contact seemed to go on forever, filling her belly, her throat.

Caitlin shuddered, grabbing hold of him, scraping a nail

along his flesh. She bit into the muscles of his shoulder without knowing what she was doing, tasting the salt and the scent of him in arousal. She heard a startled cry deep down inside the core of her and, at that moment, her inner muscles clamped down on him.

She was on fire. She only felt the beginning of his explosion as she came in every part of her, crying out and trying to merge herself with his hard, jetting flesh.

Later, much later, when her mind had returned to her satiated, supine body, she put a hand up, her fingers gently stroking the line of his jaw.

Samuel put his hand over hers. "Now you know."

"Now I know," she repeated, as if those three simple words, and only those words, were a true and solemn pledge.

How could she ever have doubted?

Chapter Fourteen

November opened with rain. Day after day, the sun hid behind massed, spitting clouds. Morning, noon and night, the eaves of the houses dripped steadily, the gaunt limbs of the hardwoods were a line of coursing drops, and through all the vast reaches of pine and cedar the pattern of rain kept up a dreary monotone.

Rain or shine, the work drove on. From the peep of day until dusk shrouded the woods, axes thudded and the thin, twanging whine of the saws rose.

Log after log slid down the chute. In the waters beside and lining the stream floated innumerable logs, confined by boom sticks, hundreds of trunks of fir, forty and sixty feet long, four and six feet across the butt, timber enough, when it had passed through the sawmills, to build four such towns as Fairbanks.

The wind and rain rattled about the depot at night like a malevolent spirit, and by day stung the faces of the loggers as they struggled between limit and depot, snatched at their clothes, fought a battle with them for their very breath. The racketing wind made Caitlin think of the old Chinaman's voice—full of portent.

At night the loggers trooped home, soaked to the skin, to hang their steaming woolen coats around the bunkhouse stove. When they gathered in the messroom, they filled it with the odor of sweaty bodies and profane grumbling about the weather.

Calling into the blockhouse one afternoon, Caitlin doffed her oilskin and handed Mulligan a packet. "Foul weather, but this should cheer the men. I brought the mail."

"This ain't nothing," Mulligan told her. And as the wind whipped down the stovepipe, sending clouds of smoke into the blockhouse, he was off on a string of yarns—the taste a dead cow's carcass had given a certain water hole, the time he'd *crawled* fifty miles of desert after a bullet had smashed his leg, how the water was so scarce down Mexico way that the oxen melted away to shadows, just ten sets of horns still plugging along, bound down to Panama.

"This bullshit gets any deeper," Moses Livingstone shouted over the laughter, "we'll have whip marks in the gravy."

"I declare, Mulligan, you've had more adventures than Marco Polo! Why don't you write them all up? Call it *Memoirs of a Dissolute Gastronome.*"

Mulligan grinned. "Sorry, mate, I can't read or write—and if I could, I'd rather call it *The Bad Egg.*"

They were good men, Caitlin decided as she trudged back to the house, superbly qualified for this business of timber cutting. Stalwart, hardy, they faced life with a cheerful grin.

If they could, so too could she—even if it was difficult in this weather. The wind ripped one end of the oilskin cloak and slapped it against her skirt. Gray daylight had slid subtly into night, a gradual dimming to a twilight of wind-driven rain, when she pulled the door to and hung her cloak over a drying rack.

With hands that had grown quick and sure, she laid a cooking fire. Soon Samuel would be home. He would appreciate the hot savory pie made from ground venison, the pickled apples....

There was comfort in the routine of preparing a meal as she mulled over the situation. There was a new tension in Samuel that she could not explain, and she had to admit it made her uneasy.

She knew the dam project had been initiated to regulate the flow of timber through the lower Aroostook River and so alleviate pressure at log booms on the Saint John. It had been and still was being bitterly opposed by some of the timber cutters, who saw the sorting and holding of logs this side of the border as a threat to their livelihood.

There'd been a series of aggravations—sabotaged log drives, delays in sorting, confiscations—that led to violence. When Morgan's boom was busted for a second time, Samuel had set a watch at the dam site. Hitherto, Sagamore had made no move, but everybody in the district knew he was biding his time. The question was not if, but when.

A door banged. There was a squishing of wet boots across the drawing room, and a very wet and very tired-looking Samuel walked into the kitchen. He rubbed his head. "Where did you get *that* thing?"

Caitlin looked at the hanging basket that Samuel had walked into. "Winter Moon made it for me, Li Foo filled it with soil and plants, Silas screwed a hook into the ceiling, and Moses hung it on that little piece of chain." She grinned. "They all had boils that needed lancing."

Samuel poured some water into a basin. Dropping his galluses over his shoulders, he stripped off his bedraggled shirt and began to wash himself in the scalding water. He rubbed the copper-red hair that crisped in short curls over his chest.

"Sorry I'm late. Water levels are rising, and I wanted to complete the ditch line before the night watch took over."

Caitlin felt a stab of fear. She tossed her head, angry with herself. A bit of flour sprayed across her skirt. With the back of her arm, she brushed it off. She measured lard out into a big blue mixing bowl, quickly cutting it into the flour. "The dam's almost finished. Surely you can drop the night guard now?"

"Don't want anyone to think they can jump the dam. Sagamore's given us fair warning."

"Good of him to give you a warning." Caitlin pushed angrily on the dough. "Proves he's not just an obstructionist trying to hold back progress for his own selfish ends."

Samuel shrugged, grabbed a towel off the drying rack, threw it over his head and began to rub his hair dry. "Don't let his charm fool you. He'll maybe hide behind some young hothead. That's the way the devil does business." His voice came out muffled.

The fire crackled in the grate, the logs moving against each other like uneasy lovers. Caitlin covered the dough with a cloth and set the bread to rise. "He'll get his just deserts. When he needs a doctor, the trade-off for medical help will arise. It'll happen one day—just you wait and see!"

Samuel sensed, rather than saw, her ironic smile. Loggers were coming with all sorts of minor complains—boils, headaches, ingrown toenails. In payment, they left some little thing to make her life more comfortable—a leg of ham, a bowl of blueberries, a dozen eggs, some trout…and now a bloody hanging plant.

A gust of wind blew down the chimney, and a plume of smoke bellowed under the rim of the fireplace and wafted gently toward the ceiling, filling the air with the fragrant scent of burning pine.

"Come on, Samuel, sit down." Caitlin took the towel and handed him a clean shirt. Green light came from inside her eyes, the fragrance of honeysuckle from her hair. The lamplight in her hair was like gold thread glinting in a coal mine.

Samuel sat on the edge of the chair and pulled her to stand between his legs. She placed a calm, warm hand on his wrist, so lightly that it seemed her palm merely lay upon the fine golden hairs of his arm. He felt his body tighten at the touch.

"It's not as bad as you think. There's a wind sprung up. It'll blow the rain away. Who knows? It might blow some sense into Henry's head. Life's like that." She teased, moving her body toward him, nestling.

She raised her arms and slid them round his neck. Her night-black hair swung in a heavy arc away from her cheek. Her lips were so curving, so close, so warm. Utterly desirable.

It's an ill wind— The foolish phrase ran in his mind, and he stopped himself. He felt the sure, heavy warmth begin to fill his loins. He sought her mouth, and she opened it to him.

He shook his head, still faintly disbelieving of the lucky chance that had put the wrong name on his marriage proposal. "A man doesn't prove himself in one day or one night, it's the years that show the truth." He could hear his own breathing now, harsh and ragged.

Caitlin groaned, her only answer.

A long cloud had been building; it lowered, darkened, emptied sudden rain. Samuel crouched in his saddle, water spilling from the broad brim of his hat.

He started down the slope into the light timber and forded the creek. It was swollen, already carrying away the shower's runoff to Presque Isle Stream. The dam had been finished without mishap, and without being blown up, which had come as a surprise. There'd been a time he thought Sagamore was going to do just that.

Sagamore's opposition to the dam did not deter him. Threats did not disturb him. He simply set his jaw and pushed forward with the project. But he did not deceive himself. He stayed alert. At any hour, the opposition might flare out in explosive action.

Samuel's thoughts drifted easily, slowly, as he headed

his mount toward the depot. He was very pleased at the precautions he had taken, especially now that Ned Flaherty was on their side. Ned was hotheaded—you had to watch him.

Caitlin had been right. No man likes to beggar his pride. And Sagamore was a proud man. A proud man did not give up because of blows dealt to him from the outside. The surrender had to come from within.

Samuel rode along thinking of her. There was a richness to what they were together that he had never anticipated....

The images flashed across Samuel's mind before he could stop them, of Caitlin and himself sprawled on a rug before the fireplace, her naked body straddling his, her fluid hands savoring the heat of his body, exploring every inch of him. Using the pads of her thumbs, then her tongue, stroking him gently in a slow, circular motion.

A crooked cluster of pumpkin pine hugged the black ribbon of the wagon road. The wind seemed much colder, its gusts stronger. As the rain eased, the light changed and the shadows moved, like clouds changing their shapes before the wind. There was something unexpectedly seductive about clouds.

Thinking of that word... Time slipped wildly by him, turned treacherous. Caitlin's warm tongue licking the skin around his nipples, tasting the salt from dried perspiration before moving lower... Everything came back to him, so very clearly—

Silken-soft lips licked under his arms, at the base of his belly, where the fine red hair thickened and spread. Now her nimble fingers touched him as lightly as a single feather and she exhaled her warm breath along the sensitive skin of his manhood.

Ripples of pleasure surged through him. He arched his hips upward as the core of him begged her, pleaded to be held, touched, and at last she gripped him gently with both hands, bringing her mouth down to engulf him. She licked, slowly, circling the head of his full hardness until his pelvis lurched and spasms racked his frame.

Time slipped again. Now she straddled him, the sleek sinews of her body pulling him deep into her, devouring him with her heat, the sensation unlike anything he had ever known before, a fulfillment, a totality. He raised himself up, burying his face in her neck, breathing her, licking her skin, seeking her lips.

He listened to her moans, her breath exploding in little panting bursts on his cheek as he lifted her up on the arch of his own body, penetrating her, enslaving her, as in a single movement he rolled on top of her without breaking their connection. Their tongues entwined, as his body thrust into hers time and time again....

It was not quite dark. Ahead, he saw, the rise along the lip of the cliff had broken loose. Great boulders had tumbled down, along with mud and grass, to block the roadway. He could discern the wet glimmer of the road, and far down upon it a blur that might have been a rider mounted on a pale horse.

Samuel dismounted. As he paused, a shadow flickered. He started to lead his horse round the debris...and the shadow erupted into whirlwind motion.

Realizing he was about to be ambushed, Samuel feinted left, hurled himself bodily to the right. A sharp pain shot through his forearm. A heavy body crashed through the bushes. At the same time, the sound of running feet. Something struck him on the shoulder blade with a blow that felt like a hammer strike. His back erupted into agony, and he fell to his knees.

For a long moment, he lay perfectly still. The heavy scent of moss and leaves drowned him. Dampness seeped into his palms and through the cloth of his trousers at his knees. His mind refused to work. It was as if he were stuck in tar.

In the blackness, there was a stirring. The sounds of

movement, furtive and stealthy. Ignoring his pain, Samuel pushed off the ground and sprang to his feet. His assailant had already struck twice. If he allowed another blow to land, it might be the last he ever felt.

Before he had moved, a deafening sound leaped into the night. At the same moment, his vision became one searing flame of white. With one swift motion, the shadow shifted. Something hard caught him in the side. The sharp clack of teeth cracked through Samuel's head, and he felt the lattice of pain lance up into his neck. He seemed to lose all energy. His shoulders slumped heavily, and his forehead rested against a knee.

Rain spattered the sitting room windows, a gray sameness that had begun to seem natural. Caitlin felt sorry for Samuel, who was out in that. Sorry, and worried for his safety. He didn't seem to understand what it was like for a woman to stay at home and wait, not knowing what danger awaited her man.

By late afternoon, she felt a return of tension, a knot of worry in her stomach. Her sure intuition told her Samuel was in trouble. On her fifth trip to the front door, she pulled down a duck gun from the wall rack and ran down to the stables.

The mare picked her way daintily along the tote road. It was nearly dark. Somewhere a night bird was calling. The rain had passed, but the intolerable wetness still clung to everything. A cool wind, not hard but persistent, flowed from the north. A long strand of hair had become loose. It whipped against her throat, but she ignored it.

Up ahead, Caitlin saw a narrow defile, as if a great knife had slashed into the rock face of the mountain. Suddenly there rose a brief clamor. She stifled a scream. What was happening?

A horse whinnied softly. In the dead silence that followed, she heard a thud, a panted oath, sounds of a struggle.

"Samuel?" Then, more urgently, "Samuel!" Fear lent a shrill note to her voice. Throwing the fowling piece to her shoulder, she pulled the trigger, and the shotgun filled the air with noise, flame and smoke. Like an invisible giant, the recoil sent her reeling sideways, and at the same instant the mare reared wildly. She dropped the fowling piece in favor of both reins. Somehow she had discharged both barrels at once.

Samuel got his breath back. He was lying by the side of the road, half-stunned, when he heard a hoarse shout, flailing, a clatter behind him, a curse, a startled neigh. He raised his head slightly. Something loomed over him so suddenly that he recoiled. It lived and breathed, a monstrous form straight from hell.

Silhouettes, shapes and shadows, grotesque, sharply defined into a sudden vivid image of Caitlin, gray cloak flapping like huge wings as she hauled on the reins of the rearing horse. Then the horse, hooves clattering, breath steaming, was at his side.

Caitlin threw herself down beside him. Soft hands stroked his chest, and he was cradled in a warm lap, drawing strength from the contact. The familiar smell of Caitlin's perfume filled his nostrils.

"Samuel, can you hear me?" Her hair fell about her shoulders, a dark, dusty cloud. It blended with the shadows, so that he saw only her face. Her eyes seemed to glow, even in the shadows of dusk.

Samuel nodded, winced. He took a deep breath, let it go slowly.

Caitlin shot him a wild glance. "Who did this to you? Did you see a face?" Her voice was flat, as if she were swept by a fear so powerful it choked her.

There was a great deal of activity around him, just outside his field of vision. Cool hands touched his forehead. Exploring fingers passed over his sprawled limbs. A touch on his arm. A soft exclamation.

Samuel took a breath and, in that instant, felt a searing pain. He twisted his head, saw the hilt of a small dagger protruding from his shoulder, tore it out, cursing, heard dimly the clatter as he dropped it.

Caitlin was beside him. "Does it hurt much?"

"Some. Know I've got an arm." He scowled in confusion. "What sainted breeze brought you here?"

She gave him a wan smile. "Please don't be angry. I couldn't wait on my own."

Best to ignore that, he decided. "I'm not angry," he said around a thick tongue. It must be shock. His heart was pounding like a wild thing caught in a trap. "Lucky for me you came along 'n' scared the beggar off."

"Listen!" Her head swung toward him. There was a new brittleness in her voice, like splintered glass. Tangled locks of hair framed her face. He was surprised at how pale she had become.

Samuel was silent, his breathing harsh and irregular. The rumble of wagon wheels going over disintegrated quartz drifted to them. Music to his ears.

"LeFeuvre," he said, in something resembling a normal tone of voice. He breathed deeply to regain his wind. "He'll take us home, Cat."

Twenty minutes later, they were back at the depot and Samuel was limping into the surgery. While Caitlin made her preparations, he sat on the table, with his shirt off, and leaned on one hand, his eyes closed. He had a ridiculous feeling that if he let go of himself he would faint.

Caitlin bent over him, working on the wound. "Come, let's get this done with." Her voice was soft as the night wind. Even now, when he was safe, there was still a tendency to speak softly.

"How far did it go in?"

"To the hilt. Lucky it was but a wee thing, and not a great bowie knife." Blood leaked from the wound to trickle down his back. Carefully she probed and poked and cleaned and moved things.

Samuel said nothing. What was there to say?

"Reckon there's been some queer happenings around here lately. It might be time for the women to take action." She began to stitch the wound closed, having already cleaned it thoroughly.

He kept his body very still. "Don't get any ideas of meddling, Cat."

"Keep still." Her fingers closed down on the corded muscles of his upper arm. He went rigid. She finished the stitching. His eyes opened as she began to apply a dressing over it.

Caitlin went over and put a kettle on the hob. A word was exhaled, farther away, so that he heard the breath but not the meaning. It took no great intelligence to know that she was mad as a hornet. While the water began to heat, she busied herself with her equipment.

Lifting his head upward to ease the ache at the back of his neck, he watched her. Followed her as she unscrewed bottles, jars, flagons, flasks, pouring first this liquid, then that powder, into the pot on the hob. Out of one container, she produced a solid object from which she cut a piece and, using a mortar and pestle, ground it up. That, too, went into the pot. Her face was wearing a smooth, serene look.

Samuel frowned. It amazed him, the transformation of Caitlin from tempestuous woman to matter-of-fact medical practitioner. She seemed out of place in this role of physician, attending to an emergency in a cool, calm manner, every inch the imperturbable doctor that Samuel's father still was. Was the incongruity of it, he asked himself, because of her beauty? Because she was a woman?

Caitlin went to the hearth, lifted the steaming teakettle from the iron hook and poured water into the pot. She worked rapidly. There was peace in simply watching the quickness of her movement, in concentrating thoroughly on each lift of the arm and bend of the back.

"So much trouble for a harmless little cut," he said, wincing at the telltale hoarseness in his voice.

His words did not soothe Caitlin as intended. They incensed her. She glared at him, her eyes were very green. "Harmless! It was getting down to the real thing when I happened by."

Samuel stared at the ceiling and said nothing. What was bothering him? It was merely a fight. *Merely?*

It wasn't until after she had obliged him to down the foul-tasting concoction that he realized that the serenity was a mask. Her eyes had shadows under them, and her smile was strained.

He smoothed back the silky hair at her temples. There were little hollows there, delicately scooped to the bone. He ran his thumbs along her cheeks, feeling the sharpness of the bones beneath the perfect skin. Her whole body was taut, even though he barely touched her. Fear did that to a body.

There was only one remedy.

He twisted, then, oblivious of his pains, and pulled her onto his lap. His hands were lost in the night forest of her hair, clung there.

"How fast can you remove that gown?" he said, his voice sounding a trifle breathless.

"Faster than you can remove your trousers."

"Hold up! Stop everything!"

Wood chips whirring and spinning, Samuel was forced to shield his eyes; it was easy to be blinded by dust and debris.

Willy Carson doffed his battered hat. His hair was mouse-colored and shot with gray. The land agent had a harassed and anxious look, as well he might, Samuel

thought, for he was helpless to prevent or control the dis-
orders that so gravely afflicted the district.

"Mighty nice to have you here, Carson, what with us all
wondering how things are going to break," Samuel said,
without any palaver.

"Break?" Carson asked cautiously.

"Seems like it can't go on like it is."

"Buckmore tells me there's been a bit of argumentation
between Canadian and Yankee timbermen over who owns
what along the border. He says there's talk of war. Came
to tell you, we won't countenance that kind of debate, nor
any lawbreaking."

"We're not trying to break the law, Carson—we're
merely seeking to hold the borderline, to protect Maine's
right to the timber."

"That's not how Buckmore sees it—and he's got the ear
of people in Washington."

Samuel had heard several conflicting versions of recent
trespass operations and illegal timber being rafted down-
river, but was not convinced that the surveyor George
Buckmore's account was the most accurate.

"Then I suggest that the wisest course would be to bring
in additional agents, from outside the district, to your as-
sistance." Samuel hardened his voice intentionally. He suspected he looked as furious as he felt, for he had no will
to hide it. Did these government bureaucrats actually know
what they were about?

"Perhaps I present things a bit awkwardly," Carson said
stiffly. "I assure you, the government is serious. Webster
is negotiating with Ashburton, and we don't want to make
an enemy of the British."

Samuel was uneasy, and easily rattled. He was tired, after
a passion-filled night with his wife and a nerve-racking argument this morning with his doctor. His arm and back still
hurt, and now his head ached. Caitlin was right. He should
have stayed in bed.

* * *

The sharp wind scoured Caitlin's cheeks, and the sky was so full of clouds it looked like a down comforter. The stream was silver-gray, set in dark gray bluffs and fog.

Caitlin ran, as she always did, past Li Foo's garden. Up the rickety steps to the Chinaman's house, where she was always welcome, where, after the first time she showed up unannounced, he had never asked the reason why she had come.

"Li Foo, if there were any choice of fruit for dessert...Samuel would enjoy something special for his birthday."

Li Foo had a most conspiratorial look. "I do think there's some fine preserved cherries, which Master Samuel very much favors. Li Foo put by several extra jars for just such an occasion."

Cherries. Out of season. Splendid.

"Li Foo, you're incredible."

The old man's face disappeared into a mass of wrinkles. "You will make me vain with your kind words, little missy."

"It is only the young and foolish who are vain, Li Foo."

"True, little missy. When Li Foo was young, he exulted in what he thought he was. Even the emperor was pleased to call Li Foo friend, to flatter a young man with a talent for both politics and business. When Li Foo fell from favor, he was forced to flee his native land. In death he will wander for all eternity with the lost souls."

"Li Foo, whatever you are, whatever you become, I cannot believe that God would be so cruel as to exclude you from heaven."

They wandered into the orchard, a dozen or so trees twice the height of Caitlin, a mixture of apple, pear and plum, and Li Foo carefully inspected each one.

"Li Foo is a Buddhist. For him, there is no heaven, no hell."

"Then what?"

"A beginning," Li Foo said. "All things die. Death is not to be feared, little missy."

He said it with such openness that Caitlin was taken aback. "Your death means nothing to you?"

"Oh, yes," he said, "it means something. But it is insignificant compared to the rivers that flow to the sea."

"Meaning?"

"Those who are able to cease action, as well as initiate it, will long endure. All others are doomed to die young."

Caitlin looked at the old Chinaman. You never knew with Li Foo, that was the problem. He was often so subtle, so obscure, that it was easy to miss what he was trying to say.

Li Foo studied a small patch of green mold on the trunk of one of the plum trees. "This old man is far from home. When the time comes for Li Foo to join his ancestors, will little missy say the words?"

"What words are they, Li Foo?"

Something passed across his face. "The ones that must be said if the spirit of Li Foo is to ride the winds back to China."

"What will become of your spirit if the prayers are not said?"

Li Foo settled himself like a bird upon its perch. "Li Foo will wander with the soulless forever, a shadow, a thing of air and darkness.... It torments him even to think of it."

Caitlin nodded gravely. "I will say the words."

Whereupon, for the rest of the afternoon, Caitlin devoted herself to learning the strange and foreign words, while Li Foo helped her prepare the cherries. They set to work, a bottle apiece, carefully removing the cherries from the spirit-sweet preserving liquid with a long spoon so that the fruit was not bruised.

The aroma of the reddish gold juice filled Caitlin's nose.

She put out her tongue and licked at the cherry on her spoon. It was cool and deliciously tart. She broke into a fit of coughing.

"Lady in Heaven! It's sweeter than Mulligan's apple brandy."

Li Foo licked his spoon. "Delicious."

"How do you say 'delicious' in Chinese, Li Foo?" She popped the cherry into the bowl, licked the liqueur-coated spoon, felt the sweet sticky liquid unroll its carpet of warmth along her throat and into her stomach.

"Little missy must roll her tongue, like so." Li Foo took up a whole spoonful and swallowed.

Their eyes met, and they began to giggle. It became a game. By the time they had removed all the fruit, Caitlin's hands and lips were sticky and she could count to one hundred in Chinese. Her accent was perfectly atrocious, but Li Foo found this absolutely hilarious.

"Samuel will consider this the best birthday present ever," she said with a sense of satisfaction. Her words sounded very slurred.

Li Foo was highly amused, very pleased with their solution, and he bowed twice before leaving. Samuel was not amused.

"Holy saints, Caitlin, look at you." He called her by her Christian name only when he was angry with her. "You're drunk!"

Caitlin felt light-headed, as if she could float away on a moonbeam. "No, not drunk. Cherries from Li Foo for your birthday. Couldn't waste the juice." She waved an arm expansively. From somewhere she produced a metal cup, which she blew into perfunctorily before filling it halfway. "Sit."

Samuel had to set his cup down in order to clear away the bowl of cherries and jars of leftover liqueur. He hesitated with them in his hands.

"Oh, drop them anywhere." Caitlin leaned forward, elbows on the table, fingers steepled. The room seemed to spin around her. She put her forefinger against her lips, thought for a moment.

"That night when you kissed me." She gave a little hic. "On my sixteenth birthday, you know, you could have gone on—" she told him.

Samuel made a small noise, almost a hiss. He sat very straight, swirled the liqueur slowly and said nothing.

Caitlin licked her sticky fingers, and unbound her hair so that it fell thick as a forest, long, swirling about her pale face. Traces of cherry brandy glistened in her hair, iridescent and unreal.

She stood up, came to stand behind him, began to massage the thick muscles of his upper arms. His back arched slightly as he felt her breasts press into him as she leaned over.

"Ten years—what a waste of time," she whispered in his ear. Through the fabric of her clothes, the contours of her breasts and thighs, at once soft and firm, defined themselves against him.

The scent of her hair, of woman, of sweet cherry brandy, filled his nostrils. His whole body responded. Samuel had the distinct feeling that he was losing control of the situation.

"Of course, there was the devil to pay from Papa as it was." Caitlin moved her breasts from side to side against his back. Her breath ran in warm puffs against the side of his face. "He never did believe I tried to seduce you." Her fingers moved down along his spine, slowly circling. The stroking became rhythmic.

"Now, just imagine if I had." Her fingers moved lower. Strands of her unbound hair brushed lightly against him in concert with her hands. Her fingers made wider circles on his body, the pressure more insistent. "Would you have counted your blessings—or accused me of meddling?"

Her lips touched his ear, the corner of his mouth. They

were moist, cherry-sweet. She made a little sucking sound.
Blood pounding, Samuel sank into the kiss, gathering her
close.

"Scheming witch—meddle all you like."

Chapter Fifteen

Rain or sun, the work went on. Timber felling continued apace, the gangs working at top speed. Up in the near woods, the whine of the saws and the sounds of chopping kept a measured beat. The smell of an ax grinding turned the air sharp. Caitlin could hear, faint and far-off, the voices of the felling gangs crying, "Tim-berrrr."

It was midmorning. Samuel was out back, chopping wood. When she protested, he had said he needed the exercise, since she wouldn't yet permit him to join the sawyers, and he was blessed if he was going to stay housebound.

She had busied herself about the house, deliberately seeking a multitude of little tasks to occupy her hands and her mind. Since Samuel's attack, she had been filled with a restless energy from which there was no surcease.

Caitlin found it in her heart to envy the sturdy loggers. They could forget their troubles in the strain of action. She said as much to Raoul LeFeuvre, who was standing, hands resting on his hips, watching the bank where, a little beyond the blockhouse, a big mechanical device spooled up the cable that brought string after string of logs down to the stream.

Curling his fingers into fists, Raoul shrugged one shoulder and replied. "This is a primitive country, ma'am, where passions run high and license abounds. What I can't understand is why anyone would want to bring trouble on himself."

Caitlin's stomach gave a tiny flip. "What do you mean, Raoul? What are you hinting at?" she asked breathlessly.

Raoul's eyes turned to her slowly. His lips compressed. "Time to chew the rag a bit. From what you're whinin' about, I don't reckon you got any engagements you have to keep immediate."

There was a drawling note of amused contempt in his voice that made Caitlin grimace. She stamped her foot in exasperation. "Talk so I can understand you."

LeFeuvre's lips widened into a thin smile. "Don't say I agree with this notion, ma'am, but the lads have voted that you accompany the team to Quaggy Joe. Heavens knows, this weather is an accident waiting to happen, and close medical help would be handy, even if it is a woman what gives it."

It did not sound precisely like a challenge, but Caitlin became aware all at once that Raoul LeFeuvre had paused and was looking at her. "Certainly," she said, hoping there was no betraying quaver in her voice.

"Good," said the teamster. "Tell Sam what you're about, get your kit, be up on that mare in five minutes, don't complain when the goin' gets tough—and don't get in the way of a falling tree."

Samuel was in front of the shed, splitting wood. The light cruiser's ax went high in the air, with his powerful body arched like a bow, feet spread wide. The ax flashed in the low winter sun like a mirror tilted, and the halved pieces of wood spilled off the block.

Caitlin skipped in front of him. "Raoul has invited me to join the team! He wants an outdoor surgery." She turned to leave.

"No." The word fell like a gauntlet between them.

Caitlin halted as if she had been pulled short by a rope. She did not move at all for a moment, then she spun back. "Samuel, let me go."

Samuel's eyes bored into her, so intense that, for a moment, she felt as though a weight were pressing against her heart. The silence stretched out until it became painful.

"All right—but I'm coming, too." He flexed his shoulder. "I want to check out the pulp cutters' pile. Liam says the cutters are bunching the logs too haphazardly. I need to find out why."

Caitlin grinned. "Moses says it's to make the bucking-board figures look good." She flew into the house to get ready before Samuel could change his mind.

A narrow fringe of brush and scrubby timber separated the temporary mess camp from the actual work. Caitlin killed time with partial success until noon. Several times she was startled by the prolonged series of sharp cracks that heralded the thunderous crash of a falling tree.

She had just decided that she was going to go into the woods that afternoon and watch the men work when, covered with grease and sawdust, Silas Crane arrived at her makeshift surgery. He was clearly shaken.

"There's been an accident."

"Accident? What kind of accident?"

He rubbed his forehead. "I don't know. Accidents are a way of life among the trees, ma'am. It's a very accidental profession."

On her way to the scene Caitlin mentally went through her satchel, checking off each item. Bandages. Scalpels. Needles. Thread. Raw alcohol.

The whine of the saws had died away, and the donkey engine had stopped. There was no shouting now, and the cessation of noise was quite shocking. A flat wagon lay on its side, its load scattered. It appeared to Caitlin's inexpert eye that the wagon coupling was connected by driving belts to the hoisting engine, and that the loss of weight on its rear end had sent the vehicle toppling off the track.

"What happened?"

Raoul said one instant it had been there, howling as if in frustration. The next, the empty air had been singing in its place. It seemed the horse had stumbled. Perhaps its load had been too heavy or its foot had slipped on a patch of mud. It didn't really matter, that part. What mattered was that a thousand pounds of deadweight had come crashing down on Tom Barsby.

Caitlin knelt beside the huddled mass and looked at the battered remains of what a few moments earlier had been a man's face, quick with life. No second glance was necessary to see that he was beyond help. Tom Barsby had been a harmless fellow of many quips and jests, a single man without kith or kin. She straightened the twisted body, and covered the face with a square of linen cloth.

Raoul gave orders for the men to return to work. Caitlin retreated a little and sat down on a root. Off to one side she saw the tree fellers climb up on their springboards. Presently arose the ringing whine of the thin steel blade.

No matter, she thought, that death came to one, that injury might hover near. The work went on apace, like action on a battlefield. Farther away could be heard the chuck of axes where the swampers attacked a fallen tree. The rhythmic hacking soothed Caitlin's shattered sensibilities. It was such an ordinary sound.

It was not good, and Caitlin knew that it was not going to get any better. The rain had mizzled all day, dampening what it didn't outright soak. It stippled the muddy puddles, drummed against the sides of the wagons, dimpling the oiled tarpaulin that covered them. The wind seemed stronger. Gusts whipped the horses' manes and tails.

"I haven't got a lick of sense. Why did I ever complain about being left behind?" Caitlin sighed, realizing how achingly tired she was. The barest gleam of light tinged the horizon. Soon it would be dark.

Evening had settled over the mountains when the wagons began their homeward journey, creaking and squelching through patches of mud and crushed pine needles. The wind grew stronger. Lightning crackled and danced all around them until the air smelled like burning zinc, and the rain dashed so hard on the ground that it set up a fine spray that covered the banks of the stream like mist.

There was a roll of thunder so loud that Caitlin felt as if the sky were going to collapse on top of her. A gust of wind, harder than the rest, hurled rain across the stream. She heard a clatter behind her, a curse, a startled neigh. As she turned, she had a sudden, vivid image of men, horses and wagons, black against the lightning flash.

Samuel rode up. Rain was pelting against his back, plastering his shirt against his muscular body. He dismounted, left Livingstone and Crane to bring the horses and wagons and set out with LeFeuvre, Caitlin hard on their heels.

"We've got to get across before the stream floods!" he shouted, and moved ahead, disappearing into black nothingness.

The riverbanks here were flat and muddy. The road builders had been laying down retainers of intertwined saplings to prevent the soil washing away and clogging up the river, which was already brown with silt. Lightning crackled all around them, and rain sheeted across the path ahead, so that Caitlin found it impossible to see where she was walking. The deluge had turned day into the pitchblackness of a well.

Fighting the wind, her eyes shielded by her hand from the rain, she followed the patch of color in front of her—a logger's red shirt. She slipped, went down on one knee, scraping it hard against a stone outcrop. Her skirt dragged in the mud.

Raoul LeFeuvre led the way down the slippery bank to

the edge of the river, his boot heels sliding in the mud. He peered into the darkness, turned, and yelled, "Run for it! If we go now, we can make it!"

Caitlin climbed onto the woven saplings and, in trying to scramble down the embankment, slipped and fell face-first in the mud. As she struggled to her feet, she scraped her hands.

"Move, lady!"

She said a word she'd heard one of the loggers use when he didn't know she was listening. She didn't know what it meant, but it sounded just right for the occasion.

Another flash of lightning that lit the sky allowed Caitlin a second's worth of clear viewing. Raoul's hat was drooping with rainwater, and his beard had formed a bedraggled point, but Caitlin could see the look of respect on his face.

After taking a deep breath for courage, she shouted, for the elements were now quite loud, "No one in their right mind would cross that!"

"Truth is, takes a set of balls even to *decide* to go." A crack of thunder underlined Raoul's words. He grinned, and hawked and spat. "If you can't keep up, lady, you'll have to stay here. Understand?"

Caitlin wasn't about to remain where she was. Fighting the wind for control of her hair, which had slipped out of its coil and was flapping about her head like a wild banshee, she nodded.

"I suppose you're thinking that this hulking great creature would be just the kind of gallant who would carry you across the brink?"

Caitlin turned around and stared at LeFeuvre for nearly half a minute without saying a word. Then she hastily pushed the hair away from her forehead with the back of her hand.

"You mean you're offering?" she asked, as if the idea had never even occurred to her. Sleet whipped her face. "I hope very much that this isn't a practical joke. I don't like getting my feet wet."

Raoul laughed, a short, sharp, shout of a laugh, and then leaned forward to slap her on the shoulder. The blow nearly felled her.

"You've courage, lady, and a sense of humor to go with it."

Samuel's deep voice came out of the clotted, inky darkness. "I'll teach you to lay hands on a woman, LeFeuvre. I'll knock your block off!" Lightning came again. Samuel had hold of the lumberman's shoulder with one hand, the other was drawn back in a fist. His expression was murderous.

"Idiot! Raoul was trying to help me!" Caitlin caught at his arm and shouted up into his rain-lashed face, before the dark again hid him. "Come on, we're wasting precious time!"

Samuel didn't spend time arguing with her. At the next lightning streak, he grabbed her around the waist and threw her over his own shoulder. Seconds later, he was half running, half sliding down the slippery slope. Terrified of falling, Caitlin clutched his torso, closing her eyes, thankful that it wasn't her modest sister who was forced to undergo this humiliation. She felt the complex coordination of muscle, bone and tendon as her husband carried her down the bank.

Caitlin felt the rushing of the wind and rain in her face and hair. She opened her eyes and almost passed out as a wave of vertigo swept over her. The world rushed by in a blur of brown and green and black. "Samuel!" she shrieked. "Unhand me!"

Samuel shifted his grip and continued carrying her. He had the men moving now; momentum itself was a tonic.

"Put me down!" She was struggling very hard, all curves and tension. An elbow jammed into his solar plexus. She was a handful, he thought as he waded into the turgid stream—and he was the only one allowed to have his hands full of her.

He'd waded across the swollen stream. His boots were seeking purchase on the crusty slope of the bank. It was getting difficult now. The water was lapping his thighs. She kicked him in the groin.

He dropped her. There was a great splashing.

"Samuel! I can't swim!"

"Invention is the mother of necessity." Samuel held his voice expressionless. "Seems to me if you put your dainty little foot on the ground, you can stand up and walk. It goes like this." Samuel lurched a step backward, as if the muddy ground had given way beneath his weight.

"Stop making fun of me!" She scrambled up on all fours. Rain danced off her face, flew through her hair, as if both were part of the wind. Her lips opened. "I can't stand this!" she cried, panting like a hunted animal. "It's beyond endurance!"

She took a step toward him and checked herself, rocking on her feet. Samuel crossed back in two strides, seized her shoulders and held her upright with his superior strength.

"Caitlin, I only wanted to—"

"I don't care what you wanted!" She began to retreat up the sloping bank. She stumbled. "I don't know how I ever could have cared!"

He pulled her back. She was shivering uncontrollably. *I'm in serious trouble,* he thought. "What d'you want me to say to that?"

"If it hadn't been for you wanting to cut timber in this weather," she cried wildly, "that poor man'd be alive today!"

Samuel knew that. He wasn't stupid. He looked down at Caitlin. It was very dark, and the rain swept away what clear vision there might be. "It's not a comfortable business to be in."

"It's simply not safe here. What if it was you? What if

I was pregnant? What are the chances of my going back to Cornwall?''

Samuel discounted that as a threat. That wasn't the Caitlin he knew—the one who'd loosed both barrels of a shotgun in defense of her husband. Still, it didn't sound encouraging. Perhaps a dose of bluntness would help.

''I'm sure the same considerations that brought you here still apply.''

''What considerations?''

''Why, your undying love for me, for one thing.''

''Huh!''

''I suppose you could go back, if you want to.''

''And leave you here to chase anything in a skirt?''

Samuel grinned. She was working herself into a fine state. It did not surprise him to see his men staring at her in openmouthed wonder. He felt inclined to do the same. She was far angrier than he could have imagined. He decided to pursue the matter, hoping to get her stirred up enough to forget the discomfort and danger.

''Reason enough to stay. I trust you are quite finished, or are you merely out of breath for the moment?''

A clap of thunder, darkness, and then a spit of lurid lightning illuminated her face. She snatched her arm away, and the sodden seam of her sleeve gave way, exposing an expanse of pale flesh. ''Now look what you've made me do! Just like a man. Get me out of here.''

They were on solid ground now. Time to call for peace. ''Forgive my impropriety,'' he said. ''I'm sorry for everything.''

''That is not the point. *Said* and *did* aren't even brothers, Samuel. Forgive my mistaken notion that this was a civilized country. At the very least, we're polite in Cornwall. We don't act like bandits or shoot people over philosophical contracts. Now, if you—''

By the time Caitlin had ceased her lecture, they were almost home, and Samuel suspected that both the weather

and his wife's tongue had done their worst for the time
being. The rain must have stopped for some while before
he even noticed, there was so much water dripping and
blowing from the leaves generally above them.

It was a hard journey. The going was rough and ex-
hausting. A trip that normally took scarcely two hours
stretched out to an interminable five, and it was half past
ten by the time they came within sight of the depot.

Samuel came around to Caitlin and caught her by the
waist, swinging her down, holding her. One of his hands
rested at the small of her back, pressing her into him,
against his chest and his hips. He bent his head and kissed
her lightly on the lips.

"Well, you'll be glad to be home safely, at any rate,
even if you do resemble a drowned rat." As a joke, it fell
flat. Caitlin wedged her hands in between them and shoved
him away.

"You tend the horses. I'll go put on the kettle."

Don't bother me, he decided that meant. Unharnessing
the horses in the grainy half-light, Samuel did not think he
had ever been so thankful a day was over. Tom Barsby was
dead, he'd alienated LeFeuvre, and now he'd offended
Caitlin. He hadn't done at all well today.

With the end of the storm came a bright, cold sky and
frost—a nipping cold that laid a thin scum of ice on every
patch of still water. A line of geese, black against the white
of the wintry sky, made their way toward their winter feed-
ing grounds. They appeared to have come from the shadows of the mountain range in the near distance. As she
pegged the washing, Caitlin could hear their honking.

As if nature wanted to show off her wares, that was the
winter of big snow. Early in December, Samuel sent out a
big boom of logs with a hired tugboat that was no more
than out of Presque Isle Stream before the snow came. The

sleety blasts of a cold afternoon turned to great moist flakes by dark, eddying thick out of a windless night.

At daybreak, it lay a foot deep, and it was still snowing hard, with no surcease. For three days the snow fell without ceasing, blotting out hills and sky, tracks and road, all but the nearer buildings, a swirling mass of featureless whiteness. The white, feathery stuff piled up and piled up, hour upon hour and day after day, as if the deluge had come again. It stood at the blockhouse eaves before the break came.

Necessarily, all work ceased. The tote wagons were shapeless mounds of white, all the lines and gear buried deep. A man could neither walk on that yielding mass nor wallow through it.

Samuel decided he'd better attend to his mail, which had arrived a week ago. Several catalogs, a few bills and one personal letter. He opened it with his thumbnail. Shadows and light played over the paper. Holding it up to the light, he could almost see through it. Almost.

He walked over to the window to read it, not, he thought, because he needed the light, for the candles cast a golden glow. His mind was clouded with memories. The sea. Waves crashing. The scent of salt. Gulls wheeling. Calling. A girl's laughter, light and liquid. Her eyes so full of promise.

Samuel flipped the page, figured out he'd stopped reading the second time somewhere in the middle of it, and turned it back, with a dogged effort to concentrate on the text, and to make sense out of the cramped handwriting. A quick pang of guilt struck him like a sharp slap to the face, and he swore under his breath.

"Is something wrong, Samuel?"

He folded the letter. "It's from Caitryn."

Caitlin had to ask. "May I see the letter, Samuel?" He got that funny little half smile on his face that meant she was meddling again and should beware the consequences, but he said nothing. He simply crossed the room and handed it over.

She began to read aloud. "'Samuel, you are the only person in my life who has not lied to me at one time or another. When you said you loved me and would never forget me, I believed you. Grief passes, they say, and in the holiness and peace of the cloister, my childish ambitions and carnal desires are set to rest all the quicker for knowing you are wed to my sister.'"

But this was *Caitryn*. She recoiled from her own thoughts, shook herself and read on.

"'Caitlin loves you, too, and her need is greater than mine. In spite of her twists and turns, I trust Caitlin completely, and you should, too. She has a hard time containing her emotions and she hates having her will thwarted, but she won't let her passionate nature prejudice her dealings with you. Recognize this truth and you will deal well together.

"'Love has many faces, Samuel, and you are now truly my brother in every sense of the word. Perhaps you will be willing to undertake a commission. Please forgive Caitlin her trespasses, as she would forgive you yours. God bless you both. Love, Caitryn.'"

"God bless you, indeed," Caitlin muttered. She folded the parchment and tucked it back neatly into the envelope. "I had not thought..."

The words stuck in her throat when she saw the look upon Samuel's face, the effort he was making to hold himself from speaking. She pressed her hands to her mouth and shook her head. What was the meaning of this strange missive from her beloved sister, who had seemed so happy to join the convent?

There was a thick silence.

Samuel was not looking forward to the tongue-lashing he would receive. It took no great skill to see that he had married into an impossible situation, that the confrontation that was bound to come was of his own making. Mostly, he was angry with himself.

He felt Caitlin's hands close around his forearm, and heard her whisper, "You know, Caitryn was right about you. You're—"

"Caitryn!" Samuel heard himself cry with harsh, raging laughter, out of control now, hardly aware of what he was saying. "Holy saints! If I'd not been such a fool as to confuse your names, she'd have been my wife—not you."

There was a terrible, tense pause. "I don't believe it," Caitlin said in a low, tremulous voice. "Is that true?" She made a sharp, distressed gesture. "Is it true?" she repeated.

Samuel's eyes came back to Caitlin's and held there, fully. She stood unmoving. Her face was white and rigid. She stared at him out of eyes filled with green fire. She was trembling, but he could feel one final hawser, somewhere deep within her, refusing to let go.

He'd meant to hold his tongue, never to speak of his mistake. But he'd always been afraid it would happen. And now it had. "Cat, I'm sorry. I never meant for you to know."

"Really?"

Slowly. Take it slowly. That was what Caitryn would say. He winced internally. Why was he thinking of Caitryn right now? He raised a hand to his forehead and rubbed the crease that had appeared above his nose.

"All things considered, I believe we could both do worse than to pretend this never happened. I know you were not my first choice of bride, but you came, and it is true that I have learned to care for you."

Caitlin's eyebrows snapped together. She was looking at him, but not seeing him. "I understand. You love my sister. You look at me and think of her, always."

Very carefully, he said, "I wrote to a girl I had not seen in ten years. It did not matter that you were a bogus bride, that Caitryn had gone into the arms of the church. You came. You were willing.''

Caitlin opened her mouth, shut it again, and headed for the door, her face set.

Where did he *go* from here? He was invaded by a sense of utter hollowness, of all things toppling, crashing...

''Caitlin—wait...''

''There's nothing to explain.'' Her face was white, the green eyes were clouded. ''I understand all I need to.''

Inside Caitlin rested a hurt so great she knew of no way to ease it. She loved Samuel, yet wished she did not. That love caused her to be completely devastated by his confession, crushed by the discovery that he did not want her, had never wanted her.

It seemed like the end of all things. Destroyed: the memory and the fantasy and all the unspoken desire, like a bright sky-colored window breaking into hundreds of pealing pieces.

As she passed him, he put a hand on her arm. ''Please wait,'' he entreated her.

''I've always waited. I've waited for you too many times. Far too many.'' Unable to accept the truth—praying she'd heard him wrong—she raised her hands to the sides of her face, as if the action would keep all her foolish illusions captured within her. Yet a clear picture of falseness and betrayal sprang to a mind even more reluctant to accept the truth than her aching heart.

''Won't you even let me speak? Try to explain? Won't you—''

Caitlin shrugged and looked away. ''Words are too often lies. You know that as well as I do.''

Here it was, then—the end of the dream, the final realization that the love she had envisaged had not remained crystallized for her, waiting for her to come happily and claim it. What had seemed so beautiful, so promising, was all a lie. He had stood in the church, held hands and repeated vows. Vows meant for her sister.

She was a pawn. She thought her heart might well burst from the hurt and anger it held.

"Caitlin—"

She lifted her head now, proudly, fiercely, and stared at him, saw there an appeal for understanding, and more.... She shook with rage and self-disgust. How dared he reduce her to a pawn? How dare he take her for a fool? And oh, God, she hated herself for letting him.

Her sanity required her to retreat, to seek some place to lick her wounds. She needed to think long and hard about what to do about her marriage, if she even had a marriage left to worry about.

Samuel's expression grew intense, his gaze traveling up over her, from her hem to her waist to her breasts and lips. Rich lamplight seemed to catch fire in his eyes. More than any other feature, it was his eyes that Caitlin loved. They burned like the inner heart of a furnace.

"Samuel, I didn't force you to marry me, you chose to do so. Perhaps you don't love me, Samuel, although I don't believe that for one moment, but at least you can treat me as a wife, and a woman, and someone whose fate you freely decided to take charge of."

Samuel stood still, feeling weightless, breathless. He didn't say anything. He couldn't. How could a man talk when he'd stopped breathing? She stood there with studied correctness, her hands folded at her waist, almost as if she were posing for her portrait.

Why did I let my own passion take over, my own pride? I've gone too far, he thought. She would leave him, he knew. *She'll never forgive me—what woman would? I've lost it all.* He felt as if his heart had abruptly sunk into his boots.

After a long time, he said, "I should have told you."

Caitlin bent her head so far down that he could not see her face under the fall of her hair. She took a deep breath.

"I need—" She broke off, as if struggling to regain control of her thoughts.

In the silence, he could hear her breathing, soft and steady. Her calmness was unnerving. She lifted her head. Her chin was high. She took two quick steps.

"I need to think, Samuel." Then she was out the hall door at the same pace. She shut it. Hard.

Caitlin paced the kitchen. Samuel still was her husband, right or wrong. *Until death us do part.* Year after year, loving him and waiting for him, being there when he needed her, or even if he didn't. After a lifetime of feeling him in the very marrow of her bones, she did not know him. It was all so unlike Samuel. Dissembling, lying. It wasn't his way at all. But it couldn't have sprung out of nowhere...

Easy to say she did not know him. She had known and loved a boy. This was very much a man. But he was the only man she had ever known who attracted her in the slightest.

There was no way to make this right. And she knew that, even if for some reason of his own, Samuel feared the possible consequences. Once again she brought out her husband's proposal letter, although she knew it by heart.

She began to read.

My dearest Caitryn, I have written to your father asking for permission to marry you...

Caitlin carefully put the letter into her pocket and then sank into a chair. *I thought he'd made a mistake. I thought he meant me. In my arrogance, I didn't even tell Caitryn the letter was addressed to her. Now, I have wrecked three lives!*

She saw her reflection in the polished silver teapot. The

world went abruptly liquid, glittering and unclear, and the past, the present and the future all rose up to overwhelm her. She buried her face in her hands and wept.

Chapter Sixteen

Samuel seemed willing to leave her to her own thoughts, not wanting to tread on her sensibilities. As if he were sorry he'd wandered into the mess. Or maybe it was in the hope that she would come about, like a ship in the wind. Well, she damned well couldn't—which gave her no comfort at all.

It was a whole day before Caitlin began to come to grips with her seesawing emotions. Gone was the mood of relief and challenge and hope that she had enjoyed since she arrived in Maine. In its place was loss—mixed with a terrible anger, and a consuming, raging desire to throw something at the wall.

All next morning she thought of Samuel and Caitryn and Summer Dawn, and every time she did, she thought about shooting Samuel. Or maybe stabbing him. Or whipping him. Or spending two weeks in bed with him.

Idiot, she thought. She was stuck with him, but—she reluctantly admitted to herself—she wanted to be. She did not want to be rid of him. No matter how deeply he had hurt her, she remained his, heart and soul.

When she spoke of her ambivalence to Li Foo, he nodded wisely. "Time will ease the hurt, little missy. Love endures.'' He cleared his throat and murmured. ''Like the mountains and the seas, love never dies.''

She had crossed an ocean to come here.... Why? What drove her more than others? Why had she come to Maine, and not Caitryn, as had been intended?

''I'm so afraid that Samuel will grow to resent having me around, a bogus bride who'll keep house, warm his bed, give him healthy children. I don't want to be married for these reasons. I want to be married because he can't live without me. I love him so.''

''Perhaps love is all that keeps us going at times, no?''

Caitlin, never taking her eyes from the slow progress of clouds across the sky, nodded wordlessly.

Caitlin played with her food, and lingered over a sweet milk pudding. Her glossy dark hair spilling around her shoulders made Samuel think of a blackbird in flight. All that he could glimpse of her face was a slice of small, firm chin. He stopped even pretending to eat. His appetite was off. He forced himself to drink a cup of tea, excused himself and went to bed early.

When Caitlin came into the bedroom she immediately doused the lantern. Samuel felt her get into bed beside him. Her head was so close to his that he could smell the fresh scent of her hair.

''Cat—''

She turned on her side, away from him. Her soft body, swathed in a cotton shroud that said, ''Don't touch me,'' curled into a tight little ball. Tempted as he was to touch her, he desisted. He must give her time, he decided. He would have to restrain himself, he thought firmly. He would have to give her time.

He wanted to find some way to break down the wall she had built between them. Any reaction was better than the silence that had gripped her since she slammed the door in his face the evening before.

He cleared his throat. "Last night. We were saying things— I wish I hadn't," he said in a desperate voice he did not recognize.

"I'm tired," she said. "Can we not talk?"

"We've not been talking since I opened my big mouth and mentioned Caitryn," he pointed out. "It's not very pleasant." He waited a moment, then cleared his throat. "It also serves no purpose."

"Samuel," she said softly, "I have lost you twice over. Once to Summer Dawn. Now to Caitryn. Once was bad enough. Twice was dangerous. A third time would be fatal."

"To you or me?"

"Caitryn." She stirred beside him. "My sister is everything I ever dreamed of being—beautiful, pure, innocent, a true angel. When we were children," she said in that faraway voice she got when speaking about the past, "I knew you loved her."

She turned on her back, and because he could see the glitter of her eyes, like moonlight on water, he did not feel as emotionally distant from her. "The thing about Caitryn— The thing is, she did—does—love you, I think…not as I do, not with every thought, but quietly and gently."

There was silence for some time. Samuel was aware of their breathing, aware that a different kind of barrier had risen between them. He pulled himself into a sitting position, and wrapped his arms around his knees. He watched the shadows dancing on the planes of her face.

Caitlin rolled over, stared at the ceiling, but really, her eyes were turned inward. "I thought I would die with the pain, when you told me there had been a mix-up in the names. It hurt…" She paused, reliving in her mind that particular moment. "I thought you loved me, you see."

Samuel did not speak, but Caitlin picked up his moment of awareness, and answered it. "Of course, that is no excuse."

Why was she alone cursed with this unnatural desire? *Why is this not enough?* Her feelings for Samuel were like a fire that, once started, was impossible to extinguish. It seemed odd that she might want them to end.

Didn't he love her? Of course. No man could share himself with such passionate zeal as Samuel did without some sort of emotion that went beyond the physical. So, what about Caitryn? Summer Dawn? Didn't he love them, too? But how could he possibly love three people at once? It seemed impossible, contradictory.

Caitlin felt shredded into a million pieces, unable to find her own center. And then it occurred to her that perhaps Samuel was feeling precisely the same regrets. He was an honorable man. It was true he had lost his own mother as a boy and he had loved two other women. Was it because they reminded him of the Madonna?

Was loving three women such a terrible sin? It would be, Caitlin thought, if the others were available and he had to choose. They're both so different from me, they could be from another planet, she thought. How could he choose between them? *Whom* would he choose?

That choice had been taken out of his hands, she thought guiltily. He did not know it yet, but she had been instrumental in altering his options. In changing his offer of marriage from Caitryn to Caitlin, she had altered both their destinies. The deception had been a calculated gamble on her part. She had known of Samuel's reading problem for years. His father said it was one reason he had not written. Impetuous as ever, she had assumed that he had confused their names. She had assumed wrongly.

Reaching out, Samuel gently brushed a few stray wisps of hair from her face, as if trying to see her face in the darkness. "Cat?"

Caitlin felt the need in his touch, and responded to it. She put her hand over his. "Perhaps it was meant to be. When your letter came, Caitryn said she had been thinking

of joining the convent for years. Since that time we were
stranded in the cave...you remember? She said it brought
home to her then how puny man was against the might of
God."

"If I had ever really loved her, do you think I would
have married you?" he asked, covering her lips with his.

Caitlin sighed as her whole being responded to his kiss.
What sweet words. The words of a gallant. But she
wouldn't be swayed by mere utterances. "And you are
willing to settle for a bogus bride?" she persisted, not quite
able to believe it.

"It's not good enough for me!" The groan of aroused
hunger that emanated from deep in his throat caught at her
senses. "I will have for my wife only a woman who is
willing to *be* a wife...no holds barred!"

Hadn't he pledged his love and affection? Words were
only words, but actions spoke true. He had given all of
himself and his energies to her. It was a heady sensation,
to know that she was capable of all the passion he wanted—
and more. Still, it was scary, just a little, to know that she
was the one who had deceived her beloved.

It might help to tell him of her deceit, she suspected, but
she could not. She tried twice, but was as helpless as a
mute. If she kept her secret, he need never know.

Caitlin knew now what she must do—abandon herself to
selfishness. It was either that or die. He was her lifeline;
only he understood her, only he could save her, his strength,
his power, seeping into her. "Samuel, sometimes I'm afraid
of myself...of the chaos inside me."

He laughed, and she felt the vibrations through his big
body. "Don't talk such folly. End of discussion."

Caitlin raised her face and kissed the hard line of his
jaw. She wrapped her arms around him and, with sensuous
abandon, pressed her breasts against him. She felt her nipples stiffen, begin to ache with her need, and she saw this
inevitable end to the day, almost as if it were predestined.

"Samuel?"

Big hands came up and tugged her hips into contact with his groin, and she gasped, feeling his taut muscles jump through the tantalizing second skin of her soft cotton nightgown. She bit his shoulder, and he made a sound deep in his throat, a rippling sound of hunger and pleasure.

They played with each other for the longest time, touching and stroking and kissing. Samuel slid the nightgown off her slowly, down over her breasts, hips, thighs and feet, following the wash of moonlight over her skin with his tongue, pausing to savor the taste of her. His lips brushed her arms, along her collarbone, that soft indentation at the base of her throat.

In the clear winter's night, with the room lit as if by a chandelier from the full moon, they watched the changing expressions on one another's faces. He crushed her breasts to his lips with so fierce an intensity that his sucking pulled at nerve strings all the way to her toes.

Samuel spread her thighs with his until they encompassed his hips and pushed into her. She trembled, grabbing hold of him. Her eyes closed, and she took a deep shuddering breath.

"Samuel, I love you!"

He plunged deeper, pushing himself up inside her until there was nowhere left to go. "I don't want to lose you," he moaned thickly.

"I'm not going anywhere."

Caitlin's legs held him tight, and her hips made a circular motion, until they were as close together as two human beings could get. She wanted desperately for this to last, for it never to end, but the sensations were overrunning her.

She wanted, in her ecstasy, to deliver up to him those dark corners of herself, to share with him the terrible wrong she had done. Him! Her beloved! But she did no such thing. She merely cried out loud and long, delivering herself up totally to the pleasure sweeping through her as Samuel began to spasm above her.

It lacked a week till Christmas. The snow lay even and deep, so white it looked almost blue, glittering in the late-afternoon sun. Beyond it, the woods were black and still.

Standing at the well, with her hand on the brass handle of the pump, Caitlin watched a deer approach across the clearing with a tentative stiltlike gait, its eyes oval and huge, looking at Samuel, out beyond the woodpile, holding an apple in his hand.

The doe stepped forward and sank hock-deep into the snow. It snorted, the steam bursting cloudlike in the still air. Another step, and another. Samuel stood immobile.

Stretching out its neck, the doe took the apple, pranced up and reared. Hooves flashing daintily, it bounded away into the long, blued shadows at the edge of the clearing, its scut swaying whitely.

Caitlin blinked. A snowball had just struck the pump, spattering white fragments. She dropped the bucket and skittered to the other side of the hawthorn hedge, slipping and staggering.

Kneeling in the soft snow, she made a ball and threw it at the woodpile. She peeped over the low barricade. Samuel was nowhere to be seen.

Another snowball struck the hedge.

Caitlin sneaked around to the rear of the woodpile, slipped on the slick grooves left by the sled and went into a series of pinwheeling gyrations. Miraculously, her plunge was intercepted by a snowdrift, so soft that it absorbed the impetus of the fall.

Samuel's face appeared on the far side of the woodpile. He waved at her, shouted something, and a snowball hit her square in the derriere.

"Give in?" His breath steamed the air.

"Never!" Caitlin laughed and started making snowballs

as fast as she could, firing them at random, flinging snow in all directions.

"You leave me no other choice."

Samuel made a big, sweeping motion with his arm, and pelted another snowball. His accuracy was abominable!

Laughing helplessly, Caitlin sank to her knees in the snow, head waggling, arms flung crazily skyward. "I can't...go on. I surrender!"

Samuel put his hands on her shoulders and swung her to her feet. Swaying, she grabbed his shoulders for balance. "Let me help you back to your boudoir, my lady. I can see a rest is called for."

She leaned forward to wrap her arms around his neck, "It'll have to be quick. The surgery opens in half an hour." Her smile became a gasp of pleasure when he flexed himself hard against her.

Samuel chuckled as his hands found and teased her breasts. "What I have in mind won't take long."

Caitlin's eyes widened and her breath caught in a rush of sensual awareness that was as elemental as breathing. She shivered at the caress of his fingers, like tiny tongues of fire licking over her. "If you don't stop, we'll never make it to bed. I'll melt where I stand," she whispered.

As he swung her into his arms, his mouth came down over hers, and the steam of their breath twisted between them like a bridal veil.

Samuel felt the sun on his back as he bent over the pile of logs. He spotted Sagamore's double-anchor symbol on a stick riding at the frozen waterline and, fetching a cant hook, pried it away from the pile.

He felt the small hairs at the back of his neck stir. He was certain this was trespass timber, else how had Sagamore's logs gotten tangled with those from his own limits? The water level where Sagamore could legally cut was considerably lower.

Bending his knees to gain momentum, he turned the cant hook and watched the log disentangle itself and purl away, a dark stain upon the ice. He put the cant hook away, climbed over the mound of logs and jumped onto the toe piling that braced the dam wall.

Near midafternoon, he strode into the kitchen, sniffing happily. "Smells good." He dipped a finger in a bowl, licked it appreciatively, and rolled his eyes upward as if thanking heaven for its bounty. "Mmm, gingerbread."

Caitlin looked up from a frothy mass of yellow stuff that she was stirring in a pan. "Better invite Liam for a meal. He's stewing over the notion that Kate might give birth before he gets back to Fairbanks. I tried to tell him she's got five weeks to go yet, but he's not convinced."

He stood looking down at her for a second or two. His lips parted, but he closed them again over whatever rose to his tongue and passed silently through the kitchen and into the living room, where Liam Murphy had been waiting for him for a matter of ten minutes. With a muffled sigh, Caitlin concentrated on preparing the meal.

Liam Murphy agreed to stay for dinner, but refused their offer of a bed. He would shack down in the bunkhouse with the crew overnight. Both Samuel and Liam ate quickly, silent for the most part. Gingerbread steamed and breathed fragrance into the air as Caitlin served the coffee and Samuel cast his bombshell.

"I've got it fixed."

"Got what fixed?"

"Why, this log business," he said. "Come spring, we'll lay a boom across the river, and when the ice gives way, we'll work the timber down the river—Sagamore's crew on one side and ours on the other."

"Are you out of your mind, Sam, allowing that scoundrel near our boom?"

"In truth, it seems to me the only course likely to meet

with any degree of success. That way, we keep an eye on each other.''

There was silence, while they all three sat there, staring at one another. Then Liam crashed his fist down on the table and swore, savagely and at length. ''Damn it to hell, Sam, there has to be a better way! Ned might be Kate's brother, but he is a young hothead and up to all sorts of mischief, and why would you trust Henry Sagamore, even if he did agree to a coordinated drive? It's too big a risk.''

Samuel shook his burnished head. ''Each move we make is a risk, and if we think too long we will not move at all, for fear of what may come. I've decided to break the deadlock, and have set out to beat Henry Sagamore at his own game.''

''Jesus, Sam. What do you mean?'' Liam's boyish cheeks were flaming red, and there was a shine in his cornflower-blue eyes.

''It's simple enough, Liam. We can control Henry by giving him just what he wants. He'll be like a donkey to whom we feed carrots. I've asked Ned to play the spy and blab as much as he feels Sagamore needs to know about our operations.''

Liam found this a particularly foolhardy notion, and made no bones about voicing his opinion. He shook his head. ''Bloody hell, what'll Kate say? Dammit, Sam, you know Ned's a bad risk, without any additional excitement.''

''There's risk in everything that pertains to either Flaherty or Sagamore.'' Samuel cleared his throat. ''In this case, I don't think we have a choice.''

There was a silence, broken at last by Caitlin. ''Samuel, if you don't mind me saying so—''

The corner of Samuel's mouth tugged up, softening his expression. ''I probably will, Cat, but you'll say it nevertheless, so go on.''

''You're just putting Liam's back up. Let me try to explain.''

Samuel gave a grunt. "As you wish. It hasn't done me a damn bit of good yet."

Caitlin had a brief hallucination that he was suppressing laughter, but dismissed it. She took a deep breath and let it all out in one huffing blow. "Now, Liam. You are to be silent and still."

Liam shook his head again, but he said nothing.

"Samuel feels that if a coordinated drive is successful, then the politicians might see this as a solution to the current border problems."

There was a long silence. Liam did not move. He might have been carved from stone, so still was he. Samuel felt as if an icy finger had traced a path down the length of his spine. He looked for a moment into Caitlin's liquid eyes, saw to his surprise only faith in his idea.

Liam raised one sandy brow. "Have you thought about what you're doing, Sam? Truly thought?"

Samuel nodded. "I think it's worth a try."

Liam gave it some more thought. "Would you step back now, if you could, Sam?"

Samuel shrugged. "What else is there? Henry is prepared to risk everything to fulfill his contract—his own life and ours."

Before this is over, it may come to just that, Caitlin thought. Samuel is taking a terrible gamble. Impulsively, she reached out, and Samuel put his hands in hers.

"So, you're going through with it?" Liam asked.

"Why not? We all deliver the logs. We all need the money."

"And if your scheme fails?"

The pause that followed was brief. "It mustn't fail. We mustn't fail. Not this time."

"Why, then, if that's what you want, Sam, I'm content. I don't see what else we can do."

Samuel grinned. "I'll ride over to Westfield tomorrow, and talk to Henry."

Caitlin pressed her cheek against his shoulder. She didn't want him to see the fear in her eyes. "Talk to him—and hold your temper," she whispered fiercely.

"I promise."

Liam Murphy merely made a rude noise in his throat.

It lacked a good hour until full daylight when the tocsin began to clang. The alarm was only to be rung in the event of a disaster. Samuel came off the bed and onto his feet in a single motion.

Caitlin was a little slower. "What is it, Samuel?"

"Sabotage at the dam!" His voice was curt.

Suddenly, before Caitlin could ask another question, there was an explosion within the woods. A great light shot into the sky and vanished, there was a dull rumble, as of falling timbers and debris, and she could see that Samuel was already half-dressed.

"Stay here! Do you understand?"

Caitlin nodded in acquiescence, but she caught her lower lip between her teeth and worried the soft flesh nervously until she could no longer hear the jingle of sleigh bells through the snow-blurred forest.

There was a single road from the depot, narrow and twisting, cutting into the promontory. Samuel drove the roans hard and fast. This was a nightmarish trip in the dark. There was a moon but, because of the ominous cloud cover, its light was wan and diffuse. A cutting wind struck icily through his jacket and trousers.

Here and there, constant use had broken up the snow. Rubble and muddy earth covered in a thin scum of ice was strewn in slippery patches across the road. Encountering the first of these, the sleigh fishtailed dangerously. A massive tree trunk reared into his vision range as the vehicle continued its skid. He pulled the reins desperately. The horses responded, and the runners found traction.

A fireball lit the night, struck tiny gleams from stumps

that were now white-capped pillars. What was that? Samuel
wondered for half a heartbeat. Something rattled and
popped and echoed through the forest. His ears felt the
shock of an explosion, but it was distant. Sound, echoing,
seemingly a long time after.

A veil of black smoke rolled along the dam wall, carried
on a stiff wind. The stink of blasting powder floating like
a miasma, bitter and choking. Through the pall of ashy
smoke, he saw someone running, a single fair-headed figure—

Even before his brain identified the shape, Samuel
grabbed the lantern, sprang to the ground and ran, dislodg-
ing slides of ice and gravel, slipping and sliding and losing
skin on his hands. Liam, he realized in a heartbeat, and he
continued to run toward the figure. He met Liam at the dam
wall, gasping for breath as he caught himself against a
snow-covered boulder and hooked the lantern on his belt.

"Get out of this. Get clear, Sam. The dam could collapse."

Samuel chose not to hear Liam. There was a thick stench
of blasting powder. At that moment, he guessed what might
have happened—what must have happened—and he stared
into the darkness with a feeling of incredulity and dread
that he hadn't felt since Summer Dawn died. "Who's down
there?"

"Sagamore—and Ned Flaherty. I think they're setting to
blow the dam."

Samuel felt—he didn't know what, then. An impact to
the gut. He lit out again, scrambling down the sloping wall
into the blinding smoke. It was not a time to think clearly,
to consider options. He heard Liam behind him, skidding
on shards of ice and pebbles, swearing at him and telling
him he was a fool, to get back, not to risk himself, that
Ned was *his* brother-in-law.

When he reached the buttress, Samuel unhitched the lantern, lit it and held it aloft. He peered into the incline, but

all he could see was denser dust. Dark as the entrance to hell, he thought. Something caught in his throat. The stench of blasting powder was even stronger here. He was about to descend when Caitlin's voice stopped him.

"Samuel! Are you crazy? Don't go down there! It's dangerous!"

"Damn it, woman. Didn't I tell you to stay behind?"

"I couldn't stay."

"And I have to go."

"Why? For God's sake, Samuel, come back!" She was pleading with him, rigid with fear for him. "There can only be destruction down there!"

"My father used to quote an old Cornish saying he was fond of—'Let all the blood be on the front of you.'" Samuel hooked the lantern into his belt again. "It's my responsibility. If I don't go down, Cat, there will be blood on my back." He took several deep breaths, calming himself, then went over the dam wall.

Sliding down the cable hanging loose from the hoist engine, hand over hand, his breath sounding in his ears, the pounding of his heart sounded overwhelming. Once his boot slipped and he hung by his arms, his other leg bent painfully, until he could find purchase. Every breath he took smelled of the suffocating dust and blasting powder.

At the lower end of the incline, the dust had stopped swirling, and as he lifted his lamp, he could see that it hung suspended in the air, like the silt from the bottom of a stirred-up pond. From somewhere close at hand, a heavy dripping made its doleful presence felt. A crack in the dam wall, or normal leakage?

Shadows enshrouded the site. There was still the faint smell of powder smoke mingled with the dampness of mud, debris, and the smoke from his lantern. Samuel could make out a dark smudge on one of the pilings that formed the lower buttress of the dam wall. He made his way to it, although his horror of what he might find was absolute. He was trembling.

Slowly, the patchwork of light and dark ceased to swirl and a pattern began to coalesce. Three bodies lay upon the pockmarked piling, two obviously dead, the other still alive. Samuel could hear the thick raling of the man's breathing. Crouching, he reached out a hand, felt the warm, sticky wet, and knew who it was before the inconstant light deciphered the mounded black form in front of him.

"Oh, my God! Henry Sagamore!"

Chapter Seventeen

The first explosion had caught one of Henry's men, hurling him into the center of a black-and-red plume. Henry, who had taken cover alongside the explosives expert he had employed to sabotage Jardine's dam, could not see through the smoke and explosions. Where was Flaherty?

"For Christ's sake, watch that bloody powder, Simpson."

"Winter's not the best time for this kind of action, boss. Hard to judge how much powder'll do the job."

"You told me you were a goddamned expert."

Henry hadn't intended anyone to get hurt, especially the boy. He'd just wanted to give Sam Jardine a taste of his revenge. It was a game really, tit for tat with Jardine, like moves on a chessboard. Now Ned had gone and put himself in the middle of what, God help him, *he'd* planned. He'd poked his head out from behind the shelter of the piling, seen what was left of Brown—not much more than a rag doll on the pockmarked buttress. There had been no sign of Ned.

He'd moved gingerly across the structure toward the spot where Ned had been standing. Then the world had been collapsing on him, with the shriek and wail of matter rend-

ing itself. The strut had vibrated underneath his boot soles
then come up and smashed against his stomach.

Henry lay for a time, dazed, his head full of noise, re
verberating on and on. It was all crazed. Shadows chasing
after shadows, extending themselves along all sides. The
pain in his head! He was aware of his heart beating, the
blood coursing through his veins. His ears were ringing
and there was a stink of blasting powder in every breath
he drew.

Then he opened his eyes. Blackness mutated into charcoal, a whiff of grit blown into his face. He began to choke
on the smoke as the gray began to swirl, coalescing light,
bright, like splinters of glass in his eyes. A corridor of
shadows was opening up in front of him. A figure, hair on
fire, crouched over him, shaking him, shouting at him.

"What?" he slurred. "What?"

The flick and pop of an oil lamp, close to guttering.
"Goddammit, Henry! What the bloody hell are you playing
at?" Jardine!

"It's the hour for ghosts," he muttered. "That's if you
believe in them."

From out of the darkness, Sam Jardine's voice, "I guess
the real thing is always much worse than you can ever
imagine, Henry."

Mist was swirling, as substantial as dust. It turned the
area around them into a ghostly facade filled with sinister
shapes. Samuel grabbed him round the waist, trying to pull
him up, onto his feet.

"Goddammit, buddy, get your ass in gear, now!"

It seemed Jardine had no intention of letting him rot here
in the mud and slime. Pain laced his consciousness like a
web. He waved Jardine away as small landslides of gravel
showered them with rock chunks and dirt. "You're a damn
fool, Sam Jardine. Get out of here before the wall col-
lapses."

"You underestimate my engineering skills, Sagamore."

Henry dug his fingers into Jardine's massive shoulders. "Ned. He's gone, Sam, and I'm responsible."

"It's too late to worry about that now," Jardine grunted. "What's done is done."

Then Liam Murphy was there beside him, on the other side, and he was being lifted to safety, and delivered into the hands of the doctor. He heard her say something about taking it easy, opened his mouth to tell her to go away, but knew it was useless.

"Dear God! What happened?"

"Sagamore thought he could blow up the dam. He was wrong."

Henry looked up, willing the ghosts of blasting powder, dust and smoke and the white noise of the percussion from his burning ears away, up into the face of Caitlin Jardine.

"How bad?" Samuel asked, hunkering down beside her.

She shrugged, made a gesture. Henry was in pain from the rubble that had landed on him, his skin was chafed raw, and his leg hurt. He'd taken that as a good sign; he was still alive.

The first light of dawn was upon the land, vaguely yet, but through the swirls of mist, the trees began to outline themselves, white spires against the morning sky. One last star hung in the sky like a far-off lamp. Caitlin was contemplating it, and when she spoke, her voice was as low as if it had come from that distance.

"It's too soon to tell. Perhaps I should amputate."

"The leg stays *on.*"

At which Caitlin made a tentative probe that sent Henry's head back and his breath hissing through his teeth. "Sorry," Caitlin said, and stood up. "There's nothing I can do without a patient's full consent. The male doctor at Caribou might be able to do something to save the leg, though by the time he gets here, gangrene will have set in for sure."

Henry tried to look away from her face, but could not.

She was worrying her lower lip with her small white teeth. It was *bad*. The slightest movement sent waves of pain through his leg, left him weak and nauseated. Hate leached from his heart. The inescapable truth was that he'd done irreparable harm, and would pay the price.

"Do whatever you have to, Doc."

Caitlin frowned and drew in a slow breath, seeming to think about it then. She shot him a queer look. "Perhaps I am not making myself clear, Mr. Sagamore. I'm the medical expert in this valley, the only person who might save that leg."

Henry's hands tightened into hard-knuckled fists. For an instant, his heart stood still. A blaze of fear seized him. But he controlled that. Pride forbade him betraying himself. "So?"

"I know what I am, but it is important how you see me." Her voice was soft, with no trace of anger or recrimination.

"Why do you say that?"

Caitlin painted her most concerned look on her face. "I would have thought that obvious." She was well aware of the difficult ground she was on. She must not, under any circumstances, give Henry Sagamore any hint that his leg was not broken, only badly bruised and lacerated.

"I suppose in an emergency, a man might call in a female medic, then renege as soon as he's on the mend and want a male doctor. Oh, well, that is, of course, the tragedy of all this."

Henry's head lolled back, and he closed his eyes against the jetting spasms of pain. "Forgive me, Caitlin."

"What is it you want from me, Henry?" Caitlin mustered a smile that was purely facial. "I cannot absolve you of your sins. I am not a priest."

"Forgiveness for my arrogance is all I ask," he said.

"Why?"

"I have put—" Henry's voice was a rasp "—my trust in you."

"But *why?*"

"Because——" He had to stop. The effort just to make himself understood was immense. He reached out, grabbed Caitlin by the hand. She waited, unmoving. He forced himself to relax his leg and hip, let the pain have its way and so more quickly subside. "Because you are a doctor, and from all accounts a good one. Whatever it costs, I'll pay. Just save my leg."

Caitlin thought for a quick minute. "We'll negotiate later on terms of payment. In the meantime, I'll put a temporary dressing on the leg, then get you back to the surgery. You'll need stitches."

For an instant, Henry looked quite stricken. He met Caitlin's eyes, quickly recovered, even gave her a hint of a rueful smile. "Whatever you say, Doc."

The purple shadows of evening were creeping down the lowest notches of the mountains when Kate arrived at the Presque Isle Stream depot. In front of the wangan store, a rime-whitened log lay across two or three fenceposts. She dismounted clumsily and hitched the reins around the log. Her mind was one urgent question mark, and there was a physical pain behind her breast.

Recognizing one among the line of the men who were stringing toward the bunkhouse, home from their work in the woods, she hailed him. "Lofty! Word came to Fairbanks that there was an explosion and two men were killed."

"Aye, at the dam. Sagamore thought the fuse had gone out, so he went back to see. Only it hadn't."

"Was Ned with him? My brother," she added, in case the timberman did not remember.

Lofty Howard looked directly at Kate Murphy. She had a funny look on her freckled face; her blue eyes stared blankly at him. He took her hand. "I'm afraid that it's quite bad news, ma'am. Some giant powder went off by mistake.

Sagamore was there, close enough to be hurt. Heard tell Ned was somewhere nearby.''

"Ned! Is he hurt?''

Lofty squeezed her fingers. They felt cold, even through the trim leather of her brown kid gloves. "He's dead, I'm sorry to say.''

"Oh, my God!'' whispered Kate. And then, without warning, her legs collapsed; she fell to her knees on the ground. Her chipstraw bonnet fell off, and the cold wind caught it and blew it fitfully across the snowy ground, until it caught in a tangle of bushes.

Kate could hear someone screaming. The rim of the sun cast a sudden, fierce gleam over the mountains across the stream, flaming gold. The bonnet's red ribbons were fluttering like the wings of a wounded bird.

"Ned?'' Silas Crane wrinkled his forehead. "Are you certain, Lofty? I heard he was pulled out alive.''

"Let me assure you that he is very much alive.'' It was Liam's voice, behind them. They spun, and stared at him as if he had sprouted gills. He laughed. "Seems your brother has more lives than a cat, but he's using them up fast, Kate.'' Liam pulled Kate to her feet, hugged her close.

"What happened? Tell me, quick.''

"It's quick told, sweetheart. Ned's a man in love with risk-taking. He pretended to go along with Sagamore's plans. They were ready to blow the dam at daylight, but at the last minute he disabled the fuse cable. He saved the dam, but the blast blew him over the wall. Luckily, he landed in a pile of soft snow. He'd have bought it otherwise.''

Kate gave a gasp, clutched his shoulders, pressing her swollen abdomen against him. Suddenly she sagged, and her arms went slack.

"What is it, sweetheart?''

"The baby!''

Liam swung her into his arms and headed for Caitlin's surgery.

It was a long night. In the kitchen, the candles had burned low, and some of them had gone out. The fire popped and flamed, licking the base of the kettle. Samuel stood in front of it, warming his hands. Liam sat in a chair nearby, white-lipped, unnerved, shaking.

Li Foo arrived and made tea, lacing it with some of Caitlin's medicinal brandy. He turned to Liam with authority. "Drink this! Don't spill it, now! Little missy not like this special mixture wasted."

Standing there, Samuel had a sudden piercing, anguished recollection of another such scene, of another much-loved woman trying to give birth, being carried inexorably into death, beyond the reach of the man who waited in helpless agony. Only then, three years ago, he had been the man, sitting where Murphy was now.

Summer Dawn was a memory, part of his past, part of himself as a youth, just as Caitryn was. It was Caitlin who belonged to his present. It was Caitlin whom he would love and cherish as long as there was breath in his body.

The clock on the mantelpiece chimed the hour. Two o'clock! Liam made a restless movement, then his hand went out, feeling blindly upward. Samuel's grip encompassed it like a band of iron.

Caitlin found them like that when she came in. She smiled tiredly. In the crook of her arm lay a tiny, red-faced, crumpled little creature, whom she transferred to Liam.

"Merry Christmas, Liam."

The infant stirred a little, blinking deep blue eyes, half opening a tiny triangular mouth, and then settling again into immobility. Liam looked up at Caitlin, who was still smiling.

"You have a strong, healthy son. You can go in. Kate is fine."

Liam's eyes were very bright, and his voice was very deep. "What a Christmas gift! I wonder if she'd mind if we called him Noel?"

Caitlin was sitting beside her dressing table, brushing her hair, when Samuel came in. He perched himself on the footrail of the bed and watched her. It was a familiar trick of his. "Will you be pressing charges against Henry?" she asked.

"No. I think he's learned his lesson. You wait. By and by, Henry Sagamore will become a very pillar of the community, donating money to build a church, and helping with the new schoolhouse."

Caitlin drew the brush mechanically through her heavy hair. "What is there about moneymaking that warps some men so, makes them so grossly self-centered?"

"You use the conventional measuring stick on him," Samuel answered, with that tolerance that so often surprised her. "Maybe his ways are pretty crude, but he's just a man, after all, with a man's tendency to go to extremes now and then. I kind of like the beggar's ambition and energy. We'll be extending our timber operations next fall. As well as coordinated drives, it's worth considering joint use of men and equipment."

The implications of what he was saying took a moment to sink in. Samuel still puzzled Caitlin a little at times; there were odd flashes of depths she could not see into, a quality of unexpectedness in things he would do or say. The man was honorable and sensible and capable and an expert, not given to letting minor grudges override his judgment.

She swung about on him, and gave him a sharp glance. "Joint use of men and equipment with Henry Sagamore?"

"It's just an idea." Samuel shifted his back and shoulders. "Something to give him back his honor."

"Honor—" Caitlin whirled, hands stiff at her sides. "Don't talk to *me* about honor! Henry Sagamore gave up his honor long ago—and other people paid for it. In blood…"

"Cat, it'd be just a token, a—"

"No!" Caitlin chopped at the air sharply once, with the edge of her hand. "No, Samuel. God knows you've taken on *his* responsibilities long enough. The ones he threw over. Have you no pride or self-respect?"

"Yes. Both aplenty." Samuel crossed the room at a bound, caught her by the shoulders and pulled her to her feet, facing him. The silken folds of her peignoir fell away from her hips. Shadows stroked her slender thighs, curving inward to keep from him her secret delta. The anticipation was a hard knot in his stomach.

Samuel's lips touched Caitlin's. "It's not like you not to be generous, Cat. Besides, rehabilitating Henry might earn us some time off purgatory."

Her fury evaporated. "Generous?"

"Yes—you've always been so generous."

Caitlin was instantly warmed by the unexpected words. Her mouth widened happily. He drew her close to him, stroking tenderly the glossy black hair that flowed about her shoulders. He kissed her forehead. She moved her hands up to the column of his neck and began a circular motion.

"Is that opinion based on discretion or discernment?"

His lips wandered to her earlobes, then slowly down her neck, to her throat and then lower still. His tongue discovered the silver chain, and his lips and teeth closed around it, slowly pulling at it until, from the lace-edged bodice of her peignoir, there escaped the little crucifix he had given her so long ago. It was warm from her flesh, and he kissed it.

"It is prudent to take into account a wild card like Henry. In taking this step, we will have effectively hobbled him. Does that answer your question?"

She wrapped her arms around him and, arching upward,

pressed her breasts against him. "That depends on your point of view."

He laughed. "Yours or mine?"

"I don't have any," she said. "And you have too many."

He made a sound deep in his throat and gently bit one of the velvety peaks that rose beneath the silk. Pleasure speared through her, arching her back in a primal response, tearing his name from her throat.

Samuel swept her into his arms, blew out the one remaining candle whose flame burned straight and tall, and tumbled with her onto the waiting bed.

Late one afternoon about a week later, a burly lumberman came in, asking if Caitlin could get a splinter out of his finger. He was short, powerful, muscular, with a face as ugly as a gargoyle's. He pulled off his tight woolen cap.

"Had it in for five days now, ma'am," he said. "I'm tree felling at Sagamore's block. I've had dozens of splinters in me time, and I've always been able to get them out. It's a right one, this, got itself buried in deep. Had several goes with a knife, but it's stuck tight."

The finger was about four times its normal size, and badly inflamed. Caitlin frowned over it. Why on earth had he let the finger get into such a state? There was a danger he could lose it.

She poured some hot water into a bowl and laid some clean strips of linen on the kitchen table. "I'll have to lance it."

"Prune if off if you have to, Doc," the man declared cheerfully. "I'll still have enough fingers left to get on with me tree felling."

"Take a deep breath. This will hurt."

The lumberman boasted he was not afraid of a bit of pain, but he lost all his color when Caitlin had cut the finger and he saw the yellow muck oozing out. "Bloody hell," he muttered, casting her a stricken look.

Caitlin bandaged the finger, issued strict instructions for bathing it, and then gave him a mug of coffee and one of her biscuits. As he was leaving, the lumberman handed Caitlin a covered wicker basket.

"I don't have any ready cash for payment, Doc, but I brung somethin' I thought the little 'uns would like."

Gingerly Caitlin lifted the lid and gazed at the small wriggling bundle. She put down the basket and picked up the squirming puppy, who was doing his best to devour her, in his excitement at being in the open air again. Her throat closed up and her eyes stung. White Cloud must make his decision soon.

"He's ten weeks old, and we've been callin' him Rascal, on account of his mischievous nature."

Caitlin held him up to her face. "He's beautiful," she gasped as the mite's sharp little teeth just missed her nose. "Zoe will love him." The child was becoming a real part of their lives. She hoped White Cloud could see how she and Samuel truly loved Zoe.

"Mr. Sagamore said there's no better surgeon in Maine than you, ma'am. He was right," the lumberman said gallantly.

When the lumberman was gone, Caitlin took the pup down to the garden, where Samuel was fixing up a trellis for Li Foo. It was nearly dark. The day was waning fast, but the air was completely still. Shadows were everywhere. They spread across the snow-crusted furrows and into the small orchard. The last fingers of lemon light played across the very tops of the snowcapped pines.

"Look, Samuel!"

Samuel reached over for the dog and stroked its small black head with gentle fingers. Rascal licked his hand with great enthusiasm and, after spying a curling wood chip, fell with a sudden wriggle to the ground, in brave pursuit of this mysterious object.

"It seems Henry Sagamore is giving me grand references. He must even have told everyone how we're hoping the Abnaki will share Zoe with us. Zoe will love Rascal, don't you think?"

"Sure, as long as every customer doesn't give us a pet, else we could well end up with a menagerie." Then he said, very softly, "A pet for every child. White Cloud will see some significance in that idea. Sometimes the Lord's ways seem strange."

Caitlin caught her breath. "What has the Lord to do with it?"

"He has to do with all things."

Zoe squealed with delight and clapped her hands when Caitlin told her of the planned trip to Fairbanks to christen the new babe. Her long braid swung from side to side like a rope.

"Oh, goody! An' we'll take Rascal. He'll enjoy the ride, too."

Winter Moon chuckled. "One doesn't take an animal to church, Zoe."

The child's face registered disappointment. "I could hold him on my lap."

Caitlin noted with some amusement that Zoe was beginning to develop her own personality. How wonderful it would be to watch her grow up. "Well, I don't suppose one small dog will make much difference." Caitlin gazed into Zoe's glowing face and grinned. "Rascal might not want to go, though."

"I'll tell him, so's he'll be all ready." The child rushed out to inspect the pup, whose tilted head and wagging tail indicated he was willing. Caitlin laughed, entranced by Zoe's effervescence. She was so easy to love.

Caitlin patted the little dog, picked Zoe up and hugged

her tight, said goodbye to her aunt and hurried up the path to the depot office. There was more to be done before she could be a true wife and worthy mother. She skirted Li Foo's garden, which was still shrouded with snow. There was a strong smell of burning joss sticks. Li Foo must be appeasing his ancestors again.

Samuel was contemplating the buckingboard figures when he turned suddenly and saw Caitlin crossing the threshold. His face immediately lit with joy, and he stepped forward, arms reaching toward her. She shrank back, clasping her hands on her breast.

"Do you know what this is?" Her whisper was almost inaudible.

Samuel stared at her, at the envelope she held in one hand. A muscle jerked beneath the skin covering his cheekbone. "Is something wrong?" Caitlin was fighting the swirl of emotions that threatened to engulf her, and she found her hands clenching till the nails dug deep.

"What I have to do is not easy, and I should like to get it over. I believe it's time you saw this." She handed over an envelope, a queer tense look on her face.

Samuel took it, and stared at it blankly, but did not open it. There was a profound silence. He imagined that he could hear motes of dust falling.

"Read it," Caitlin said.

Samuel stared at her. He knew what was in the envelope. Why would he want to read his own proposal of marriage? The hackles at the back of his neck began to stir. A sudden reluctance born of intolerable uncertainty, of a feeling that he could only characterize as fear, sprang full-fledged into his mind.

"Read it," Caitlin said again.

Samuel felt a sickening lurch in the pit of his stomach as he flipped open the envelope. He did not know what he was expecting, but it certainly wasn't this. He stood stricken, staring absently at the sheet of paper in his hand. It was unbelievable, beyond reason.

"Samuel?"

In time, he raised his head. He could hardly bear to look at her. That pale, clear-cut face framed in raven hair, the full mouth, the luminous eyes under winged brows that met his own with such trepidation. He finally found his voice. It was clotted with rage and disbelief. "What have you done to us?"

"I thought you'd made a mistake."

"You lied to me." Oh, God, give me strength. He wanted to grab her and shake her. It was the ultimate, the culmination, the deceit to end all deceits, and he didn't know how he felt. Angry? Hurt? Betrayed? All of the above, or any?

"I didn't lie. I just didn't tell you the truth. There is a difference."

Samuel moved around the room, abruptly uncomfortable with excess adrenaline. He felt a desperate urge to touch the table, chair, shelves, solid objects, dense and substantial, that would remain immutable even in the face of her deception.

Caitlin swallowed. "Please don't be angry."

He exhaled, aware that he had been holding his breath. "I'm not angry," he said around a thick tongue.

"Why did you marry me, Samuel, when you loved Caitryn best all the while? Why? Why?" A little half-strangled sob escaped her.

That stopped him. It was like a blade sliding wickedly through his defenses. He shot her a sharp glance. Now he could see her pulse actually making her high collar quiver rhythmically. She was as wrought up about this conversation as he was. That helped, in a way.

"I love Caitryn. I loved Summer Dawn. I also love music and good wine, the mountains, rivers and trees. I've got many loves—and one wife," he said slowly, groping for a reason that he couldn't see very clearly himself. Some dark memory brushed him with its wing and flew away again. "Besides, what sort of a man would I have been if I'd packed you off home again?"

"A man of honor, as you have always been." As Samuel watched Caitlin chew her lower lip, a flood of longing rushed through him. He could feel the feral beating of his heart, as heavy as the thrumming of the waves on the shore. Her lips parted as she altered her stance subtly. He had to fight the instinct to move in response.

"Tell me true, Cat. Why did you do it?" he asked, knowing why, but wishful to hear in words what her eyes shouted.

"Pride. Anger. Envy. Lust. Covetousness."

"Five out of seven ain't bad."

Caitlin ignored the humorous note in his words. She still had enough spirit to aim a blow at him. "Is that all you have to say? You have a wife who has just confessed to the most heinous of sins, Samuel Jardine, and you joke about it?"

"It's a shame to spoil a good gesture, to be quit of all the uncertainties, all the useless regrets—or maybe I'm just a fool." His voice was sorrowful, and he had the face of a much-put-upon man, but she could see the flame that glowed in his eyes.

"It is I who am the fool. It is the only explanation of why I would connive and lie and cheat and jeopardize my immortal soul for love of the stupidest man in all of America." The astounded look on his face ended Caitlin's tirade. She cursed, then, lifting her skirts slightly, went to hurry out of the room. His next words stopped her.

"Why confess now, Cat?" he asked quietly. "You could have destroyed the letter. I would never have known I hadn't made a slip of the pen and mixed up your name with Caitryn's. That I'd asked your father for the wrong girl."

She turned reluctantly to face him, one hand on the doorknob. "I don't know, but I wanted it all out in the open. I wrote to Caitryn and told her it was she whom you had really wanted to marry. She wrote back that if she was once unhappy because of what I did, her joy within the convent far outweighed it a hundredfold."

"Don't flatter yourself, Cat. That is not the reason."

The poignant truth of that struck home to her miserably. It was not a matter of reason or logic, of her making any sacrifice for her conscience's sake. "I also wanted there to be absolute truth between us, Samuel. And forgiveness. For you have forgiven me, haven't you?" Her voice shook.

He looked across the room at her eyes, green eyes glittering with desire for him, and all thoughts left his mind. He opened his arms to her. She flew into them.

"Do you go with us when we raft the logs, Sam, or are you going to start on the new schoolhouse for the Abnaki?"

A moment or two elapsed before Samuel answered. His gaze fixed on the plate in front of him, he went on arranging and rearranging a little pile of cherry stones with the point of his knife.

"I am doing neither," he said at last. "I'll leave both those chores to you and Henry. I am going to England."

There was a curious deliberation in his reply that brought Liam's eyes quickly to his face. "With any definite object?" he asked.

Samuel looked up slowly and nodded. "With a very definite object," he said quietly. "I am going to visit my father—mend some fences. I also want to take Caitlin home to visit her family. It's not a little thing to tear a woman's life up by the roots, and drag her away from her own people. White Cloud understands this. He has consented to Zoe spending more time with us when we return so she'll grow up knowing her dual heritage."

There was a little pause when he stopped speaking. It was Caitlin who spoke first, her smooth forehead wrinkled with perplexity. "Why have you never mentioned this before, Samuel?"

Samuel shrugged slightly, without looking up from the cherry stones. "I never knew for sure, until you confessed your heinous deception. I was sure I had taken a bogus bride, but I couldn't do anything but stand back and trust you to find out what quicksand you were building your castle on."

"Oh, Samuel, you have a capacity for reckless undertakings. You'd never have married me if you hadn't." Caitlin glared at him balefully.

Samuel looked at her, a little chuckle deep in his throat. "And miss out on the best bargain of the century? A wife, a doctor, and a miniature tyrant, to boot? A chance to live happily ever after?"

"What use to demand reason of a man? You know we'll vex each other, be at cross-purposes. You know what a nag I am when I get going. We'll fight again."

He felt a warmth about his heart, a great welling up of love. "And again and again. Well, those arguments will remind me I have something money doesn't buy. A *real* wife." He pulled her onto his lap. "What do you reckon, Liam?"

"Grand it is, Sam, that miracles *do* happen."

* * * * *

Harlequin®
Historical

A clandestine night of passion
An undisclosed identity
A hidden child

RITA Award nominee

Miranda
Jarrett

presents...

THE SECRETS OF
Catie Hazard

Available in April,
wherever Harlequin Historicals are sold.

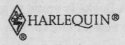

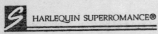